BLACK CABS

Also by John McLaren

Press Send
7th Sense

BLACK CABS

by

John McLaren

SIMON & SCHUSTER
A VIACOM COMPANY

First published in Great Britain by Simon & Schuster UK Ltd, 1999
A Viacom company

1 3 5 7 9 10 8 6 4 2

Simon & Schuster UK Ltd
Africa House
64–78 Kingsway
London WC2B 6AH

Simon & Schuster Australia
Sydney

A CIP catalogue record for this book is available from the British Library

ISBN 0-684-85826-6

Typeset in Palatino by SX Composing DTP, Rayleigh, Essex
Printed and bound in Finland by WSOY

Dedicated to the memory of Sean Conroy, cystic fibrosis sufferer and son of a London cabbie, who died on 18 May 1995.

Acknowledgements

I am hugely indebted to Nick Webb, Martin Fletcher and Glen Saville of Simon & Schuster, Jonathan Lloyd and Nick Marston of Curtis Brown, and Tim Bevan and Natascha Wharton of Working Title.

There are many good friends I want desperately to thank, beginning with Katharine Road, Karen Mistry, Roger Lewis, Sylvie and Bernard de Lattre, and:

John Barker	Mike Galvin	Steve McCauley
Laura Bishop	Alan Gibson	Margaret McLaren
Jeremy Black	Miriam Gillinson	Derek Myers
John Bligh	Caroline Gornandt	Angela Nolan
Jamie Borwick	Lucy Heinink	Richard Nourse
Angelika Brozler	Ted Howell	Anne, Kirstin and
David Charters	Pete and Mark	Stewart Smith
Michael Conroy	Johnson	Rod Stentiford
Tom Enders	Jacqueline Koay	John Towner
Lorne Forsyth	Judy MacDonald	Nigel Williams
Clement Freud	Dena and Gordon	Tammi Woods
Matthew Freud	McCallum	Peter Yao

1

If it hadn't been for the subsidized mortgage, the pension plan and the season-ticket loan, Jo would cheerfully have buried the heavy-duty stapler in his overpaid skull. He snapped again.

'Come on, *come on* . . .'

The banker stood menacingly over her as she stapled the thick documents together, his smooth, handsome features monstrous with rage.

'. . . And you'd better have checked that my taxi's still waiting.'

'It is.'

Jo's voice smouldered with resentment. All she could risk was catching the eye of her neighbouring secretary, Janice, and pulling a mocking face. As soon as the last of his precious documents were stapled together, she'd be shot of the toffee-nosed tosser for twenty-four hours.

When it was done, he ripped them from her grasp and sped back to his desk to stuff them into his briefcase. Grabbing his mobile phone, he hurried past the other desks, pausing only to yell again at the junior executive whose unforgivable error had held up the process. Scurrying out to the broad bank of lifts, pointedly ignoring the older colleagues waiting there, he jabbed hard at the little button.

'Come on, come *on*.'

At last the lift finished its hesitant ascent to the eighteenth floor. He stormed in and turned, flinging a glare at the others for wasting valuable seconds shuffling inside. His luck was out, and the lift stopped at floor after floor, each pause bringing fresh muttered curses from him. The moment the doors opened at the ground floor, he barged his way though the scrum, his sharp-cornered case banging painfully into one girl's knee. With no time to waste on apologies, he raced on across the marble foyer, out of the tall glass doors and into the blustery, chilly embrace of the September evening.

'Shit.'

There were eight or nine taxis waiting there in Throgmorton Lane, with no sign which was his. He banged on the window of the first. The driver looked up from his crossword and slid the window down. The banker snarled,

'Ford?'

The cabbie pressed a button on his electronic display, and shook his head. The banker dashed on to the next. And the next. And the next, swearing louder with every denial. The sixth was his, a new-style TX1 . He got in and slammed the door so hard it stress-tested the welds. The cabbie winced and took a look in his mirror. As he moved off, he pressed the intercom switch. A red light came on in the passenger compartment and another on the dashboard. The sound was thin and reedy.

'You'll never guess who I 'ad in the back of this cab yesterday.'

The banker rolled his eyes. All he needed was a talker.

'I've *no* idea. If you don't mind, I've got some calls to make.' He started punching in the number on his mobile.

'*You.*'

'Me what?' This guy was driving him crazy.

'You. It was you what was in this cab. Picked you up at the City Airport. Don't you remember? You was with a tasty blonde number.'

'Oh yeah . . . Grace. Sorry, I can't chat. How long will it take us to get to the airport?'

'What time's your flight?'

'Seven forty.'

'Oooooh, tight, very tight. Been 'orrible everywhere today, and they're down to one lane on the 'Ammersmith flyover. Reckon it'll be the best part of an hour and an 'alf.'

'*Shit.*'

'The last thing I want to do is rob myself of a fare, but if you

2

really need to be on that flight, you'd be a lot quicker on the Tube.'

Oh yeah, thought Ford. He would rather miss *any* flight than risk bumping into another banker and be thought the type who went to Heathrow by Tube.

'Just do the best you can, okay . . . ?'

He hit another button on the phone.

'. . . Jo, it's me. The cabbie says I won't make it. Can you get me on another flight? . . . I know it's the last Stuttgart flight, but there must be some other way of getting there. Via Frankfurt, or Schipol maybe. If there's nothing, you'll have to charter a jet. However you do it, *get* me there. Now, put me through to Simon Black . . .'

He glanced through the drizzle at the road ahead. They were swinging round the Blackfriars spur that loops down to the Embankment. He prayed it would be moving freely. Further round the bend the cab pulled up sharply. A sea of brake lights shimmered before them. *Fuck.* His fists clenched involuntarily. Then a voice came back on the phone. Jo had tracked down Simon Black.

'Simon? Marcus. I'm off to Stuttgart. I got a message from Robert Quilley suggesting we might bring Foxtrot's bid forward to Thursday. Can you call and persuade him to stick to next Monday?'

*

It was gone eight by the time they got to Heathrow. To Ford's chagrin, there *was* a scheduled connection through Frankfurt, and the only seat left was in economy. He wouldn't tell Sophie that. He'd called her to let her know he might charter a plane. Busy as she was watching the nanny bathe their kids, she didn't have time to be impressed. If she heard now what had happened, she would laugh like a drain. Rich bitch. How he would love it if her father tripped up and lost a few millions. Most other wives he knew would be delighted to have a husband who was a director at thirty-four and making half a million a year. Not Sophie, though: she called it his 'pocket money'.

3

As the cab climbed the ramp to Terminal One, Ford was still on the phone, this time to someone in the bank's New York office. Still talking, he clambered out of the cab without a word of thanks to the driver and made his way into the building.

The bald, middle-aged cabbie paused for a while until the banker disappeared, and then drove off. Including all the waiting time, the meter had wound itself up to seventy-six pounds forty, his personal record for a flyer. In the twenty-odd years since he'd got his badge he must have been out to Heathrow hundreds of times, and never broken the sixty-five mark. It was quite a start for the evening. Even if it was slim pickings for the next few hours, he should be able to knock off by midnight with at least a hundred and fifty in his pocket. And maybe the smartarse had left him a little tip, too?

He drove over to the feeder park, took a ticket, parked to wait for the call to one of the terminals, and dialled.

*

The floodlights scorched through the gathering mist. In the old days the loyal band of supporters would have huddled together for warmth near the centre line or behind the goals, but all-seater stadiums didn't permit that. And when it was as cold as this, the thin plastic seats numbed the buttocks. Getting any kind of atmosphere going was hard, and any cheers were uncoordinated and passionless. The players seemed to catch the same mood, and the game was dully mired in the middle of the field.

Without warning, the stalemate was broken. Red-shirted defenders made a mess of an offside trap, and a striker in claret and blue sprinted in pursuit of a long-floated ball. The goalkeeper raced out to narrow the angle, spreading his limbs wide, but the striker deftly slid the ball between his legs and it rolled to a muddy halt eight yards from the naked goal. All three hundred home supporters roared as the attacker athletically hurdled the prone goalie, swung back his right leg and thumped the ball clean over the bar.

The groans of the little crowd were interrupted by a mobile phone going off. The resident wag got there by the second ring.

4

He pointed to the striker, whose face was still buried in his hands.

'That'll be 'is missus, tellin' 'im not to come 'ome.'

The phone rang and rang. Finally the owner succeeded in fishing it out of his scuffed leather jacket.

' 'Ello.'

'That you, Terry lad? You at West 'Am?'

'Yeah. It's a reserves game against Charlton. Nil-nil. Bleedin' terrible, it is. What you want, Len?'

'You got the *Directory of Directors* in your cab?'

'I'm sittin' on it. Only way to keep me bum from freezin'.'

'Do me a favour. Look up Robert Quilley in the index. I got it from a punter at Skidder Barton. Company's code name is "Foxtrot". You know how dumb these bleedin' bankers are. I'll give you even money the real name begins with an "f", too.'

'Wait a minute, I'll take a look . . . Oldfield, Oswald . . . Penfold, Roberts . . . Quarta, Quilley. Yeah, that's the fella. Managing Director of Furnival Engineering. Says they make parts for cars, lorries and trucks. What's goin' on? Will they get bid for?'

'Nah, they're the *bidder*. It's to be launched Monday; could even be this Thursday. To be on the safe side, we should get Einstein to work out the target tonight and buy shares tomorrow. I'll give 'im a bell.'

'You forgotten? Tuesday's their nookie night. Einstein and Ruth never answer the phone Tuesday nights.'

'Will you nip round there, then? We could do well out of this one, Terry.'

'I'm supposed to 'ave a drink with Marcie after the game. You know what she's like if I'm late.'

'Better show 'er who wears the trousers before you get wed. Come on, Terry lad, there's only eighty shoppin' days to Christmas, and if I'm to get decent presents for Poppy, I need some of the needful.'

'Okay, I'll drop round there. If Marcie gives me attitude, I'll tell 'er it's down to you.'

'You do that. If Einstein works it out, call me back and let me know, there's a good lad. 'Ow much you want on this one?'

'Can't afford a lot, Len. I just got a new exhaust for the Cossie. Cost me an arm and a leg. Put me down for 'undred and fifty.'

*

Terry drove the four miles to Newbury Park as fast as his old Fairway cab would carry him. It was almost ten when he opened the creaking low wrought-iron gate and walked up to Einstein's front door. All was in darkness downstairs, but a hint of light escaped from the bedroom above. He rang the door chime. It always made him smile. Einstein had modified it to play the first notes of the theme from *Exodus*.

Silence. He tried again. Nothing. He stepped back a pace or two and looked up. The glimmer had gone. Good. They were in, anyway.

Up in the bedroom they waited. Whoever it was should leave now, and they could resume.

'King's bishop pawn to bishop 5.' Her voice was dry and tense.

'You devil. King to rook.'

'Mmmm. Let me think. Rook to queen 6.'

What a move! His hands tightened on her breasts.

'Okay, you scheming vixen. Queen's knight's pawn to bishop 4.'

She was finding it harder to think straight, but somehow she had to counter him.

'Queen to bishop 4. Check.'

Einstein almost squealed with delight. It was a feeble parry, taking her nowhere. The gentle rhythm of his motion turned rougher. Now it was time to *truly* surprise her.

'*Bishop to knight 4.*'

She groaned in baffled ecstasy.

'Your gorgeous mind.'

She was well away now. Einstein was getting there too, but his thoughts were still sharp. Time now for some different thrills.

'Ruth, talk *dirty*.'

She smiled in the darkness.

6

'Okay. Copulating queen to fornicating bishop 2.'

It was a rotten move, but, by God, it sounded *good*.

Now Einstein's brain was leaving him too, as the force took over. He could no longer imagine the board so clearly. Oh, to hell with it.

'I'm going to spank your queen's bottom hard all night long. I'll thrash your Russian defence. I want to . . .'

The tempo was picking up now, their breathing getting more ragged, the final crescendo near at hand.

Down below Terry strained to look at his watch again. He'd given them nearly ten minutes since the last chime. If they'd been in the middle of anything when he rang the bell, they should've had plenty of time to finish off. He reached into the tiny rockery and picked out a few small stones.

The bed was being shaken to its foundations. Ruth had managed another desperate move, but it was all *wrong*. In one last burst of lucidity, Einstein saw how to finish her off but delayed the coup de grace for a few more seconds. She sensed it was coming too, almost *wanted* it now, as she felt the waves rising within her. They were close, almost there.

'Jacob *darling* . . .'

Crack.

They both froze, the ecstasy draining away.

'What the *hell* was that?' She sounded genuinely alarmed.

'No idea . . .'

He had been *seconds* from checkmate. Unless they got going again soon, they would lose the mood altogether.

'. . . Must have been a bird flying into the glass. Don't worry about it.'

He buried his head back in her little bosom.

Crack.

His head flew up again, alert now.

'What the . . . ?'

A distant stage-whisper voice entered their senses.

'*Einstein . . . Einstein . . . You awake, mate?*'

Ruth started in fury.

'Is that bloody Terry?'

'Might be. Ignore him. He'll go away.'

They lay there, still panting slightly, for a few trial seconds.

'*Einstein . . . Einstein . . .*'

The voice was louder, more insistent, his stage whisper getting closer to a shout.

Einstein knew it was blown.

'I'll murder him.'

Crack.

Ruth's dander was up, too. 'He'll break the blooming windows if he goes on like that.'

Growling furiously to himself, Einstein pulled himself out of bed, yanked back the curtains and threw open a window.

'*Piss off.*'

He banged the window shut again, closed the curtain, and stumbled through the darkness back to the bed. A minute passed: cautiously, he tried nuzzling a nipple.

Crack.

Ruth reached over and switched the bedside lamp on. She picked up a tall glass of water, stomped over to the window, opened it and threw the contents down at Terry. He had his wits about him and stepped neatly aside.

''Ello, Ruth. Sorry if I caught you at a bad moment, love.'

'Get lost.'

'Len's found a big one. We need Einstein's 'elp.'

'What's wrong with tomorrow?'

'Too late. Len says we got to do it tonight.'

'Well, tell Len to piss off.'

'He *needs* this one, Ruthie. Wants to get Poppy some things for Christmas.'

'*Christmas*? It's bloody *September*.'

All the same, the mention of Poppy seemed to have some effect. Ruth disappeared and a light came on in the hall downstairs. The door opened to reveal a sullen, dishevelled Ruth in a plum-coloured bathrobe, with an even more unhappy Einstein trailing downstairs after her in a matching outfit. It was the first time Terry had seen him without his thick glasses. Einstein marched to the door and eyed Terry coldly.

'If this isn't good, you're in deep shit.'

Terry grinned inwardly. The idea that anyone could be in deep shit with eight-stone Einstein was funny. What was he going to do? Attack him with a modem?

'Len's well keen on it.'

'Okay, come in, then.'

Einstein fished in his pocket for his glasses and led the way into the front room. He sat down in front of his computer and turned on the power. As it ran through the warm-up routines, he asked, without turning round,

'So . . . ? What's Len's big story?

'Furnival Engineering.'

'Wait a sec . . . Okay, we have it. Sales of two billion, pre-tax profits two hundred and seventy million. Market value two point six billion. Looks expensive. Are you saying they're going to get bid for?'

'Nah, they're going to *make* a bid, accordin' to Len.'

'Who's the target?'

'That's what we need you to tell us.'

'Mmmm.' Einstein's irritation was fading fast. He enjoyed their little investment club – at least when it didn't interfere with Tuesday nights – and the way Len and Terry prized his help. Warming to the task, he whizzed slickly from page to page of his much-customized computer database.

'Is Len sure it's a UK company? There are four or five listed companies on the Continent in the same product areas. Two in France. One each in Switzerland, Holland and Germany.'

Terry scratched his genitals pensively. 'Len didn't say, but it sounded like he *thought* it was British.'

'If so, there are only two possibles. IFK and Burton. Burton's closer in product terms – clutches, friction materials and spark plugs – but I don't see it. If you look at their share price, it's at the

9

very top of the trading range. Furnival couldn't justify paying a premium on top of that.'

This was stretching Terry's brain to its limits, and anyway it was hard to concentrate when he thought of the bollocking Marcie would give him. She must've been at the Spreadeagle for a good half-hour now, and would be working herself up into a right little fury. He didn't want to stand here *discussing*. All he wanted was the answer, so he could be on his way.

'What you mean, a premium?'

'If one company bids for another, they have to offer the shareholders more than market price: otherwise, why should they sell? Bidders usually offer at least thirty per cent above market. They difference between market price and the offer level is called a "takeover premium". If it didn't exist, how would we ever make any money out of this racket?'

'Is *that* 'ow it works? I thought it was like bettin' on the 'orses. You get a tip, put some cash on the nose, and Bob's your uncle. Does Len understand this *premium* stuff?'

'Of course he does. I explained it to you both ages ago but you weren't listening. You probably had your mind on some piece of skirt.'

'What you mean, "piece of skirt"? I 'ope you're not referrin' to my fiancée?'

'No, this was one of your other "fiancées".'

'Oh, *Julie*? That was only a bit of fun. Hey, you 'aven't said anything to Marcie about Julie, 'ave you?'

'You'd know about it if I had, wouldn't you?'

'S'pose I would. Talking of Marcie, she's waiting for me now down the Spreadeagle, and she'll skin me alive if I'm any later. Could you maybe work it all out and give Len a bell in the—'

'Ahhhh, *this* is more like it. Take a look here . . .'

Einstein pointed excitedly to a new graph that had appeared on the screen.

'. . . See, IFK's profits are down twenty per cent, and their share price has halved. That's the one, I'd lay money on it. I *will* lay money on it.'

10

Ruth came into the room bearing mugs of sweet tea. Terry shook his head.

'No thanks, love. Got to be on me way. What time is it? Oh, *Jesus* . . . IFK, right?' He picked up a pencil from Einstein's desk and scribbled the name down. '. . . So, 'ow much you want to put on it?'

Einstein swivelled round on his stool, took his glasses off for a quick face rub, and put them back on.

'What d'you think, Ruth? How much can we afford?'

Ruth looked doubtful. Their last two sallies into the market had gone badly awry. Either their information must have been wrong or something had changed at the last minute to blow the bids off course. The three cabbies had lost a bundle and all but wiped out the gains they'd made since starting this lark back in January.

'I don't know, Jacob. I don't think we should risk more than a hundred.'

Terry couldn't stop himself smiling. Einstein's real name didn't suit him at all.

Einstein looked pleadingly at Ruth. Investing in shares had uncovered a gambler's streak buried deep within him. He'd never been tempted by the horses, and the thought of someone like him going inside a casino was ridiculous. But this new sport had really got hold of him.

'Surely we can do a couple of hundred, Ruthie? There's not much risk here. The IFK share price is so bombed out, I don't see how it *could* fall any further. Even if they're not bid for, we can't lose a lot.'

Ruth held her mug to her lips and considered. She was unconvinced. Then the thought of that masterstroke – bishop to knight 4 – came fleetingly back to her mind, and she knew she couldn't refuse him.

'All right, then, two hundred. Not a penny more.'

Through his thick lenses, Einstein's eyes shone their silent thanks. Terry looked mightily relieved they'd reached a decision.

'Okay then, I'll phone Len, and tell 'im to get onto the broker

11

first thing. Bye now. Sorry again for disturbin' you. Don't bother, I'll see myself out.'

They let him do that, and seconds later heard the raucous clatter of his cab's diesel engine starting up. Einstein looked one more time at the IFK share graph, nodded, and began the switching-off procedure. As he was waiting for it, a voice came from behind.

'Anagram. Twelve letters. T ... N ... R ... O ... I ... N ... S ... I ... R ... C ... U ... E ...'

As the screen flickered and died, Einstein whispered back, 'Insurrection.'

'Oooh, your *gorgeous* mind.'

By the time he swung round, his arms outstretched, Ruth had flung the sides of her bathrobe triumphantly aside, and stood there gloriously, exultantly, skinnily, for him to take her right there on the carpet.

2

When the call came that Friday morning, Marcus Ford felt profoundly flattered. However dented Charles Barton's reputation might be, he *was* still Chairman and Chief Executive, as well as a member of one of England's grandest banking dynasties. Proudly, Marcus ordered Jo to cancel his lunch date with an old Oxford friend.

The food in the Chairman's personal dining room was the same as that served in the many client dining rooms at Skidders. But in Barton's room the service was that bit more deferential and the wine more select. Normally, Marcus made a point of not drinking at lunchtime and had developed the habit of casting sly, pitying glances at any sad colleagues who felt the need. However, when he saw Charles Barton accepting a glass of Montrachet from the formally clad butler, he thought it churlish not to join him.

For a while they swapped small talk. Then Barton talked expansively about the bank's future. Marcus couldn't suppress a measure of private amusement. The word in the City was that Charles Barton's strategy was a disaster. After too many years of twiddling his thumbs, he had sold a twenty per cent stake to the mighty Zuricher Bank, confidently believing that this would give Skidders a much-needed international edge. However, the market divined Zuricher's real intentions: to grab total control of the English bank when the first chance came.

Midway through the main course, Barton edged his way closer to the nitty-gritty.

'Sorry to hear that your Stuttgart trip was wasted.'

'Yes, the rumour that the owners of Porsche were willing to sell turned out to be false. Still, you never can tell: it was worth seeing if they needed a bank.'

'Indeed. More important – Furnival's bid for IFK. You're all ready to launch first thing on Monday?'

'Yes. For once, there doesn't seem to have been a leak. We should hit them out of a clear blue sky. Robert Quilley will call their Chairman just before we announce it. Sir Reginald's not an early riser, by all accounts, so we've got hold of his home number.'

'Marcus, I can't tell you how much I appreciate the way you've pulled this bid out of the fire. When the team handling it defected to Merrills, I had a hell of a job persuading Quilley to give us another chance. But here we are, two months later, and you've got him eating out of your hand.'

'I could never have managed that without all the support you've given me.' Marcus came close to tacking on a 'Charles'. Not just yet. Give it a few more days.

Barton smiled and continued. 'I dined with Quilley last night. If this bid succeeds, he's already got his next move planned. I'll tell you more about it some other time, but believe me, it's breathtakingly audacious. He's a real visionary, that man: he has *balls* . . .'

Marcus was so surprised by the sudden jock talk that a mouthful of fish went down the wrong way. Barton politely ignored his splutterings and went on to the next subject.

'. . . If you don't mind, I'd appreciate an off-the-record chat about the corporate finance department. I know you're the youngest director there, but you've been at Skidders for five or six years now and you've worked closely with all the older directors. What do you think of them?'

Marcus lifted up his glass again to buy a few seconds of reflection. This was a real googly. If he had a clearer idea of where Barton himself stood, he could echo his view, in suitably considered and statesmanlike terms. Without that guidance, he could go a hundred and eighty degrees the wrong way. Simply giving an honest opinion was *far* too dangerous.

'They're certainly a very experienced group. Safe pairs of hands everywhere you look.'

'Mmm-hmm.'

Damn – he hadn't smoked Barton out. He'd have to inch

further out of his crease.

'It's probably true that their expertise is mainly limited to the UK domestic market.'

'*Precisely.*'

Sounded like a lucky strike. Better press home the advantage.

'Very few of them are interested in Continental work. I don't believe any of them even speaks a language.'

'Exactly.'

Yo! Thank God for that French 'A' level. Not that he'd got round to unleashing it on any clients – or anyone at all, beyond waiters and girls.

'How do you rate Richard Myers?'

This was even trickier. Myers had been head of the department for a couple of years. He was a perfectly competent corporate financier who couldn't manage his way out of a paper bag.

'Richard has his strengths.'

Barton smiled at the cautious reply.

'Yes, that can't be denied. However, those strengths may not be the right ones for today's increasingly international environment. Frankly, Marcus, the jury's still out on whether Richard will make it . . .'

For a second, Marcus dreamt that the dazzling prize of Richard's job might be offered to him. Barton saw that thought flicker across his face and ploughed hastily on.

'. . . I've been thinking this over for some time, and I've had a chat about it with Ernst Lautenschutz. I must say, I do find the alliance with our Swiss friends refreshing. They have such an *international* outlook. Together we concluded that the department would benefit from some widening of perspective, and I've made an offer to a team from Morgan Stanley in New York. Does the name Rosco Sellars mean anything to you . . . ?'

It didn't, but Marcus faked it and nodded.

'. . . I was sure you would know him by reputation. Then you'll be aware of his leading role arranging financing for takeovers.'

'Naturally. How many guys will he be bringing with him?'

'Seven or eight initially. They're not all "guys", as it happens.

15

One of them is called Julia Daventry. English, actually, and not unattractive. That won't concern a married man like you, of course, but I wager she'll break a few hearts in the department.'

'When will this be official?'

'I'll tell the directors at the Monday meeting and the team will join one week later. I had a spot of bother over where they slot in. When I told Richard Myers about the plan, he was very insistent that Sellars should report to *him*. Sellars was having none of that. After much to-ing and fro-ing, it's been agreed that they'll be joint heads of corporate finance.'

Marcus was digesting this news, trying to work out what it meant for him. He suspected that there was something in the tail: if not a sting, then at least a message. He didn't have to wait long.

'I would appreciate you doing your best to make sure this is well received in the department. Some of the old guard may find it rather threatening, and could try to undermine the new team before they have a chance to prove themselves. However, if the younger, more dynamic directors like you get behind it, I'm sure it could be made to work . . .'

Marcus nodded gravely and speared a triangle of Camembert. In principle, he was happy to help. However, one part of the equation was still missing: what was in for him?

'. . . Looking to the future, we would never want an American in *sole* charge of corporate finance. If Richard Myers doesn't work well with Rosco and we have to choose a successor, age won't be a barrier.'

Excellent. Now the equation was satisfactorily completed, the trick was to avoid showing how totally he had been bought.

'I'm sure Richard *will* make this work. And of course I'll do my best to make the junior staff view the change positively.'

'I appreciate that. Now, tell me, are you going to take your son and daughter with you to Courchevel, or will they be staying with your nanny?'

*

They call it Green Badge Valley, that triangle of Gants Hill, Wanstead and Newbury Park. Every street has at least one cabbie

16

in residence, and there are some you can drive down and see nothing but cabs parked in the drives. There are a few yellow-badgers living there too. Yellow means suburban. The living's almost as good, and of course the cab's just the same, whether it's a classic Fairway, a Metrocab or a new TX1. The problem with being a yellow-badger is *knowing* you're second-class. Doesn't bear thinking about. What's the point of going through the aggro of getting the badge if you can't hold your head up and say you're a real London cabbie?

Terry was from good cabbie stock and never contemplated going for yellow. Born and brought up in Wanstead, he had three uncles who were cabbies, so it sort of ran in the family. His Dad had tried the Knowledge when the building trade had one of its downturns. But he got fed up freezing his balls off riding around on a moped, memorizing routes, so as soon as things improved he went back to bricklaying. The moped didn't go to waste, though, since Terry used it when his turn came.

Becoming a cabbie had been the natural choice for Terry after he gave up the football. As an apprentice at West Ham, he'd had talent to spare, and there were high hopes for him. If only he'd taken it seriously, he could've have been a star. He never had the discipline, though: all he was interested in back then was girls. As he drove along Romford High Street, he laughed at himself. He hadn't changed very much: his head was as full of girls as ever. In fact, he was planning to be a bit naughty that very evening. Marcie was going on a hen night somewhere up the West End. Usually they started at Quaglino's. The girls all loved it for being so sophisticated. After that, it would be high jinks at some male stripper club, and they'd all come rolling home, pissed as duchesses.

It helped that Marcie and Terry lived separately, even though they were engaged. With Marcie's Dad being the layabout he was, there was no chance he'd cough up for the nuptials, so it was down to the couple to save for it themselves, and that would take time. Terry had rented a flat in Canterbury Gardens, Redbridge, reckoning they could shack up there, try it out for size for a few years, and worry later about the legal bit. But Marcie was sharp

17

and realized that once she parked her slippers in Canterbury Gardens, she might not progress from tiny diamond to gold band.

Not that she had any objection to using Terry's place for nookie. Even though she stayed resolutely resident in her Mum's and Dad's semi in Chigwell, Marcie didn't enjoy bonking in her bedroom there, since she could never cure her Mum of the habit of wandering in unannounced to offer them a nice cup of tea.

So most Fridays and Saturdays they'd start with a few at The Spreadeagle, have a Chinese or Indian, and end up in Terry's sweaty bed. But if Marcie went out with the girls, like this Friday night, she would go straight home to Chigwell, leaving Canterbury Gardens safely and deliciously available.

That thought was not far from Terry's mind as he drove his pride and joy, his metallic blue RS 500 Cosworth Sierra, into the Spreadeagle car park, checked his breath in a cupped hand, and ventured inside.

There she was, early. That was a good sign.

' 'Ello, love. Don't *you* look a picture? What can I get you?'

'Already got a Bacardi and Coke. You don't look that bad yourself. Wondered if I'd recognize you, it was that dark in *Faces*. I was really pleased you phoned, you know. It's the first time I've gone out with an older man.'

'You call twenty-eight *older*?'

'From where *I'm* standing, it is. Twenty two's been me oldest up to now. Tell a lie, twenty-four, but that that was so quick it don't count. Twenty-eight's *ancient*.'

'Why d'you come then, if I'm ancient?'

'Fancy yah, don't I? By the way, one of me mates, Carol – red hair, big thighs, remember? – saw you down Tesco's with some blonde gel. When I say *blonde*, Carol says she was black as the ace of spades at the roots.'

'She must've got me mixed up with some other fella.'

'No, she was positive it was you.'

Terry hesitated. He looked at her lovely slender legs and her proudly jutting bust. The contrast with Marcie was striking: even at twenty-seven Marcie's tits had embarked on their long southward voyage.

'Blonde, with dark roots, you say? . . . Could be me sister, Lorna.'

'Oh . . .' She was more or less convinced, if only because she wanted to be. '. . . So where we goin' tonight, anyway?'

'Thought we'd have one or two here, then there's this film I want to see.'

'A *film*? You said we'd go to a restaurant. I'm famished.'

'We could always get a takeaway.'

'What? And eat it in the cinema?'

'This film's not actually *on* at a cinema, so I got it out on video. Thought we might watch it at my place.'

Terry grinned. The girl slapped him in the face, but it wasn't a proper slap, more like an 'I know your game' sort of slap. He reached round and put an appreciative hand on her buttocks. They gazed into each other's eyes for a few seconds. Then she glanced over his shoulder towards the pub's main door.

'Now *that's* what I call roots.'

Terry turned round to clock this newcomer. *Jesus.* He darted behind a pillar. The teenager followed him.

'What's the matter, Terry? You look like you've seen a ghost.'

'It's me . . . sister.'

'You goin' to introduce me, then?'

'Not tonight. We had a tiff. Tell you what, I think I'll slip out the back door. See you in the car park in about three minutes. *Shit*, she's coming this way. I got to run.'

Terry had been miserably unlucky. There was no reason for him to guess that the relationship being celebrated was not rock-steady, nor that the girl in question would choose that afternoon to uncover evidence of her fiancé's dalliance and call the thing off, leaving her cronies short of a dinner at Quaglino's and back on home turf, all dressed up with nowhere to go. He was even unluckier that Marcie's short sight was compensated for by the eagle eyes of her best friend, Lucy.

19

Lucy's finger pointed, and Marcie marched imperiously up to the hapless young girl.

'Where's the fella you was with just now?'

The girl played for time.

'You're Terry's sister, in't you?'

Marcie's eyes flashed a thousand volts.

'I'll give you "sister", all right. Where's 'e gone . . . ?'

Meekly, the girl indicated the passage to the back door and the toilets.

'. . . And what was you plannin' to do together, eh?'

'Watch a video at Terry's place.'

Marcie shrieked and marched, footsteps like thunder, towards a showdown.

Terry rattled the bolt again, but the back door was definitely locked. He dashed back down the scruffy corridor, skidding to a halt and darting into the gents when he saw Marcie turn the corner. Christ, what was he going to do now? There was only one thing for it: the window.

It was high and small. Pushing past three pissers, he jumped up, wriggled his shoulders through, and tried to lever the rest of his body out.

The door swung open and a bloodcurdling yell rang out. Three startled men pissed all over their shoes and trousers.

Marcie strode forward and grabbed at the kicking legs. Terry strained every muscle, but only succeeded in getting more stuck. He would just have to talk his way out if it. That wasn't easy: he couldn't twist his head around to speak to her, so he had to shout to the outside world in general and hope that his voice would carry back inside.

'That you, pet? I can explain. I needed some fresh air, that's all.'

'I'll give you *fresh air*.' She sounded *very* sure of that.

Four minutes later, Marcie emerged triumphantly from the gents, bearing a pair of black leather trousers and jockey shorts of an exotic pattern. She carried her spoils straight to the bar and addressed the cheery old publican.

'Des, give me an empty ice bucket, one of them lighter refills, and a box of matches.'

With due ceremony, she turned to her friends.

'Guess what, gels? That's a second one broken off tonight . . .'

She stuffed the underwear and trousers into the bucket, doused them in fuel, and struck a match. The flames leapt up, blue and yellow. Lucy pressed a vodka and orange into her hand. Marcie raised it high.

'. . . To freedom, and bollocks to men. They're all cheatin' bastards.'

She drained her glass and caught sight of the mystified teenager, who was still rooted to her spot, and gave her the evil eye. Then she softened a little, stepped over and put an arm round her.

'It's not your fault, love. I'm sure 'e told you a right pack of lies.'

'So you ain't Terry's sister, then?'

Marcie looked down at the red line the engagement ring had left on her finger.

'See that? That's where I wore Terry's ring.'

'Oooh, the dirty lying so-and-so. What you done with it?'

'Gave it 'im back, didn't I? Only Terry's 'ands weren't free, so I 'ad to stuff it wherever I could.'

And Marcie began to giggle, then creased with laughter. Lucy followed suit. So did Des, and his wife Janet, and everyone at the bar. Even the young girl did, when she finally got it.

*

'Len, that you?'

'Hi there, Terry lad. Don't worry, I called the broker.'

'That's not why I'm callin'. Do me a favour, Len? Can you come to The Spreadeagle right away?.'

'Sorry, mate, not tonight. Thirty quid's all I've taken so far. I got to work for another four hours, minimum.'

'Len, I'm in a real spot of bother. Someone's got to bring me a spare pair of trousers.'

'You crapped yourself or somethin'? What's wrong with Marcie? Why can't *she* run your errands?'

'Len, *please.*'

'Terry, I'm in Fulham. I couldn't be there much before ten . . . Anyway, I ain't got a key for your flat, 'ave I?'

'Don't matter. A pair of yours'll do fine.'

'Bollocks, you could fit in mine twice over.'

'Len, I'm *desperate.*'

'Okay, but you'd better 'ave a bloody good reason. See you in the bar.'

'Can't, mate, I'll be in the gents. Cubicle nearest the window.'

Len switched his phone off and chuckled. Terry was always getting into scrapes, and girls were usually involved. He was looking forward to hearing this one.

*

The traffic was lighter once was he was clear of the centre, and Len pulled in front of his house by half-nine. He'd tried to give his missus a bell to let her know he was coming back early but his battery gave out on him after the first two or three rings, so if she was rogering the neighbour she'd get a big surprise. Not that Jean was the rogering type. Sex had never interested her very much. While Len heaved and panted, Jean would fill in the time gossiping away to him. When he got close, Len would tell her to belt up, which she never minded, bless her heart, and as soon as he was done she'd start chatting again. It wouldn't have suited every man, but Len had got used to it. Of course, when they saw folk having sex on the telly it was never like that. But who was to know which was nearer to normal? Truth to tell, Len was losing interest himself these days, what with working late and Poppy coughing away in the next room. Didn't do a lot for the libido.

He walked up the herringbone drive that they'd had put down last year and turned the key in the door. He half expected Jean to leap straight out into the hall to check it was him, but it seemed like she hadn't heard him. It was hardly surprising, what with the music that was blaring away from the lounge. What the hell was she up to in there?

Intrigued, he pushed the lounge door ajar and put his head round it. Jean had her back to him. She was wearing a leotard, and waving her arms wildly about. Then she put her left leg out, then the right, wiggling them around, hokey-cokeyish. Len looked past her to the source of the noise, the TV set. It was an aerobics video, with all the women about half Jean's age and girth. Jean's awkward movements bore no obvious resemblance to what they were doing.

Len stayed as still as he could, grinning broadly. Jean sensed something and swung round.

It was hard to know who got the bigger shock. Jean nearly had a heart attack, of course, but the awesome sight of his wife's facial pack almost did for Len, too. He recovered the power of speech first, and raised both arms above his head in surrender.

'You are welcome on Planet Earth.'

'Jesus Christ, Len, you frightened the life out of me. What you mean, sneaking up on me like that?'

'What do *you* mean, cavorting round like that with goo all over your face?'

'It's not *goo*, it's aubergine oil. It's good for wrinkles. Mum gave it me for my birthday, that and the video. Thought I'd try them out in peace and quiet. Didn't expect you back for *hours* yet. What you doin' 'ome at this time anyway? You're not sick, are you?' Jean had already reached for a box of tissues and was busy smearing her face clean.

'Terry's in a spot of bother down The Spreadeagle.'

'What kind of bother?'

'All I know is the lad needs a new pair of pants. Promised I'd take a pair of mine along.'

'That'll cramp Terry's style all right. Can't see 'im picking up many gels in your smelly old trousers.'

'Thanks a bunch. I better be off. 'Ow's Poppy?'

'She's not been too bad tonight. I think she's asleep now. She won't say it, of course, but the poor little thing's worried sick what that doctor'll say next week.'

'She's not the only one.'

3

It was Ruth who'd got Einstein back to the synagogue, and now they went every Saturday. He'd been brought up strictly and had his bar mitzvah and all that, but when he rebelled against everything else, it made no sense to make an exception for religion.

He never got back on speaking terms with his father, not even when his mother died. His father just couldn't get over his disappointment, his feelings of betrayal after *all* he had done.

Einstein had the misfortune of having too big a brain. By four he was reading the newspapers and by ten he could knock off the *Times* crossword. At thirteen he started breezing his way through his 'A' levels, passing eighteen in total, just for the hell of it. It wasn't just school stuff, either. He was a whizz at chess and had a talent for piano which, if he'd nurtured it, could have led to the concert hall.

Being an only child, he was the constant focus of his parents' attention, and his father, who hadn't made much of himself, devoted every spare hour to training his son. When Einstein was accepted for Cambridge at the age of fifteen, it seemed that the whole world stood at his feet, encouraging his father to live vicariously through him more than ever. He gave his parents no early warning of the feelings that were building up inside him, though his mother had occasional forebodings and would try to rein back her husband. But how could you persuade a man to ease up when his only pleasure in life came from musing on whether his son would be a Nobel laureate or a Cabinet minister? She did what she could to lighten the load, to introduce other topics of conversation or to suggest that Jacob should invite some friends to the house. Her husband dismissed the very idea that Jacob would want to idle time away in the company of those childish halfwits, when there was so much to do that was far more fulfilling. It was all hypothetical, anyway. The lad had been a freak for too long for any normal friendship to function.

Cambridge was where the explosion came. Disoriented and isolated, away from his father's baleful watch, he gave up any semblance of serious study halfway through the first term. Some of the undergraduates entertained themselves by plying him with alcohol, soft drugs and fags. Everything collapsed before the end of the first year. The tutors' patience was wearing thin, and various counsellors failed to make any headway with him. Before the final blow fell, the college wrote to his parents.

His father couldn't decide whether he should rant more at the teachers or the student. Could it be true that Jacob really was performing so dismally, or were they all too dim to recognize his genius? He travelled to Cambridge to interrogate the suspects in person. It was his son's bad attendance record at tutorials that convinced him of the awful truth. So the son got the blast, and a few blows too, till he promised to pull his socks up. At the time he would have said anything to get rid of the man, and had no intention of ever opening another mathematics textbook. Three weeks later he was sent down and he ran away, living rough on the streets of London for over a year.

His late teens passed in much the same way. The dole gave him enough to pay for a squalid bedsit in Kilburn. He was back in touch with his mother by then, and she would quietly welcome him round for a few hours in the daytime if he felt like it. This was kept secret from his father and Einstein had to be gone long before that terminally disappointed man came home from his job at the sorting office.

It was his mother's gentle persuasion that got him to try for a teaching diploma, and not long past his twentieth birthday he enrolled at a local college. Most of his fellow students were pleasant enough, though they never invited him along to the pub or to parties. The course was a doddle, and even his teaching experience at a friendly, traditional school in King's Lynn went well. The kids took a bit of a rise out of him, but their instinct for

25

obedience was too deeply ingrained for things to get far out of hand. This even gave Einstein a first hint of confidence: when the kids clubbed together and bought him a jokey farewell present, it brought tears to his eyes.

Oh, the contrast when he began teaching for real at Hackney. There was already uproar when he went into the class of fourteen-year-olds. His attempts at quelling it were risible and soon missiles were thrown at him. If he hoped that getting on with the lesson would bring order, he was misled, and a black eye was his reward for trying to break up a fight. He persevered grimly for a few more weeks, but that first-day defeat had been fatal. Most of the boys simply walked out of his lessons and the girls ignored him, forming small gaggles in his classroom to discuss nail varnish, underwear, and conquests.

So by twenty-three it was back to the dole. Another year on and he took the first of a series of dreary desk jobs, from the DHSS to insurance, and spent evenings and weekends in front of his computer surfing the Web. He had no friends to speak of – unless Internet friends counted – and by his thirtieth birthday had still never laid a passionate finger on a member of the opposite sex.

His unhappiness finally became so acute that he *had* to do something, and plumped for that great standby of lonely hearts, an evening class. He didn't intend to actually study anything, so he enrolled in a chess class, posing as a beginner.

And who should walk into the classroom that first night but the girl of his dreams, an instant soulmate in a fawn cadigan, with tight little black ringlets, specs just like his, and the sweetest, shyest smile you ever saw? They went for a drink in a pub afterwards, and laughed themselves silly when they found they were both at the same game. They never went to the chess class again, and married one month later. Ruth took three weeks off from her job at a pharmaceutical research lab and they had a wet but enchanting honeymoon in Galway. Everything about Ruth was wonderful, and her parents eventually warmed to him, relieved that he was a Jewish boy even if he didn't fully match their idea of a 'good' one.

It was Ruth who first saw that becoming a cabbie made sense for a loner like Jacob, blessed as he was with extraordinary powers of memory. Unsurprisingly, he passed the Knowledge in some new record time. It was only his actual driving that needed any real work.

Later on, the golf was Ruth's idea, too. She thought it would be nice for him to know some other cabbies, and was aware that they often struck up friendships through fishing or golf. Einstein was too uncoordinated to have a natural aptitude for either. They talked it over and concluded he would be less of a menace to himself and mankind with a stick and a ball than with a line and a very sharp hook.

Ruth bought him a half-set of clubs in the sales and they went off to Hainault Forest Club. He had a few lessons, which yielded no discernible benefit, and a few weeks later he embarked on his first solo round. As a precaution, he took along two dozen balls, but found he'd used them all up by the fifth hole. He persevered unpromisingly for another few weeks, and was close to abandoning the whole project when he ran across Terry and Len.

It was the investing game that brought them together, after that first friendly drink anyway. Terry blabbed something about stocks and shares. Len looked daggers at him, like he was giving away some big secret. Terry didn't seem to notice and went right on saying it was a pity that they didn't understand the 'rudimentals', because there must be good money to be made from what you overheard in a cab.

Einstein had never bought a share in his life and knew nothing whatsover about investing. What he *did* know was that he could master any subject in no time at all.

And so it began. Within a fortnight, Einstein had digested the key textbooks – and the cabbies' investment club was successfully born. Len called him 'a bleedin' Einstein' and the name stuck. Ruth was so pleased for her husband that for many months she put aside any qualms about the propriety of what they were up to. However, the Saturday after Terry's unwelcome visit, she ventured a question as they walked home from the synagogue.

'Jacob, the stuff you do with Len and Terry, it is *legal*, isn't it?'

'Legal? I *think* so. Never really thought about it, to tell the truth. It's not like we're being given information in confidence or anything, is it? We just pick up snippets and piece them together. There *is* something called "insider dealing", but I don't think that can possibly apply to cabbies. In fact, I can't think of a group that's more "outsider". And even if, strictly speaking, it *was* illegal, no one could prove how we came by it. As long as we claimed that we were investing based on my research, they couldn't touch us.'

'If you're sure, that's all right then. Just as long as there's no risk of you losing your badge.'

'Don't bother your lovely brain about it. Now, how about a game of Scrabble when we get back?'

'Standard rules or ours?'

'Ours, of course. The standard ones are for dimwits.'

*

Marcus Ford was passing his Saturday more strenuously. He had been in the bank since early morning, overseeing armies of lawyers and bankers who were putting the finishing touches to the long press release that would tell the world of Furnival's bid for IFK. The final decision to proceed would wait till Monday: no one in his right mind would take a risk for a whole weekend that there would be no nuclear accident in Russia, no earthquake in Japan, no untimely demise of the American President. In the meantime, there were hundreds of 'i's to be dotted and 't's to be crossed.

Robert Quilley looked in on them for a couple of hours, then drove to his weekend place in Somerset. Richard Myers turned up too, to check that 'his' team was doing okay, but everyone was too busy to bother with glad-handing. After what Charles Barton had told him, even Ford barely offered him the time of day. So Myers went too, leaving Marcus undisputed king of the castle, with his assistant director, Simon Black, and junior executive, Grace Chesterfield, there to wait on him hand and foot.

By nine in the evening it was all but done. The whole bunch

agreed to rendezvous back at Skidders at noon the next day, just in case, but with luck they could look forward to a fairly peaceful Sunday. The trio went back to their desks to tidy up. Ford was in no special hurry. When Sophie had heard that Marcus would be working at the weekend again, she grumpily cleared off with the kids to her father's huge pile in Oxfordshire, pointedly ignoring the more modest address in Wiltshire which was all Marcus could afford so far. God, that bugged him. It had cost the better part of a million to buy and do up, and still it wasn't good enough for Lady Muck.

Keeping Grace there by sending her on some superfluous errand, he propelled Simon Black back to the grateful embrace of his new wife, and dialled the number for Marco Pierre White's latest flagship restaurant. This would be in the nature of a working dinner, so there was no earthly reason why the corporate Amex shouldn't take a good hammering. Grace didn't need much persuasion, and within the hour they were tucking into a bottle of Krug '85 and browsing contentedly through the menu.

It wasn't the first time they'd dined together. A while back, when Sophie had been groaningly expecting for the second time, Marcus and Grace had shared a business trip to Paris. A jolly dinner that night had ended with some mutual exploration in her hotel bedroom. On the train back to London, Marcus had feigned dire remorse, both to excuse his callousness at betraying his pregnant wife and to avoid any risk of slipping into a protacted entanglement.

As they progressed sumptuously from langoustines to oxtail, from Condrieu to Cheval Blanc, his recollections of Paris flooded back. She'd been far more relaxed in bed than his wife, and her breasts were three times the size of Sophie's ungenerous offerings.

Marcus ordered a half bottle of Yquem to go with the pear *tarte tatin* and lasciviously assessed his dining partner. Was it his imagination, or had she stealthily freed another button on her shirt?

'So, Grace, enough of the glories of Furnival. Let's hear some of the Chesterfield dirt. Which lucky man are you seeing these days?'

'Why should I tell you?' The tone of her voice was all come-on.

'I thought I could give you some avuncular advice.'

Grace laughed outright. '*What*? With a whole six years' age difference? Anyway, if my memories of Paris are correct, you make a thoroughly undependable uncle.'

'Paris was fun, wasn't it? Must be, what, two years ago?'

'Almost. Mind you, Marcus, that was before you became such a superstar.'

Ford made a feeble attempt at a modest smile. Grace continued.

'. . . And I, too, was a mere executive back then, whereas today I have risen to the dizzy heights of . . . executive.'

'But a particularly good one, if I may say. Not only that . . .' He paused to flick off some cigar ash. '. . . I think I may be able to help you make faster progress through the ranks.'

'Really?' Her voice was still doubtful, but her eyes were dancing.

'People are noticing your work for Furnival. If you work on one more big deal, you'll be a sure thing for promotion next spring. At my lunch with Charles yesterday, he told me that IFK won't be Robert Quilley's last bid. In fact, we start soon on his next project. If I told you what it is, I'd have to kill you, but it's *mega*.'

'Wow. And will it be the same team, I mean you, me and Simon?'

'Between ourselves, I'm not one hundred per cent convinced by Simon. He's rather too political for my taste. And, since you do most of the grunt work, and I give all the strategic advice, frankly I was wondering if we *need* an Assistant Director next time.'

He looked meaningfully into her eyes. She smiled back.

'I'd love to try that. Thank you, Marcus.'

'Another thing Charles and I discussed is confidential too, but since it's going to be announced on Monday, there's no harm in telling you now. Have you heard of Rosco Sellars of Morgan Stanley? . . . Really? He has a *huge* reputation in New York. Very big in acquisition finance. Anyway . . .' He lowered his voice to a whisper. '. . . Rosco's going to join us as co-head of corporate finance. He's bringing a team of seven or eight with him.'

'Interesting. What does this mean for Richard Myers?'

'Basically, he's toast. There's no way he can compete with a big swinging dick like Sellars.'

'Do you think he'll leave?'

'Well, he *ought* to, if he has any sense. Whatever happens to Richard, I think my own star may be rising. I can't go into details, but Charles wants me to play a big part in integrating Rosco's team. One of them's a girl called Julia Daventry. Maybe you could make a point of making her feel welcome. I'll tell Charles you're helping me on it.'

They had already leant close together. Grace's hand bridged the small remaining gap and touched his hand gratefully. Marcus held onto it.

'So . . . you were going to tell me who you're bedding, remember?'

'I never said that.'

'But there *is* someone, right?'

'Yes, there is, but he's not usually around at weekends. If you don't have to rush home to call your darling wife, how about a nightcap in Kensington? I don't have anything to match this Yquem, but I can probably rustle up a whisky.'

'Why not? As long as it's a decent malt.'

'You can tell me what you think of it over cornflakes.'

4

The top management of IFK had passed an agreeable Sunday. The weather had turned warmer again. The Managing Director played golf, the Finance Director took his family for a spin in the Cotswolds, and the Chairman, Sir Reginald, torched a great pile of leaves in his garden. After a few bloody months, things at the company were beginning to look better. They had taken some painful decisions about the Lancashire plants, sold off one large loss-making division, and restructured tiers of middle management to bring on some fresh blood. It would take time for the improvements to show up in the profits, of course, but they had definitely turned the corner. Within a few months, the patience of their shareholders should be rewarded with a strong rise in their share price. As each of them woke to greet a bright Monday, they were blissfully unaware of the danger they faced from a group that had already gathered at Skidder Barton.

This group were using the largest meeting room, which – incongruously in this uncompromisingly modern monolith – was panelled in rich mahogany. Charles Barton had left Gloucestershire before crack of dawn, silently abandoning his sleeping wife and daughters. He wanted to be there to offer moral support, but placed himself discreetly at the far end of the long polished table, leaving Quilley and Ford to star.

They began by asking the stockbrokers, Cazenove, to comment on market conditions. Happily the American President had passed an uneventful weekend, Far Eastern stocks had gone sideways, and there was nothing to suggest that London would open sharply higher or lower. That gave the bid the greenest of lights, and the only thing left was the pricing. IFK's management was too weak to mount a spirited defence, even against a low bid. The problem was the risk of a white knight.

The moment any hostile bid is announced, investment banking vultures all over the City flock overhead, searching for bones to pick. They try to persuade other buyers to enter the fray, outbid the predator, and pay the bank a big fee for suggesting it. The company under siege is so grateful for being 'saved' that they welcome the second bidders and dub them 'white knights', though the intentions of the knights are rarely any purer than those of the first bidder.

Then the predator has to join in an auction or walk away beaten. In the testosterone-ridden, ego-filled world of big business, succeeding with a hostile bid is one of the most admired martial arts. For Robert Quilley, the bid for IFK was little more than a dry run. He couldn't run the risk of fumbling it, and it didn't take long to decide to offer fully forty per cent above IFK's Friday stock price of five pounds.

By convention, bids are announced just before half past eight, immediately before stock market dealings begin. At eight-fifteen, the team huddled round Robert Quilley as he prepared to call Sir Reginald Hitchens. This was the only customary act of civility in an unotherwise unchivalrous world. There was a moment of levity when Lady Hitchens said he was on the thunderbox. They had to wait for five minutes before he completed that operation and picked up the phone.

'Hitchens here. Who's that?'

'Good morning, Sir Reginald. Robert Quilley, Chairman and Chief Executive of Furnival Engineering .'

'I take it this isn't a social call?' Hitchens might have been a blimp but he wasn't a fool.

'Not exactly. As a matter of courtesy, I wanted to let you know that we will shortly be announcing an offer to your shareholders.'

'I see . . .' He was trying to collect his thoughts. '. . . At what price?'

'Seven pounds, a premium of forty per cent on Friday's close. That puts a value of six hundred and eighty-five million pounds on the company. We believe it's a very full offer.'

33

'You'll have to forgive me if I reserve my position on that. What are your plans for our workforce?'

'Until we get in there, we cannot possibly give any under-takings.'

'Slash and burn, that's what you'll do, just as you've done at Furnival.'

Quilley kept his cool. He could afford to; he knew he was going to win, and within six weeks Hitchens would be out.

'Sir Reginald, I don't think this is the time for this sort of exchange. I'm sure you'll be wanting to get in touch with the rest of your board and your merchant bankers. Naturally, we hope you'll consider our offer positively and recommend it to your shareholders.'

'At seven pounds . . . don't hold your breath. You know damn well it undervalues us.'

'Why don't we let your shareholders decide that?'

'Very well. I suppose I should thank you for this call though, for the life of me, I can't think why. Goodbye.'

'Goodbye, Sir Reginald.'

And so it was launched. Time would show that it wasn't one of the City's livelier contests. All the financial press supported Furnival. No white knight cantered into view. The IFK board soon rolled over, Robert Quilley got a new train set to play with, and Skidder Barton banked eight million in fees. Everyone was satisfied.

*

It was Terry who heard the news first, about ten o'clock that Monday while he was driving down Marylebone High Street. He phoned Einstein and Len, who was busy trying to put up a shelf in Poppy's bedroom for her TV and video. As soon as he ended the call, she quizzed him.

' 'Ow much this time?'

'What's that, Poppy love?' Len was back to concentrating on getting the brackets screwed in place.

'That was Terry on about another investment, wasn't it? Lose

34

another packet, did you?'

Len turned towards Poppy. 'No, I didn't, you cheeky little whippersnapper. Matter of fact, looks like I'll make eighty quid or so. If you're a good gel, I might buy you a Christmas present with it.'

'If I last that long.'

'You shouldn't say things like that, Poppy, not even as a joke.'

'Why not? It's *me* I'm talking about. I'm not takin' the piss out of anyone else.'

'Well, anyway, *don't*.'

'Dad, what will they say tomorrow?'

Len turned back to his work. He didn't want his face to give anything away. He twisted the screwdriver a few more times before replying.

'. . . Oh, nothin' special. Give us the results of them tests, I s'pose.'

He glanced furtively back at Poppy. She had turned her head to face the wall. He put the screwdriver down, went and sat on the bed, and took hold of her frail hand.

'You're not worried, are you, Poppity? It'll be okay, you know.'

'Like it was with Tommy, you mean?'

'Things've got better since then. They're discovering new things about CF every day.'

'So why can't they cure me, then?' Her head was still turned away.

'Those things take time, but I bet by the time you're twenty-five cystic fibrosis will be a thing of the past.'

Abruptly she turned and fixed him with a severe look.

'D'you think I'll live to be twenty-five? *Honest?*'

Shit, what was he supposed to say, knowing there was every chance that tomorrow's news might be ghastly? He smiled the widest, most reassuring smile he could muster, and gently stroked her pretty red hair.

' '*Course* you will, love. Twenty-five, and thirty, and forty, and bleedin' ninety.'

'You're lyin'.'

'If I *am*, let the good Lord strike me dead . . .' He looked up theatrically at the ceiling and held his arms out to receive the blow. Nothing happened. He looked at Poppy and winked. '. . . See, that *proves* I'm tellin' the truth.'

'You're *sad*. There ain't no God.'

''Course there's a God.'

'Crap. And even if there is, why should God give a toss if some fat old cabbie tells lies?'

'Maybe you're right. Maybe God's too busy frettin' about a thirteen-year-old whose language is somethin' terrible. I don't know where you get it from.'

'From you, Mum and the telly.'

'You shouldn't watch them sort of programmes.'

'Bollocks. They're all like that and, anyway, what else've I got to do?'

Len was grateful that they'd got out of the deepest waters, and wanted to escape before Poppy got serious again. He put the TV up on the shelf, with the video tucked in below it, and switched it on for her.

'There, you should be able to see better now. I'll put all your Michael Owen posters back up later. I got to get on now.'

'Thanks . . . Dad?'

'What, love?'

'I'm not scared, you know.'

'Scared of what, Poppity?'

'Of dyin'.'

'There you go again.'

'I *mean* it.'

'Stuff and nonsense. You'll outlive us all. Now, I *got* to go.'

Len kissed Poppy quickly on the forehead and made it out the door. He didn't go downstairs until he got a grip on himself. It wouldn't help if Jean saw him like that.

*

Monday's investment news didn't come a moment too soon for Terry. He'd had a miserable few days. On Friday a copper had

36

stopped him for having a smoking exhaust, so he'd wasted the whole day at the Carriage Office. Then on Saturday, after watching West Ham get beat by Blackburn, he'd gone round to Marcie's house to patch things up.

They'd had spats before. The girl had a temper, no two ways about it, but twenty-four hours later she was usually over the worst. She'd still need a spot of cajoling, but afterwards she'd accept a little kiss, and only ten minutes later they'd be having a consoling roll in the sack. True, she'd said he was on his last chance, but he hadn't actually *done* anything this time, had he? He hadn't bedded the girl. Come to think of it, he hadn't even bought her a drink, what with her getting to The Spreadeagle before him. All he'd done was be sociable for ten minutes. That was no reason to go around breaking off engagements, was it?

The more he thought about it, the more he saw himself as the injured party. Marcie, who'd no business being anywhere other than up West, had marched into the pub, clocked him and the girl, added two and two together to make five, and left him dangling from a window, naked from the waist down with a ring up his arse. By the time he stopped his cab outside her house in Chigwell, most of his old confidence had come steaming back. Not all of it, but a lot.

Marcie's mother opened the door. She was a big lady, a ghost of Marcie's future, and today there was something odd about the way she looked. Her chin was sort of waggling from side to side and her eyes and nose were screwed up. The overall effect wasn't exactly welcoming.

'You've got a bloody cheek, turnin' up 'ere. What d'you want?'

'Where's Marcie?'

'None of your business, you lecherous little turd.'

'Come on, Deirdre, that's not what you should be callin' your future son-in-law.'

'My future *what*? You ought to be 'ung, drawn and quartered for what you done to my poor gel.'

'Look, Deirdre, I know you're upset an' all, but if you let me 'ave a quick word with Marcie, we'll get this sorted out in no time. Then we can all make up and be friends again.'

Marcie had been listening from the upstairs landing, and her powerful voice bellowed down the stairs.

'*Piss off. I don't ever want to see you again.*'

Terry selected his softest, most charming voice.

'That you, Marcie darlin'? You ain't still cross with me, are you . . . ?'

There was a squeal of ear-splitting intensity. Terry decided he'd better try another tack. He edged a few inches across the threshold to make sure Marcie would hear.

'. . . I brought you the ring back, love.'

He pulled it from his jeans pocket. Deirdre swayed back in disgust.

'. . . What's the matter? I *did* wash it.'

A door slammed violently upstairs, and Terry heard a bedroom window being opened. Before he could work out what was going on, the Princess Di figurine he'd given Marcie for Christmas smashed violently on the paving stones behind him. It was followed by the entire catalogue of his presents, from Delia Smith and *The Joy of Sex* to the Boots eau de toilette, the crotchless panties and the vibrator.

As soon as she'd chucked them all out, the window banged shut again. Terry turned back to where Deirdre was standing, arms crossed, looking grimly satisfied.

'Let that be a lesson to you, and don't ever come 'ere again.'

Terry knew when he was beaten. Without a further word, he turned and began to walk away.

'. . . And another thing . . .' Deirdre yelled at his retreating back. '. . . I 'ope you enjoy Monday's *Sun.*'

Terry got back into the cab. Before he left, he cast one last glance up at Marcie's bedroom. If, despite everything, she still loved him, her tear-stained face would be at the window.

There was no sign of her.

Terry drove off feeling very low. He and Marcie had been

together so long, life without her would feel strange. Looking on the bright side, he could now chase skirt without always fretting about being seen. All the same, he felt like he'd lost a limb.

And what was that crap about the *Sun*? Had Marcie put in an announcement that the engagement was off? How could she have arranged that so fast? Hang on, though, one of her friends called Sharon worked on the *Sun*. *She* might have pulled a few strings.

Not feeling like being on his own, and anxious to test-drive his new freedom, Terry drove straight from Marcie's house up to the West End. His chat-up routines went badly, though, and he came nowhere near scoring. Maybe it was that *Sun* stuff putting him off. It was still niggling him while he worked on Sunday.

On Monday morning, he got up at six-thirty, shuffled along the damp street to the corner, and flicked through the pages of the *Sun* before he left the newsagent. On the fifth page his horrified eye spotted a very unflattering photograph of himself in the centre of a huge splash. The headline read:

CABBIE CHEAT: BUM DEAL FOR ROMEO RAT.

Two hours later, when Terry went into the cabbies' shelter at Temple for a cuppa, he found himself very much the centre of attention. The other cabbies didn't let up taking the piss until, red-faced, he left. And when he rang Len with the word on the bid, even *he* couldn't resist a few digs. If Terry had heard of Brutus, that's what he'd have called him.

*

Soon after the Monday meeting broke up, the Skidders corporate finance department was awash with opinions on the significance of the impending arrivals. The old guard were fiercely against it. For many a year they had enjoyed an almost cloistered existence. Decisions were taken so collegiately that, if any of the twelve directors had a strenuous objection to any proposed course of action, it was quietly abandoned. This gave each one a remarkable degree of influence, even power, that they saw would

39

not survive this upheaval. So they gathered in whispering clutches to consider what counter-measures they could adopt. As Sellars and his team were due to arrive the next week, any decisive action would have to be quick. There was talk of a mutiny, of a united front to present Charles Barton with a choice between Sellars and them, or possibly even a move of the whole team to another bank. It turned out to be all talk. A few calls went out to headhunters, but no one wanted such a large team, especially from a bank whose reputation had taken such a battering.

Below director level, most people were more positive. Many of the executives and Assistant Directors thought the bank was too old-fashioned and needed to change. They all knew that the leading US houses – Goldman and Morgan Stanley – were way out ahead of the pack. Injecting some of those American techniques *had* to make sense. So, when the directors bitched about the new hires before they arrived, their opinions were taken with a large pinch of salt.

Word somehow spread that Marcus Ford had been instrumental in approaching Rosco Sellars. Planting this story was a calculated gamble: it brought him new respect from the younger guys, at the price of being cold-shouldered by Myers and company. The first dividend of his approach came quickly: Charles Barton had invited Rosco Sellars and his team out to Gloucestershire for Sunday lunch to celebrate their arrival in England. Marcus was thrilled to be asked to join them.

Generally, he was on a roll. He had called up a financial journalist and discreetly traded some dirt on another banker for a positive personal comment on his role on the IFK bid. Things like that were important, and this was the first press mention he'd ever had. Clippings could play a big role in career development: headhunters devoured them enthusiastically, and other bankers had a remarkable memory for them. Legends were easily created: if a banker was described as a star more than once, it was taken as gospel. Press reports had a big impact in generating job offers and lubricating negotiations on pay and promotions.

Best of all was a signal from Robert Quilley. Although the IFK bid had only just been launched, it was screamingly obvious they would win and Quilley's restless mind had already moved on. He invited Marcus for dinner at the Connaught and gently unpeeled the real apple of his eye.

'Jowell.'

Jesus, thought Ford, Jowell's *huge*. The biggest engineering company in the UK. It must have a market value of . . .

'Fourteen billion pounds . . .' Quilley guessed what Marcus was thinking, and provided the answer. 'And that's before we pay a premium. Jowell has very loyal shareholders. I don't believe it will fall for a penny less than twenty billion. Will you do it with me, Marcus?'

Marcus reached out and shook Quilley's hand. Quilley smiled warmly.

'Okay, I want you to take a quick look at the numbers and visit me tomorrow for a first discussion of bid strategy.'

As he forked seared foie gras into his mouth, Marcus's face bore a look of supreme contentment. The thing which thrilled him most was that Quilley had raised it direct with him, and not through Charles Barton. However well his own relationship with Robert Quilley was coming on, until that dinner he had belonged to Barton. From this moment onwards, Quilley was *his*.

5

The news of their quick profit on IFK got Einstein thinking. If he and the others took investing more seriously, he could go for a better cab. He and Ruth had put every penny they had into the mortgage, so there wasn't anything over to spend on a fancy cab. Unlike Terry – who was fiercely loyal to the classic old Fairway – Einstein definitely wanted the new TX 1. It was more comfortable and economical and, apart from its habit of letting rainwater in through the 'Taxi' sign on the roof, more reliable.

Unfortunately, it was pricier, too, particularly if you went mad on the options list. Metallic paint, for example, would set you back five hundred and fifty quid, and air conditioning a cool fifteen hundred. Then there was de luxe seating, walnut dash and disc brakes. Tick one box too many and you could find yourself spending thirty-three thousand. If you were buying, that was. But there were all sorts of financing deals, and Einstein calculated that if he could keep up payments of a hundred and eighty a week, a fully loaded, brand spanking new TX 1 could be his.

*

The atmosphere in the Bishop household that Tuesday morning was subdued and nervous. Jean put cornflakes in the microwave and tea bags in the coffee maker and got generally muddled. Len, who'd slept half an hour at most, cut himself shaving and stood around in the kitchen holding cotton wool to his face.

Poppy was really too sick to go, but she insisted, so Jean got her dressed. Len cradled her sickly thin form, set her down carefully in the back of the cab and tenderly arranged a blanket about her. They set off early and got to the hospital half an hour before they were due. What with that and the usual delay, they were waiting

42

in the corridor for the better part of two hours.

To Poppy's noisy annoyance, she was made to wait outside with a middle-aged nurse, whose good-natured questions she answered witheringly. Throughout these exchanges, her attention was focused on the frosted glass door for any words that might escape through its panes. At first there was nothing, then the sound of a distant hubbub. If she couldn't catch the words, she could certainly hear the sound of her father losing his cool and her mother trying to restrain him. After that, there was silence again. Poppy knew it was bad news when the doctor didn't come out at the end and say hello. Her Mum looked frantic, her Dad furious. He walked towards her.

'Come on, Poppy, let's get out of this place.'

'Tell me.'

'Later.' There was something in his voice that stopped Poppy making an issue of it. Len scooped her up, and carried her back to the cab.

With brittle cheerfulness, Len said they'd treat themselves to a Haagen-Dazs. For Poppy that was another worrying warning sign. She bided her time while Len drove there, bought scoops of her favourite flavours, and joined them in the back of the cab.

Poppy took a few licks. She knew her mother was the better actor, so she fastened her beady eye unwaveringly on her Dad and aimed her first comment at him.

'So it's kick-the-bucket time, is it?'

'That chocolate pecan tasty, love?'

'I want to know. *Now.*'

Len and Jean exchanged glances. Instinctively Jean realized that soft-soaping wasn't an option.

'It wasn't all great news, pet. The tests weren't good. Your poor little lungs are worse. Doctor says the only thing left is the big transplant job, but they're not sure they can do it.'

'Why not?'

'They think you're so weak your system might not stand it.'

'So I was right all along, and Dad was lyin' to me. Then I want

43

to be left in peace to die at home. Promise you won't make me die in *there*.'

Jean turned away and pulled out a handkerchief. Len swallowed hard. The only one who was not feeling sorry for Poppy was Poppy. She was watchful, wary, still scared of a final betrayal. Tommy's last days were etched in her mind. Many years back, with a young will of steel, she'd resolved that when her time came it wouldn't be that way. She bloody well meant it.

Len's voice turned gravelly.

'You ain't goin' to die, love, we ain't goin' to let you. Maybe there's not a lot they can do 'ere, but there's some new treatment they got in America. It don't cure the CF itself, but it builds up your health so you can take the operation. That's what we're goin' to do with you.'

Poppy looked unsure. Was this a cock-and-bull story?

'Is that where the doctor wants to send me?'

'Not exactly.'

Jean managed a chortle.

'Your Dad lost his rag when the doctor said there was nothin' to be done, and shook the bugger till 'e told us about this American treatment.'

Poppy giggled. 'So are the Council goin' to pay for me to go there?'

Len and Jean looked at each other. It was Len's turn again.

'Prob'ly not. But that don't make no difference. You're goin' anyway.'

'How come?' Poppy had a pretty good grasp of the Bishop finances. 'Who's goin' to pay for it?'

'*We* are.'

Poppy snorted. 'Come on, Dad, we've 'ardly got a pot to piss in.'

Jean looked appalled.

'*Poppy*!'

Poppy was unabashed. 'It's true. Everything we've got is on credit. The cab, the leather suite, Dad's stereo. 'Ow much are we talkin' about, anyway?'

'I said, we'll find it.'

'And I said, 'ow much?'

Jean touched Len's hand.

'You might as well tell Poppy, Len, she'll find out in the end.'

Len looked doubtful. He was sure it was a mistake, but he knew that glint in Poppy's eyes. Once she had made up her mind to get something, she always wheedled it out of them. He sighed.

'Okay, it's not cheap. 'Alf a million dollars.'

''Ow much is that in real money?'

'Three 'undred thousand. Bit more, maybe'

Poppy whistled through her teeth. It was so far beyond anything they could afford, it was funny. Pathetic, anyway.

'Dad, 'ave you lost your marbles? You'd 'ave to work in the cab for the next thousand years to make that sort of money.'

Len was lost for an answer. Jean tried to help out.

'We can all do our bit. If you was away in America, I could look for some work.'

Poppy bridled. 'Doing *what*? You're a bit old to go on the game.'

Len's eyes flashed angrily. He wagged a finger an inch from Poppy's nose.

'Don't you *ever* say a thing like that to your mother.'

Poppy was regretting it and it showed in her eyes. Jean kicked Len, who nodded sullenly and returned to the subject.

'I don't want any more arguments about the money. It's down to me to find that. You concentrate on keeping your 'ealth up so you can manage that flight to San Francisco.'

Poppy's face eased a little. She knew they could never raise the money, but she could see how hard this was for them. She'd just have to be strong and play along. Maybe she could daydream a little, too. Since she'd been all but bed-ridden for a year now, the TV set was her only window on the world and one of her favourite programmes was set in San Francisco. It looked so lovely, with its swooping hills, its deep blue bay and its dizzy bridges. She'd love to see it.

She took a lick of blueberry and gave them a big smile.

*

45

Marcus summoned Grace for the first working session. She gasped when she heard Furnival's new target. It would be one of the biggest public bids in UK corporate history. Even if Skidders didn't do another bid for twelve months, this would guarantee them a high position in the corporate finance league tables for the year.

For four or five years, Skidder Barton had been sliding ever lower in the tables. Back in the good old days, the top few places were fought over by Schroders, Warburgs, Skidders and Morgan Grenfell. Sometimes a Kleinworts, Rothschilds, Baring or Flemings would pop up there for a year or two before resuming their natural places in the upper reaches of the second division. The pattern of domination by the home-grown banks was occasionally interrupted by a guest appearance by one of the Americans, but those were flashes in the pan and the next year they would be nowhere to be seen.

It all started to change in the mid-Nineties. Barings, Warburgs, Morgan Grenfell and Kleinworts were all too busy changing their names and owners to concentrate on their work, and the Americans, stuffed fat with profits from their home market, started waving their chequebooks in earnest at bright City people. If the British and European banks had got their act together, they could have given the Yanks a much harder time. As it was, the coastal defences were unmanned.

Once the Americans had established a bridgehead, nothing could stop their tanks rolling across the countryside. They were much slicker at marketing, paid their staff better, and took no prisoners. Working for them could be a harrowing experience, but at least you felt part of a winning machine.

Many of the talented Oxbridge graduates who had joined Skidders in recent years were now voting with their feet. If Skidders' decline turned into a free fall, the bank's name would become a liability on their CVs. Grace herself had been close to leaving. She saw immediately how this could transform Skidders's prospects.

'I want you to begin by getting hold of all the latest brokers' reports on Jowell and having a first stab at a break-up value. Furnival will certainly want to keep automotive, robotics, and power-generating gear. They'll sell defence electronics, satellites and missiles. I doubt that the numbers will work unless we can net eight billion pounds from those disposals. Then you need to draw up a list of potential buyers for those divisions and do a schedule of what prices similar businesses have fetched in the past . . .'

Grace went through the motions of taking notes. This was all routine stuff.

'. . . After that, you should analyse Jowell's shareholder register. Concentrate on their biggest five or six institutional investors. Try to get hold of the name of which individual is responsible for that investment at each of those institutions. See if they've been active in that stock recently, buying or selling. And, most important, check how they've behaved when other major stocks in their portfolio have been bid for . . .'

Grace nodded and smiled prettily.

'. . . That brings me on to the question of acquistion financing. This will have to be underwritten – the full twenty billion.'

'Do you think Zuricher will do the whole lot?'

Grace asked the question doubtfully. Under the agreement Charles Barton had struck with the Swiss, they had to be offered first bite at any financings. Skidders' experience with them so far had not been encouraging. They were slow, bureaucratic and risk-averse.

Ford pointed out the window,

'See those pigs flying past?'

Grace actually turned round to look, then laughed to cover her embarrassment at being so dumb. Marcus pressed on.

'. . . Frankly, I'd rather not depend on them for *any* of it. No, this one's so big, it's going to require a very sophisticated international financing. The timing couldn't be better: it's precisely what Rosco's good at. We'll have to bring him into the loop. Apart from him, I've agreed with Charles that inside the

47

bank, information about this bid will be shared on a strictly "need-to-know" basis.'

Grace looked puzzled.

'So only Charles Barton, Rosco Sellars and Richard Myers will be informed, then?'

Ford frowned.

'I don't think we need trouble Richard, do you? As you know, he's only co-head of the department now. As long as Rosco knows, that's enough, surely . . .? Now, code names. I see no reason why we shouldn't continue to call Furnival "Foxtrot", but we need a name for Jowell. Any ideas?'

'Jupiter?'

'Okay, Jupiter it is. Now, when can you get back to me?'

*

Len and Jean didn't get Poppy to sleep until midnight. Half an hour later she was awake again, shaking convulsively with a dreadful coughing fit. It died down by two and Jean drifted off. At about five-thirty Len gave up trying to get to sleep and went to the kitchen to make himself some tea.

By his third cup, the first inkling of an idea had come to him. The amount that was needed was much too high to even *consider* working for. Crime was the only answer. Anything white collar was beyond him, and he could hardly go around mugging grannies. Robbing a bank might make sense. All it would take was an imitation shotgun, a bag, and a pair of Jean's tights. Driving to the bank in his own cab would be asking for trouble, so he should use a pedal bike or pick a bank close to a Tube station. As long as his bag didn't say 'Swag' and he took the tights off his head when no one was looking, he could be down to the platform and onto a train before the first squad car arrived. Better buy a ticket before going in to the bank, in case there was a queue.

By the time he'd downed his fifth cuppa, the cuckoo clock in the kitchen had struck seven. He remembered he was supposed to be playing golf, the last thing he felt like. Better call Terry quick and cancel.

It was easier said than done. Terry had known him for a good few years, and Len had confided in him about Poppy's tests. He sensed right away that something was up, and coaxed and cajoled until Len changed his mind.

Len's form was appalling, with every drive wildly sliced. He didn't seem to care, didn't even bother to look for the balls. He just took the penalties and dropped new ones. Terry pestered him the whole time, but it wasn't until the fourteenth that he got it out of him. He was horrified by Len's news, and gobsmacked by the cost of the treatment. All the same, he saw something had to be done. It wasn't a question of being a good friend to Len; he loved little Poppy to bits himself and often went round to see her. She flirted with him outrageously, and was always thrilled to hear the lurid details of his tangled love life.

As they walked up the fairway, he listened sympathetically to what Len had to say, until they got to the great bank robbery plan. Then Terry laughed right out loud.

'You daft bleeder. When was you last in a bank?'

'Not for a while. I always use the cash machine at Tesco's.'

'*Exactly*. There ain't any money in the banks no more: it's all in them machines. What'll you do'? Chisel one out and shove it in your pannier bag?'

Len said nothing while he fluffed his next approach shot. It bounced on a bank and squirted into a deep bunker. Terry had hurt him a bit with this comment. He wouldn't have been surprised if the lad had warned him of the dangers of being caught or attacked by a security guard. But to mock him like this . . . it was uncalled for. He went on the offensive.

'So, you got a better idea?'

To his astonishment, Terry shot right back.

' 'Course I 'ave. In fact, I got a bleedin' brainwave.'

'What's that?'

'Reach into your golf bag, pull out your mobile – and tell Einstein to get that scrawny little arse of 'is round to the clubhouse.'

6

Charles Barton cancelled all his meetings for that Friday morning. He badly needed peace and time to prepare himself for his lunch with Ernst Lautenschutz.

Before Zuricher had become shareholders in Skidders, Ernst and his Swiss colleagues had been models of charming restraint. Disarmingly, they insisted that they knew too little about the peculiarly Anglo-Saxon art of investment banking to play any active role. Of course, they would be happy to offer assistance if sheer financing muscle would help the much smaller Skidder Barton win business. Naturally, it would be interesting to have a seat on the Skidders board, but Charles Barton could rest assured that Zuricher would be thoroughly supportive in all board deliberations.

Now Charles privately regretted letting these Swiss cuckoos into his nest. At every Skidder board meeting Ernst Lautenschutz produced a lengthy catalogue of gripes, and when a real setback – like the fiasco in fund management, or the painful loss on Russian bonds – was reported, his histrionics were appalling. And it wasn't as if Zuricher were actually *helping*. The anticipated flow of Swiss business for Skidders hadn't materialized, and getting finance for Skidders's corporate clients was like getting blood from the Matterhorn. Worst of all, Lautenschutz was forever hinting that if the Swiss were thwarted on a major issue, they might slap a takeover offer for the bank on the table.

Barton knew only too well how vulnerable Skidders would be if this happened. When the bank went public back in the Seventies, it seemed they could have their cake and eat it. The broad Barton family controlled more than half of the shares – their Skidder counterparts having died out in the late nineteenth century – and large blocks of the rest were lodged in the amiable hands of old-fashioned English insurance companies. However, little by little the security of the shareholder base crumbled. Over time, more members of the Barton clan needed cash for this reason or that, and Skidders regularly had to arrange discreet share placements in the market. The collective family holding was now down to twenty-six per cent, still powerful but no longer an impregnable bulwark.

The insurance companies, for their part, had come under growing pressure to maximize returns on their investments. The chummy relations that Sir Miles, Charles's father and predecessor as Chairman, had enjoyed with those groups counted for little now, and many of them sold. It was when the last of those blocks of shares came onto the market that Charles Barton made his move with Zuricher.

Hiring Rosco Sellars and his team was something the Swiss had insisted on, contemptuous as they were of the softer-edged English approach. Barton knew that these interlopers could change for ever the style of the bank, especially as Sellars's team was going to the corporate finance department, the bank's listing flagship. If they had been joining global markets or fund management, they would have been a more containable threat. This move went to the heart of the whole machine, and could lead to glory or disaster. Barton was playing double or quits with two hundred years of family history. As he paced up and down awaiting Lautenschutz's arrival, he hoped devoutly that by agreeing to pay the Danegeld of hiring Sellars he had at least bought himself a little respite. By the time that Lautenschutz had turned up and was tucking into his seafood starter, that hope was already being crushed.

'So, Charles, Rosco Sellars will start work on Monday?'

'That's right. There are eight of them in all.'

'But that is only the beginning, yes? Sellars will be hiring more, naturally?'

'Probably. The first batch will need to settle in first.'

'I hope they don't take too long about it. If Skidders is to

51

improve its performance, we need better people and *fast*. This gives you the perfect opportunity to get rid of some of dead wood. I have now met all the directors in that department. They are nearly all – what is that word you have? – fuddy-duddies.'

Charles Barton thought this was *very* unfair. He knew for a fact that Lautenschutz had spent no more than five minutes with any of them.

'That's certainly not true of all of them. Some of the younger ones – Marcus Ford, for example – are as good material as you'll find anywhere in the City. I grant you the older ones are like some wines: they do not travel well. However, this side of Dover, they do a perfectly satisfactory job.'

'If that is so, how do you explain Skidders' poor showing in the UK league tables? Answer me *that* . . .'

Before Barton could try to do so, there was more.

'. . . And anyway, Great Britain is not any more "the market". We must learn to think globally, Charles. Only the Americans seem able to do that.'

Barton noted the insult, but resisted rising to the bait.

'I can assure you, Ernst, if Rosco makes a good case for more hirings, I'll be the last one to stand in his way.'

'Good. And we may also want him to take a look at the bank's overall structure. The way you are organized is too parochial. We need to move to the American pattern, with cross-selling across the group. If the current staff accept such changes, well and good. If not, to use your own expression, they cannot stand in the way.'

This was outrageous, thought Barton, as the butler cleared away the starters. The *cheek* of the man, to behave as if he owned the place and that he, Charles Barton, could be spoken to like hired help! He lapsed into a hurt silence.

Lautenschutz's antennae twitched enough to detect this. He had nothing but contempt for Barton, who was patently there through nepotism, whereas he, a farmer's son, had succeeded through his own efforts. It was too early to let this show, though. He had pushed the man too hard and needed to row back a little.

'Please understand, Charles, my own board puts *me* under

pressure to get the best out of our investments. I was the one who sponsored the idea of buying the shareholding in Skidders, so I do feel the weight of that responsibility. Forgive me if I sometimes get carried away in my enthusiasm to help you.'

Barton nodded, slightly mollified. Lautenschutz took that to mean that the damage was mended. Good, he could press on.

'Enough of corporate finance. Let's discuss your fund management business. I have some interesting ideas about how your managers could be more helpful to our analysts in Zurich.'

Barton sighed. He didn't how much longer he could put up with this tiresome little man.

*

Einstein had been thrilled to get the call. He didn't ask what it was about: as far as he was concerned, any time his friends needed advice, he was glad to be there for them. As he set off in his cab for the golf club, he guessed it was about Poppy. He knew how worried Len and Jean had been, and he'd seen for himself how much the poor kid had weakened. For over a year now, Poppy had been too sick to go to school, so the council had sent round private tutors to the Bishops' house in Gant's Hill. By the time Einstein got to know Len and his family, that system had all but broken down. Poppy hated the lot of them and would lash out, asking what was the point of learning useless facts if she was going to die anyway?

Despairing of finding a teacher she would work with, Jean had the notion of sneaking Einstein in there. Since he was just another cabbie, it wouldn't occur to Poppy that he might be a teacher in disguise. And Einstein was clever about using games to instruct, so that his wayward pupil learned without realizing it. To begin with, Einstein didn't actually like her very much; he, too, had to learn to see past her bad language, her feistiness and her tantrums, and understand the frustration and the bouts of blind terror that lay beneath that scarred surface. Within two or three months he found himself adoring Poppy as much as everyone else did. So if this *was* something to do with her, that was most definitely all right with him.

As he drove into the car park, Einstein saw Len and Terry walking up the eighteenth fairway, so he went into the clubhouse, ordered three teas, and had them all sugared and ready by the time they joined him.

Terry sketched out the background, including, to Len's embarrassed annoyance, a ribaldly embellished account of the bank-robbing plan. Einstein listened silently until the end, sipping his tea, then nodded sagely once or twice, prompting the others to ease themselves forward to the edge of their leatherette chairs to hear what the oracle would pronounce. Instead, Einstein asked questions.

'Len, what's the difference between what your house is worth and the amount you owe on the mortage?'

'Maybe forty thousand on a good day.'

'Do you own anything else that's worth much?'

'Not really. Like you know, the cab's on finance. I suppose I could save a bit by changing back to a Fairway.'

'Okay. Terry, how about you?'

'Me? I ain't got two pennies to rub together.'

'What about the Cossie?'

'What d'you mean, "What about the Cossie?" '

'I mean, what's it worth?'

'I never thought about it.'

'Well, *think*.'

Einstein surprised himself with how assertive he sounded.

'Twelve, fourteen grand, I s'pose . . . Why d'you want to know?'

Len had already got there.

'I can't let either of you do this . . .'

Terry's confusion was becoming monumental.

'Do *what*, for fuck's sake?'

Einstein ignored both of them. He was preparing for the moment when his master plan would be unveiled.

'Len, if you switched cabs, and took out a second mortgage, you should be able to raise at least twenty thousand. We'll do the same with our house. Ruth won't be too thrilled, because it's mainly *her* money, but when she hears what it's for, she'll come round. Put our forty grand together with cash that we'll get from flogging Terry's old banger and . . .'

'*Banger*? That's a Sierra Cosworth RS 500 you're calling a "banger". One of the finest road cars ever built. Two point three litres of race-bred, turbocharged thoroughbred. The ultimate modern classic. There was only five 'undred of 'em ever made.'

Einstein was unsympathetic. 'Good, then there'll be lots more to pick from when we earn the money back.'

Terry's nostrils flared like an angry stallion's.

'Piss off, Einstein . . . Anyway, even if we *did* scrape together fifty-odd grand, that's still a drop in the ocean next to what Len needs.'

Len couldn't disagree; he was a bit lost on that, too. Einstein explained.

'It's stake money, like buying chips at a casino.'

Len looked worried. 'You're not suggestin' that we . . .'

'No, no. Of course, we can't hope to make half a million dollars without taking *some* risks, but it has to be somewhere we have a competitive advantage. That can only be the stock market.'

''Old your 'orses . . .' Len was disappointed. He had expected something cleverer from Einstein. '. . . I know that IFK did us proud, but, apart from that, our track record is pretty patchy. And try as we might, we don't get good gen *that* often. We might not pick up anything worthwhile for *months*.'

'I agree, which is why we have to up the ante.'

Terry was confused. 'Up the who?'

'All three of us work in the City at most one-tenth of the time. If we target it full-time, statistically we should get ten times more leads.'

'That's true.' Len could see it would make a big difference. Even Terry found something positive to say about it.

'Yeah, and we could work Canary Wharf as well the Square Mile. They got Morgan Stanley, Credit Suisse First Boston, and loads of other banks there.'

Einstein was pleased. 'You're right there, Terry. I haven't had a chance to think this through yet, but I'm sure I can get information from the Internet about which banks do most of the big bids. And if I do a search for articles about takeovers, we might even be able to work out which individuals in those banks have handled some of the recent bids. If we had one of them in the back of our cabs, we would know to prick up our ears more than usual.'

'Yeah, that's a real good idea.' Terry was warming to the notion. 'If only there was some way we could know when them fellas were bookin' cabs.'

Len scratched his bald head. 'There *could* be, you know. Either of you been to the Control Cabs centre in Ealing?'

They both shook their heads. Control Cabs was the radio dispatch company they all worked for. Occasionally they would pick up a punter on the streets, but most of the time it was through the radio computer link.

'I went there once. There's thirty or forty gels what sit there takin' the calls, and feedin' them into the computer. Two or three minutes before the cab is due to turn up at the punter's address, the computer uses the satellite system to automatically pick out which cab is nearest, and that lucky little cabbie gets the fare.'

Terry was back to being puzzled.

'I'm sure that's fascinatin', Len, but what's it got to do with *our* problem?'

'Just wait and I'll tell you, won't I? There's no way to fiddle the computer system. Even if one of the gels at Control Cabs *wanted* to give the order to a particular cabbie, she couldn't, because it's the computer what chooses. But if that same gel let a cabbie know exactly where to be and when, the computer would automatically choose 'im.'

Einstein smiled. 'So all we need is a volunteer to make friends with one of the Control Cabs girls, and we solve the problem.'

'Yeah, that's true', added Terry. ''Ere, why are you two grinnin' at me?'

Len laughed out loud. 'Sorry, lad. Einstein and me are both

56

married men. If it was last week, when you was engaged, it'd be a different story. Now you're fancy-free again, though . . .'

'You must be jokin'. What if they're all old bags?'

'Nothing wrong with the love of a mature woman, Terry. You might learn a trick or two. And there's thirty or forty to pick from. You'd be like a kid in a sweetie shop.'

'I don't *need* a woman. I just got a new blonde bombshell. Nineteen, she is, fresh as a daisy. And, as it 'appens, she *works* in a sweetshop.'

'Some of them gels at Control Cabs might be nineteen, too.'

'Yeah, that's true, I s'pose.'

'Good.' Einstein thought it was time to bring the meeting to a resounding close. 'Let's vote on it, then. Who's in favour of the new investment plan?' He held his own skinny arm aloft. 'Len?'

'Fellas, I appreciate all this, but I'll 'ave to leave the decision to you.'

'Okay, Len. Terry, it looks like it's down to you.'

Terry looked downcast, his shoulders hunched tightly together.

'Would I *really* 'ave to sell the Cossie?'

Einstein was in no mood to negotiate. 'Sorry, Terry. Even as it is, fifty thousand's not much to play with.'

Terry stared at the floor. It was the worst dilemma he'd ever had to face. He looked up and shrugged.

'Okay, count me in. If the Cossie's got to go, I want to get it over with. I'll call *Exchange & Mart* on the mobile and put an ad in right away.'

Len turned and patted Terry on the thigh.

'Thanks, mate . . .' Then he looked to the other side of the coffee table, brushing one hand quickly past his eyes . 'And you know what *you* are, Einstein? A bleedin' genius . . .'

7

Marcus Ford spent a busy Saturday in Wiltshire. He'd hoped for a quiet day to think through how to play lunch at Charles Barton's. However, it wasn't until early evening that Sophie exhausted her list of tasks for him and allowed him out for a pint at the local pub.

None of their friends could work out how the Ford marriage ticked. All of Marcus's previous girlfriends had been bubbly, dim Sloaney types, quite different from the clever but caustic Sophie. Money was assumed to have played a large part in his passion, but this was only a half-truth. It was not so much the money as her father's amazing connections. What he overlooked during their whirlwind romance was the downside of acquiring such a father-in-law. If ever he walked out on Sophie, that man was capable of ensuring that business doors would slam mercilessly shut in his face.

Sophie, too, had in the past been drawn to other sorts, usually saturnine artists who treated her badly. When she began to get broody she was faced with the depressing reality that no man she fancied would make a half-decent father. Just then Marcus appeared on the scene with his clean-cut if unindividual features, his gym-toned physique and his attentiveness, and pestered her into taking his ring.

Having married in haste, Sophie was now destined for a life in a gilded cage. Her father was of Catholic Irish stock and, whatever he got up to on the side, he was intemperately of the view that marriage was for life. Sophie's younger sister had tried to call his bluff by walking out on her guitar-playing husband – and found herself cut off without a cent. Sophie had seen from her sister's experience what penury meant, and didn't like what she saw.

Marcus drained his pint, glanced at his watch and wondered if he could risk another. No, he'd better get back.

*

Terry put his Saturday night to good use. Len had told him there was a pub only fifty yards from the Control Cabs office, and he reckoned that any telephone girls at a loose end after their shift might go in there for a quick one. So he ordered a tonic water and picked a bar stool that had a view down the road. Shortly after nine a bevy of women came out of the gates. Some walked the other way towards the Tube station; half a dozen came along the street and paused by the pub. Terry could vaguely hear the sound of arms being twisted, and eventually the whole menagerie came bustling in.

Terry sized them up as they ordered. Three were well past forty and so stout as to be well beyond the call of duty, even for Poppy's sake. One was mid-thirties, and looked borderline attractive until Terry caught a glimpse of thighs like prize-winning marrows. The other two were younger. The one with dark, greasy hair was a definite paper-bag job, but her redhead friend might do. Terry couldn't abide bulky women, and this one was tastily slender.

He was battle-hardened enough to know he had no chance if he tried to get something started while the whole gaggle was there. They'd take the piss out of him, and even if the girl was interested, she'd be too embarrassed to show it. So he quietly ordered another tonic and bided his time, having no choice but to run the risk that they'd all leave together.

His luck was in. The oldies went first, taking marrow-legs with them, leaving only the beauty and the beast. Sadly, they were sitting the wrong way round, with the plug-ugly pointing his way, so giving the old eye was out of the question. He'd have to wait for their tanks to fill up. Hopefully, the back of the bus would feel the need first, giving him a couple of minutes alone with the redhead.

Bollocks. They were going *together*. He could understand women who hadn't met up for over a year wanting to gossip over the

59

cubicle walls, but why did two girls who'd been chatting for the last half-hour need to do synchronized peeing?

Five minutes later they reappeared and came up to the bar together to order another drink. They were standing no more than three yards from him. The redhead glanced in his direction. Now he had her on radar lock. Better move in.

' 'Scuse me, ladies, you don't by any chance work at Control Cabs, do you?'

The girls looked at each other. The ugly one was wary, the redhead mildly curious.

'Yeah,' they replied simultaneously.

'Wonder if you could 'elp me? My sister wants me to find out if there's work there. I looked in earlier, but I couldn't see anyone to ask.'

They weren't too sure about him, but went through the motions of debating it between themselves. The redhead tried to sound helpful.

'What you think, Dot? Are they looking for girls at the moment?'

The greaseball responded grudgingly. 'Might be a chance if she don't mind nights. Nine till six. She got any experience of phone work?'

'Not to speak of. She takes the calls at the salon sometimes.'

That turned the plug-ugly's alarm on, and her voice turned aggressive.

'If she works in a salon, what would she want with Control Cabs? It ain't well paid.'

The redhead chipped in. 'Maybe she feels like a change.'

Great. She was on his side, but both girls would need more convincing. He had a brainwave.

'Tell the truth . . .' He leaned in conspiratorially. '. . . It's 'er 'usband.'

'Thought you said it was 'er what wants the work.'

Terry nodded. 'It is, but 'er 'usband won't leave 'er alone. Got a sex drive like a bull. Wants it four or five times every night . . .'

'Ooooh', commented the redhead.

'Pig', added her friend.

'. . . That's why she's lookin' for night work, to get a bit of rest, like.'

By now the redhead was well satisfied with the tale and her friend was so outraged by the husband's unnatural demands that she mislaid her scepticism, and chipped in.

'They 'ave application forms at the reception, if that's what she wants.'

'Is it still open now if I want to get one?'

' 'Course.'

'You wouldn't go there with me and show me where to find them, would you?

The girls looked at each other.

'S'pose we could, after we drink up.'

'I'm a cabbie meself. If you like, I could drive you both 'ome afterwards.'

'Me and Daph always go on the Tube.'

Hatchet-face sounded like she meant it. This would wreck everything. Daphne rode to his rescue.

'Come on, Dot, it's more than 'is badge is worth to try anything on.'

Terry agreed enthusiastically, and the doubter was swayed. The three chatted more as they finished their drinks, then went to pick up the form at Control Cabs.

The big problem, both for Terry and an increasingly keen Daphne, was how to deposit Greaseball first. Sod's Law dictated that she lived further away than Daphne, *and* in the same direction. Terry had to pretend to get so carried away talking with them over the intercom that he forgot where he was going. Neither of the girls was remotely convinced, and in the mirror he could see Battleship scowling and the redhead smirking knowingly. Even when they got to Dot's drop-off address, it was the devil's own job to get her out of the cab. Daphne had to put up with a dozen variations on the themes of 'You sure you're all right?' and 'Let's make 'im go back to your place first' before Dot

61

was persuaded. Her parting shot was to tell Terry that she had his badge number and if he so much as laid a finger on Daph, she'd have him for breakfast.

With a huge sigh of relief, Terry drove off, slipping easily into full chat-up mode as he went. As they neared their destination, he made a noble effort to collect his thoughts. Both Len and Einstein had pleaded with him to take it easy the first night. They reckoned the best chance of getting the right help was a slow-starting old-fashioned romance, which would first smoulder and only later burst into the full fire of love. The last thing they needed was for Terry to pick up one of his usual flippertigibbets and be straight into her Marks & Sparks on the first night. He might have a high old time, but it would be over within a week, and the girl wouldn't lift a finger to help.

They drew up in front of Daphne's house. Terry switched off the engine and they chatted a while. He was getting more attracted to her by the minute, and it *was* Saturday night, after all, and this was hard. Daphne let the conversation run on, waiting for him to try something. She wasn't sure what she'd say if he asked to come into the house. He was obviously a Romeo and not to be trusted. But he did have nice curly brown hair, he looked good in his tight black jeans, and he made her laugh. And it *was* Saturday night.

When, instead of making a pass, he asked for her phone number, she was so astonished that, before she knew what she was doing, she'd invited him up and was making a coffee for him.

Terry swore to himself that he'd leave when he'd drunk the coffee and only sat next to Daphne on the couch to be sociable. He didn't mean anything by it when he reached over to see what her hair felt like, and the first kiss was mainly out of politeness.

His iron resolve only started to weaken when her black uplift bra surrendered its captives, and his will-power came under even more pressure when her white frilly knickers joined the bra on the floor.

62

It wasn't all bad news, though. At least they were still talking on Sunday morning.

*

If the driveway from the road to the Barton establishment was neither as long nor as imposing as that at Sophie's father's place, it ran it a close second. The house was eighteenth century, with lovely proportions and gently flaking honey stone. As Marcus's BMW braked to a halt, the air was filled with the barking of two dogs, pursued by a fresh-faced girl of around twenty. She apologized for the fuss that the labradors were making and escorted Marcus through to the library, where Charles Barton was already having a drink with his new white hopes. He looked up as Kate led the way in.

'Ah, Marcus, you found us all right? . . . Thank you, Kate. Now, will you join us in a glass of champagne, or would you like something else? . . . Good. Now, let me introduce you. Ladies first. Julia, Marcus Ford.'

'Hello.'

'Hi.' Julia offered a friendly but cautious smile.

'And now to the gentlemen. This is Rosco.'

Sellars was about the same height and build as both Ford and Barton, but he exuded so much energy that he seemed much taller than either of them. He shot out a strong, firm hand. Marcus half missed it and made a second grab. He didn't want to be dismissed as an English wimp.

'Hi, Marcus. Charles's been telling us a lot about you. Sounds like you're one of the stars at Skidders.'

Marcus blushed slightly, but was delighted to hear this. He wasn't sure that Barton's thumbnail sketches of the other directors would be as positive.

'Good to meet you, Rosco. We're all looking forward to working with you and your team.'

'Well, I can tell you, we're all up for this. It's going to be a fascinating challenge.'

Barton swept him on along the line of superfit, clean-cut men.

For fifteen more minutes they made small talk about settling in London. Sellars was the only married one among the newcomers but his interior-designing society wife was staying on in Manhattan, so he too would be looking for a bachelor pad. As that topic ran its course and came to a natural end, Charles Barton's heavy-hipped wife, Patricia, entered the room and apologized that other business had prevented her being there to welcome them earlier. The 'business' was the *Sunday Times* crossword, and she'd remained in the smaller sitting room, together with twenty-two-year-old Emma, until Cook sent word that the consommé was ready.

Patricia Barton had grown very bored with the triumphs or tribulations of Skidders and she had banned banking as a topic of conversation in their house. Once upon a time her husband's career had engaged her, but with the passing of the years, that interest had faded. Apart from her daughters, what gave her pleasure now were the gardens, the animals and the glorious swathe of countryside their house surveyed. For the life of her, she could not understand why her husband put up with the dreadful pressures of that job, the criticism from his crotchety father and the slings and arrows of outrageous journalists. Why on earth didn't he have the sense to wash his hands of it, and remain here in this tranquil setting? But no, off he went back to London each Monday, and lived alone in Knightsbridge, while she stayed in Gloucestershire and tended her roses.

Their weekends were unstressed. Charles respected the conversational no-go zone. One advantage of having such a beautiful house was that Emma and Kate liked to come at weekends and, even if they were away, the place was rambling enough for Patricia and Charles to pass the time pleasantly without bumping into each other too often.

However, it was mightily annoying to mother and daughters alike if Daddy wrecked their plans by inviting boring business-men. In this case there had been a stand-off when Emma wanted to bring a new squeeze for the weekend, and Daddy had the temerity to say no. It took more than an hour of cajoling for him

64

to talk her round, which Emma deftly turned to advantage by making him promise to rent a house in the Caribbean.

The girls tried to keep away from the lunch party altogether, but were moved by Charles's pleading and agreed that one of them should be present. Kate lost the toss.

They sat down. Naturally, Rosco was in the favoured position on Patricia's right, with Julia in the equivalent slot next to Charles. Marcus was halfway down the table among the young Americans. However, the distance did not stop Rosco Sellars from addressing some of his questions directly to Marcus.

'So, tell me, Marcus, how do most of your colleagues in corporate finance feel about us coming? I want the truth, now.'

Sellars looked back at Patricia and winked, making her feel like throwing up. She had disliked this man on sight. He was too smooth and self-satisfied by half. Not only that, he had no conversation. She'd tried everything: plants, dogs, country walks, the *lot*.

'The younger guys, below director level, are pleased. They've been wanting some new ideas for some time. It's been great to see someone take decisive action . . .'

Marcus glanced in Barton's direction to signal who deserved the credit. Kate saw this and caught her mother's eye to confirm an instant shared opinion on this crawler.

'. . . Among the directors, it's more mixed. Some of the older ones may feel threatened. It's not that surprising. The department's been like a private playpen for them. They have their own way of doing things.'

'But surely they see that their way doesn't work any more? Skidders has no presence to speak of outside Europe, and has slipped badly even in your home market. Charles showed me the figures. Profitability per head is lower today than five years ago; at Morgan Stanley we were *way* up over the same period. Can't your colleagues see that if we doubled the profits, their personal compensation could rise exponentially?'

'It depends whether they believe in their ability to generate those profits, especially if it means a new way of doing business.'

65

Charles Barton added his pennyworth.

'As the most ancient person in this room, perhaps I shouldn't say this. But what Marcus means is that we may have problems with old dogs and new tricks.'

Rosco nodded, and forked a whole roast potato into his mouth.

'Well, I *do* hope they realize that times are changing. Whether they like it or not, we're gonna have to turn up the heat on them. Right, Charles?'

Charles nodded. Patricia shuddered. The sooner this repulsive man left her house, the better. Would you just *look* at his table manners? What on earth was her husband doing, employing people like this? Sellars continued.

'And if they don't like the heat, they should get out of the kitchen. In fact, they may have no choice.'

There was silence for a while. Barton wasn't altogether happy about that last remark. Of course it was true, but if Sellars went around saying things like that before he'd even *met* them, he'd get people's backs up unnecessarily.

The silence was broken by Rosco.

'Boy this beef is good, Patricia. You're one hell of a cook. Charles sure is a lucky man . . .'

Patricia's only response was to fire an eye-salvo down the table at her husband. He had now been officially warned to get lunch over quickly.

Rosco kept the small talk coming.

'. . . Hey, Charles, when do I get to meet this famous brother of yours?'

*

Einstein was spending his Sunday in communion with his computer. From time to time Ruth would bring him a cup of something. She was being *so* good about it all. He could see that, as a natural worrier, she was petrified that they might lose their house, but she didn't let that override her endless capacity for compassion.

Ruth had only met Poppy once, when Einstein took her round

66

to explain how research into drugs was done. When Ruth saw how the child responded to him, it thrilled her to see what a natural teacher he was and made her want to wring the necks of those little ruffians in Hackney.

Now, when she watched her husband entranced by this latest project, so glad to be needed as the brains of the operation, her motherly instincts forced her to let him have his head. He was checking the Internet for articles about bankers and bids. Among the huge number, his eye was particularly caught by a piece in *Sunday Business* about the banker who'd handled Furnival's bid. He printed it off and called Len on his mobile. Since they had decided on their course of action, Len was working all the hours God sent to cover the payments on the second mortgage.

'Len, the banker from Skidders that you got the IFK story from . . . D'you remember his name?'

'Don't think so, Einstein. Young, 'e was – not more than thirty-five, very full of 'isself. It was somethin' to do with cars . . .'

'Ford?'

'That's it, *Ford*.'

'I've been checking the press. There's an article about him. Do you think he's worth having on our list?'

'Why not? 'E was just the sort of loud-mouthed wanker we need.'

'Okay, I'll put him down. Have you heard from Terry?'

'Not a peep. Maybe the lad's too ashamed to admit that 'e didn't score.'

'I'll leave a message for him. We need to meet later tonight to carve up the banks between us.'

'Okay. Why not come over to us at nine?'

67

8

'So d'you think of yourself as English or American?'

'I *feel* English, but sometimes I *think* American.'

'How long were you there?'

'I went often in school holidays when Daddy was in Washington. Then, later, I had three years at Harvard doing a Master's and five years on Wall Street.'

'I'm amazed you've come back. Doesn't London seem boring compared with New York?'

'I've hardly had time to find out yet. Santé.'

'Cheers.'

It was Marcus who'd arranged for Grace to take Julia for a drink at the end of her first week. They were in the downstairs bar of Chez Gerard in Bishopsgate.

'So, Julia, what do you make of Skidders?'

'I think I could get to like it. Everyone's friendly. We were all expecting to be treated like aliens.'

'In case you haven't noticed, they're friendlier to you than to the rest of the new team. It *could* be connected with your looks. You've been the main subject of conversation among the boys all week . . .'

It was true. Julia's long legs, chestnut hair, grey-green eyes and model-like features had caused quite a stir, and the executives and assistant directors had been salivating from the moment she walked in. Grace passed on further compliments without any trace of bitchiness. Although Julia was more elegant, Grace was confident that, overall, she was in the same attractiveness bracket.

'. . . What are your other impressions?'

'To be honest, it seems a bit sleepy compared with Morgan Stanley.'

'Yes, I think we'll have to change.'

'If Rosco has anything to do with it, you better believe it . . . There I go with another Americanism. I'll have to stamp them out. My parents *hate* me using them.'

'Where do they live?'

'Darkest Hampshire. Daddy retired last year. Mummy never worked, though being a diplomat's wife was almost a full-time job.'

'They must be glad you've come home.'

'Mummy seems to be and she *tells* me that Daddy is. He's a slightly sad figure these days. To supplement his Foreign Office income, he went into Lloyd's in a big way back in the Eighties and it pretty much cleaned them out. Nowadays they live in carefully disguised genteel poverty. Their house is grand enough, but it's rented from an old friend. They still owe a lot of money to our relatives. That's why I went into banking, to help bail them out. I'm still working on paying it all off.'

'So those guaranteed bonuses will come in handy. Did you work with Rosco Sellars the whole time you were at Morgan Stanley?'

'No, not at all. For the first three years I was at the wrong end of the food chain, doing economic forecasting. Then I got my break in the high-yield group and was transferred over to Rosco's team about ten months ago.'

'You know, I oughtn't to say it, but someone in the Skidders office in New York is spreading the rumour that you and Rosco . . .'

'Rosco and I *what*?'

'You know . . . have a thing for each other. They say that's why he's left his wife and kids behind.'

Julia shook her head wearily, and took a deep draught of champagne. *Fuck*, that was just what she needed. She *had* succumbed once, at the end of a very drunken evening celebrating a deal. Word – or at least speculation – had spread and had found its way to her manfriend, a corporate lawyer who got very unhappy. She had lied her way out of it and made absolutely sure that Rosco understood there would be no return match.

After a while, the gossip died down, and she'd hoped that was the end of it. She smiled at Grace.

'Don't you find it amazing how gossipy men are? They simply don't believe that girls like us can work in a bank for five minutes without falling for some other banker. I *bet* they make up stories like that about you all the time. Come on, tell me which of the Skidder boys they think *you* drop your knickers for . . .'

Grace smiled too, impressed by how skilfully Julia had hit the ball back over the net without actually denying the tale.

'Tell you what, let's get off men. Where do you hail from, Grace? Do I detect a tiny remnant of "oop north" in that sophisticated banker's voice?'

'You do indeed, *and* I'm proud of it, whatever anyone else thinks. If you haven't noticed yet, the boys tease me mercilessly. "Ee ba goom, trouble at mill", et cetera.'

'So where are we talking, up north?'

'Beverley, near Hull. Ever been?'

'I *have* been north of Watford, but I've always leapfrogged Yorkshire and gone straight to Scotland. Mummy's family have a small estate in Morayshire.'

'Well, if you ever get the chance, Beverley's not such a bad place. We have a lovely Minster and . . . well, that's about it, really. My dad works for BT up there as a telephone repairman. I can tell you, not many of the executives at Skidders have telephone repairmen in the family.'

'And if they did, they'd never let on.' Both girls giggled prettily. 'They must be thrilled with what you've achieved.'

Grace put on a heavily Yorkshire accent. 'They are *that*.' She returned to her normal voice. 'I was always good at school, and got a scholarship to Cambridge. You should have seen the jig my folks danced when the letter came through. And then when I got a First, they nearly climbed the Minster spire and put bunting round it.'

'And now . . . all this.' Julia nodded at the champagne bottle.

'I've had to stop telling them how much I'm paid. It's *so* much more than my Dad gets, it's embarrassing.'

'Yes, the English seem to have a real problem with big salaries. No one in America is bothered by it.'

'I can understand it. It's hard to see why we should be paid more than brain surgeons. Mind you, that doesn't stop me enjoying it. My gods are brands, champagne and five-star hotels. I want it all.'

'What does "all" mean?'

'A great life. That doesn't mean just career. I'm happy to work as hard as the next man for a few years, but the last thing I want is to be forty, stressed out, and on my own.'

This topic was uncomfortably close to home for Julia. At thirty-one, she wondered increasingly whether that would be her own fate. Though she'd never been short of well-heeled professional admirers, she hadn't come across anyone she could dream of marrying.

'So what *do* you want, Grace?'

'A successful, obscenely rich husband. If I can't reach obscenity, very rich indeed will do.'

'How about Charles Barton's brother, Guy? According to the *Daily Mail*, he's just dumped his supermodel girlfriend.'

'He's far too glam to look at the likes of me. Anyway, he doesn't seem to be the marrying kind, and I can't waste time double-checking. You must see things differently, but *I* plan on being married by the time I'm thirty.'

'Which is how far off?'

'Fourteen months.'

'Then you'd better get your skis waxed, unless of course you've already got your hooks into some suitable victim.' Julia smiled enough to blunt the barb.

'I'm working on it. I know it must sound awful to you but, when we were growing up, money was always a worry for my parents. It still is. I'm scared of ending up the same way.'

Julia nodded. That was enough girl talk for now. Usually her instincts were pretty dependable and her first impressions stuck. She *thought* she liked Grace, but was finding the admixture of couth Northerner and titanium-tipped City girl hard to assess. In the meantime, Grace could help her understand the Skidder topography better. Her fellow newcomers were all finding the place comically old-fashioned. Whenever they weren't being overheard, they mimicked the English accents and made lots of jokes about passing the port. Marcus Ford would have been horrified if he had known that, far from being an exception to this, there was a rich seam of Marcus jokes, all suggesting that he was keeping Rosco's rear in a state of moist cleanliness.

'Grace, I'll have to run in a moment, but there's something I want you to fill me in on. Richard Myers and the other directors are *saying* all the right things to us, but do you know what they're really thinking? And what's Charles Barton's reputation in the bank?'

*

Marcus Ford had enjoyed a pretty good week. Being at that lunch at the Bartons' had positioned him handily, and Rosco Sellars had latched onto him as a source of intelligence. Whenever he wanted to find out how things worked, he strolled along to Marcus's desk and asked. This got noticed, and Marcus's stock rose further among the young opinion-formers. None of them believed that Sellars would share power for long, or that Myers had any chance of winning the inevitable struggle, and they were all watching who would emerge as Rosco's leading lieutenant. It was already obvious that the other directors had no chance. Whether out of loyalty, habit, or failure to see how the tide had turned, they wore their support for Richard on their sleeves and so ruled themselves out. Marcus only had to play his own cards well, and the prize would be his.

He was also pleased with his progress on the bid. The numbers were looking good. Their estimates showed that, after disposing of unwanted divisions, there should be enough cashflow to service the debt. The problem for the Skidders team was that Jowell's long-time boss, Albert Austin, supplied the market with minimal information and gave no data at all on the profitability of his individual businesses. This made it hard to build up a detailed picture.

However, there were some useful straws in the wind suggesting that Austin's stewardship was coming into question. Looked at over a five- or ten-year span, he had unquestionably delivered fabulous results for his shareholders, but Jowell's recent performance was less stellar. His failure to cultivate brokers' analysts was now counting against him, and the perception was gradually spreading that, at fifty-nine, Albert Austin was past his best.

In the course of the week, Marcus visited Furnival's offices more than once, and the good progress on the bid consolidated his relationship with Robert Quilley. On his last visit that week, he and Quilley talked detailed timing for the first time. Ever since the IFK board had surrendered, completing that deal was mere mechanics. Never a man to let grass grow under his feet, Quilley wanted to go after Jowell when no one was expecting another move from him. He and Marcus worked through the practicalities and put a large red circle round Monday the ninth of November. After that, the biggest issue to be resolved was how quickly and stealthily they could bolt together the financing. As he rode back in a taxi to Throgmorton Lane, Marcus concluded that, by any standards, Rosco Sellars now 'needed to know'.

It was the last thing he accomplished before leaving on Friday. Sellars gave an impressed whistle. Marcus was mightily pleased that even a dude like Rosco was impressed by the size of the project. He offered to begin helping first thing on Monday. His only question was who else knew about it. When he heard how small the list was, and that Richard Myers's name was not on it, his dark eyes narrowed and his mouth widened into a broad, cool smile.

*

That same Friday evening, Len, Terry and Einstein met up at Piccolo's, the cabbies' subterranean café near Marble Arch, to review an altogether less satisfactory week. They queued to get something to eat, while around them another sixty or seventy

73

drivers drank tea, played the pinball machines, read the taxi newspapers, or just chatted. The trio found an empty table and sat down.

'So when will we know if she'll help us, Terry?' Einstein asked through his bulging baguette.

'Not sure. Another week or so, p'raps.'

'Did you *ask* 'er yet?' Len's body language was none too friendly.

'Not . . . in so many words.'

'So what do you two talk about, then?'

'We don't talk a lot. All she wants to do is shag. She's like a bleedin' rabbit. I'm knackered, I tell you.'

Len grinned and thumped Einstein in the ribs.

'If Romeo 'ere ain't up to the job, maybe you and me could 'elp 'im out. We could work a rota, keep the gel satisfied, eh?'

Einstein grinned sheepishly and kept on munching. Terry fired back.

'You keep out of this. I got to time it right; we *are* askin' the gel to put 'er job on the line.'

Einstein was unimpressed. 'No one's going to find out.'

As he was talking, a sliver of bacon fell out of his baguette. Terry grabbed it and held it aloft.

''Ere, what's this you're eatin', eh? Does Ruth know about this?'

Einstein grinned back. 'Don't you dare tell her. She'd kill me. I love the stuff.'

Len started wagging a finger. That always meant reminiscence time.

'When I was at school . . .'

'In the last century.'

'Piss off, Terry. When I was at school, there was different dinners for the Jewish kids and the rest of us. We queued up in two lines, so we'd get our pork and they'd get salt beef or whatever. Then, when the dinner ladies wasn't watching, we'd all swap over. Them kids was as bad as you, Einstein.'

The focus now off him, Terry relaxed.

74

'Funny thing, a religion based on not eatin' bacon. Is that 'ow you Jewish boys imagine 'eaven, then? Angels, 'arps, and not a rasher in sight?'

Einstein smiled, swallowed the last bite, and wiped his mouth clean.

'Okay, back to business. Len, anything?'

'Nothin' much. I waited at Canary Wharf and picked up a few punters from Morgan Stanley, but they was mainly chattin' about their own pay. Then there was a couple from Lazards that I took to the City airport. I *think* they were discussin' some deal, but they didn't mention no names. You do any better, Einstein?'

'I got one possible. A big-mouth from Lehmans, bragging over the phone to his woman. Said they were selling some gin brand, and getting offers three times higher than expected. I checked on the Internet. A big spirits company, Drumalbine, bought one of its competitors recently, and the authorities in America are making them sell off their gin. I think it has to be that. The newspaper reports at the time valued it at four hundred million quid, but if it fetches more than a billion, Drumalbine's share price should shoot up by ten or twenty per cent. I think it's worth a small punt. Maybe five thousand pounds or so.'

Len didn't want to put Einstein down, but he couldn't see the logic in doing that.

'Sounds a good lead, Einstein, don't get me wrong, but if we make a grand or so on it, it's neither 'ere nor there, is it? The doctor says if we don't get Poppy over to San Francisco within three or four months, she'll be too weak to travel. Shouldn't we do somethin' bigger?'

'Of course you're right, Len, but I think there's a way to get better returns on our investments. I've done a bit of homework on something called "options". Instead of buying shares, like we always do, you can buy an *option* to buy shares. For, say, five thousand pounds, you get the right to buy a much larger block of shares – more like a hundred grands' worth – for a fixed time.'

' 'Ow long?'

'Usually forty-five days. The share price you can buy at is fixed from the start, so if the shares go up, your profit is on the whole hundred grand and not on your five thousand quid.'

Terry's brow furrowed deeply. Einstein could see he would have to go through it more simply, and slipped into his teacher's voice.

'Take the example I gave of the drinks company. We buy a forty-five-day option and during that time they announce the sale of the gin brand for a very high price. Their share price goes up twenty per cent, so a hundred thousand quids' worth of shares is now–'

'Worth 'undred and twenty, so we make a profit of twenty grand!' Terry looked triumphant, and Einstein took care not to spoil his moment.

'Almost. You have to deduct the five thousand cost of the option, so our profit would be fifteen thousand.'

Terry looked perplexed. '*Why?* If you win at the 'orses, you get your stake money back.'

Einstein thought of explaining, but it was going to be too hard.

'These City boys make up the rules to suit themselves, I suppose.'

Len had been taking all this in.

'Einstein, what 'appens if the share price *don't* go up?'

'Then the option is worthless, and we lose our stake.'

'Well, *that's* like the 'orses, anyway.' Terry was happier again.

'Look, fellas, you're right that it's risky, but we've no other choice. We're simply not going to turn fifty-five thousand into half a million dollars in three months without taking some calculated risks.'

Len considered, then nodded.

'I s'pose you're right.'

'Good. Terry, we haven't heard from you yet. That is, if you've found any time for working between bouts in the sack.'

'One of my punters was that fella from Skidder Barton, Ford. I got a job pickin' 'im up from Furnival's offices. There was a tasty blonde with 'im. I was all ready to listen in, but they banged the window shut and switched the intercom off.'

76

Len tried to cheer him up.

'Don't worry, Terry mate, they was probably just takin' care of the tag ends of the IFK deal.'

Einstein stroked his chin thoughtfully. 'Hold on. That doesn't make sense. There's nothing secret about that bid any more. Why should they bother to close the window? Unless . . .'

Len watched him carefully. 'Unless what, Einstein?'

Einstein's voice went very quiet, as if he was talking to himself. 'Unless they're planning *another* bid.'

Terry nodded thoughtfully. 'Pity they noticed the intercom was switched on . . .'

Einstein and Len looked at each other. Einstein grinned. Len shook his head frantically.

'No way, Einstein, that's a bridge too far.'

Einstein kept grinning.

'It's the *only* way, Len.'

Terry's head was swivelling left and right, like he was watching a tennis match.

'*What's* the only way, for fuck's sake? I ain't got the first bleedin' clue what you geezers are on about.'

Einstein ignored him.

'Len, where did you get your Technics stereo?'

'Tottenham Court Road. One of them Paki places.'

'Good, we'll go there tomorrow first thing and get what we need.'

'Get *what*, for Gawd's sake?'

Len slapped Terry hard on the back. 'You concentrate on rogering Daphne, mate. Leave the rest to me and Einstein.'

9

Rosco, Marcus and Grace got to the Hotel Am See in time for dinner. Their meeting with Ernst Lautenschutz at Zuricher's headquarters wasn't until nine the next morning so they could relax and enjoy themselves. They ate well and lingered over a digestif. Marcus was torn between luxuriating in the opportunity to spend so much time with Sellars and the hope that, like most clean-living American bankers, he would turn in early, leaving Grace and him to themselves. There had been a few more private sessions since that Saturday at Marco Pierre's, and Grace was looking exceptionally succulent tonight. It helped that they were all on different floors, so it should be possible to slip down to her room without any risk of bumping into Rosco.

But no: Sellars talked on and on, and it was Grace who left first, without enough of a glance in his own direction to make Marcus sure she was willing to chance it. He champed at the bit while Sellars demolished another large cognac. Finally, Rosco yawned, stretched, and they walked to the lift together. At the second floor, he got out, slapped Marcus on the back, and bade him goodnight.

In his own room on the fourth floor, Marcus paced the room. Damn, it was now so late that Grace might have got fed up waiting and be sound asleep. Should he sneak down to the third floor and tap gently on her door to see if she was still awake?

Marcus was uncertain. Grace could be hard to read. There were times when she was hot, beyond doubt, but at others she played harder to get. It was partly his own fault. One time recently, in the full flood of passion, he'd got carried away and let his dick rule his head, spouting some meaningless crap about a future together. When it came back to him the next morning at her flat in Kensington, he'd been obliged to dilute the effect with a large dose of calculated coolness.

He looked at his watch. It was nearly one-thirty. If he was going to go for it, it had to be now, or he would never get any sleep. He brushed his teeth, cursorily sponged his genitals and pulled on the next day's ration of clean underwear. Then, grabbing a condom from his overnight bag, he made his way down to the third floor and tapped discreetly on Grace's door.

Inside the room, Grace tensed in the dark.

Marcus waited a few more seconds and tried again. He pressed his ear hard against the door to listen for tell-tale sounds. Nothing. He gave it another half-minute, and tried one last time. The third knock was sharper and was accompanied by a breathy, insistent 'Grace'.

Shit. With a last pleading look at the door, he wandered disconsolately back along the corridor and up the stairs to his bedroom. There was nothing for it but the soft-porn films. He would have to make sure that he checked out before the others so they didn't overhear the girl at the cash desk announcing the extras on his bill.

It was a pathetic German story of two nurses on holiday, one he'd seen twice before. He got it over with as soon as possible and switched off the lights and the set.

*

It went without saying that Rosco would lead the meeting with Lautenschutz. Over breakfast he took Marcus and Grace through his strategy. Marcus concentrated intently on every word, making it all the easier to ignore Grace.

'Okay, this is how we play it. Marcus does the presention on Furnival, including their plans for integrating IFK. After that, Grace majors on the business-by-business analysis of Jowell. Then back to Marcus for the bid timetable. Don't assume that Lautenschutz understands much about takeovers: they scarcely exist in this well-ordered country. Finally, I'll handle our ideas on financing. It's not only that Skidders is required to offer Zuricher first bite of the cherry: the US banks now regard Zuricher as being virtually our parent company, and if they don't back this deal, we'll have no credibility in their eyes. We need them to commit for a very big slice. If they do, I'll have zero problems getting the rest together. By the way, I should tell you that I've brought one more person into the loop.'

Marcus looked worried. Sellars moved swiftly to defuse his concern.

'Only one. Julia Daventry. After she joined my group at Morgan Stanley, I had her help me in acquisition finance. She has a big contribution to make here. . .'

Marcus nodded approvingly. Since that lunch at Charles Barton's, he'd had little chance to talk to her and was too dignified to join the back of the queue of Skidders guys trying to invite her to lunch, dinner or *anything*. Working with her on a project – *his* project, as it happened – would provide a more natural opportunity to get to know her better.

'In fact, she may come with us when we go over to New York to present this to banks.'

Marcus looked very pleased. Grace smiled cautiously, not sure whether the 'we' included her.

At eight forty-five on the button, a Mercedes appeared at the hotel and whisked them the few miles to Zuricher's grand head-quarters. They were ushered to the top floor and installed in a large meeting room to await the arrival of Ernst Lautenschutz. Ten minutes later, he swept in.

'Ah, Rosco. How good to see to you again.'

In good hierarchical fashion, Lautenschutz ignored the underlings until the main man was comprehensively greeted.

'Are you settling in well? I hope our English friends are responding positively.'

'Yes, very well. Ernst, I believe you once met Marcus Ford, one of the corporate finance directors.'

'Did I? Oh, yes, perhaps. Forgive me, there are so many directors in your department.'

He shook Marcus's hand perfunctorily.

Marcus felt a rush of colour to his face. He'd talked with Lautenschutz for fully ten minutes, and had exaggerated that timespan generously when lying in bed with Grace. Sellars continued.

'And this is Grace Chesterfield, the executive on the project we want to discuss with you. She does a great job.'

'I'm sure she does . . .'

To Marcus's irritation, Lautenschutz clung on to her hand for an age, and clearly *noticed* her.

'Well, Rosco, what exactly *is* this project?'

As the session proceeded, Marcus's mood became darker. He had expected to be the star of the show and to be treated accordingly. Instead, this infuriating Swiss jerk insisted on addressing all his questions to Sellars, even when it concerned aspects which Marcus was presenting himself. Rosco then called on Marcus to answer, but had the annoying habit of adding a sentence or two to each of his responses, conveying the impression that he himself was in charge of the whole operation. But it was a different story when bloody Grace had her turn. Lautenschutz had no trouble at all speaking directly to *her*.

Once the formal presentation was over, Lautenschutz asked for more guidance on the English takeover rules. What blocking actions could the target company take? He was patently surprised to learn that, apart from being able to rubbish the bidder's record and talk up their own, there was little they could actually *do*, short of crossing their fingers.

'I am glad it is not like this in Switzerland.'

Marcus was irritated enough to point out that Switzerland now had a takeover code of its own. He had mugged up on this specially, so as to explain all the better. Now he wanted to use it to put the man down.

Lautenschutz smiled patronizingly.

'You are right, dear boy, we do have takeover rules. However, having them and *using* them are different things. It is true that one or two naive companies have suffered at the hands of these rules, but most of our corporations and, I'm happy to say, banks have placed enough shares in friendly hands to ensure that our feathers are never ruffled. However, if I understand you correctly, in England it is merely a matter of price. Is that what you think will happen with Jowell, Rosco?'

Sellars didn't even defer to Marcus this time.

'Basically that's right, Ernst. The PR battle will be important, too.'

'And under your rules, once a bid has been made, do other potential buyers have to sit out the dance?'

Marcus opened his mouth to elucidate, but again Rosco got in first.

'Not at all. In any bid situation there's a risk that a so-called "white knight" shows up. This particular bid is so large, every investment bank in the goddam universe will be trying to find one. After all, the total fees they could earn on this will be over a hundred million sterling.'

Lautenschutz looked seriously impressed.

'Is that what Skidders stands to make if Furnival succeeds with this?'

'Absolutely. That's one of the reasons we'll be recommending Furnival to make a knockout bid, to make sure they win.'

'Mmmm. So this single transaction could double Skidders's annual profits?'

'You have it in one, Ernst. That will make you a very happy shareholder, I imagine.'

'Indeed. Tell me, which other companies theoretically *could* come in as white knights?'

Rosco was way off the pace on this one. Unfortunately, so was Marcus. Grace had done the legwork, so when Sellars passed him the baton, he had no choice but to sling it on to Grace. She passed round copies of a schedule.

'As you see here, there are very few industrial buyers who

match the profile in product sectors and financial strength. With the possible exception of the Mitsubishi group, there's no one from the Far East, and in North America there is only Allied Dynamics. Moves like this aren't their style. We see nothing in France, Scandinavia, or the UK. All that leaves is Lerber from Germany and the Burlikon group from Switzerland. Of the two, Burlikon has the better product match, but we find it hard to imagine either of these companies wading into a battle between two UK companies. Overall, the coast looks pretty clear.'

'Thank you, Grace. That's very encouraging . . .' Lautenschutz smiled warmly at her, and glanced at his gold Rolex. 'Okay, we should move on to the financing. I have only fifteen minutes before my next meeting. Let's try to finish in ten minutes. Then I want a private word with Rosco about something else.'

After the ten minutes were up, Lautenschutz said goodbye to Marcus and Grace with varying degrees of warmth and asked them to wait in the meeting room while Rosco went through to his office with him. As soon as the door closed behind them, Grace began.

'What did you think? Sounds to me like Zuricher will go for it.'

'Yeah. What a creep, though.'

'I thought he was rather charming. What d'you think he and Rosco are talking about?'

'How the hell should I know?'

They sat in silence for a while. Eventually Marcus broke it.

'Did you get a good night's sleep?'

'Not bad. You?'

'Okay. I came down to your room, actually.'

'Really? About what time?'

'Half past one.'

'I assumed you were enjoying spending time with Rosco. I put my head down and was out like a light.'

At that moment Rosco Sellars came back into the room and they all left to head back to the airport. When Grace was out of earshot, Marcus gave Rosco a chance to confide about his private chat with Lautenschutz. He didn't seem to notice the hint.

Rosco Sellars had made sure his new secretary had arranged a separate car to travel back into London. Though it was only two o'clock when they landed, he didn't plan to go back into the bank. Today was the day he was finally getting out of the Berkeley hotel and into the majestic apartment that Skidders were renting for him.

As he rode in, he reflected on the day's events. Marcus Ford had definitely failed to grow on him. He had sulked so badly when he wasn't given centre stage that he had resorted to scoring cheap points. It could have turned the whole meeting against them. Fortunately, Lautenschutz was still in the honeymoon period with his American hires, and he obviously liked the look of Grace. Those factors, plus the undeniable scale of the bid, had carried the day. Another time it might have been different, though, and Sellars resolved never to take Marcus to a presentation again unless he had no choice.

The car drew up outside Rosco's new abode. He had selected his rental agent solely on looks and was glad to see that she was there, waiting for him. Five minutes later, he'd booked her for dinner that night. He intended to have fun in London. He disliked his wife wholeheartedly, and cared little more for the two kids they'd spawned. However, Marisa had always threatened him with financial carnage if they divorced and parting with forty or fifty million dollars was more than Rosco could bear. Marisa was no keener to make it official. Manhattan was choking with wealthy divorcees, most of them pathetically unable to persuade anyone to remake an honest woman of them. That was the problem with the spread of prosperity: the price of companionship constantly outstripped inflation. Provided her allowance was generous enough, it suited Marisa better to maintain the fiction of marriage, and indulge herself freely with the many lithe bohemians whose artistry could be purchased with loose change.

Rosco planned to treat London like one big candy store. He was rich, moderately powerful, physically fit, at forty-four still young enough, and none too bad-looking in a vaguely Mediterranean way. Nature had treated him well: recently he'd started returning the favour, paying an LA snipper to spirit away the first hint of jowls.

There were already some promising prospects. The rental agent, a foxy banker he'd met on the Concorde – and Grace, of course. Plus, now that Julia had been prised away from her lawyer friend she might be less fussy about resuming relations. If he found ways to keep her working late at the bank so she developed no social life, then loneliness, if not his own charms, should smooth the way to removing again those delightfully stuck-up panties.

As Rosco strolled round the flat and took in the grand view from the master bedroom, his mind wandered involuntarily away from sex. Lautenschutz had privately pointed out two very interesting things. First, since Furnival's bid for Jowell had been conceived before Rosco arrived, Skidders wouldn't pay him his fat slice of the fees. Second, whatever Charles Barton might think, the future of Skidders was definitely Swiss.

The agent had thoughtfully provided a bottle of Dom Perignon. They poured themselves glasses and clinked. She was thirty-six, no great beauty, but definitely sexy. Boy, life had improved. Only nine months before, Sellars's star had been fading at Morgan Stanley and word had begun to seep onto the street. If he hadn't moved fast and found these European schmucks in time, he would have been history. Yet look at him now the darling of a deep-pocket Swiss bank, with the jerks at Skidders hanging on his every word, not to mention three years of guaranteed bonuses big enough to make his accountant's eyes water.

10

Buying three Walkman recorders was the easy part. Wiring them up was something else.

Einstein did all the work in Terry's garage, now sadly empty bar the ghost of the Cosworth. Both Einstein and Len had decided not to worry their wives any more than was necessary. Neither knew whether taping punters' conversations was illegal, but they were pretty damn sure that if they were caught, their green badges would be gone for good.

Einstein had hoped to get his own taxi rigged up in one afternoon and then replicate the operation on the other two cabs the next day. In the end it took bloody ages and two more trips to Tottenham Court Road. It was hard to wire it so the sound fed direct to the tape recorder when the intercom was off. Einstein had to construct a mechanism that overrode the main system and was powered off the Walkman so it could be disconnected and hidden if the police stopped the cab. It worked pretty well, but at the price of a vast power drain on the Walkman's batteries. They agreed there was nothing for it but to carry spares at all times.

*

Len had been finding it a strain, hanging round in the City during the day for interesting titbits, and then working until the small hours to make enough dosh. It all meant he was seeing less of Poppy.

Poppy's spirits seemed okay, but her health was awful. Some nights when he came back at two or three, he would creep in to make sure he didn't disturb her. As he walked up the stairs, though, he would listen out, and if he heard her hacking away he would push the door open and sit with her for an hour or so, holding her hand, chatting in whispers.

Len and Jean couldn't work out whether Poppy believed in the San Francisco plan or was humouring them. They often remarked how the illness had made her grow up prematurely. She seemed to bear the burden of the whole world on her frail shoulders, and was always able to see through any attempt to varnish the truth.

The way her cough sounded, they were worried she'd end up in hospital this side of Christmas. They knew how Poppy feared that if she went in again she'd never get out. What could be done about it, though, other than to hope and to pray, and to show every ounce of love and affection? Since she'd stopped going to school, a gap had grown between her and her friends. They visited less often and, when they came, they seemed awkward with her sickness, uncertain whether they could behave normally. The time Terry and Einstein spent with her helped fill the void. Jean and Len had their own routines with her, of course. Jean gave her two essential hours of physiotherapy every day, and the first thing Len did of a morning was to take up her enzymes, all her other pills, and a cup of her favourite Ribena.

'There you are, Poppity.'
　'Thanks, Dad.'
　'Did you get much sleep, treasure?' He stroked her hair gently.
　'A bit.'
　'What you been drawin' there? Is that the Dartford Bridge?'
　'No, you div. It's San Francisco.'
　'Oh, of *course*. They got a bridge like that, too, ain't they?'
　Poppy rolled her eyes and grimaced.
　'We'll make sure you're all dressed up smart for your trip and for sight-seeing afterwards, when they fix you up. Shall I go to the shops today and get you some new trainers? I forget what size you are.'
　She rolled her eyes again. 'Dad, don't you know *nothin'*? Trainers used to be cool. Now they're sad.'
　'What's that mean, *sad*?'
　'Sad's like lame.'
　'You've lost me again, doll.'

'Trainers are for divs.'

'I 'aven't the first idea what you're on about, love, but I take it you don't want no trainers?'

'Halleluia . . .' Poppy's eyes became beadier. Lez recognized the warning sign. 'Dad, the money for California: what exactly are you doin' to raise it? I got a right to know, since it's in aid of me.'

'No, you bleedin' well ain't. As long as we get it, it's no concern of yours.'

'Yes, it is. I want to know why Terry sold the Cossie. Did you take that money?'

'What, *me*, take money from Terry? I ain't took a brass farthing from the lad.'

Strictly speaking, it was true. All Terry was doing was investing. Poppy watched her father's face for a few moments, assessing, then handed down her judgement.

'You're lyin'. And, since you and Terry couldn't organize a piss-up in a brewery, Einstein must be involved too. Come on, Dad, you might as well tell me. I'll find out anyway.'

Len suddenly felt the urge to check his watch.

'Bugger, is that the time? I got to get to work. You drink up your Ribena.'

He kissed Poppy and retreated downstairs.

*

It was exquisitely dreadful timing that, on the very day that Charles Barton was lunching at White's with his father, Sir Miles, the Lex column of the *Financial Times* should have chosen to comment on a new rash of defections from the bank's global-markets department, stating that this was 'further proof that Skidder Barton have lost their way'.

All very vexing. The bank's in-house press-relations man had attempted a major offensive to get wide positive coverage of the hirings from Morgan Stanley. The *FT* did cover it in a matter-of-fact way, but it was buried deep on the appointments page. Several of the newspapers failed to run it altogether, and the only one that described it in any detail, *The Times*, made wounding comments about 'a cheque book strategy smacking of desperation', and called into question whether Rosco Sellars was really such a big catch.

Yet here was a *much* smaller story – the departure of a dozen second-rate traders – and it was splashed everywhere, as well as picked up in several City editorials, 'crisis at Skidders' being the common thread. The share price had risen, not fallen, on the news, but this was cold comfort to Charles Barton. The buying was being driven by one thing only: the belief that the bank's performance was so lamentable that sooner or later a bid for them was inevitable.

Sir Miles had been famously short-fused in the years of his pomp, when Chairman of Skidder Barton. Now seventy-eight, time had done little to mellow him. He hardly permitted his son to swallow one mouthful of potted shrimps before wading into him.

'You've simply *got* to get a grip. It's been one catastrophe after another. When is it going to stop? *That's* what I want to know.'

Charles munched on a sliver of toast. It was so like his father to ask unanswerable questions like that. He knew from experience that there was no point in replying yet. The storm would have to blow itself out first.

'You seem to have no proper controls at all. Take that absurd nonsense in the fund-management department. How was it *possible* for an error like that to go undetected so long? And did you see the most recent takeover league tables? Sixteenth, we were. *Sixteenth* . . .' He was working himself up into such a fury over it, several fellow diners thought he might have a coronary. 'During my time, we were *never* below fifth.'

'Yes, father, but you didn't have the Americans to contend with.'

'Oh yes, we *did*. They were all here. Goldman Sachs, Morgan Stanley, Salomon Brothers. The difference then was we knew how to defend our home market.'

Charles thought of trying to explain how much had changed, but what was the use? And he did have to keep the old man vaguely

89

on-side since he controlled the trust that held the family shares in the bank. At twenty-six per cent, their shareholding was big enough to make even a determined bidder think twice. By the same token, however, if that block swung behind a bid, the fight would be over before it began. He tried to move on to a more positive note.

'Well, we are doing a lot to strengthen the corporate finance department.'

'If you mean those Americans, you seem to have made rather a tit of yourself again there, don't you? Bought a pig in a poke, by the sound of it.'

'That story in *The Times* was ridiculous. Rosco Sellars is a genuine heavy-hitter. Just what we needed. He's made an immediate impact, given the place a thorough shaking-up.'

'How much are you paying him?'

Charles was tempted to lie, but the figures would have to be published in the bank's annual report in due course and his father had a very good memory for things like that. There was, however, no need to go into the Byzantine off-shore arrangements for paying Sellars' special fee share. He would restrict himself to the figures that *would* find their way to the taxman.

'His package is about four million, if I recall rightly.'

His father's face, which had briefly faded to vermilion, resumed its deep purple hue.

'Four million *pounds*? You've taken leave of your senses, Charles. The most I ever made as Chairman was–'

'Yes, I know, father. Times have changed.'

'For the worse, clearly. How can you possibly hope to make worthwhile profits for shareholders if you are going to pay individuals as much as that, eh?'

' It's quite simple. If Rosco Sellars is half as good as he looks so far, he will make so much money for the bank that his package will seem cheap.' Before his father could snap back on that, he rushed on. 'And let me tell you, the pipeline of business in that department is looking better than ever. There's one deal they're working on that should net us a hundred million pounds.'

His father had the decency to look impressed. In the early

Eighties Sir Miles had personally brought in a fee of ten million. He was so proud of it, he still trotted out the story ten times a year.

'Did this Sellars fellow bring it in?'

'No. He's involved in the deal now, I believe, working on the financing. As it happens, it stems from a relationship that I cultivated myself.'

'Hmmm.'

It was clear that the old man was torn between his greed for the increased dividend such a profit might bring and his dislike of his personal record being broken. He changed the subject abruptly.

'Have you spoken to Guy?'

'Not for a while. How are the preparations going for the jump?'

'Well, I think.'

Guy was Charles's brother, younger by one year. He had started off life as the black sheep, getting into scrapes at prep school and being expelled from Eton. He spent a few months in prison for marketing soft drugs, and on his release ran away and joined the French Foreign Legion. The whole family was mortified. Meanwhile, Charles gathered golden opinions and was in every way the model son. Upon graduation, he was sent to a blue-blooded Boston bank to learn the trade, and brought into Skidders at twenty-six. By twenty-nine he was promoted to director, and ten years later slid comfortably into his father's seat when the old man reluctantly reached sixty-five.

Over the same period, Guy had surprised the whole lot of them. Returning to London in his late twenties, he set up his own company, trading commodities between Europe, Asia, and Africa. Though sceptical, the family felt obliged to lend some help, which Guy repaid richly when the company reported its first million-pound profit. Two decades later, Elixir Ltd had grown enormously, making Guy Barton wealthy and a darling of the financial press. Not only the financial press, either. He had the same handsome features as Charles, but his perma-tan, fuller head of hair, and wicked sense of humour offered greater allure. Throw in his fortune and his bachelor status, and it was not hard to see why he figured regularly in the society pages.

In recent years, his interest in parachuting had propelled his fame even wider, until he was now a true household name. He had already participated in a record-breaking 'canopy' formation jump, and now he had switched his attention to high-altitude, low-opening 'HALO' parachuting. The world record for this extreme form of free-fall jumping had stood since 1960, and Guy was obsessed with shattering it. That required lots of specially designed equipment. The whole crazy project was costing a mint, and it was widely believed that Guy Barton spent more time working on it than running Elixir.

Not that this seemed to have any damaging effect on the company's performance. It appeared that he'd mastered the art of how to set strategy, motivate staff, delegate fully, and then keep out of their way. Indeed, as Elixir continued to grow and Skidder Barton declined, the press could not resist the temptation to compare the track record of the two brothers and shrilly suggest that, if Skidders' management was to stay in family hands, no time should be wasted asking Guy Barton to shoulder the dynastic burden and ride to the rescue.

Guy enjoyed poking fun at his strait-laced brother, and those in the know said that the styles of the brothers were too incompatible for them to work together. The universal view was that bringing Guy Barton into Skidders would soon result in Charles being booted unceremoniously out, not that many commentators seemed overly concerned about that.

Charles Barton had to wait while Sir Miles wolfed the bulk of his Dover sole before discovering whether Guy's name had cropped up for a reason. The old man wiped his mouth roughly with his napkin, shoved a signeted pinky finger into his mouth to act as a toothpick, examined it for results, and resumed.

'I've been thinking. When does Guy get back from this parachuting lark?'

'The jump itself is on Christmas Day. I think he's coming back from Morocco as soon as he's done it.'

'It's all damn-fool nonsense, if you ask me, but he seems to enjoy it. It's made him something of a minor celebrity, I suppose.'

92

Sir Miles swelled with pride. He had always known that Guy would come good. He'd always said so – or, if he hadn't, he was sure he'd *thought* it.

'Not so minor. He's hardly out of the papers. Guy seems to have developed a taste for the public eye.'

'Mmmm . . .'

You jealous little *nothing*, the old man was thinking. The only time *you* get in the papers is when you've buggered something up. Sir Miles had to struggle to stop his contempt showing too much.

'Anyway, when he *does* get back, I think we should put him on the main board of the bank.'

The intake of breath from Charles was audible. Sir Miles knew he needed to be careful over this. He didn't want Charles flouncing out in a huff and handing over the reins to someone not family.

'In a purely non-executive capacity, of course. And certainly not spending more than a day a week at the bank. Two at most.'

There was a pause. Charles seemed more interested in toying with his vegetables than replying. Sir Miles could stand the suspense no longer.

'Well, what d'you think?'

It was a tricky one to handle. If Charles accepted this, his authority at Skidders would be shot to pieces. If, on the other hand, he batted it away too firmly now, the old man might turn terminally against him. What Charles needed was time to shore up his position and to demonstrate that the changes he'd instituted were working. If the defections stopped and the profits began to improve, he would be in a far stronger position to resist boarders. He might not need to wait for long. The moment Furnival's bid for Jowell was announced, the lustre would start to return to the firm's name. And that was only, what? A couple of weeks away. He surprised his father by nodding.

'I think it's a rather *interesting* idea, father. I've been wanting to strengthen the non-executive part of the main board for a while now, and putting Guy on it might work very well. I'd like to mull it over, if you don't mind. In any case, I don't think Guy's mind will be on anything but parachuting between now and Christmas. It would be pointless to bother him before then.'

'Hmmm . . .'

Sir Miles had wanted it settled. However, that was mainly because he was convinced that Charles would have to be bludgeoned into accepting it. If, after all, he wasn't going to oppose it, perhaps there was less need for haste.

'All right, then. How are Patricia and my two darling grand-daughters?'

Charles went on autopilot to tell him, grateful only that this dreadful occasion was nearing an end and that he had something to look forward to. For that very evening the little creature who lit up his life, who always understood, who listened tirelessly and intelligently to his troubles, who never browbeat or belittled him, who touched him in bed like Patricia had never touched him . . . was coming for supper.

11

'It's looking good, Robert. Everything went well in New York.'

'Is it done? Have they committed?'

'In principle, yes. They won't sign firm until the last business day before we launch.'

'Since we're launching on the ninth, that means next Friday, the sixth?'

'Exactly. Zuricher will sign up the same day, though that is of course a pure formality. Since the US funding is conditional on Zuricher coming in, we'll get them to sign early that morning so we have a full business day in New York to collect all the other signatures.'

'Good. Marcus, can you run me through the rest of the financing arrangements?'

'If you don't mind, I'd like to ask Julia here to explain all that. In the end I couldn't take time off to make the trip to New York, so Julia and Grace went with Rosco Sellars to all the meetings. . .'

He hid it well, but Marcus was still fuming over the way Sellars had manoeuvred him off the trip. The thought that Grace had now flown Concorde and he hadn't bugged the hell out of him.

'. . . I was hoping to bring Rosco today, so that you two could finally meet and he could report in person. Unfortunately, there's a big internal meeting he can't get out of.'

Robert Quilley found that surprising. How could *any* internal meeting take precedence over a twenty billion bid? Sounded to him like Skidders had their priorities all wrong. Still, as long as they were getting the job done . . . And, anyway, it wasn't his style to show that he felt slighted.

'Makes no odds to me. Shoot, Julia.'

'Thanks, Robert. As you know, the first thing we have to take care of is the full cash alternative for the bid. That will require a short-term facility of the entire twenty billion pounds. Our own shareholder, Zuricher, has agreed to provide eight billion of that, and the rest will be syndicated among a group of US banks led by BankManhattan. The term sheet is at appendix one in the pack of papers . . .'

Quilley flicked through the pack, found the right tab, took a quick look, and closed them again.

'. . . We've looked at the likely split between Jowell investors who will accept the cash offer and those who will prefer to take shares in the expanded Furnival group. We believe at least half will opt for the shares, so the drawdown on the financing facility will be ten billion maximum, and possibly much lower. Obviously, you'll need time to assess all the Jowell businesses, and to sell the parts you don't want. Our best guess is this process will take nine to twelve months. Assuming these disposals bring in at least seven or eight billion, your long-term debt shouldn't exceed three billion, leaving you with a very comfortable debt-to-equity ratio.'

Quilley nodded.

'And the providers of the long-term debt will be?'

'Zuricher and BankManhattan, on an equal basis.'

'I'm happy with that. Thank you, Julia. It sounds like you did a good job.'

'Rosco has long-standing links with BankManhattan, which helped smooth the way.'

'Good. So, Marcus, what else do we need to cover today?'

'I think we're in pretty good shape. The draft press release is nearly done. The biggest remaining issue is whether to consult your own major shareholders in advance.'

'What's your advice?' Quilley knew his own mind, but wanted to hear Marcus's view first.

'On balance, I'd recommend against. I don't think we should do anything that increases the chance of a leak.'

Quilley nodded, more in acknowledgement than in agreement.

'I see the risk, Marcus, but the relationship with our top three shareholder institutions is very close, and, as you know, there was no leak after we told them about IFK. I think I *have* to speak to them. However, I'll keep it to that small group, and I won't do it until, say, the fifth, so the risk is minimized.'

'Okay.' Marcus wasn't happy that Quilley had spurned his advice, especially in front of Grace and Julia. 'Well, I think that's about it for today.'

Quilley smiled and stood up. 'Thanks for coming round, everybody,'

Marcus, Grace, and Julia filed out, took the lift, and stepped into the taxi waiting downstairs. Marcus gestured to Grace to close the glass divider and make sure that the intercom was switched off.

'Okay, he seemed happy with the financing plan. I may try again to stop him talking to his shareholders. It's not a leak I'm so worried about; what if the buggers *oppose* the bid? I wonder if they also have big holdings in the target? If so, maybe we can persuade Robert it's too risky to tell them. Since Jupiter's market value is fourteen billion, they're bound to hold *some* shares in it. Can you check, Grace?'

Marcus used the rest of the cab ride to issue more instructions. As the cab drew up in Throgmorton Lane, he squeezed out ahead of the girls and dashed into the bank.

The cab moved off, and promptly stopped again round the corner. The skinny, bespectacled driver pulled from his pocket what looked like black string with two buttons attached. He stuffed the buttons into his ears and reached down to fiddle with something, then looked straight ahead again as he listened. A few minutes later, he repocketed the buttons, picked up a pink newspaper and glanced down the stock market pages. Companies with values of fourteen billion weren't that common. Where should he look? Automotive? Nothing. How about engineering? Were there any Js? Not only was there one: it was the only company in that whole sector with anything like that market value. *Jesus.* He picked up his mobile and dialled. A sleepy voice answered.

'Len? Sorry, did I wake you? . . . I think we've just hit the bull's-

97

eye. We need to meet this afternoon. Can you call Terry and get him to come to the café in Gresham Street? Two-thirty all right?'

*

After they left, Robert Quilley sat down at his broad oak desk, bare apart from a sleek telephone, a computer, a folder of papers his secretary had left for signature, and a wooden-framed photograph of a strikingly attractive young woman. He glanced fondly at the picture, then transferred his gaze outside to the rooftops of EC1. Jowell would be the crowning moment of an improbably successful career. French by blood and by birth, Quilley had been ripped from his native land at fourteen, when his father had wearied of trying to make a living farming in the Dordogne and had set off for fresh pastures in America. Robert had arrived there with a knowledge of English limited to 'Coca Cola' and 'Beach Boys'. It was fortunate for him that he was able to take care of himself, as more than one bullying Midwest teenager found to his cost.

That same penchant for the physical took him into the US Special Forces. It was scarcely a job for life, and at just past thirty he took a business degree and tipped into industry. No one expected much of him. They were wrong. He soon showed a flair for management, cutting costs ruthlessly but inspiring fierce loyalty in those who survived. His strategic grasp was strong and under his stewardship, companies grew.

What he was attempting now was breathtakingly audacious. For any other manager, securing and integrating IFK would have been enough to chew on for years. But Robert Quilley saw little merit in a patient step-by-step approach. Opportunities like Jowell didn't come along every day. The battle would be hard and it would be personal. It would turn on the market's view of who could manage the Jowell assets better, Albert Austin or himself. The loser would be mortally wounded, his reputation irretrievably damaged. The stakes could not have been higher. Quilley liked the smell of battle. He was looking forward to it.

*

98

By the time Marcus Ford got back to the bank, the directors' meeting had been under way for ten minutes. Sellars and Myers were co-chairing it, but by now everyone knew what that meant. Richard had realized that, in order to survive in the short term, he had to dance to Rosco's tune.

'Rosco and I have talked things over and decided that we need a fundamental rethink about responsibilities in the Department. Until now, we haven't marketed systematically to the leading companies in the UK and on the Continent, and we've been rather feeble in defending *our* client relationships against attacks by other banks. This will have to change. As we all know, the market trend is towards sectoral expertise. It's far easier to talk to a telephone company, for example, if you know something about telecoms.'

Peter Elton, one of the diehards, rolled his grey head agitatedly.

'Richard, that's fine for someone who actually *knows* about telecoms, but what do you want people like me to do? Call the head of BT to prove that I know how to use a phone?'

There was a nervous but supportive titter from round the table. Most of them were in the same boat. Myers turned to Sellars.

'Rosco, would you care to comment?'

Sellars looked cold but detached.

'No, Richard. Why don't you go on?'

'Okay. We already have a sector-led effort among the junior executives. What Rosco and I are proposing is to extend this to director level. Each of you will take on a sector and concentrate exclusively on that.'

It was the turn of Julian Lithgow to join the resistance. He was still in his thirties, and fairly mobile, so had less to lose than the oldies. He didn't even bother to address his comments to Myers.

'Forgive me, Rosco, but London isn't New York. Most of our clients don't want to discuss their widgets with us, they just want good, straight corporate finance advice.'

Sellars saw that he would have to slap Lithgow down before he encouraged the others to make a stand.

'You may be right, Julian, but the fact remains we *are* losing market share to banks with a sector-led approach. Have you ever considered why firms like Morgan Stanley or Goldmans make so much money? Do you really think those banks could afford to pay their top guys five or ten million dollars a year if they were wasting their time handling transactions or giving *advice*? Their job is to haul the client in the door, then kiss goodbye until the deal's ready for signing. Sure, they may call him up once in a while, or have lunch with him to maintain the illusion, but they're *salesmen*, for fuck's sake.'

Lithgow was so repelled, he found this almost amusing.

'So if I've understood you right, Rosco, investment banking is basically a high-class conjuring act?'

If he thought Sellars would be abashed, he'd underestimated the man. Rosco shot right back.

'Who said anything about high-class?'

This one shook them and the temperature in the room started rocketing. Rosco didn't care. It looked like the cultural gulf between his style and theirs was even greater than he'd realized. Maybe it was good that it came to a head. If he won, he would have a free hand; if he lost, Skidder Barton would have to pay him off handsomely.

Lithgow jumped back in. 'I can't speak for anyone else round this table, but *I* didn't sign up here to be a salesman.'

Perfect, thought Sellars, the guy had played right into his hands.

'That's fascinating, Julian. So tell me, then, why *did* you sign up?'

Lithgow paused for a second. He sensed that he'd made a mistake.

'The intellectual challenge mainly, I suppose . . .' Even to his own ears, it sounded lame. His colleagues, who'd admired his line up until then, stared down at the table or up at the ceiling. He couldn't stop digging himself in deeper. 'I enjoy solving knotty problems for clients.'

There was a short, embarrassed silence. Sellars savoured the moment as he lined himself up for the kill.

100

'I *see* . . . So it had nothing to do with the money?'

Lithgow had seen it coming, but couldn't see a way out of the trap. Admit that he *was* there for the money, and his previous comments would sound like pretentious crap. But deny it and, come bonus time, his negotiating position would be shot.

'I'm not saying that money's unimportant, it's just that . . .' His voice tailed off.

Sellars was firmly in command now.

'Well, in that case, Julian, you should be pleased to hear how your compensation will be determined in future. Each director will be given a quota of fees that he'll be expected to bring in. The quota will depend on how long he's been a director, with the highest quota for the most senior directors. For the first year, starting in January, quotas will be relatively modest, but they'll rise after that.'

Sellars glanced round the room again. He could see they were shitting themselves over this. At his side, Myers hung his head, ashamed of the Judas-like role he was being made to play. Supinely, Elton asked Sellars for an indication.

'Well, Peter, a senior director like yourself should expect a quota of around ten million pounds of fees in the first year. The good news is that if you hit that number you'll be well paid and if you overshoot it you will do very well *indeed*. However, if you make only five million, don't expect any bonus, and if you come in any lower than that, you shouldn't need Richard or me to tell you what your next move should be.'

Resistance was crumbling, but it wasn't all gone yet. Julian made one last attempt to regain credit in his colleagues' eyes.

'It's fair enough to pay us according to what clients we bring in, but basing it on actual fee *income* is absurd. In corporate finance, almost all the jam comes from success fees. We often put *months* of work into a transaction which gets cancelled at the last minute by the client. Through no fault of our own, the bank receives almost nothing. Surely we have to look at swings and roundabouts.'

Rosco's eyes glinted. 'Julian, in case you haven't noticed, the

101

days when this bank was run as a funfair have just come to an end. I'll tell you what to do with a client who doesn't want to go through with a transaction. Pester the motherfucker until he *does*.'

That was it. All opposition was crushed and it was time for the collaborators to speak up in gushing support of the new approach. Marcus Ford went first, followed by the second-youngest director. The rest looked sullen or cowed. Richard Myers ran through some more minor points and brought the meeting to a close. Julian Lithgow went straight back to his desk and telephoned three headhunters to let them know he was on the market.

*

It was quarter to three by the time Terry, Len and Einstein had collected their mugs of tea and found a quiet table at the café in Gresham Street. Einstein was heavily pregnant with his news, and spouted it out while the others took their first sips.

'A lucky hit, that's what it was. There was nothing doing at any of the banks so, on the off chance, I hung around outside Furnival's offices. I'd only been there ten minutes when I got a booking to take some punters from there to Skidder Barton.'

Terry looked excited. 'What name was it booked in? Ford?'

'No, the booking name was Chesterfield. But Ford got in, with two girls.'

Len chipped in. 'Was one of the gels about five foot five, shoulder-length blonde hair, big lips?'

'Yes.'

'She's called Grace something. I picked 'er up once at the City Airport with that Ford. Sexy little number, she is. What's the other one look like?'

'Brown hair, a bit taller, more the elegant sort.'

Terry smirked. 'Did they both 'ave big knockers?'

Einstein shrugged. 'You can't tell in those business suits.'

'I can.'

Len looked exasperated. 'Give it a rest, will you, Terry? Come on, Einstein, what did they say?'

102

'I've got the recorder in my pocket. Want to hear it?'

'In *'ere*? You must be *mad*. Tell us.'

'They were talking about another bid. They were calling Furnival "Foxtrot", like before, and the target was "Jupiter". On its own, that wouldn't have helped much: "Jupiter" could have been anything. But Ford went on to say that it has a current market value of fourteen billion pounds. So I checked the *Financial Times*. There are only six companies with about that value, and just one that's anywhere near the same industrial sector as Furnival. And guess what? It begins with a 'J'. It's called . . .' He lowered his voice to a tiny whisper. '. . . *Jowell*.'

'What?' Terry cupped his ear. 'Speak up, Einstein, I can't 'ardly 'ear you.'

Len slapped the back of Terry's head.

'Shoosh, you daft berk . . . I didn't catch it either, mate. Write it down.'

Einstein rummaged round in his pocket, and unearthed a stubby chewed pencil and a scrap of paper. He wrote the name down and pushed it across the table.

Len nodded. Terry looked unimpressed.

'Never 'eard of it.'

Len looked like he wanted to strangle him.

'Of *course* you never 'eard of it. They don't make condoms or footballs, so why should you?'

'Bet you never 'eard of it, neither.'

'Yes, I 'ave.'

'What they do then, if you're so smart?'

'Einstein'll tell you.'

'They're an engineering conglomerate. They make all sorts of parts for cars, trucks, and trains. They're big in electronics, too, and they have a large defence business. I checked what's being said about them. Basically, they've done very well, but the share price has gone sideways for a while. It says in the papers that the boss, Albert Austin, is getting a bit long in the tooth.'

' 'Ow old is 'e?' Terry had spotted an opening.

'Fifty-nine.'

103

Terry grinned. 'Then it won't be long before Len's ready for the knacker's yard too, eh?'

Len thumped the back of his head again. 'Einstein, gettin' back to them bankers, did they say when they would make this bid?'

'No, more's the pity, especially as we need to buy options, not shares. We *must* find out when they plan to launch it. Terry, how's the rabbit shaping up?'

'She's got me more exhausted than ever.'

'Did you ask her?'

'Yeah, last night. I think it'll be okay.'

'Good. Len, if we can find out the timing, do you agree we should go for this in a big way?'

'Definitely.'

'Terry?'

'Me, too.'

'Okay: there seem to be three people on this Skidders team, and we have two of their surnames, Ford and Chesterfield. We need to find out the other girl's name, then get the bunny to let us know whenever any of them books a cab, so one of us is always on the spot when the computer does its stuff.'

12

Julia was surprised to get the invitation. She had got to know Grace better while they were in New York, sharing asides, giggles and a little furtive shopping. All the same, she was taken aback by Grace asking her up to her parents' house. Both girls had expected to be stuck in the bank again all weekend, and hadn't bothered to make any social plans.

This was a bigger sacrifice for Grace. Julia was out of touch with old friends from school and Oxford days, and was artfully dodging the squadrons of 'nice young men' her mother tried to introduce. That only left the offers from the single guys at Skidders, and Julia wasn't going to repeat the mistake of mixing work and private life. In fact she'd avoided romantic invitations altogether in the first few weeks after she got back to England. She'd agreed with her American lawyer friend to have a stab at a long-distance love affair. It was soon obvious that there was too little feeling on either side to sustain that, and the torrent of phone calls that marked their first days apart dwindled to a trickle. Away from his alluring physical presence, Julia saw he was little more than a particularly handsome example of the only sort of men she met in Manhattan: high-achieving, self-obsessed white professionals, with a smooth, caring style gleaned from magazines and an unshakeable belief that the measure of a man is his bank balance.

Grace suggested it late on Thursday when it was clear that they weren't needed at the weekend. Julia thought it sounded more fun than hanging round London on her own and by seven on Friday night, they were throbbing up the M1 in Grace's new Alfa Romeo GTV, heading for the bright lights of Beverley.

The traffic was so wretched that halfway through Leicestershire they gave up trying to make Yorkshire without a break, pulled off the main road and ate greasy food in some dire pub. They finally made it to the Chesterfield house after midnight, where Grace's Mum had predictably ignored her daugter's telephoned command and stayed up to ply them with cocoa and biscuits. Grace took her younger brother's old room and let Julia have her own. It was tiny but cosy, its narrow bed still draped in a coverlet with a Paddington Bear design. The pink-patterned wallpaper was half hidden beneath framed certificates and group photos from her comprehensive school and Cambridge. It took Julia time to pick out Grace, and she was surprised when she found her. Judging by Grace's scholastic success, she'd expected to see a swotty, spotty duckling, who only in her adult years had loosened up into today's voluptuous swan. But no, there she was at fifteen, with bright scarlet lips, buckets of mascara, and hair that looked like it must have been a higher priority than any examination.

Julia slept as well as she ever did in a strange bed. She felt like getting up right away and having an early shower, but the lock on the bathroom door was broken and she didn't want Mr Chesterfield stumbling blearily in. So she lay on in bed and counted the openings and closings at the bathroom until it sounded as if everyone else had taken their turn. She was about to throw off the blankets and make a run for it when the bedroom door was pushed open and a large mug of tea made its way in, followed by Grace's Mum.

'Thank you, Mrs Chesterfield, that's really kind of you. You're spoiling me.'

'It's a pleasure to have Grace's friends here to stay. Did you sleep well? It's a small bed, that, more for a kiddy than a big lass like you.'

'I had a wonderful night.'

'You won't say the same about the day. Shall I open the curtains?'

106

'Please.'

Grace sat up higher in the bed to see how it looked. It was dry, but over the roofs of the council estate, big black clouds billowed.

'Tom says the forecast is bad. It'll rain in this afternoon. If you want to see the Minster or take a drive in the country, best do it this morning.'

'I'll get up, then.'

'Oh, there's no rush. Grace is downstairs, but she's still in her dressing gown.'

'I liked seeing all the pictures of her.' Julia inclined her head towards the wall.

'We're proud of Grace. Her brother Paul's a nice lad, but he was never clever academically. Mind you, it wasn't always plain sailing with Grace either, I can tell you.'

'Really?'

'Oh, she wasn't a *bad* girl, and she never got involved with drugs, which these days you have to be grateful for. Her problem was boys, right from the start. Whenever she fancied she was in love, her studies went right out of the window. She had me and Tom sick with worry at times.'

'But she did brilliantly in the end, didn't she? Getting a First at Cambridge is quite something.'

'Until she was sixteen or so, we often had to lock her in the house so she didn't stop out all hours with one lad or another. After that, she pulled her socks up a lot, it has to be said.'

'What changed her? Was it just growing up, or did her teachers inspire her?'

'No, it wasn't that. She saw where she'd end up if she kept on that way . . .'

Mrs Chesterfield's voice faded away. Julia stayed silent, wanting neither to pry nor object if Grace's mum chose to say more. It seemed she didn't. Slowly, she got up from the end of the bed where she'd been squatting.

'Well, I don't suppose the breakfast will make itself, so I'd better go down.'

107

'Thanks for the tea. I'll have a quick shower.'
'Take your time. How d'you like your eggs, love?'

The house was on the outskirts of the little town, so as a precaution against the threatening rain, they took the Alfa for the short ride to the Minster. In the daylight the estate looked like a long line of ugly women with overbright make-up. All the doors were painted in searingly vivid oranges, reds, yellows and lime greens. The houses themselves were drearily identical with small metal-framed windows and square concrete canopies over the front doors. A few occupants had broken defiantly free from the architectural strait-jacket and applied token Tudor, Georgian or Mediterranean touches.

As they drove out of their cul-de-sac, Grace nodded at the houses.

'What do you think?'

Julia hesitated. What on earth could she say? She didn't want to hurt Grace's feelings. 'It's . . . very . . .'

With a chuckle, Grace volunteered,

'*Revolting.*'

Julia burst out laughing in relief. 'I don't think it'll win any prizes for architecture. Unless, of course, the Georgian bits appeal to Prince Charles.'

'Ever since I can remember, this place has given me a burning desire to get as far away as possible . . .'

Approaching the Minster, Grace noticed a parking space, braked abruptly, and reversed in neatly. She switched off the engine, but didn't get out.

'When I was about fifteen, I fantasized about eloping with my boyfriend. We'd lie on the fields in the summer, looking up at the sky, and talk about starting a life together in California, or some-where. It didn't matter where, as long as there was money and sunshine.'

'Did you ever actually run away?'

'No. I realized I'd only be swapping one type of poverty for another. I was right, by the way. He's married with three kids now, and on the dole.'

'And this just came to you in a blinding flash?'

Grace looked away.

'Something like that . . . Let's go and see the Minster.'

The rest of the weekend was filled with rain and a strengthening north wind. On Saturday night they drove to a country pub, where they ran into two men who'd been in Grace's class at school. Julia took to them and would have been happy to share a drink but, after exchanging a few reminiscences, Grace ushered her away to a small table near the fire.

They got up late on Sunday and sat around with the papers until Mrs Chesterfield's gargantuan roast beef lunch was ready. After that, it was time to load their things into the car. Mrs Chesterfield hugged Julia warmly, then wrapped her chubby arms around Grace and held on for an age. Mr Chesterfield, who'd hardly spoken during their stay, was more restrained in his farewells. Solemnly, he shook Julia's hand and thanked her for coming. He bestowed a single quick peck on Grace. But there was warmth in his eyes, and Julia could see how much love was there.

As they headed for the main road, Julia reached across and touched Grace's left hand as it rested lazily on the gearstick.

'Thank you. I really enjoyed myself. Your parents are kind.'

'You weren't too shocked, seeing how the other half live?'

'Come on, Grace, it isn't exactly a mud hut.'

'It's the next best thing . . . I think you're the poshest person ever to cross that threshold. My dad was terrified of you. I could see what he was thinking: the less said, the less risk of saying the wrong thing.'

'That's *terrible*.' Julia was genuinely upset. 'Am I really so off-putting?'

'Of course not. You're just different from what they're used to. Mum likes you a lot. She thinks you're beautiful and refined.' For that last word Grace added the accent. Julia wondered for a second if there was a hint of chippiness there. 'She says you're a living porcelain doll.'

They both laughed.

'Well, whatever you say, I liked them, and if ever they come to London, I hope I can return some of their hospitality.'

Grace grunted. 'That's good of you, but you needn't worry too much: wild horses wouldn't get them down again. They came once, soon after I started work, and hated every moment.'

Julia nodded and changed the subject. 'Well, are you all revved up for our big deal? I don't think either of us will have much social life over the next few days. Not that I'm getting too many offers at the moment, apart from the boys at Skidders.'

'How about Rosco?'

'I think he's found other fish to fry.'

'Tell me more.'

'Until recently, whenever he was at a loose end, he tried to get me out on the town. From the lack of calls recently, I presume that he's stepping out with some other number.'

Grace smiled. 'And you have no one? Really?'

'Remember that night I played hookey in New York? I had dinner with the man I used to see there. It was more of a wake than a date. We gave our relationship a decent burial. How about Grace? Is Grace in love?'

'Grace is always in love. Trouble is the men I pick.'

'What sort of problems do you have with the current one?'

'Oh, nothing too serious, nothing I can't handle.'

'Like what?'

'Like a wife.'

'Aaah.'

And they lapsed back into silence and stayed that way for most of the rest of the slipping, splashing drive home.

*

On Monday night Einstein came back from a marathon slog. It was fruitless as far as information went, but handily cash-generative. He had taken over two hundred and twenty pounds, well above par for twelve hours. Ruth's day at the lab had been long, too, so they were recovering in the bath together, Ruth resting the back of her head on his swirly-haired chest, and Einstein twiddling the taps with his toes while his fingers played absent-mindedly with her nipples. They were well through a game of square roots when the cordless phone rang. Einstein let go of one breast and reached for the phone. He listened carefully, saying little, put it back down, and replaced his hand on Ruth's breast.

'Who was that?'

'Terry. He's found out the name of the other girl. He can be quite crafty when he wants to.'

'If women are involved.'

'He bought a calculator and kept it in the cab. The next time his little friend from Control Cabs tipped him off that Chesterfield had booked a cab back from Furnival, he dropped the three of them off at Skidders and hung around outside for a couple of minutes. Then he went to the receptionist and told her that one of the girls had left a calculator in the cab. He described what they looked like, and waited while they sorted it out. Three minutes later he'd got the name from the receptionist, dropped off the calculator, and was gone. Those girls must've laughed when they saw it. Bankers often use calculators in cabs; they're always big Hewlett Packards. Terry's cost sixty-five pence and had blue bears all over it.'

'Did the bankers say anything more about timing?'

'We don't know. The twit forgot to check his batteries. They were dead.'

'What was the last name?'

'Daventry.'

'Another place name. Like Chesterfield.'

'I hadn't thought of that.'

'Okay, let's have a game. Who can remember the most English place names beginning with a particular letter? Starting with "A".'

'Abercorn, Aberfan, Aberystwyth . . .'
'I said *English* . . .'

*

They met in Paris. Rosco wanted to keep well away from the famous Right Bank spots for fear of being seen, so they picked the Verneuil, a gorgeous jewel box of a hotel near the Musée d'Orsay. By arrangement, Sellars and Lautenschutz got there half an hour before their guest.

'So, how keen is he, Ernst?'

'As I expected, he's been watching Jowell for years, but was not aware that it might become . . . available.'

'I know this is stating the obvious, Ernst, but you do realize, don't you, that if Furnival's bid goes ahead, Skidders can't act for anyone else? Burlikon would need to appoint another bank.'

'In that case, Rosco, we would simply channel the work to a friendly bank.'

'What do you mean by "friendly"?'

'A bank that would have no scruples about sharing their fees with us. Discreetly, of course.'

'We need to sort this out before Manz gets here . . .' He looked anxiously at his watch. 'At our private chat in Zurich, it was you who pointed out that, since I played no part in getting this project started, I wouldn't get my normal forty per cent cut. If I'm helping you out like this, I want you to confirm that – whatever other bank is involved – I get my full share.'

Lautenschutz had a sip of Earl Grey and smiled reassuringly.

'My dear Rosco, don't concern yourself. We will work out some satisfactory arrangement. Trust me.'

'If there's one thing my years in banking have taught me, it's to trust no-one . . . Now, if you have no objection, I've had my personal lawyers draw up this simple memorandum. Take a look. Until that gets signed, I'm not getting into detail with Manz.'

At that moment a tall, severe-looking businessman arrived at the reception desk. From where they sat, they could see him being directed towards them.

112

'Better make up your mind, Ernst.'

Grimacing fiercely like a troll, Lautenschutz grabbed the paper and gave it a cursory glance. He pulled a Mont Blanc ballpen from his jacket pocket and scribbled a signature on the bottom seconds before Dieter Manz reached their table. Then he jumped to his feet.

'Ah, Herr Doktor Manz, welcome to Paris. It is good to see you.'

'The pleasure is mine, Herr Lautenschutz.'

'May I introduce Rosco Sellars?'

'Good afternoon, Mr Sellars. Dieter Manz.'

'Hi, Dieter. Good to meet you.'

Lautenschutz waved at a waiter.

'What can we arrange for you, Doctor Manz? Will you join me in some English tea?'

'How appropriate.' Manz sat down and opened his slim black briefcase. 'Gentleman, if you will forgive me, I have very little time. May we get right down to business? Mr Sellars, I understand that Jowell is for sale.'

'Well, yes, in a manner of speaking. It's what we call "in play", which means it's going to be bid for.'

'But, Mr Sellars, isn't Furnival too small to do that? Surely, it's a *fraction* of the size of Jowell.'

'Furnival may be small, but the management is highly regarded. The transaction is highly leveraged, of course, but it *will* fly.'

'And Zuricher intends to put up a lot of the money?' He looked, somewhat harshly, in Lautenschutz's direction.

Sellars nodded. 'That's the plan.'

'Then it is fortunate that you told us. If this had come out of the blue, we would have reacted very negatively . . .'

Sellars thought this was taking Swiss solidarity pretty far. It must have shown on his face. Manz spat a question in Swiss German at Lautenschutz, who shook his head. Manz moved forward in his seat.

'There is one thing that Herr Lautenschutz may not have explained to you. In Switzerland we believe that the destiny of our companies should not be threatened by interference from outsiders. To that end, many of us have discreetly placed our shares in safe hands through nominees, trusts, and offshore companies.'

Sellars couldn't see what the guy was driving at.

'Dieter, I don't exactly see the connection . . .'

'Then let me spell it out. Several years ago when the laws changed in Switzerland, Zuricher Bank began to fear that it could become vulnerable, so it bundled together a large block of its shares and sold them to another Swiss group for safe keeping. That group was Burlikon.'

'Aaaah . . . I see.'

'Yes, I thought you might.'

This was all very interesting, but Rosco wasn't sure he liked the way he was being treated like some idiot boy. He decided to go on the offensive.

'So tell me, Dieter, which safe hands control Burlikon?'

Lautenschutz shot bolt upright in his chair, bridling at Rosco's presumption, unsure whether the man was being deliberately offensive or just American.

'Rosco, that's a very indiscreet question.'

Manz seemed to be less fazed.

'As someone once said, Mr Sellars, there is no such thing as an indiscreet question, only an indiscreet answer, and I'm sure you don't expect to get one. However, to put your mind at rest, I'm happy to tell you that over forty per cent of our shares are controlled by one of the largest Swiss institutions. The Chairman and I were at school together, so I don't have to lie awake at night worrying about our share price performance . . .'

Manz and Lautenschutz exchanged smug, knowing smiles.

'Now that you understand our private arrangements better, you will see that, as long as we have a possible interest in acquiring Jowell ourselves, we would not wish Zuricher to assist any other buyer. If, after studying this opportunity, we decide not to proceed, that would be a different matter'

'And how long would this study take?'

'Two months, perhaps three. It depends on how much

114

information we need to digest. Then, of course, we will visit Jowell's plants, go through their management accounts, interview their executives. It is – what? – the third of November today, but there is the Christmas break to think of. We could let you know by the end of February.'

Sellars was shaking his head incredulously. This guy was smoking dope.

'Dieter, first up, you seem to have no idea how hostile bids work. This is *not* a negotiated sale. There will be no plant visits, no interviews with executives, no inspecting the management accounts. Think wartime. Did Eisenhower and Churchill invite Hitler over to London to check out the D-Day plans? You better get used to the idea that if you want to go hostile, you'll have to make do with whatever information is publicly available. Also, I don't think Ernst has given you a clear enough picture of the timetable we're working to. Furnival is planning to announce its bid for Jowell next Monday, the ninth.'

'Well, change the timetable. Tell them to wait. Say that if they want Zuricher's money, they have no choice.'

Sellars was getting riled now. He didn't know whether it was Ernst's fault for failing to brief the guy properly or whether Manz was too arrogant to care.

'And what do you suggest we tell Furnival? That they have to wait in line until Burlikon makes up its mind?'

Manz had little sense for irony.

'No, that would not be wise. Say whatever is necessary. It is not my concern.'

'Forgive me, Dieter, and you, too, Ernst, but this isn't gonna work. I've never met Robert Quilley, the CEO of Furnival – indeed I've deliberately avoided doing so – but he sounds one neat guy. He'll see right through any story we concoct. Market conditions for Furnival's bid couldn't be better. And although Skidders can *advise* Quilley to delay the timing, in the end he'll call the shots himself. As long as there's no glitch on the financing, there is nothing we can do to stop him proceeding.'

Manz was impassive. 'Then it is simple. *Create* a glitch.'

'Like what, may I ask? The US banks I've lined up are hot for this deal.'

'But what if Zuricher changed its mind?'

'Let's assume I call Robert Quilley right now and tell him Zuricher's pulled out. Know what he'll do? Drop Skidder Barton and appoint fresh advisers. Within two or three days they'll find another other big European bank to replace Zuricher and get another US syndicate together.'

Still Manz was unmoved. He turned towards Lautenschutz.

'When do you commit formally to this financing?'

'Friday this week.'

'Very well. Mr Sellars, would things be different if Zuricher waited until Friday to pull out?'

Rosco considered. 'That would certainly cause bigger problems. The launch would have to be postponed, probably by at least a week. However, if markets stay in good shape, and the US banks had no reason to get spooked . . .'

Lautenschutz interjected. 'But they *would*, Rosco.'

'I don't get it, Ernst. Why would they?'

'Because we would tell them that we had withdrawn for some good reason. Even American bankers are conservative fellows, Rosco: if they feel unsettled, they rarely proceed.'

'And how would you plan to tell them that, Ernst?'

Lautenschutz smiled at Manz, and then back at Sellars.

'Oh, we wouldn't. *You* would do that for us, wouldn't you?

And he reached down to the low table before him, gently touching the memorandum he'd signed.

116

13

As the week rolled on the cabbies were getting anxious. The good news was that the Drumalbine share price was rising steadily, a sure sign that word of the likely price for the gin brand was spreading. The trio were already well in the money with a paper profit of eight thousand pounds. The bad news was that there was no news on Jowell. The flurry of movement between Skidders and Furnival continued intensively, making the cabbies suspect that something might be imminent. As a group they got more than their fair share of the rides – so much so that they feared being recognized. Happily, the bankers were too caught up in their own world to bother about taxi drivers. However, the tapes revealed nothing about timing. Any thoughts the cabbies harboured of taking their chances and plunging heavily into the options were dismissed when they contemplated the dreadful prospect of getting it wrong and unloading the lot. As a compromise, on Wednesday they agreed to buy ten thousand pounds' worth, so they wouldn't lose out altogether if the bid went ahead. Apart from that, they clung on nervously, desperate for a signal.

It came, at about three-thirty on Thursday, thanks to Marcus Ford as he rode back from Furnival with the Chesterfield girl. As soon as the two of them got into Len's cab, Marcus banged the sliding window shut, and told Grace to ring the PR advisers and bring them into the picture. As he said it, he intoned the magic words 'Monday's launch'.

Len fairly whooped with delight when he heard the tape, but cautiously played it through once more before calling Terry and getting him to phone their stockbroker. By quarter past nine, they had dealt, with every remaining penny of the fighting fund invested in a forty-five-day option on Jowell shares, expiring on the twenty-first of December.

*

At four o'clock on Friday morning, Robert Quilley gave up trying to sleep. Although there were still three days to go before the launch, his rapidly accumulating fatigue was no match for the cascade of adrenalin. As quietly as possible, he slipped away from the bed where his girlfriend lay and went down to make himself a coffee.

He hadn't felt this hyped up since the days of his Special Forces covert operations. He knew that the pressure would be far higher than at the time of the IFK bid. The management there had been so feeble that no one had taken their claims seriously and their attempts to blow poison darts at him had failed pathetically. Albert Austin would be a different matter. For two decades he had done well for his company, building steadily, strongly, leaving his long-term record to speak for itself. Yes, he had gone off the boil recently. However, he still had many friends, and was sure to fight ferociously.

On Thursday evening, Quilley had met with fund managers at their largest three institutional shareholders. All of them were astonished that he was going for something so big so soon. The response was mixed. One was for it, another against, the third undecided. This hung jury left him free to proceed if he wished, but without a level of support that would shift one ounce of the responsibility from his own shoulders. If it worked he would get most of the glory: if it failed, all of the blame.

The financing should be sewn up by the end of today, and Marcus Ford had assured him there would be no problem. Then there was only the weekend to get sleeplessly through. He drank down the dregs of his coffee and went back to lie on the bed, open-eyed, for another hour.

*

118

Julia was the first to get windy. She suggested to Marcus that they check what was happening. Zuricher hadn't sent confirmation that they'd signed, and they were twenty minutes behind schedule. No cause for major alarm yet, but good reason to get slightly jumpy.

Marcus called the head of credit approvals in Zurich. Amiably, he told Marcus that it was probably a technical hitch and the faxed signature should be through shortly.

Julia sat at Marcus's desk and waited, both of them growing slowly more agitated. When the multi-time-zone clock on the wall reached eleven in London, Marcus announced that he would call Lautenschutz himself. He was trying to get through when Jo gestured at him and mouthed that Robert Quilley was calling. Irritably, Marcus waved her away.

It took five minutes to get Lautenschutz's secretary, who told him curtly that her boss was in a meeting and couldn't be disturbed. When Ford attempted to cut up rough with her, she did the same back. He tried the head of credit again and threw quite a fit when he learned that the fellow had gone out to lunch. All attempts to find anyone else who was dealing with the matter failed.

By noon there was a full-scale flap. It was getting harder to stall Quilley. What was needed was someone senior enough to get through to Lautenschutz. Rosco Sellars was travelling, his mobile permanently engaged. Charles Barton was with their largest fund-management client, who had complained about loss of focus at Skidders and was threatening to withdraw the account. Marcus swallowed his pride and asked Richard Myers whether he would make the call. Myers coolly questioned him, and when he found that such a major transaction had been kept from him, sourly bade Marcus to do his own dirty work.

At one o'clock, with New York now wide awake, they were forced to admit to Robert Quilley that there was a problem. He announced that he was coming round to the bank. That was the signal for full-scale panic and, to the fury of his fund-management staff, Charles Barton was wrenched from his

119

meeting, sealing the fate of that account. Marcus explained and stood by him as he put in the call.

This time Lautenschutz's secretary seemed willing to produce her boss. Barton only had to wait two minutes.

'Ernst, I'm calling about the Jupiter bid. I'm told there has been some sort of hold-up in Zurich and, if your confirmation does not come through in the next half-hour, the whole financing will be jeopardized. I'm sure it is only a technical matter, but I would appreciate it if you could help us cut through the red tape.'

Lautenschutz paused before replying.

'Charles, nothing would give me greater pleasure . . .'

'Thank you.'

'. . . *If* it was a technical matter. Unfortunately, it is not. I have only been informed myself five minutes ago: our credit committee has turned down the loan.'

Barton looked aghast.

'But that is not possible . . .'

Lautenschutz's voice was dry, unemotional.

'Sadly, it is.'

'But you gave us your assurance that all would be well, which we passed on in good faith to our client . . .'

'Yes, at the time I was confident there would be no problem, though I recall telling that young man – Ford, was it? – that all credits ultimately have to be authorized by the committee. I am sorry if this causes you embarrassment . . .'

'*Embarrassment*? Why, it may wreck the entire transaction! And *you*, of all people, know how important a deal it is for us. At the very least, you can tell us why.'

'Certainly. Our committee has been concerned for some time that our bank's exposure in the UK is too high. Also, they received some information that shook their confidence in the management of Furnival.'

'May I ask *what* information?'

'Unfortunately I am not at liberty to tell you.'

Charles Barton felt lower than at any moment in his

professional life. This wretched Swiss was immovable and unembarrassable. It was time for his parting shot.

'Well, If Zuricher wants to keep *any* shred of credibility in the London market, I suggest that you ring Robert Quilley and explain this yourself. He is currently waiting in one of our meeting rooms. I'll transfer you now . . .'

Barton said it in his most magisterial voice. It didn't work. Calmly, Lautenschutz interrupted.

'Charles, unfortunately that won't be possible. We have an all-day board meeting today, and I only came out to take this one call. If it would help, I will write to him on Monday.'

'I'm sure nothing would please him more. Goodbye.'

Barton put the phone down, close to tears. The awkward silence was broken by a ringing phone. Marcus picked it up. It was Grace, saying that BankManhattan had picked up a rumour that Zuricher was withdrawing because of unspecified problems at Furnival. Unless Skidders could flatly deny this, they were pulling out, too.

Marcus passed it on, and looked straight at Barton.

'That's it. It's dead.'

Barton asked one last question.

'Do we think there's any chance of raising the money elsewhere?'

Marcus shook his head. 'Not unless Rosco pulls a rabbit out of a hat in the next hour.'

'Where the hell *is* he, anyway? Why isn't he here with you?'

'I don't know. He's travelling somewhere or other. We can't get through on his mobile.'

They tried the number again. Now it was switched off altogether.

Barton sighed miserably. 'It doesn't sound like there'll be any rabbits today. What *are* we going to tell Quilley?'

Ford looked at him harshly.

'When you say "we" . . . ?'

'Well, I don't mean to interfere, if you think it's better to do it yourself . . . I just thought you might want some moral support.'

121

'Charles, I've sweated blood over this. What's destroyed the deal is *your* relationship with those pathetic Swiss. We could have got this financed *anywhere* if we hadn't been forced to go to them first.'

'So what are you saying, Marcus?'

'That I think it's down to you to go into that meeting room and tell him. Down to you and *no one* else.'

'I see. Very well. Thank you for all your efforts, anyway.'

And Marcus stomped haughtily out of the room.

When Marcus got back to his desk, Jo was fielding a call from someone who refused to give his name, but insisted he was a close personal friend of his. Marcus grabbed the handset and barked violently into it. Then he fell silent and listened. He put the phone down, walked over to Jo's desk and told her he was off for some lunch.

The cab Marcus hailed in the street dropped him off on the south side of Tower Bridge. He walked through Butler's Wharf until he found the Cantina del Ponte. It was a simple, informal Italian place. Bankers giving their corporate credit card pre-weekend exercise might visit its swish neighbour, Le Pont de la Tour, but the Cantina was cheap enough to be safe from their prying ears and eyes.

Marcus went inside. There he was, at a quiet table at the back, looking calm, almost pleased with himself. Eyeballing him aggressively, Marcus pulled back a chair and slumped down.

'I thought you were supposed to be travelling.'

'I *am*. I came all the way from Belgravia, didn't I?'

'So I presume this means you know what happened.'

Sellars reached inside his jacket pocket and took out a fat cigar and a gold Dunhill clipper.

'You don't mind?'

Marcus didn't respond. Rosco sliced the end off, warmed the tip with a match and puffed hard until it was firing on all cylinders.

122

'Yes, I heard. Ernst Lautenschutz called me.'

'So *kind* of him to find time in his busy schedule. I suppose it proves how highly he values you.'

The sarcasm was wasted.

'Yes, it does.'

Marcus was still in attack mode.

'But you knew before today, didn't you?' Sellars drew deeply on his cigar and nodded. 'Tell me, Rosco, I *really* want to know, why did you wreck my deal?'

'I haven't wrecked it.'

'What the fuck d'you mean? As we sit here, Charles Barton is telling Quilley it's over, and probably getting his scrotum removed in return.'

'Oh, it's over for Quilley, all right. But the acquisition itself will go ahead. The only difference is that the bidder's name will change.'

'To what?'

'I'll tell you shortly. First of all, let's order something.'

'I'm not hungry.'

'Suit yourself. *I* am.'

He ordered a salad. At the last moment before the waiter left them, Marcus grabbed the card and chose a lobster pasta.

'*So*? Who's your new mystery buyer?'

'Marcus, remember that directors' meeting when that cocksucker Lithgow said that horseshit about why he's in banking? Well, I prefer honesty, and I think there is only one reason why anyone does this chickenshit job. *Money.* There's no bank left in the world that gives a monkey's toss for its employees and any guy who says he cares about his bank is a liar or a fool. The only strategy worth thinking about is how to position yourself to make the most cash. Think of bankers as tapeworms. Do you honestly think any tapeworm with an above-average IQ will crawl up the ass of an underfed weakling, who might up and die on him any minute, when it could go for some fat guy? That's what we all have to do: be smart, ask ourselves the right questions. Will your bank make enough profits to pay well? If

123

not, *leave*. And if it will, are you positioned within it to get your fair share? If not, *leave*.'

The food arrived, prompting Sellars to stub out the cigar. He demonstrated again his ability to communicate while nourishing himself.

'Now, let's start with Skidders. Under present management it's on a one-way road to nowhere. How long d'you think it can survive as an independent bank?'

Marcus swallowed a mouthful of lobster. 'Two, three years. Longer if we're allowed to complete some deals.'

Sellars ignored the jibe.

'I give it six months, tops. The fund-management business is losing accounts hand over fist, global markets is haemorrhaging its best people, and you know the state of corporate finance. Net result: Skidders is dead in the water, just waiting to be taken out.'

'If it's in such a bad state, why should anyone want it?'

'Rarity value. There are precious few investment banks left to buy and for foreign commercial banks, buying is easier than building.'

'So who'll buy it?'

'It's obvious, isn't it? Zuricher.'

Marcus laughed dismissively. 'Are you seriously suggesting that Zuricher can succeed in investment banking?'

'Zuricher? You gotta be fuckin' joking. They couldn't devise a strategy for opening a Toblerone bar. Give them five years and they'll destroy every bit of value in Skidders. Who cares? They have plenty of cash to acquire it, and they'll need to make sure that the key guys stick around by paying us obscene amounts of money. Now, the question you've got to ask yourself, Marcus, is where will you be sitting when that gravy train pulls out of the station? In the first-class dining car with me, sipping a glass of vintage Bordeaux, or clinging to the outside of a second-class carriage?'

Marcus was calming down. He was struggling to keep his expression non-committal, but his eyes were telling another story. Sellars saw that and pressed on.

124

'Now, let's get on back to money. If your Furnival bid had succeeded, the bank would have made a hundred million pounds. How much of that would have found its way to your pocket?'

'You know how our bonus system works. It's not linked directly to any one fee that we generate. Having said that, I would've expected a pretty chunky cheque this year.'

'Like how much?'

'Last year my bonus was half a million. I don't know . . . seven, eight hundred, a million maybe?' It sounded a lot of money to Marcus.

'And you would be satisfied with that?'

It was hard to know what to say. Marcus *would* have been happy, bordering on delirious, to get a million-pound bonus. However, it was pretty clear that this wasn't the right answer.

'I wouldn't say *satisfied*, no.'

'Well, I'm relieved to hear it. For a moment there I thought I was dealing with a boy scout, and I *despise* boy scouts. Let's move on to the new arrangements. When I joined Skidders, there were a lot of rumours flying around about my package. As usual, those stories got exaggerated. However, it *is* true that I get a twenty per cent share of deals I bring in. That means if we revive our project with *my* buyer, I stand to make twenty million from that deal alone. Now, I have a proposition to put to you. I can't do that deal without help. We have to move fast before Jupiter's share price moves up, and there isn't time for some other director to get up to speed. Plus, you're the only one I trust.'

Marcus had come to the Cantina intending to tell Sellars what he thought of him. Instead, Rosco's words were making a warm glow spread inside him.

'If you will commit to work with me, Marcus, I'm willing to offer you one third of what's coming to me.'

Marcus couldn't stop himself gulping. Jesus Christ, did he really mean six point six million pounds? Sellars watched him making the calculation and smiled.

'Yes, it *is* a lot of money, isn't it? And that's only the start. Once the Swiss get control of Skidders, there are bound to be a lot of changes. I suspect they may want me to take on something fairly senior, so there'll be a vacancy as head of corporate finance.'

'*Co*-head', Marcus reminded him.

Sellars smiled. 'I don't think so. Surely you don't see a future for Myers in the new world? I guess we'll just have to pack him and the others in a crate and ship them to Jurassic Park.'

Marcus chuckled at that one. He had to admit, this was beginning to sound . . . interesting. From the change in Marcus's body language, Sellars could judge it was time for the kill.

'So what's it to be? Sign up and we'll get right into details. Hesitate or say no and we call the whole thing off.'

'Count me in.'

'Good man.' He reached across the table and shook Marcus's hand.

'Right, let's order some coffee and get to work.'

*

Charles Barton went back to the office all but broken. Robert Quilley hadn't ranted or raved. He'd heard him out and asked one or two questions. Throughout the conversation there was a chilling, intense anger in his eyes, which was far more frightening than any violent temper. When it was done, Robert stood up, icily confirmed that Furnival's links with Skidders were severed, and shook Barton's hand. It was all too clear to him that Barton was a powerless pawn in this game, and his departing glance was filled with contemptuous pity.

Barton called Patricia to say he wouldn't be joining her after all. He couldn't stand the thought of driving down to Gloucestershire and facing a whole weekend of her lack of interest in his troubles. To sit at table with her, enduring endless drivel about bays, Barbours, and beeches was more than the human spirit could bear.

The only good thing that happened on that most wretched of days was when he called that special number and, with kindness which moved him beyond words, she offered to come to Knightsbridge that evening to cook something simple and give

126

him a soothing massage.

She later proved as good as her word. The grilled chicken breasts went supremely well with the magnum of Pommery. The lavender oil caressed Barton's senses and, ignoring his protestations that she must be tired too, she carried on deliciously with it for over an hour. When at last she lay down beside him and told him to take her, his heart overflowed with emotion and, emboldened by the champagne, he spoke heady words, going beyond anything he'd said before.

Marcus Ford spent his Friday evening with Sophie. He didn't go into much detail, just let it slip that his big deal would be postponed. Sophie replied with a snort which, in the private language they'd developed, meant 'I couldn't care less, but typical of you to screw it up anyway'. Then he hit her with the figure. She actually stopped playing with their daughter for a full fifteen seconds, until the brat bawled at her to resume. Finally, he'd impressed her. Even to Sophie, six million was real potatoes.

He let her digest it while he wandered into the kitchen and made himself a large gin and tonic. Sellars was tricky, all right, but, my God, he was focused. With Zuricher willing to underwrite the entire cost of the acquisition, there was no doubt at all about Burlikon's firepower. It amused him that Rosco had quietly put one over on the Swiss by using Hawk, the international private-investigation company, first to discover the identity of Manz's school friend and then to dig up some dirt on that guy. Rosco called it his 'little insurance policy'. It sounded as if Gerhard Muller's rise to the Chairmanship of the immense Alps Insurance had not been solely on merit. If Hawk's information was right, a slender shaft of daylight, if shone upon his past, would cause a shock, both to Alps and the Swiss business community, that would be right off the Richter scale.

From Rosco's account, it seemed that Hawk had shown laudable entrepreneurship, loosening tongues in the Swiss underworld and even indulging in a touch of freelance burglary. Sellars amused himself and Marcus by speculating how Muller must

127

have felt, returning with his wife from a weekend away and discovering their safe gaping open. He would have been actually *relieved* that the thieves had taken her jewels, and be hoping desperately that the papers they had also removed would be meaningless to them.

Marcus was less amused when Sellars insisted that Hawk's special skills would be needed in England, too. However keen they were to do the deal, Burlikon were apparently disinclined to proceed with so huge a transaction without more information on what they were buying. Rosco assured Marcus that here there would be nothing as crude as robbery. All that was needed was to find some friendly soul at Jowell who, in return for a pay-off or the prospect of future preferment, would give them a little helpful guidance on what the internal projections looked like.

Marcus knew that these were swirling currents which might engulf him. Such action was massively illegal and, if discovered, would bring down everyone involved – and probably the bank itself. Why had Rosco told him? To bind him still tighter into the Faustian pact? Probably, but there was another likely motive, too. If this sort of detailed data had emerged unexplained, Marcus might have reacted hastily. At least this way he had time to make up his mind and back out. Or not. It certainly provided ample reason for Rosco to limit the information flow even more than before. What need was there for Charles Barton to know anything about the deal? Now that the financing was taken care of, Julia could be out, too. Grace would be needed, of course, and she should have an incentive too. Fifty thousand ought to secure her cooperation and confidentiality. Better not tell her about the Hawk stuff, all the same. That should stay between Rosco and him.

11

Zuricher was on Guy Barton's mind as his Gulfstream V landed that Friday in Sacramento. Their proposal was insolent but not untimely. Elixir had suffered a sharp downturn. The group had a hefty debt position and, if there wasn't an improvement soon, they would be very exposed. As a privately owned company, they would be able to suppress this news for a while, but sooner or later their banks would get twitchy. If things got serious, an injection of the sort Zuricher were proposing could make a big difference. There was no need to do anything yet, but playing them along would do no harm. If in the end he accepted, it would irritate Charles magnificently.

In the meantime, there were more interesting things to think about. He was coming to California to inspect the equipment he'd commissioned: a jumpsuit with integrated oxygen mask and a pressurized balloon. At that altitude, there was no plane which could safely open a door. The balloon would use only pure helium. The suit was, if anything, even more critical, since it had to withstand both freezing temperatures and the turbulence of the descent. Barton had got the same Sacramento company to design both, and was throroughly looking forward to trying them out over the weekend.

He reached in his pocket and pulled out a battered black-and-white photo. His new girlfriend, a slinky black soul singer, looked over his shoulder and asked Guy who it was. A true pioneer, was the answer. Joseph W. Kittinger. Back in 1960, free falling eighty-four thousand feet was impossibly brave. It was astonishing that he'd survived, and he still held the the world record. Barton believed firmly that, with the technology of today, he should be aiming to do a lot better. Nothing less than a hundred thousand feet of free fall would satisfy him. Equally, it might kill him. But then, that was the nature of experiments.

*

Einstein and Len spent the weekend in a state of high excitement, but not poor old Terry. He had to spend most of it thinking about his state of health. Once in a while, if he was pissed, lazy or carried away, he got forgetful about condoms. He'd been pissed more than once recently, both with Daphne and the girl from the sweetshop. The two females began to itch about the same time he did, so it was hard to say which of them was to blame. The sweetshop girl needed three swings to connect, though the power was there when she did, as Terry's rainbow-hued left eye testified. She wasn't a huge loss, being so weak in the conversation department that even her basketball tits had begun to pall.

Daphne threw some crockery and gave him some serious attitude. That might've been a disaster if he hadn't been lucky with timing. What with Len's news, they shouldn't need her help again. Still, it wasn't the ideal way to sign off, not what you'd call *stylish*. He felt more than a little abashed as he sat waiting in the clinic in Ilford, shrivelled by the thought of some Paki doctor checking his dick like a dipstick.

Len and Jean invited Einstein and Ruth round for a drink on Saturday evening and were thoroughly surprised when Terry called up to say that his date was cancelled and could he come over too? Though they hadn't altogether abandoned keeping the plan from Poppy, she'd worked out so much by now that it seemed sort of pointless, and that evening Len carried her down so she could sit by the electric flame-effect fire, wrapped tight in a blanket, and be part of it all.

Poppy was bewildered and thrilled that the money was going to be found. They wanted to send her to California right away, but the wilful little thing had set her heart on spending her Christmas at home and wouldn't be swayed. So Jean booked a flight on the twenty-seventh of December. If Einstein's calculations were anywhere near right, their profit from Jowell options should be over four hundred grand: enough to pay for the treatment and have cash to spare. Len and Jean could go too, and stay there until Poppy was ready to come home. Terry tried for a while to disguise the cause of his facial injury but buckled in the face of general disbelief. When he came clean, his account of how he and the two girls had reacted to discovering their symptoms had the others in stitches.

Before the end of the evening, they agreed that they should all be together for the big moment. The IFK experience had taught them how early these things were announced. A merger of this size should hit the radio news by nine. They would gather at the Bishops' house at that witching hour, with an ear to the radio and one eye on the TV teletext City pages.

The goodwill of that Saturday night took them through on a high until Monday. Even Terry hadn't minded a day of enforced celibacy. They came early, Terry, Einstein, and Ruth, who'd taken a day off specially. They started guessing how far the Jowell share price would rise. Terry wanted a sweepstake; Len thought that was tempting providence, so they just had tea and toast with strawberry jam, chatting like excited kids about to set off on a school trip.

At eight-thirty they switched the teletext on. The market was off a few points. There was little movement in any of the larger shares. Jowell itself was steady, the calm before the storm. How those dealers would be jumping around any minute now. Jean topped up their mugs.

Terry wondered out loud if there was usually such a delay getting stuff up onto teletext. The others were too busy checking the radio was tuned right to listen to him.

There was nothing on the news, and nothing on the teletext, at nine, quarter past or half past. They began to sweat. Len called their broker; he had heard nothing either. The ten o'clock news doubled their fears and the eleven o'clock bulletin confirmed them. They stayed on until noon. When that news was over, Len turned round, and spoke gravely.

131

'Terry, lad, you'd better get round to Control Cabs as fast as your Fairway will carry you. However scratchy, spotty or scabby that sad little dick of yours may be, it's got to be back up Daphne by sunset. Go to it, mate. Dip it in chocolate, tie flowers around it, garnish it with herbs, sprinkle it with perfume, dangle sapphires from it . . . *Whatever* it takes, get it back in the trenches.'

For once Terry knew what to do. Without another word, he drained the last drops of his coffee, flew down the short driveway, hopped into his taxi and was off on his journey to Ealing.

Terry drove into the little car park at Control Cabs. It was full of cabs available for hire by the day or week to their drivers. Five or six cabbies were hanging round in the reception area. When they saw Terry arrive carrying a bunch of roses, they gave him whistling encouragement.

It took plenty of smiles, compliments and persuasion to get the receptionist to interrupt a girl at her work, and more of the same when at first Daphne refused point blank to come out. In all it was fifteen minutes before she marched through the swing doors, righteous indignation igniting every step, and stood in front of Terry in a hostile pose, fists planted firmly on hips, elbows horizontal.

'What you want, eh? I'm surprised you've got the nerve to show your face.'

' 'Ello, love. You look nice today.'

'What 'appened to your eye? 'Er, was it?'

Terry hadn't admitted that there *was* another woman, and this wasn't the moment to change tack.

'Bumped into somethin' in me garage . . .'

Daphne's expression spoke volumes about her trust in this story. Terry produced the roses from behind his back.

'Brought you these, doll.'

'Very *nice* of you . . .'

Daphne took the tall stems in both hands and flayed Terry's face with a fine, grunting combination of backhands and forehands.

'Oh dear, what a *pity*, all the petals seem to 'ave fallen off. They

132

must've been cheap.'

'What d'you *mean*? They cost me ten quid.'

'What you want, anyway?'

'Look, love, I'm sorry about your itchy whatsit, but I've been missin' you somethin' terrible. Thought we could kiss and make up, maybe go for an Indian after you get off . . .'

'So you can come bonk me afterwards and give me whatever you picked up *this* weekend? Is that your game?'

'We don't 'ave to do nothin' unless you feel like it, and if you do, I promise to use a johnnie. Look, I brought one . . .'

Daphne's eyes flashed and she stomped to the waste bin to retrieve the throny stalks. Terry held his hands out in alarm.

'No, love, not *again*. We could just chat if you prefer.'

'And swap stories about 'ow it feels to 'ave your privates prodded?'

Terry had almost agreed when he spotted the sarcasm.

'Nah, we could talk about other things.'

'Like *what*?'

There was only one answer that had a chance.

'Like . . . our future together'

'Oh, *yeah*?' Her face wore a challenging, mocking smile. 'And does that mean goin' out, livin' together, or gettin' married?'

He was getting in deep here.

'Well . . . livin' together . . . yeah, I'd vote for that.'

'But that's as far as it goes, right?'

'You never know. If things went well, we could always think of gettin' married later. Why not?'

Daphne snarled triumphantly.

'I'll tell you why not. Because wild 'orses wouldn't drag me up the aisle with a rat who can't keep 'is flies buttoned, *that*'s why not.'

Terry was relieved, if not flattered.

'Okay, suit yourself. That won't stop us goin' out together, though, will it? Tell you what: I can see you're still pissed off, and p'raps it'll take a while before you want me back. But even if it takes forever, I'll wait for you . . .'

Daphne didn't believe one word of this but, in spite of herself, that childish charm of his was easing away the sharpest edges of her temper.

'And, while I'm pinin' away, could you see your way clear to 'elpin' me out for one more week? Two at the most.'

'Piss off.'

'Please, Daph, I love you *so* much.'

That ought to do the trick, thought Terry. Ridiculously, it did. She kept him on tenterhooks for a while, then eased into a smile.

'All *right*. I must be soft in the 'ead. Only two weeks, mind. After that, you're on your own.'

'Thanks, love.' Terry moved forward to give her a kiss; Daphne stepped smartly back.

'You keep your distance – I don't want to catch anythin' else from you. Go on, get out of 'ere.'

Terry blew her a kiss and walked over to the door. Daphne called after him.

'Tell that other gel from me . . .'

'*What* other gel? . . .' Terry still had his wits about him.

'Pull the other one. Tell 'er well done. It's an 'umdinger, that eye of yours.'

She turned and disappeared. Terry left too, enduring a further commentary from his fellow-cabbies on the way. He got into his cab, and fired up the mobile.

'Len, we're back in business.'

'Well done, Terry mate. Me and Einstein'll get right on over to the City. See you for a cup of tea in Gresham Steet at five.'

*

Julia was mystified. The more she thought about it, the way the Furnival financing had collapsed was odd. She didn't have the remotest understanding of Zuricher's internal processes or why they might have turned down the deal. What she *did* know, though, was that it was a perfectly bankable transaction, and if Rosco had tried hard enough he should have been able to salvage something.

The most perverse part was how Marcus Ford and Grace had

134

reacted. Marcus had come back late in the afternoon on Friday. She'd expected to find him drunk and planning to quit on the spot. In fact, he was quiet, but not *that* agitated. She went over and asked how he was feeling; all she got was some philosophical twaddle about setbacks being good for the soul.

Grace was something else. When she first heard, she was inconsolable. To have done all that work, night after night, and have this happen was too much to bear. Julia took her out for a coffee and did her best. Grace seemed to calm down a fraction when someone called and evidently invited her out for the evening. Grace only stayed in the office for another hour and was gone before Marcus came back.

Julia tried to reach her over the weekend, but none of her messages were answered. She wondered if she had gone up to Yorkshire on Saturday to lick her wounds at her parents' comforting hearth. However much balm that might offer, Julia was sure that by Monday Grace would still be hungover, metaphorically and literally.

That seemed to be correct, at least early on Monday. However, later that day, things changed. If someone had given her a motivational chat, it had worked. It seemed that she had been put on some new assignment, and was too busy and distracted to have a drink, so instead Julia pressed for an introduction to Shipshape, Grace's health club in Holborn. The only time Grace could manage was seven the next morning.

They met at the club's reception desk. A blond god answering to 'Marti' turned round the book for Grace to sign them both in, and gave Julia a wad of literature and application forms. Marti looked caught between giving Grace meaningful looks and trying to make a strong first impression on Julia. They changed in the locker room and went through to saddle up on two adjacent exercise bikes. It was soon obvious that Grace was much the fitter. Julia had to snatch breaths just to speak.

'What's the story with Marti? Looks like he has a thing for you.'
Grace pulled a face. 'Don't get too friendly, he's *weird*.'

135

'Did *you* . . . get too friendly?'

'I got one-cup-of-coffee friendly. I thought I fancied him, in an earthy sort of way. As soon as we sat down, he started on about sex . . .' She glanced around to make sure no-one was hovering. 'Kinky stuff. Handcuffs, black leather, whips . . .'

'Whatever turns you on.'

'It turned me right *off* and when I wouldn't see him again, he started writing me strange letters.'

'Where? To Skidders?'

'No, thank God. If my secretary had opened one of them, it would've been all round the bank in ten minutes. He got my home address from the club records.'

'What did you do?'

'I ignored the first few. When they kept coming, I told him to stop. After a while, he started up again.'

'Why didn't you tell the police or change clubs?'

'I didn't see why I should be forced to leave. It's the best club in the City. And going to the police would've been overreacting. He's probably lonely. He hasn't been in London long and he doesn't have any friends here. Mind you, in case he ever does anything serious, I'm keeping all his letters as proof . . . Watch out, he's coming over.'

Marti sidled up and said something to Grace, which she answered with a dismissive shrug. Then he stepped right behind Julia. It gave her the creeps, having a pervert a few inches from her rear.

'Your posture's wrong, Julia.' Somehow it alarmed her that he'd made a point of remembering her name. 'Straighten your back and slide your seat slightly forward.' Nervously, she tried to do as instructed. 'No, that's not it . . . like *this* . . .' Before she could stop him, he had his hands on the top of her buttocks and was pressing her forward. 'Yes, that's more like it.'

Julia flushed in a blend of embarrassment and rage.

'Thanks, I can manage myself.'

Without being in too big a rush about it, he slid his hands off and moved away. Julia turned and hissed to Grace.

136

'Does he do that to you?'

'Not any more. I yelled at him last time. It's the only thing he understands.'

The exchange with Marti had made Julia forget why she was there at this ungodly hour. She dropped her pace slightly.

'So tell me what's going on. You seem to be spending a lot of time with Marcus. Is this another of his projects?'

Grace nodded.

'Is it a takeover?'

'Yeah.' Grace looked straight ahead and began to pedal harder.

'Who's the client?'

'I don't want to say here. There are too many people about . . .'

'No one will hear if you whisper.'

Grace looked unsure. 'I'd rather not go into details. Our client's a big Continental company.'

'And is the target in the UK?'

Grace hesitated, then nodded again.

'Who are they?'

'Julia, I'd really rather not get into this.'

'Why on earth not? We work in the same department, don't we? I know how to keep secrets.'

'This one's strictly "need-to-know". They made me promise.'

'Who's "they"?'

Grace kept quiet. Julia had a stab.

'It's not Rosco, is it?' Still silence. 'Oh, that's all right, then, *he*'ll tell me.'

She hoped this would bluff Grace into spilling the beans. It didn't; in fact, she turned it neatly round.

'Why are you so keen to know, anyway? It's only work.'

It was Julia's turn to shrug.

'I'm not, particularly. Just checking up on what's going on in your life.' Damn, she'd have to drop it. She switched subjects. 'So how's the mystery man? Did you see him at the weekend?'

'Yes, we had a nice time.'

'How's it going? Are you making progress? Will you prise him away from his wicked witch, whoever she is?'

Grace smiled happily.

'I think I'm making progress. We had a good conversation.'

'And is his identity "need-to-know" too, or will you at least let me into *that* one?'

'It's even more "need-to-know". He's paranoid. He won't even let me telephone him.'

And she laughed to herself, leaving Julia with nothing to think about except pedalling the stupid exercise bike for another virtual mile.

*

Grace had a glass of champagne and relaxed. She'd worked like a slave for a week to prepare the presentation that Marcus would give to Dieter Manz. As soon as she landed in Zurich, her task would be over. Marcus, who was travelling there from some meeting in Stockholm, said that Manz wanted to see him alone. Grace was to hand Marcus the presentation at the airport and fly home again. If she felt piqued at being used as a courier and excluded from the meeting, there was compensation in a day out of the office, a few air miles, and the chance to indulge herself at the duty-free.

She came in bang on time, precisely half an hour before Marcus's SAS flight was scheduled to land. A glance at the arrivals board sent a shock-wave through her. His flight was delayed by two hours. The meeting at Burlikon was due to start before then, and it was a good thirty minutes from the airport.

She rang his mobile. The signal was poor and it was hard to hear. It took three attempts for Marcus to explain that he was stranded on the tarmac while they tried to fix a hydraulics problem. He would ring her back when he had more news.

The minutes ticked by. Ten, twenty, thirty. Grace had to avoid making other calls in case he was trying to reach her. Over an hour had passed when her phone rang. The call was on the very cusp of breaking up into digital plumbing sounds.

'Grace, I'm still stuck in this fucking plane. They've fixed it, but now they can't get a slot. I've no idea when we'll take off.'

'What d'you want me to do? . . . Marcus, can you hear me? . . . Marcus, are you there? . . . That's better, I lost you for a moment.'

'The reception's terrible. I'll keep it short. I want you to take the presentation to Burlikon, but on no account . . .'

'Marcus? . . . Marcus? . . . Hello, hello, hello. Can you hear me? . . .'

With a last beep, the line went dead. She breathed in anxiously and dialled his number. Nothing. Again. Same. Shit, what was she supposed to do now? What did he mean by that 'on no account' stuff? At least he'd made it clear that she should deliver the presentation to Burlikon. Presumably Marcus would find some way to get a message there instructing her what to do. And if his signal strength got better, he might reach her in her taxi.

By the time the taxi reached Burlikon's grimly imposing head-quarters, it was barely ten minutes before the appointment. She paid, got out, and tried Marcus's number one more time. No good. She checked with SAS, and established that the plane had now taken off. Marcus would be incommunicado for another hour. Grace prayed that Dieter Manz would be understanding and agree to see Marcus later on.

Nervously, Grace asked at reception and was taken up to the top floor where she was greeted by Manz's secretary, who looked like she might double as a paratrooper. This ogre showed no sympathy for the vagaries of international travel, and remarked that Dr Manz expected people who served him – as Skidder Barton now did – to turn up on time. She disappeared for consultations with her boss. On the way in to his inner sanctum she looked severe; on her way out, exultant.

'Dr Manz's schedule is too full for a later meeting to be possible. He says that either you make the presentation yourself or the meeting is cancelled.'

Grace was panicking.

'But I can't . . . Marcus told me that Dr Manz *insisted* that–'

The secretary's eyes were becoming ever more beady.

'Miss Chesterfield, Dr Manz's patience is not infinite. Make up your mind. *Now*, please.'

He sat very erect at his desk, every strand of steely hair perfectly arranged, and looked at her with detached curiosity, like a collector examining a rare but otherwise uninteresting butterfly. There was no trace of warmth, humour or humanity in his manner. She could tell at a glance that none of her normal feminine wiles would work.

'Do not be concerned, Miss Chesterfield. If I have any idea of how banks like yours work, I imagine that *you* did most of the work. Is that not true?'

Grace smiled feebly. 'I suppose so. All the same . . .'

'May we start?'

With voice and hands trembling, Grace started in on the valuation. The main addition to the work they'd done for Furnival was to run a simulated consolidation with Burlikon's businesses to show what the synergies would be worth. It was all fairly approximate because of the paucity of information on Jowell.

Manz let her keep on turning the pages of the presentation book, but she sensed that she was losing him.

'Dr Manz, is something the matter?'

He pouted a little.

'No . . . it is fine as far as it goes, but I expected an update on the more detailed figures.'

Grace was thrown. 'What do you mean, exactly, by more *detailed*?'

'I mean Jowell's weekly results, business by business.'

'That's . . . not possible. There must have been a misunderstanding: Jowell doesn't publish that sort of information.'

Manz was staring strangely at her.

'Miss Chesterfield, surely you are aware of the information Mr Ford delivered to us personally last week? It was very helpful. Indeed, without further similar updates, we could never proceed. We like to know what we are buying.'

Grace felt like someone had walked across her grave.

'Dr Manz, I'm sorry if I'm being slow. Would you mind showing me what Marcus brought, and then we can clear this all up.'

Manz lifted his phone and barked a command. Two minutes later, the paratrooper stormed in, handed him a file and swept out again.

Manz flicked through it, found the right part, and held it out for her to see.

'This is it. That's what I need an update on.'

Grace took the file from him. Her eyes flicked down the unfamiliar figures. What the hell *were* these? How on earth had Marcus . . .? As she turned the pages and began to take it in, she turned ashen.

15

Any last trace of huffiness that Julia felt towards Grace was blown right away by a gust of compassion when she saw how she looked on Wednesday morning. What the hell could have happened to her? On Monday she'd been busy but fine. Yesterday she had been away all day, presumably on a trip to her mysterious Continental client. Today, when Julia got there, she saw Grace talking with Rosco. Her hair was an unkempt, scruffy mess, her only make-up a smudge of pink lipstick. She looked like she'd slept in her clothes and her eyes were bloodshot, with great dark rings round them.

When Grace got back to her desk, Julia punched in an e-mail. 'you look a fright. what's wrong?'

She watched while twenty yards away Grace clicked and read it. She didn't reply, just looked for an instant in Julia's direction, her expression desolate.

Julia tried again. 'tell me. whatever it is, I want to help.'

Grace shook her head without even looking across. Julia left it for half an hour, and gave it another try. 'lunch?'

'no time.' At least it was an answer.

'then how about a coffee? I'll be in Starbucks cafe from noon.'

There was no response. At five minutes to noon, Julia got up, picked her handbag up from beside her chair, and ostentatiously walked past Grace's desk on the way to the lifts. She glanced back; Grace hadn't stirred.

For nigh on an hour, Julia nursed espressos. She grew resigned to a no-show, and it was a jolt when Grace walked in, bought a cappuccino, and stepped nervously over to where Julia sat. Grace took a seat herself, still looking shell-shocked, barely responding to Julia's gentle hand on hers.

The state Grace looked to be in, Julia feared she might drink her coffee and run off without a word. She knew she couldn't be too pushy, but if they were going to discuss it, they'd have to start somewhere. She plunged right in.

'Grace, *do* tell me. I can see that something's upset you . . . Is it something to do with your man?'

Grace nodded faintly.

'Partly.'

'What d'you mean, "partly"? What else is it?'

'I'm sorry, Julia, I can't say, I really *can't*.'

'Is it connected with work?'

Grace put her coffee down and let her head fall slowly, heavily into her hands.

'Oh, God, I wish I knew what to do . . .'

Julia put her hand on Grace's back and stroked it gently.

'Grace, listen. Whatever the problem is, there must be an answer to it. There always is, if you face up to it. Come on, can it really be *that* bad?'

Grace's head reared suddenly back up and turned accusingly towards Julia.

'Yes, it fucking well *is*. Don't bloody patronize me.'

'I'm sorry. I didn't mean to.'

Grace caught hold of her temper.

'I'm sorry, I know you're trying to help. In this case you *can't*, that's all.'

'Could you take a few days off, and maybe go up to Beverley?'

'It's impossible. I have to work round the clock the next few days . . .' She checked her watch. 'I should get back. I have a meeting with Marcus.'

Julia stepped down off her stool and made to leave too. Grace shook her head.

'*No* – don't come with me. I don't want anybody thinking I've confided in you.'

Julia shrugged. 'If that's what you want.'

Grace managed a faintly friendly smile. 'Thanks, anyway.'

'It's okay. Call me any time if I can help. Even if you don't want

143

to talk about it. I could just *be* with you for a while.'

Grace squeezed Julia's forearm and was gone. Julia sat there for another five minutes, worrying.

*

Terry had quite enjoyed his Wednesday. Len was so worried about the money he wasn't in the mood, so Terry played a round at Hainault with another pal. They started early and got the best of the day. By eleven it was clouding over and soon after he left the scruffy little clubhouse it came on to rain. He headed straight into the City to get some work done.

He needed the money. The night before, when he'd been up West celebrating the end of his course of antibiotics, he ran across a brace of very pretty twins. They'd been in identical outfits, with skirts so short the winter wind blew straight up their bums. Terry didn't have any mate with him to split them, so he chatted up both. Soon they started talking about how the pair of them liked to have fun with a single fella. They weren't up for it that night, but said they'd be back in the bar on Friday night.

He was skint and needed to use the two days to get some dosh together, to make sure he wasn't caught short if the girls wanted to go to some fancy club first. So it was good that the rain was lashing down; it meant punters were flapping their arms all over the place, desperate for cabs. Not only did he get plenty of fares on the street, Daph came through with a ride for the Daventry girl, and she yacked away on her mobile the whole journey. It was the first fare the cabbies had got with any of the Furnival team since that fateful Monday. Curious as he was, Terry knew his batteries were running low, so he didn't play the tape back right away. After the rain stopped he'd buy some fresh ones.

On and on it poured all afternoon, past seven and eight. All the shops in the City were closed now. He thought of driving a few miles west, but what with the rain the traffic was god-awful and he couldn't be bothered. Most likely he'd have no more use for the tape machine that night anyway, so tomorrow would do. He

144

stopped at a rank off London Wall. He would take one last fare, hopefully something long-distance, and knock off for the night.

When he got to the front of the queue, the punter asked to go to London Bridge station. A short ride was the last thing Terry wanted, so he pretended to have engine trouble, and broomed him off on the cabbie behind. He'd been there another two minutes when Daphne called again on the mobile.

'That you, black-eye?'

''Ello again, love. You got another for me?'

'There's one just come in for Chesterfield. It's for nine-fifteen, from Skidders.'

'Thanks, love, you're a real pet.'

''Ow's your spotted dick? Fallen off yet?'

'Piss off, Daph . . . Thanks, though, I'll get round to Throgmorton Lane in good time.'

Terry was looking forward to this. She was a tasty number all right, that Grace. He'd had her in the back of his cab a few times now, and if it wasn't for the Poppy thing, he'd like to *have* her in the back of his cab.

The call flashed up on his screen right on cue. Instead of keeping him waiting, like bankers did most of the time, she came right out, scurrying down the steps with her bag over her head to keep the rain off. As soon as she jumped in, Terry took an eyeful in the mirror. In the dark he couldn't see a lot, but she looked sort of *strange*.

'Where to, love? All I got 'ere is SW5.'

'Redcliffe Gardens . . . Only I want you to go via Holborn. I'm picking up someone at the roundabout there.'

'If someone's waiting for you out in this rain, it must be love.'

Terry thought he'd get a giggle for that one, but there was no reaction. Suit yourself, he thought as he pulled out of Throgmorton Lane and into the streaming traffic. The spindly wipers were losing the battle to displace so much water. A motorbike came from nowhere, slicing past, causing the car in front to brake so sharply that Terry almost rear-ended him.

145

'Pillock.'

'*What?*'

'Not you, love, that kamikaze biker . . . Workin' late, eh?'

'Yeah.'

'You doin' a takeover? Must take a lot of work, them.'

'Yeah.'

'Big one, is it?'

She didn't reply. Terry glanced in the mirror. She was staring out the side windows, looking nervy and worried. He decided to give it a rest.

It took another five minutes before they got to the roundabout. He couldn't see anyone. He pulled in and looked across the street, getting quite a fright when there was a sudden banging on the nearside window, and a man in a low-brimmed hat, scarf and dark glasses tugged at the door. Terry pressed the lock release and let him in. The first thing the man did was to slide the partition window shut and switch off the intercom.

Visibility being so bad, Terry had to stick his head out the window to pull safely back into the flow. Another cabbie flashed his lights and let him in. If anything, the rain was getting heavier. He flicked a glance at the man, and couldn't stop himself sniggering. *Sunglasses*, on a night like this. What a prat! A good-looking girl like that ought to do better. She was looking daggers at the fella: whatever he was saying, she didn't like it.

Bollocks, he'd forgotten to switch on the Walkman . . . His left hand reached down. He hoped the batteries would last. He went through one set of lights, and then stole another glance. It was her turn to have a go at him now, and she looked like she was coming nicely to the boil. Terry couldn't hear any of the words, but the distant tones of her fury were rumbling darkly through the glass. This tape should be make interesting listening.

One more look. She caught Terry's eye in the mirror, annoyed that he was watching. Better stick to driving. They were almost at Southampton Row, and two lanes of traffic were joining from the right, jostling for equal rights to the road ahead. A white van cut right in front of him. At the next lights, Terry drew level with it,

146

yanked his window down and yelled out the choicest of curses. The van driver leaned over to wind down his own passenger window and responded in kind. Terry was midway through his second volley when he was interrupted by the glass partition being slid back. A voice came from behind him.

'I'm getting out here. Take her on.'

Without looking away from the van driver for a second, Terry released the lock and continued.

'You know, you look like a bleedin' orang-utan. Escaped from London Zoo, 'ave you?'

The lights added amber to red. That didn't bother the van driver.

'You got the bottle to get out of that cab and say that again, eh?'

He was a big bugger. It was one of those moments when Carriage Office rules come in handy.

'You know bleedin' well that gettin' out of this cab's more than me badge is worth. Any other time I'd come over and smash that baboon face of yours.'

'Oh *yeah*?'

'*Yeah.*'

The green lights had beckoned for fifteen seconds or more, and the drivers behind were getting exasperated enough to risk the wrath of a white van. A chorus of honking started up. The van driver was more interested in continuing the conversation.

'Where you live, then? I'll be round later to put a fist through your face.'

'Twenty-two Avon Road, Cricklewood. Midnight tonight, okay? I'll get some bananas to feed you.'

The van driver growled furiously, 'You *wait*, you *fuckin'* little . . .'

Terry smirked triumphantly, made a parting wanker sign and drove off. He chortled heartily as he threaded his way through the traffic, taking good care not to get too close to the van again.

'What a dick, eh? It'll be bleedin' funny if 'e goes out to Cricklewood. Know who lives at twenty-two Avon Road? . . . One of the geezers what does the Knowledge tests. What I'd give to

147

see the look on that dick's face if 'e goes round there with a crowbar and wakes Mr Hines. Funny, don't you think?'

Grace didn't reply. He glanced in the mirror. She was staring straight ahead like she'd seen a ghost. Maybe his barney with the van driver had upset her. Girls could be like that: they hated it when fellas got involved in any argy-bargy.

'Don't worry, love. It 'appens all the time. Them van drivers are all fart and no shit – pardon the expression.'

He looked in the mirror again. She was still staring ahead. Then he realized he'd forgotten about *her* barney. Why had the fella got out again so soon? Had he dumped her? She looked in a right state of shock about *something*.

'Lover's tiff, eh? I used to 'ave them all the time with the fiancée.'

Not a word. Okay, one last try.

'Bad one, was it?'

No reply. Fuck her. He turned on Capital Radio, loud, and slipped his hand down to the Walkman controls. Somehow it had already switched itself off. Had the tape reached the end? No, it couldn't be that; it had auto-reverse. Maybe the batteries had given out. Lucky it was only a lovers' squabble.

Terry drove on to Hyde Park Corner, round Belgrave Square and along Pont Street towards South Kensington. He was still feeling sulky with her for ignoring him like that. Upset or not, a few words wouldn't hurt. After he gave up trying, he was determined not to look at her in his mirror, in case she thought he was *so* very interested in her and her stupid little tiff. Even now, as he pulled off the Old Brompton Road and into Redcliffe Gardens, he didn't look back. All he did was ask, in clipped tones, what number she wanted.

She didn't reply. He waited impatiently.

'Look, darlin', I've got work to do. If you want to argue with your fella, do it in your own time, okay?'

Still she didn't move, just kept staring ahead. Could she be a head case of some sort? The last thing he needed was a girl having a nervous breakdown in the back of his cab. Why couldn't she break up with her fella in the pub, like everyone else did?

'Are you gettin' out or not, love? I can't stay 'ere all night, you know.'

This was driving him crazy. Angrily, he got out of his cabin and pulled the door next to her open. It was still tipping down and he was starting to get soaked. Even now, she wasn't deigning to look at him.

'Okay, *out*. I said get out of my cab. *Now.*'

No reaction. He leaned further in. Up close, something in her expression sent a shiver through him. He softened his voice a little.

'You all right, love?' He put his hand on her right arm and shook it gently. 'Sorry if I got a bit shirty.'

Slowly, almost gracefully, she swayed away from him and slumped heavily to her left, hitting her head hard on the padding below the opposite window.

'*Christ.*' Terry ran round to the other side of the cab and pulled that door open. Her head was flat on the back seat, her eyes stared blankly ahead. He gulped 'Oh, my *Gawd.*'

Banging both passenger doors closed, he jumped back into the driver's seat and sped off. Where was the nearest big hospital? Was it Saint Thomas's? . . . He couldn't think straight. No, the Chelsea and Westminster was much nearer. Please God, let this be nothing serious.

Along Fawcett, down Finborough, and into the Fulham Road. There it was. Terry pulled in under the bright canopy and, with only the slightest look back to check that she hadn't stirred, he flew out of the cab, into the reception area where two or three people were waiting. He pushed past them.

''Scuse me, *'scuse me* . . .' The black receptionist broke off from her conversation. 'Got an emergency in the back of me cab. Gel's been took peculiar.'

'Where's your cab?'

'Out the front.' He pointed superfluously to the big doors.

149

'Wait a minute.' She punched in a number. 'We have an emergency on the forecourt.' She looked back at Terry. 'They'll be with you in a minute. Please go and wait with your taxi.'

Terry nodded thanks and skipped back out the door. He had no sooner got there than a pair of male orderlies arrived with a trolley and got on with the job of easing the girl gingerly out of the taxi. As they wheeled her inside, Terry trotted alongside. One of them asked him what had happened.

'Just came over sudden, like. When we stopped, I shook 'er, and she sort of fell over.'

'Okay, wait here. The duty doctor will need a word with you. He'll be out as soon as he's examined her.'

Terry sat down on an orange plastic chair. God, he hoped she'd be okay. He didn't want to tell anyone about his shouting match with the van driver. What if she was one of them epileptics? They might say he'd set it off and report him to the Carriage Office.

Why didn't the doctor come out? What was happening? With every passing minute he was getting more nervous. He kept having to rub his hands on his jeans to wipe the sweat off. When a nurse bustled by, he called out and asked her for news. She shook her head and scurried on.

Twin rubberized swing doors flew open and a man in a light green smock came over to him. Terry jumped nervously to his feet.

'Okay now, is she?'

The doctor paused for a second.

'I'm afraid to say she's not okay. She suffered a cardiac arrest.' He saw the confusion on Terry's face. 'A massive heart attack . . .'

'But she'll be all right, won't she?'

'No, she won't. She was already dead when she got here.'

'*Fuck.*' An icy wave swept though Terry.

The doctor looked straight at him.

'A heart attack is unusual in someone so young. She's not overweight, indeed she looks very fit. In cases like this, we're

150

required to call in the police. They'll be here shortly. Obviously, they'll want to talk to you. If you don't mind waiting a little longer . . .'

'No, no . . . 'course not.'

Terry slumped down on the chair. The doctor turned and walked back towards the swing doors. Just before he disappeared, a thought smashed its way into Terry's haywire consciousness, and he shouted out.

' 'Scuse me, doctor. All right if I get the mobile from my cab, is it? I need to let someone know I'll be late.'

The doctor thought for a second and nodded.

Gratefully, Terry scampered along the corridor to the reception area and out to his cab. He grabbed his mobile, and, hands shaking, began ripping out the jack plugs, switch box, earphones, Walkman and wires.

Across the other side of the road there was a litter bin. Checking that no one was watching, he started to cross over. Halfway there he froze. Jesus, what should he do about the tape? He was panicking too much to think straight. A car screeched to a halt and the driver blared furiously at him. He hotfooted it over to the other side, pressed the eject button, and dropped the recorder and the rest of the gear into the bin, burying them deep under the yucky mess.

Then he raced back over to the cab, opened the boot and stuffed the tape behind the spare tyre. As he closed the boot lid, he heard the sound of an approaching siren. He made it back past the reception desk barely seconds before the squad car pulled up outside.

16

'Old money porker pet? (6,3).' Detective Sergeant Dennis Wear scratched his thinning crown with the point of the much-chewed biro, leaving greasy blue marks on his scalp. The first word was something 'u', something something 'e', something, but he had no letters to help with the second. He tried to recall what he'd learnt at school about the names of coins in the olden days. Crown, shilling, farthing? Never mind, move on. Fourteen across. 'Day before Adam's partner (3).' He pondered, his eyes flashed with satisfaction, and emphatically he filled in the three squares. That was more like it. Sixteen across. 'Chocolate-coated god of war? (4).' Balls, why did they make them so difficult? He scanned the rest again; inspiration didn't strike. He threw the pen and the *Standard* down onto the desk.

He hated night duty at the best of times, and when it was as quiet as this, it was worse. His DI had gone off two hours ago to investigate a gang bang near Fulham Broadway; since then the phone hadn't rung once. He picked up the pen again and doodled in the margins of the paper. Life wasn't going too well at the moment. He'd been turned down for promotion and his wife was giving him grief about the hours, trying to make him give up the force and take a job selling mobile phones. Some fun *that* would be. For all the tedious stretches, he liked being a copper, especially in the Met CID.

He stared at the phone, willing it to ring, and jumped when it obliged. As he reached out for it, he prayed it would be something worthwhile. His excitement subsided quickly when he heard. They didn't come duller than checking out a common-or-garden heart attack. Still, anything was better than hanging round the nick. He rang for a car and driver and went the short

152

distance to the Chelsea and Westminster hospital. They put him in a small, cluttered office and told him the duty doctor would be along in five minutes.

'Hello. I'm Doctor Harding.'

'DS Wear. What've you got for me tonight?' He took out his notepad and biro.

'A girl, late twenties, early thirties at most. Name of Grace Chesterfield. Works at a bank called Skidder Barton. We got that from the cabbie who brought her in. There's a handbag, but we haven't touched it.'

'Is he still here, the cabbie?'

'He's waiting to see you. She appears to have died from a massive heart attack. The cabbie told the nurse she got in at the bank and later picked up some man. The man got out again somewhere along the way, and the cabbie took the girl on to South Ken. When they got there, she didn't move. She must've been already dead or dying by then. By the time she got here, anyway, there wasn't a flicker.'

'Any signs of an assault on her person?'

'Nothing obvious. We haven't looked closely yet. I had to deal with another case, a living one. If you want, I'll give her more of a going-over now.'

'Thanks. What's your feeling, though? Natural death?'

'If she was a few years older, or less fit, I wouldn't be in any doubt. Could be she's on drugs. A lot of bankers use them. Or there might be a family history of premature heart disease. We'll find out more when you speak to her next of kin.'

'Of course. Okay if I take a look at the handbag? After that, I'll interview the cabbie.'

The doctor brought the bag in, holding it delicately with a pair of forceps. He'd had similar cases before and knew not to disturb any fingerprints. DS Wear nodded acknowledgement of this, took the bag and, avoiding any contact with the clasp itself, used his pen to prise the two sides apart. There was the usual collection of junk, plus all sorts of make-up, a purse and a Filofax. The purse

153

contained eighty-odd pounds, credit cards, driving licence, and membership cards for a video shop and a health club. Wear thumbed through the Filofax. There was no obvious next-of-kin entry, so he looked through the Cs. No mention of a Mum or a Dad, but in his experience, there usually wasn't. Kids normally knew their own folks' address and phone number off by heart and didn't bother to write them down. Right at the top of the 'C' page was written, 'Paul', with a Yorkshire address. All the other names on that and other pages were neatly written out in full. Might be a brother or uncle. He thought of trying the Paul number on spec . . . No, better follow proper procedures. He put a call in to Skidder Barton and made the security guard call the home number of someone in personnel to access their records.

*

It was well past midnight when the Chesterfields were roused by the knocking at the door. Beth Chesterfield got up out of bed, pulled on her quilted dressing gown and peeped out of the window. The sight of the police car gave her palpitations. It was *Paul*, something must have happened to Paul. The boy always drove too fast, she was always telling him. Oh God, let him only be injured . . .

They opened the door and saw two of them standing there, a man and a woman, both *so* young.

'Mr and Mrs Chesterfield?'

They nodded. Beth Chesterfield's voice was already a strangled croak.

'It's Paul, isn't it? He's not . . . ?'

The man shook his head.

'No, we're here about Grace . . . I'm afraid it's bad news.'

It wasn't Beth Chesterfield who fainted. It was Tom who crumpled unconscious.

The policewoman went straight back to the patrol car and radioed for a doctor. Lights came on in the house next door and a woman in curlers opened her door to see what was the matter. She was pressed into service to make tea in the Chesterfields' kitchen,

154

and half an hour later she was still there, holding Beth's hand as she tried to compose herself to answer the policewoman's questions. Paul had been told and was on his way to comfort them and drive them to London. Tom Chesterfield sat far back in his worn easy chair, a blank, distant look on his face, retreating behind a silent wall that couldn't protect him from the shattering pain of losing the person he loved more than anyone in the world.

*

There wasn't much sleep happening in the Bishops' house, either. Terry's whispered call scared Len out of his wits, and he stopped work pronto, called Einstein to let him know, and headed home. He was glad that Terry had shown the sense to ditch the recorder, though dumping it in a bin right across the road wasn't particularly smart. What if someone had seen him? And though he knew that Terry meant well hanging onto the tape, it was a daft thing to do. There was little enough chance that the passengers had said anything about the bid, and it certainly wasn't worth taking that kind of risk. Einstein agreed and called Terry back to suggest that he break open the cassette, throw away the casing and drop the tape itself into the cab's radiator, where the scalding water would destroy it. Terry was halfway along the corridor to do that deed when he bumped right into DS Wear and was taken into the small office for questioning.

Luckily, the policeman was friendly and Terry began to relax However, after Wear was called away to the phone, he came back looking more serious and less bored.

'We've spoken to the next of kin. There's no history of premature heart disease. The body will be sent over to Horseferry Road first thing in the morning for the Home Office pathologist to take a look at. And the duty Superintendent is on his way to our nick. He'd like a word with you there, if you don't mind'

Terry snatched at his last chance to get at the tape.

'Whatever you say, guv. You tell me where it is and I'll be right over. I need to fill my tank on the way, so I might be a few minutes.'

'No. The Super says he doesn't want your cab touched. You can

155

come with me in the squad car and we'll pick up the cab later. Keys, please . . .' He held out his hand.

Soon enough Terry found himself in an interview room in Fulham police station, being introduced to a stocky, grizzled, nasty-looking copper.

It had been a while since Superintendent Hunt had interviewed a murder witness in person. He liked working with Wear and was looking forward to this.

'I've already been over all this with the sergeant.'

'Then you'll be happy to go over it again with me . . . You're *sure* you didn't get a clear sight of this man?'

'With all the clobber 'e was wearin', there wasn't much *to* see.'

'Did you have the impression he was covering his face deliberately?'

'Can't say, really. It *was* bleedin' cold, *and* there was the rain. I think *I'd* want to cover up in them conditions. And as for the sunglasses, 'e was prob'ly a poser, like fellas you see in nightclubs. Or 'e might've 'ad a black eye. The way she flew off the 'andle, I wouldn't be a bit surprised if she'd fetched 'im one before now. I bet she could do some damage, that gel.'

'Why d'you say that?'

'Because she 'ad sockin' great tits, you ask the doctor.'

'What the *hell* has that got to do with it?'

'Gels with big tits always pack a wallop. It's to do with the size of their lungs.'

Hunt's eyes glinted. He was looking at Terry's discoloured eye.

'Got a lot of experience fighting with women, have you?'

Terry smiled. 'I wouldn't 'urt a fly, but I've been thumped by gels once or twice. Temperamental lot, they are. My ex-fiancée, Marcie, could punch all right, and she's got real big . . .'

'Yeah, yeah, I get the point. The man got out of the cab while you were arguing with the van driver, right?'

'I wouldn't want to give you the wrong idea. It wasn't a real barney, more of a natter.'

156

'You didn't see a company name on the van, and you have no idea what its registration number was?'

'Look, I was givin' the fella a bollockin', not testin' me eyesight.'

Hunt cracked his knuckles. 'Can you at least describe the driver?'

'Twenty-five, thirty maybe. Red 'air. Big. Ugly bugger, looked like a monkey. Might've been Welsh.'

For a moment, the Superintendent's gloom lifted.

'You didn't tell DS Wear that. You mean he had a Welsh accent?'

'No, I mean 'is *face*. You know the way the Welsh look, like monkeys.'

Hunt's fists tightened. 'My mother's Welsh.'

'Yeah . . . well, when I say Welsh, maybe I mean more like Scottish.'

'Let's get back to your barney. While you were arguing, the male passenger slides opens the window and says he wants to get out?'

'That's right. So I let 'im out, and 'e buggers off back into the rain.'

'And you're sure he wasn't carrying anything?'

'Definitely. Apart from 'is briefcase, that is.'

'He had a *briefcase*? Can you describe it?' Hunt gestured towards the note-taking constable to make sure he got this down.

'Yeah, I saw it in the mirror. It was sort of squarish and black. Or brown, p'raps.'

Hunt ran his hand irritably through his hair.

'Let's go back to the man. When he got out at the junction with Southampton Row, did you see which way he went?'

'No, I was busy–'

'Bollocking the van driver.'

'Yeah.'

'So, you didn't see him at all after he got out of your cab? What about when he got in, or when he was inside the cab? Did you get any idea of his age, height or build?'

'Not really. Could've been any age. Like I told the other fella, I reckon 'e was about average size. About my height or yours.' He looked carefully at the Superintendent. 'Maybe a bit taller than you.'

The constable bit his quivering lip. Hunt was five foot ten, short for a copper, and sensitive about it.

'So, what are we talking? Six foot?'

'Somethin' like that. Average build, too, I'd say, though it wasn't easy to tell with that overcoat. Not what you'd call a *big* man, anyway.'

'And the conversation itself, you couldn't hear much through the glass?'

'I did catch a couple of "How dare you's" and one or two "Let me finish's"; you know, the kind of things gels say when they're barneying.'

Hunt nodded. 'Okay, that's it for now. I may want to interview you again in another hour or two. The constable here'll get you a cup of tea. After that, we'll want all your clothes off.'

Terry's gut tightened at the thought of being buggered in some stinking cell.

'What the 'ell for? I ain't done nothin'.'

'Our forensic boys will be checking your cab for fibres from the man's clothes. They need to test yours to eliminate them.'

'They won't be needin' me underwear, then, will they?'

Hunt smirked coldly. 'Oh yes, they will. There are some different tests they'll run on that.'

''*Ere*, what's your game? I never laid a finger on 'er.'

'It's only to eliminate you from our enquiries, Mr Thorogood. After all, apart from your say-so, there's no evidence *anybody* was in your cab, apart from the deceased. Sergeant Wear checked with Control Cabs. The booking only says SW5. There was no mention of any detour or of picking up any other passengers along the way.'

'There wouldn't be, would there? Not unless it was well out of the way.'

'Probably not. Still, there's no corroboration of your story, so

158

we have to check things out. Okay?'

Glumly, Terry nodded. Before now, he hadn't thought about Control Cabs. He hoped the coppers didn't smell a rat and start putting the heat on Daph. She would crumble, no question. Was it too late to come clean, admit the whole thing and tell them about the tape in the boot? He hesitated for a second, almost said it, then missed the moment. Hunt stood up and left the room to listen to what else Wear had found out.

'Nothing much, sir. He's had a green badge for four years. There's another Thorogood living in the next street, who's done time for breaking and entering. Could be related. But our cabbie himself has no previous.'

'What did you make of him, Wear?'

'He's an odd one, sir. Cocky half the time, then suddenly he gets nervy for no obvious reason. Mind you, if he'd been involved I don't suppose he would've driven the body straight to the hospital.'

It was a chance for Hunt to show the benefit of his greater experience.

'He might have had no choice. He knew that the Control Cabs records would show when he picked her up and dropped her off, and he'll have watched enough telly to know we can get a good fix on the time of death.'

'Do you mean, sir, that he might've clambered in the back of his own cab and done her in?'

'We don't yet know that *anyone* did her in. It may still be a natural. Even if it's not, I doubt he did it himself. He couldn't have planned it, given the way the calls go out on the Control Cabs system. You checked it, you know that. Our cabbie didn't get the call until four minutes before she got on board. No, I'm sure there *was* someone in the cab. The fellow gets in at Holborn, right? He and the girl have a fight, and he does something that causes this heart attack. But our cabbie sees what's going on in his mirror and stops the cab. He keeps the door lock on, so the villain can't get out. Now the villain's in queer street. If the cabbie calls the police,

159

he's finished. If he opens the window and tries to clamber out, the cabbie will get a good look at him. So what does he do? Offers our friend a thick wad to let him go.'

'But Thorogood doesn't *have* a wad on him, does he, sir? Unless it's in the cab. If so, the forensic boys will find it.'

'He had the entire journey from Southampton Row to the hospital to do something about that. He could've stopped at a cabbie shelter and slipped it to someone for safe keeping. Or he might've bought a stamp and an envelope at a shop and posted it to himself.'

Wear joined in the game, anxious to please the Superintendent.

'Or maybe the villain didn't have the money on him, and promised to meet up later to hand it over.'

Hunt nodded. 'You might be right, sergeant, and now the villain can't risk double-crossing the cabbie in case he gives us his description.'

'That would certainly fit with his behaviour, sir. Putting on a jokey act, but being in a lather under the surface.'

'Either way, we won't hear from the pathologist till nine or ten tomorrow. We could let Thorogood home for a few hours, I suppose, but I think I'll give the lad an all-nighter. Let him cool his heels for a couple of hours, then I'll start on him again. If they *do* have a rendezvous planned, we might get the cabbie to lead us to him. While he's waiting, don't let him make any calls.'

A door opened and a constable poked his head round it.

'Just had a call from Hull Police, sir. Her parents are on their way. Should be here about six. The dead girl's brother is driving them down.'

*

With the passing hours, Len's worry deepened so much that he confessed about the taping to Jean. They didn't *think* of going to bed. It was past four, and they hadn't heard another peep from Terry. Had he managed to get rid of the tape? Or had he broken down and told them the truth? If so, it wouldn't be long before they rumbled Einstein and himself too. You only had to look at

160

Terry to see he was incapable of inventing a scam like that. Jean got out of her chair and came over to the couch to snuggle her generous form next to him.

'What'll 'appen to you, Len, if Terry's gone and told them?'

'If it comes out we was recordin' punters' conversations, we'll all be suspended, and I s'pose we could lose our badges for good. Right now I'm more worried about what they'll do about them options. Even Einstein don't know if it counts as insider dealin'.'

'Oh God, Len, what are we goin' to do? I can't stand the thought of you goin' to prison. You know what your blood pressure's like; it'd be the death of you. And what would we say to the neighbours? Couldn't we go and hide somewhere abroad?'

'With a sick kid in tow? Don't be daft, love. We've no choice but to wait and see.'

The phone burst into life. Len's heart pounded as he pushed Jean's heavy form off him and made a dash for it.

It was only Einstein.

'Sorry to ring so late, Len. Mind if we come over for a cup of tea?'

' 'Course not, mate. I'll go and put the kettle on.'

*

The pathologist arrived at the lab in Horseferry Road on the stroke of eight. He washed his hands and put on his gloves. His assistant had already brought the body out of the cold chamber and it was lying uncovered on the slab. Such a pretty girl. But, sadly many of them *were*.

He started with the back and front of the neck, and then examined the arms minutely. He noted a faint contusion on the left forearm, as if someone had grabbed it roughly. The torso came next. Her body looked very fit, with a hard, flat stomach. All his instincts told him that this was no natural death. On to the legs. Nothing on the right one. The left looked unharmed too, until his expert eye noticed a tiny red mark halfway up the side of the thigh. He asked his assistant for a magnifying glass and took a good look ... Yeees, there it was, the little beauty. A microscopic

161

puncture mark, no more than three millimetres in diameter. Now he knew what he was dealing with he would go straight to the kidneys. That's where it would show up. The other tests, on her heart, stomach, blood and vagina would have to wait. If it was what he thought, they would want to know fast.

The tests on the kidneys took half an hour. As soon as the pathologist was sure, he picked up the phone and dialled the number of Fulham police station.

'Superintendent Hunt? Her kidney has clear toxic traces. It'll take a few more hours to be certain what type of poison it is. However, there can be no doubt this is what caused the cardiac arrest.'

'How was it administered?'

'By piercing her left thigh with a syringe or a spike smeared with poison.'

'You're sure about this? She was definitely killed?'

'I suppose she could've committed suicide. However, unless she flung the weapon out of the window very fast, I'd say you have a murder on your hands.'

Smartarse, thought Hunt. The pathologist continued.

'Do you want me to call you in person with the poison results?'

'I don't know who'll be handling it yet; I just happened to be on duty. It depends how much experience they want. I've investigated more murders than most men in the Met have had hot dinners.'

17

Scotland Yard underestimated the level of interest. After the story went out on the news wires, the press conference was packed to the rafters. The Deputy Commissioner opened proceedings and introduced the Senior Investigating Officer for the case, Superintendent Hunt, at forty-eight one of the most experienced detectives in the Met. Hunt spelt out the basic facts before inviting questions.

'Is an arrest imminent?'

Hunt had been there before, and the standard form of words tripped easily off his tongue.

'There are several lines of enquiry we are pursuing vigorously and I am confident we will soon apprehend the perpetrator of this vicious crime.'

'What sort of poison was it?'

'It was a very concentrated form of a poison that occurs naturally in castor-oil beans. When this poison enters the blood-stream and reaches the heart it causes paralysis of the heart muscle, prompting immediate cardiac arrest. This can easily be mistaken for a natural heart attack.'

A wizened hack from the *Guardian* had a long memory. 'Is this like the murder of that dissident Bulgarian in the Seventies?'

Hunt had been briefed on this by the pathologist. That case had involved a much weaker, more slowly acting version of the same poison.

'It's very similar. Markov was his name. The assassin put a tiny platinum pellet containing the poison on the point of an umbrella and stabbed him in the leg with it. The raw material for the poison is widely available in India and is often used in killings there.'

'Was Grace sexually assaulted?'

'There is no evidence of that.'

'So what would you say was the motive?'

'It's hard to say at this stage. It seems that the assailant was known to her, but we don't yet know whether he was a friend or a more casual acquaintance. What *is* clear from the manner of her death is that it was premeditated.'

'Can you tell us the name of the cab driver?'

'No. He's been helping us with our enquiries, but he is not, repeat not, under suspicion himself. However, you will understand that we must keep his identity confidential.'

'Is he helping you make a photofit image of the murderer?'

'We will not be issuing a photofit. We have reasons for this that I am not at liberty to disclose.'

If the murderer had any intelligence, he would guess that this meant the cabbie hadn't seen him clearly enough. However, nothing would be gained by spelling it out.

'What message do you have for ordinary people who use London cabs? Will you be recommending women not to travel in them alone?'

They'd seen this one coming, too, and agreed it would be handled by the Deputy Commissioner. He moved closer to the microphones.

'London taxis are the safest in the world. As Superintendent Hunt has said, this was clearly a planned attack which could have happened anywhere. Not only was the driver not involved, he wasn't even aware that the attack had taken place until he arrived at the destination.'

This version wasn't the whole truth, of course. Though satisfied that Thorogood was not the murderer, they were still far from concluding that he was entirely innocent. The decision to declare him clear of suspicion was purely political. Any other line would have caused chaos in the capital, a point that the head of the London Taxi Drivers' Association had made forcefully as soon as he learned of the wire story. If more evidence emerged later that implicated the cabbie, they would investigate it away from the glare of publicity.

164

There was a pause which allowed the Deputy Commissioner to announce that he wanted to bring out Grace's parents to make a brief statement, adding that they would not be answering any questions.

The Chesterfields had abandoned the original plan for Tom Chesterfield to read the statement. He would never have got through it. Paul's offer to stand in for him was quietly rejected by Beth who, despite her tears and her sobs, felt it was her own dread duty. They all shuffled on, Paul holding his mother's arm and the kindly Scotland Yard policewoman supporting Tom. Both parents looked drawn, haggard, very old. Paul stood behind while they sat, and rested a hand on his mother's shoulder as she struggled with the tangled array of microphones. She pulled out the much-used handkerchief from the sleeve of her purple dress and tried to clear her throat.

'Grace was a lovely girl who had her whole life in front of her. When she graduated from Cambridge University and became a banker, we were both terribly proud of her. It never changed her, though, and she always stayed our little Grace, with a kind word for everybody. We cannot understand why anyone should want to hurt her. We appeal to anyone who has any information to come forward, not only for our Grace, but to stop this evil monster striking again . . .'

Beth's composure crumbled. Paul squeezed her on both shoulders. Tom was too far gone to be able to help, the tears streaming down his face. Beth sucked in great gulps of air to try to get through the last few sentences. It was hopeless. The Deputy Commissioner took pity on her.

'I think we will not intrude further into the grief of Mr and Mrs Chesterfield. We will keep the press fully briefed on the progress of our investigation. Thank you for coming, ladies and gentlemen.'

*

The press conference was repeated on every news bulletin. It came as a jolt both to Jean and Len and to Einstein and Ruth.

165

Before that, it had been a bit like hoping to get Terry off a drink-driving charge. Seeing it on the telly made it hideously real, and watching the girl's poor Mum struggling to make her statement . . . it broke your heart. None of them wanted to admit to the feelings that were creeping into their minds.

With all the fuss, Jean and Len had hardly given a thought to Poppy, apart from carrying up her meals and checking she was taking all her pills. Coughing had kept her awake most of Thursday night, and she'd noticed all the comings and goings. She knew her Mum and Dad were still up at four o'clock, and when she heard the familiar clatter of a taxi engine outside and the low tones of her Dad welcoming Ruth and Einstein, it was clear to her that something odd was going on. Why wasn't Terry there too? Had he got himself into trouble? Was it another woman thing, or was it the law? Was it something to do with the money to send her to San Francisco? Terry hadn't tried to rob a bank for her, had he, the daft div?

Later, in the afternoon, she saw the news about the taxi murder. At first she didn't make the connection. The girl hadn't been robbed, so it didn't look like a fund-raising job, and she hadn't been interfered with *that* way, which ruled out Terry's only other motive. But why was everyone being so peculiar? Her Mum wouldn't answer any of her questions. And when Terry finally *did* turn up, why didn't he come up to see her, like always? Poppy reached for her worn old teddy bear, and thought.

In the kitchen, Terry, Jean and Len ate their fish-and-chip tea in silence. Although the police had let Terry go, they were keeping his cab a bit longer. Would they find that tape and, if so, would they play it? Another sleepless night awaited them all.

*

A mere four hours after the press conference was over, Superintendent Hunt convened the first evening meeting of the special murder team. There were twenty-three of them in all. He was pleased with the team, too, barring Detective Inspector Mary Long. It got up his nose, having to take a woman in that key position. All of Ron Hunt's experience told him that police-women were good for dispensing tea and sympathy, and that was as far as it went. It rankled that she'd been to university and was on the Met's fast track. At twenty-nine she'd progressed faster than hundreds of far better coppers. If she kept it up, by forty she'd be on the command course at Bramshill, hand-picked for the highest echelons of the force, and beyond anything Hunt himself had achieved. His own one-time dreams of senior glory had been crushed, and he would be taking retirement at fifty. Yet he would always have the satisfaction that he was ten times the officer a Mary Long would ever be. He'd done his time, on the beat, in the Serious Crime Squad, in the front line. He'd come up through the ranks, with no advantages of education or privilege to help him. His colleagues respected him for that. He was a copper's copper.

Long would be a passenger on this team – no doubt about that – but when he couldn't talk the bosses out of foisting her upon him, he'd swung it to his advantage and insisted on getting Dennis Wear as his own bag carrier. Wear had a good nose and, above all, was loyal to him personally. Together they would crack it.

The rest of the team consisted of three detective sergeants and a dozen detective constables, who together would do the street work and the scouring and sifting, plus a group of five civilians whose task was to log every new snippet onto the computer and cross-check it on 'HOLMES', the Home Office Large Major Enquiry System.

Hunt decided to put pressure on the girl from the start.

'So, DI Long, tell us about the girl's place?'

'It's a pretty normal flat for a girl working in the City.'

Hunt smiled. The son of a railwayman, he was genuinely curious to discover what this word meant to a barrister's daughter.

'When you say *normal*, Inspector, what do you mean, exactly? How much would the place cost to buy?'

Mary Long saw what was coming. She'd groaned when she heard she'd be working for Hunt, the biggest misogynist on the force. This assignment would be purgatory.

'I've no idea.'

'Have a guess. You know more about these things than the rest of us, I imagine.'

Mary had recently bought a sweet little flat in a nice part of Highgate, and her father had helped with the deposit. She'd tried to keep the whole thing quiet, unsuccessfully.

'Maybe two fifty, three hundred.'

Hunt looked around the room, and made sure they all acknowledged his leer.

'Nice to hear that's normal. Makes the rest of us subnormal, I suppose.'

There was a titter. Mary moved on as fast as she could.

'There was no match with any of the fingerpints we found in the back of the cab. Not that this means much if the assailant wore gloves, as we suspect from the smearing of prints on the door handles. There's no evidence of drug use. There were a lot of personal financial papers – investments and so on – which we'll analyse over the next few days. Letters from her Mum, but they don't say much. The main lead is another batch of five or six letters. There's no address or date on them, and they're just signed 'M'. Kinky fantasy stuff.'

Hunt smirked.

'How d'you mean, Inspector? Give us a few examples.'

Mary long did her best not to redden.

'There's a lot of S&M stuff, about wanting to handcuff and whip her.'

'Whipping, eh? Do women enjoy that, Inspector?'

To the amusement of all, she reddened. But she still managed to volley back.

'Depends who's doing the whipping, sir.'

There was a tightening around Hunt's lips and a mute salute in the room to her defiance. It was clear to everyone how this would unfold: the woman-hating veteran against the privileged upstart. It might be amusing, provided it didn't get out of hand. Hunt decided to get back to the subject matter, though he left a harsh, sneering tone in his voice.

'What's the big deal, anyway, if she and her man wrote dirty letters to each other? If she hadn't liked them, she would have junked them.'

'Perhaps. The letters are sexy, but they don't read like they're lovers. He rambles on about her not knowing how much she wants it, and he keeps saying that he'll never give up on her. All pretty vague, but nasty. His way of writing is strange, too, oddly formal and *correct* for smutty letters.'

Before she'd finished saying that, she was kicking herself for setting Hunt up again.

'Is that the sort of thing that university makes you worry about? Sergeant Wear, better make sure any notes you take are grammatical.'

'Yes, sir.' Wear grinned obsequiously. Long wasn't going to leave it there.

'What I'm trying to tell you, sir, is there's something artificial about the English, as if the writer isn't a native speaker.'

Hunt grudgingly accepted there might be a point.

'Are the letters from abroad?'

'No. The deceased kept them in their envelopes. They all have the same postmark. London EC1. That includes some of Holborn.'

'Okay, sounds like you need to follow that up. If it's not a lover, we need to work out how he got her home address. Could be a tradesman who did work at her flat, for instance. So check any recent repair bills. Equally, it might be a delivery boy, or someone from a courier company. Get hold of her credit card statements and check for anywhere she went regularly, like restaurants or clubs. Could be someone who worked there.'

A messenger brought in a note for Wear. He gestured to Hunt, who nodded.

'Sir, interim report from forensic. They've identified the fibres on the back seat. Black cashmere. Expensive, obviously. Apparently no way they can narrow it down to any particular manufacturer. The dye is a very common one. Not very good news on footprints, either.' Wear paused and read the rest verbatim. ' "Cab floor very dirty; many footprints, none clearly linked to the murder. Some small marks where the deceased's heels dug in, probably at the moment of the attack. Several lateral scuffings, possibly from the assailant's shoes. Likely he was wearing leather soles. If so, positive identification impossible." '

'Thanks, Sergeant. Okay, what else? We have the surveillance on Thorogood in place. Barclays Bank will let us know if there's any large payment into his account or any evidence of big expenditure. Sergeant Wear will accompany me tomorrow when I visit Skidder Barton. I'll be seeing the Chairman. Depending on what we pick up, we may need to interview the colleagues she worked closely with. Someone should also speak with her secretary – Inspector Long, that might be a suitable one for you to handle – and try to reconstruct her moves over the last few days. I think that's it for now, unless anyone has more to say?'

One of the civilian staff, a nerdy individual with greasy hair and glasses, put up a tentative hand.

'There is one thing, Superintendent.' Hunt glowered, frightening the lad out of his wits. 'I've found a piece on Terence Thorogood. He got himself in the *Sun* a few weeks ago over a bust-up with his fiancée. I'll put a copy on your desk. The article describes him as a womanizer.'

'Okay, thank you, everybody. Back to work for you lot. I've been up all night, so I'm going home.'

*

Hunt slept refreshingly well and felt in fine fettle when he arrived in Throgmorton Lane. It was the first time he'd been to an investment bank, and he hadn't the faintest idea what they actually *did*. He expected that it'd be full of snooty people who would look down their noses at the likes of him. Well, let them try. If for one moment he felt they were patronizing him, he'd give them hell.

He was surprised, soothed and flattered when he was politely, even deferentially received. The instant he and Wear arrived, they were escorted to the lift by a pretty receptionist and put in a magnificent panelled room with a glorious view over the City and the river. Fresh coffee and chocolate biscuits were brought in, and the Chairman's secretary put her head round the door to say that Mr Barton had instructed her to interrupt his meeting as soon as the Superintendent arrived. He would be along in a minute. Before she closed the door, Hunt was almost audibly purring.

Charles Barton came in only thirty seconds later. He was slim, distinguished, very well groomed.

'Superintendent Hunt?'

'Indeed.' Hunt put out his hand and administered his signature bonecrusher. 'This is Detective Sergeant Wear.'

'Gentlemen, do please sit down. You've been given coffee? A terrible thing, this.'

When he looked closely, Hunt could see from his pallor that Barton was genuinely shaken.

'Appalling. Her parents are in a very bad way.'

'Of *course*. I've written to them, and naturally I'll go to the funeral service.'

'Did you know her yourself, Mr Barton?'

'Only a little. I do try to make a point of meeting even junior staff when they join. Other than that, it happens only if we meet in connection with a particular piece of business. As a matter of fact, I *did* run across Grace on a takeover her department was working on.'

'Was she still involved in that?'

'No, that deal came to a halt . . . oh, about a fortnight ago. I'm afraid I've no idea what she was doing more recently. If it's important to know, you'll need to speak to the co-heads of that department, Richard Myers and Rosco Sellars. Would you like me to arrange that?'

'That would be very kind. I don't suppose you have any ideas or theories about who might have done such a thing?'

'I can't say I do, Superintendent. This sort of thing doesn't happen very often in the City, thank goodness. We have other ways of settling our differences here.'

Hunt smiled. He was warming to Barton. He was not at all

171

what he'd expected.

'So you don't believe it has anything to do with her work for Skidder Barton?'

'Inconceivable, I would say.'

'Even though she picked up the murderer in a taxi ordered from here?'

He was almost embarrassed to have to ask the question.

'Our rule is that after eight p.m. staff are entitled to take a taxi home, or wherever else they want to go – provided it's not John O'Groats. I imagine our more socially active young people often give rides to their friends. They work very long hours under great pressure. We try not to be over-zealous in checking up on trivial things like use of taxis.'

'Quite.' If one of Hunt's people took a taxi without the proper authorization, there would be hell to pay. However, he could see that it was different for banks like Skidders. For a moment he fantasized about another life where he himself worked in a panelled room like this, and the powers in the land came to him for his money and wisdom. Sadly, it was too late. Not for his son, though, now coming up to fourteen. If he pulled his socks up and got a few GCSEs, maybe he could get a job somewhere like Skidders. Perhaps he should stay in touch with Mr Barton and, when the time came, see if he would be willing to give the boy a chance. He wrenched himself back to the present.

'. . . Obviously, we'll need your help in examining the telephone records both from her mobile phone and her land line here. We have already requisitioned the information for her home phone.'

'Naturally, we want to do anything we can to help. Anything at all. But do tell me, how far have you got? Is there a suspect?'

'It would be premature to say very much. Confidentially, we did find some rather lurid personal letters in Grace's flat which we hope may lead somewhere.'

Barton looked shocked. Hunt was amused at the reaction of this old-fashioned gent. If he worked for the Met, he'd get used to the seamy side of life fast enough.

172

'When you say "lurid", you mean from a lover?'

'More of a weirdo. Someone she knew but probably didn't have a relationship with. It's possible he's our man. Tracking him down is our biggest priority.'

'Well, it's good to hear that you have a lead. Now, would you like me to arrange for Myers or Sellars to come up here?'

'Yes, please, Mr Barton.'

'I'm sure I can ask for your understanding on one point. Most of what our corporate finance department does is highly confidential, and we have a legal duty to maintain that. My colleagues will be able to tell you generally what Grace was doing, but they may not feel able to give you chapter and verse.'

'Of course not. I do have *some* idea of how investment banks work, big deals and so on.'

Wear looked more than a little surprised. It was a *murder* they were dealing with, and he saw no reason not to ask for any information they wanted. What was turning the Rottweiler into a poodle? Oh, well, maybe the boss had his reasons. He usually did.

*

There was drama at the Friday-evening meeting of the murder team. It started quietly. Hunt reported that Skidder Barton were being very cooperative. The Chairman, in particular, had been at pains to help, but the co-heads of corporate finance had been unable to imagine any link between her work and such a violent act. Hunt added that he thought they were right. There were better trees to bark up.

As he was finishing his report, Mary Long, who had irritated him by being absent at the start of the meeting, burst in.

'Sir, excuse me for being late. I think we've found something. As you instructed, we checked all the places Grace went regularly. One of them is a health club called Shipshape, right in the middle of Holborn. Grace was a member and went there two or three times a week. They had an attendant there from Finland who left the day after the murder, name of Marti Salminen.'

Hunt tried to avoid looking impressed. Long pressed on.

173

'Unfortunately they don't have a sample of his handwriting, but the paper they use in the office is exactly the same shade and size as that those letters were written on. And the person we talked to there said that Salminen was always trying to hit on women members. They gave us his home address: he was sharing a place in Earl's Court with three Swedes. We interviewed two of them. They say he took his things and left without a word. They've no idea if he has a cashmere coat. By the way, they're pretty pissed off at him; he owes two weeks' rent.'

'And do we have *any* idea where he is?'

'None at the moment, sir. We only discovered this in the last hour.'

'Okay, put watches on airports, stations, ferries. He may have fled the country already, but we can't be certain. Do we have a photograph of him? No? Well, get his flatmates and the people at the health club to help make a photofit. Better still, get onto the authorities in . . .' He tried to think of the right capital. It wouldn't come. '. . . in Finland. They must have a picture from his passport application. And get them to check if he's gone back there, or whether his family has heard from him. Come to think of it, better alert the police in other countries he might run to, like Spain. Let's get moving: this could be our man.'

He nearly added a grudging word of praise for Inspector Long's efforts, then thought better of it.

*

On Friday night Terry tossed and turned and got little more than one hour's sleep. At four he got up, pulled on some of his cleaner clothes and shuffled along to the kitchen to make himself a Nescafé. As he lifted the cup, he noticed his hand was trembling. He looked out the window at the dark night. A light snow was falling and there was already a thin dusting on the ground. It looked bloody cold. He went back to the bedroom and tried to get back to sleep.

He didn't succeed. At eight-thirty, he heard a taxi roll to a halt outside. There was no mistaking that sound: it was *his*. Did that mean he was in the clear, or might they be round to arrest him later in the day? The driver rang, got him to sign for it and left. When the man was safely out of view, Terry went to open the boot. Then he thought again, went back into the house, called the others, and drove through the shrouded streets over to Len's.

Einstein beat him there, and he and Len were already out in the street rubbing their hands to keep warm. Len moved his own cab out of the garage. Only when Terry's was safely in there and the garage doors were closed against prying neighbours' eyes did they turn the handle and peep inside the boot.

18

Len bore the cassette carefully in, and Einstein and Terry trooped processionally behind him. They assembled in the lounge, where Len knelt in front of the Technics and slid it into the cassette player. As one, the three of them sat down and waited expectantly through the clickings and whirrings.

Len had to wind it to and fro a few times before finding the right part. Terry apologized right away for missing the start of the conversation; he was keeping his fingers crossed that the batteries had lasted until the end.

There were a few background noises. Then, chillingly, the dead girl was talking to them from beyond the grave.

' ". . . and you're completely backtracking on everything you promised me . . . I can't *believe* it. I trusted you, loved you, and this is what I get. And now you have bloody nerve to ask me to turn a blind eye to what's happening with Jowell. I could land up in prison over it, couldn't I? Can you give me *one* reason why I should?" '

' ". . ." '

Einstein raised a hand. To Len and Terry, it had only sounded like hiss on the tape. Einstein thought he heard something *very* faint.

'Play that bit again, but turn the volume up and switch out the Dolby to make it clearer.'

Len did as he asked. Now the girl's voice was much louder.

' ". . . *reason why I should*?" '

' ". . ." '

Einstein waved his hand again. 'Again. Even louder.'

Len pressed the rewind, and turned the wick way up.

' ". . . REASON WHY I SHOULD?" '

' " . . . Half a million . . . " '

It was very quiet, but it was there, all right. They played it back twice more to be sure, then let the tape roll on, turning the volume back down so they weren't deafened if the next part was louder.

' " . . . *Fuck you*. No amount is worth going to jail for. If you had stood by me, like you said you would, I would've taken my chances for you. Not now, though. I'm not risking my neck. Unless I hear by eight o'clock tomorrow that you've changed your mind, I'm going straight to the police . . ."

' " . . . " '

The tape simply wasn't picking him up. He must have been too far from the microphone or whispering deliberately. They tried the trick with the volume again, turning it way up, and rewinding a tad.

' " . . . TO THE POLICE . . ." '

After that, something *was* audible. It was a man's voice, even fainter than before. They had to go over it several times to be sure of the words.

' " . . . you bleedin' maniac . . ." '

Len paused the machine, puzzled. The voice sounded different from the bit about the half-million. Terry looked flushed. Einstein was impatient.

'Go on, Len, see if he says any more.'

Len let the tape roll another few seconds. Again, they strained to hear.

' " . . . You're a fuckin' moron . . . " '

Einstein and Len looked more confused. Terry was anxiously willing the murderer to start talking in a nice loud, *clear* voice. The tape went back to the girl, her voice ear-splittingly loud. Len hurriedly turned the volume down to a more comfortable level.

' " . . . Don't you *dare* threaten me. I don't give a damn what you think. Unless you tell her tonight, I'm not putting myself on the line." '

As soon as she stopped talking, up the volume went again.

' " . . . Who gave you a licence, anyway? Mickey Mouse? . . ." '

The penny dropped, and Einstein and Len swung round on Terry. He wanted the floor to open up and swallow him.

'Sorry, fellas. Never knew the microphone could pick up sounds through the glass.'

Len eyed him sourly. 'It wouldn't if you didn't bleedin' well *shout*.'

Terry badly wanted to win his way back into favour.

'Don't fret, Len, mate, any minute now we'll catch the geezer askin' to get out of the cab. It'll be clear as a bell.'

Einstein gestured to Len to move the tape on. It was Grace's voice again.

'"... I *mean* it. That's my last word. Call me if you change your mind. Otherwise ... No, don't you *dare* try to touch me. Get your *repulsive* hands off me ... What the *fuck* is that? ... Keep that away from me, I'm *warning* you ... Leave my arm *alone* ... Oh no, *no*, No ... YAAARRRH ..."

'"..."'

Len had forgotten to turn up the sound again. Even before he did, somehow they had all too clear an idea of what they might be about to hear.

'"... Why don't you spend more time watchin' the road, and less pullin' your wire? Know what youu sshouldd dooo? You ssshhhouuuulddd–"'

Then there was a slight clicking sound. The tape rolled on: this time it really *was* only hiss. Terry looked horrified.

'Bugger, me batteries must've given out.'

Len was livid. 'You stupid prat, we was always on at you to buy spares.'

'I did. I used them, didn't I?'

'Then they weren't *spares* no more, were they, you daft berk? And why on earth couldn't you keep your big mouth shut long enough for us to 'ear 'im, eh?'

Einstein's brain was racing ahead. There was no point crying over spilt milk. And they'd got a real nugget, despite Terry's balls-up.

'Hold on, hold on: think why we taped this in the first place. It

178

wasn't to witness a murder, it was to find out if the bid for Jowell is still alive. From the sound of that, I'd say there had been some sort of snag, but that it's still on the cards.'

Terry was worrying about something different.

'What about the *murder*, Einstein? That tape don't come close to tellin' who done it.'

'True, Terry, but it *does* prove that the murderer knew about the Jowell takeover bid. That must narrow the field.'

Terry could see that. 'You mean it's someone from Skidders?'

'Possibly. Or it could be an investor getting inside information from Grace.'

Terry's conscience was still plaguing him.

'That's all very well, Einstein. Now we know that the murder was somethin' to do with that bid – but what if the coppers don't? The killer could get clean away.'

Einstein was unconvinced. 'I doubt it. If there are no other obvious clues, they're bound to turn that bank upside down. Once they're told what she was working on, it shouldn't take long for the police to draw up a complete list of people who knew about the Jowell bid. I *bet* they found lots of other evidence in the back of your cab, Terry. Fingerprints, fibres, that sort of thing. It shouldn't be too hard to compare them with everyone on the list. They'll track him down within days, mark my words.'

As he finished, he looked over at Len; his mood was hard to read. Terry looked uncomfortable, too. Einstein had more persuading to do.

'We *could* hand the tape over, of course, provided Terry doesn't mind doing time for obstructing a murder enquiry. Plus, we would all lose our badges and Len would lose Poppy. And all for what? Telling the police something they've probably worked out for themselves already?'

Terry nodded uncertainly.

'I s'pose when you say it that way, you might be right. What d'you think, Len?'

'To be honest, after seeing that poor gel's Mum and Dad on telly, I think we owe it to them to 'elp catch the bastard. But if

Einstein's right, and it won't make no difference . . . well, of course, I want to do what's right for Poppy.'

Einstein was relieved. He really believed in what he was saying and, having come this far, he couldn't stand to think of their project failing. Helping Poppy had been the bravest, the grandest, the most exciting thing he had ever done in his life. He couldn't let it go now.

'Okay, then. We need to go back to work.'

Terry looked aghast.

'If you think I'm askin' Daph for any more 'elp, you're bleedin' bonkers. She must know it was *that* fare. She might go to the police 'erself, for fuck's sake. Last time I speak to 'er, I tell you.'

Einstein had overlooked the Daphne angle. He paused long enough to analyse the risk.

'I know what you mean, Terry, but it shouldn't be a problem. Nobody's disputing the fact that Grace booked a Control Cabs taxi. Provided they don't suspect any hanky-panky over the booking, what could they hope to find out by questioning anyone there? And even if they did, Daphne has a job to protect, too. The *last* thing she'll want is to get dragged into a murder enquiry.'

Terry still looked doubtful.

'Whatever you say, Einstein, I'm through with that gel.'

'Okay, okay. It's probably best for you to keep away from the City, for a while anyway. Len and I will hang around Skidders. Shouldn't take long before we get some of those jokers in the back of our cabs again. Okay, Len?'

'Fine with me, Einstein. If you fellas don't mind, I'm goin' upstairs to see Poppy. I've been that distracted, I've 'ardly seen the little mite the last couple of days. Last time I went up there, she gave me the funniest look. I want to find out what's goin' on in that little mind.'

Terry looked up, more cheerfully now, and called out at Len's departing back,

'Just as long as you don't tell 'er what's goin' on in *our* little minds.'

*

180

The Chesterfields returned home on Friday to find hordes of newspapermen camped out in their street. When the couple refused to say anything more, they began to drift away on Saturday. By Sunday night they were all gone.

The funeral would have to wait until the people in London finished all their tests. It broke Beth's heart, thinking of her poor girl lying naked there on a slab, cut open for prying eyes to look at. All Tom wanted now was for his poor girl to be given a decent Christian burial so he'd have somewhere to go every day and pour out those feelings, all that love which he'd never found the right words to express.

Paul was reluctant to leave them, but Beth told him it was time he got back to his wife and his child – and to his job, for that matter. He hugged his Mum deeply, and put a hand on his Dad's shoulder. Tom looked up and thanked him wordlessly. Then they heard the sound of his car driving down the close, and he was gone.

Beth fetched a mug of cocoa for each of them and they sat silently for a while. She knew how difficult this would be.

'Tom, we were wrong not to tell them. It could be *important*.'

'We're *not* telling them, and that's an end to it. I won't have her dragged through the dirt any more. Anyway, we don't know who he was.'

'We know it was someone at the bank.'

'Aye, and a fine thing it would be if it got in the papers. Think what the tabloids would call her. *Marriage breaker . . . Promiscuous . . . Slut.* Is *that* what you want, woman? And if they get hold of that, they won't stop there. They might talk to the people at the clinics.'

'Can't you see, though, Tom, if they don't catch the murderer, and we don't lift a finger, we're letting Grace down? We can wait for a while, see how the police get on. Will you agree that, if they get nowhere, we'll think again.'

'*Never . . .*' He almost spat the word at Beth. 'Grace is dead and gone. Of *course* I want to catch the man that did it, and if there were any justice in this world, he'd be strung up. But, whether

181

they catch him or not, it won't bring Grace back. All she has left now is her good name. I want her remembered as a good, decent lass, not as something that folk will scorn. Don't cross me on this, Beth.'

She saw the look in his eyes, the fierce, wild resolve, and the rising colour in his face. She looked down at the carpet, and nodded resignedly.

*

Monday was the first time since Grace's death that Sellars and Ford had come face to face. At the emergency meeting of directors on Thursday morning, they'd noted each other's presence but had kept warily apart, exchanging no nod, no glance while Charles Barton informed them all of Grace Chesterfield's death in suspicious circumstances. Word spread throughout the bank within minutes; the staff were appalled and intrigued at the same time. Later that day, when the news of the murder filled every radio broadcast, every TV screen, the levels of horror and fascination ratcheted higher. In the City and even on Wall Street the story dominated conversations, and in their fast, sick way, the brokers and bankers were soon competing to post Grace Chesterfield jokes on the Internet.

Since then, Rosco and Marcus had studiously avoided any dealings with each other. By Monday afternoon, however, Sellars no longer had a choice. He was due to go to Zurich and needed an update from Ford, so he e-mailed him and suggested a chat in a meeting room. Sellars was there already when Ford walked in. For ten or more seconds they stared directly at each other, each trying to work out how the other was feeling.

'Weird business.'

Marcus merely nodded. Rosco continued.

'I'm not sure our hearts are in this now, but life has to go on. I'm meeting Lautenschutz in Zurich tomorrow, and I doubt he's the type to accept more than one minute's silence. You and I have to decide: do we go forward or pull out?'

Marcus stared back at him and said nothing.

'*So*? You better tell me where you stand. I can't do this bid alone, and, after what's gone on, involving any other director would be crazy.'

Still no reply. Sellars backed off for a moment too, and looked at the man, almost with admiration. His instinct told him that if Ford definitely wanted out, he would have said so right away. This silence could only mean one thing: the sonofabitch was *negotiating*.

'Marcus, don't jerk me around. Are you in or out? This is still one hell of a deal. If it's our financial arrangements that are bothering you, I'm happy to revisit them.'

Marcus looked down at the table and back up at Sellars. Sure, he felt giant contempt for the man. My *God*, he had balls, though. Marcus had spent the last day or so in a state of abject terror, waiting for his fate to overtake him. Sellars should be feeling a million times *more* scared, yet here he was, proposing that they get right back on with the business. Grace is dead; long live the deal. He didn't know what to say. There could be no going back, he supposed, but did he himself have the nerve to go forward? Sellars was starting to drum his fingers impatiently on the table, and couldn't stop himself lunging back in.

'Tell you what, I'll up your share of the fee to ten million.'

Marcus shook his head, not as a comment on the offer, simply in amazement that anyone could talk, could think in such terms at a time like this

'Okay, twelve, goddam you.'

'Rosco, know what I think about your offer?'

'Don't say it. All right, you have me over a barrel, I admit it. Fifteen million pounds. That's my absolutely final offer.'

Marcus was beginning to find something weirdly calming about the conversation. It was so surreally tawdry and mundane that it brought an odd sense of normality to a terrifyingly abnormal situation.

'I don't get you, Marcus. Even if you don't move forward on Jowell, where does that leave you? What's done is done. If we stop now, we'll only point the finger at ourselves.'

Marcus considered. Sellars was right about that. And maybe the worst *would* be over in the next few days. If they found something, he was dead meat, of course. But what if they didn't? What he would give to know what was in those police files! For the hundredth time, he cursed fortune for making him late for that meeting at Burlikon. Sellars was right, though: stopping would be riskier than continuing. He looked back at Rosco. It was *his* fault, this whole thing. If he hadn't blocked Quilley's bid and given Manz whatever he wanted, none of this would have happened. He would be looking forward to Christmas in the glow of Furnival's hugely successful takeover, and Grace would be sitting a few yards away from him, happy to slope off for a quiet Yuletide cuddle. Having blown all that, if Sellars wanted his help now, he'd have to pay for it.

'Rosco, you asked me not to jerk you around. Well, *you*'re the one who's doing the jerking here. I know damn well that your share of fees isn't twenty per cent, it's *forty*. I'm not going ahead unless we do this fifty-fifty, which, by my reckoning, makes twenty apiece.'

Sellars smiled. This guy had balls. To have the nerve to pull a stunt like this after what he'd done . . . you had to hand it to him. He kept on smiling.

'Okay, Marcus, it's a deal.'

He reached across the table and offered his hand. Marcus took it.

'I'll let you into another secret. Jowell's not the only reason that I'm going to Zurich. There will be *two* Swiss bids, not one. Lautenschutz is going to bid for Skidders.'

'When?'

'Not until they get hold of the Barton family's twenty-six per cent shareholding. If they combine that with their own twenty, they'll almost have control. Ernst's strategy is to buy the Barton shares *before* our bid for Jowell is announced because if it's known that we'll make such a huge fee, Skidder's share price will shoot up. He's persuaded Manz to hold fire on Jowell until the Bartons have sold.'

'How long will that take? The conditions for Manz's bid are

perfect now. He *must* launch before Christmas.'

'That may be tricky. Someone's told Ernst that the real decision maker in the family isn't the old man, it's Charles's brother. Apparently, Guy Barton used to be the black sheep but now he's famous he has Sir Miles eating out of his hand. You *have* seen the press comment, haven't you, saying he should take over from Charles?'

Marcus shook his head dismissively. 'Those stories are all crap. Guy Barton has his own empire. Why should he want to run a bank, specially one in such terrible shape?'

'Who knows? Maybe he's bored and wants a new challenge. I hear rumours that he's planning to sell Elixir. Or maybe it's the oldest reason in the book. Money. I can tell you, Lautenschutz is offering Guy Barton one shitload of cash.'

Marcus looked astonished.

'You mean, they've *met*?'

'Yup. Ernst hasn't told him about Jowell, but he's promised him the Chairmanship of the bank, plus a huge fee for delivering the family shareholding.'

'I don't believe this. Those financial arrangements would have to be disclosed in the offer documents. The moment the other family members saw how much he'd gained personally, they'd never forgive him.'

'Give the Swiss credit for a *little* more subtlety than that. Ever heard of numbered bank accounts? The fee would never see the light of day.'

'So, has he accepted?'

'Not yet. As you've seen in the papers, he's off at Christmas on some half-assed parachute record attempt in Morocco. He's said he'll give his answer as soon as he gets back. If it's yes, Zuricher will buy the shares immediately and announce their formal takeover bid on the twenty-ninth. Needless to say, when the Swiss take control, there'll be management changes. Ernst will appoint a new Chief Executive.'

Marcus saw it all now. 'And let me guess . . . that'll be *you*, right?'

Sellars smiled his confirmation. 'Don't forget, I'll be needing a deputy. He should be an Englishman, preferably someone with a corporate finance background. Now, we *could* look outside the bank. On the other hand, there might be a suitable internal candidate, especially if the bid for Jowell goes well.'

Marcus nodded. If only he got through the present nightmare, imagine banking a cool twenty million pounds *and* being promoted over the heads of all those old farts to be number two! In time, maybe he'd get the top slot: Rosco wasn't the type to stick around forever. A wave of excitement pushed his fear back another few inches. If it all came to pass, how he'd enjoy telling Sophie's father to put this in his pipe and smoke it. With a position so powerful, he would be able to chart his own future course without help from that obnoxious man.

'Sounds good, Rosco, I have to admit. Before we get on to my update, there's one thing I should let you know. Julia Daventry told me that Grace had a coffee with her on the day of her death and said she was worried about some work thing. Julia asked if it could be anything Grace was doing with me. I denied it point blank, of course. She doesn't know about the Burlikon bid, does she?'

'Not unless Grace told her.'

'I didn't get that impression. All the same, Julia has got it into her head that there could be a connection with the murder.'

'As long as she doesn't know anything, what can she do?'

'She could gossip about it in the bank, and someone might tell the police.'

'Okay, I'd better have a word with her. Marcus, would it make any sense to put her on the team to replace Grace? We could offer her the slice that was coming Grace's way.'

'No, Julia doesn't have the technical skills to do a UK takeover. Plus, if she's sniffing around about Grace's death, we don't want her anywhere near this deal. I'll pick another executive, a very green one, who'll be so thrilled to work on it they won't ask any awkward questions.'

19

Marti Salminen wasn't smart when he went on the run. He managed the first part, taking a train to Dover on Friday, catching a ferry and hopping on another train to Paris. There could be no tracing his journey, and if he had laid low there, continuing to pay in cash for his cheap room, they might never have found him. The hotel proprietor was none too concerned about checking pass-ports and, as long as he was paid in advance, he wasn't the sort to bother the police.

What spooked Marti was the English newspaper he saw on a news-stand on Monday. The picture of him had been taken eight years before, when he was eighteen, and bore so little re-semblance it was no kind of threat. All the same, to read his name, wanted for questioning in connection with Grace Chesterfield's murder, terrified him. And to think that his mother in Helsinski would be hearing about this too. If this murder was such a big deal, the papers up there would certainly cover the story that a Finn was a suspect.

Without stopping to think, he phoned her. She was beside herself with worry, too distracted to take in his impassioned denials of any involvement. What with his past, was she going to believe him anyway? She just told him to give himself up, to go back to England, not to make matters worse. She wanted to know where he was, of course, and it hurt her when he wouldn't tell her. It was only after the call ended, as painfully as it began, that it dawned on Marti that the Finnish police might be bugging his mother's phone. If so, they would know where he was now, would be on to the French police, and a police car would turn up in minutes. He threw his few things in his holdall, slipped quietly past the front desk, and left the hotel.

He knew he must get out of France. As he rode to Roissy, he was trying to work out where to go. Europe was now too dangerous. All his instincts said go far away. America was risky: he feared their computers. How about going back to India? The year he had spent there had been happy. Or to South America, where it was summer now? He didn't have a word of Spanish or Portuguese, so getting a job there would be hard. The Far East appealed more. There were so many young Americans, Australians and Europeans travelling in those parts that you could lose yourself happily for years. He'd always hankered after finding out whether the girls in places like Bali or the Philippines lived up to their reputations.

At the airport Marti asked around for cheap flights at several airline ticket desks, knowing that to avoid using his credit card he was limited to what was left from the money he'd drawn before leaving England. He carefully avoided all the European-owned airlines, eventually finding a Thai Airlines flight to Bangkok that was leaving in only one hour. Having no choice but to book in his own name and produce his passport, he was at fever pitch as he queued for passport control, and dry-mouthed throughout the wait in the departure lounge. It was only when they were two hours out, well away from French airspace, that he began to relax and start ogling the stewardesses. After some drinks and a meal, deep sleep captured him, and he didn't wake up until they were making their final approach to Bangkok.

The welcome committee of local police and the Finnish consul took Marti by surprise. He never got beyond the airport. The consul told him that he had no choice. If he didn't agree to return to England voluntarily, the British would apply for his extradition. The Thais would lock him up until the court sat, and there was no doubt what their verdict would be. It was plain to Marti that he was an embarrassment: the consul wanted rid of him.

Marti asked for a lawyer and was given a telephone consultation with a Thai attorney who got regular work from the consulate. In dry, disengaged tones, he echoed, word-perfect, the views of the consul. Three hours later, with no chance to shower or change clothes, he was airborne again, and for all that his return was 'voluntary', he was escorted humiliatingly by a detective from the Bangkok police. On arrival at Heathrow on Tuesday night, he was handed over, fettered like a farmyard animal.

The British police formally arrested him, stuck him in the back of a heavily armoured van and, with outriders to front and rear, drove him into London.

Hunt handled the interrogation personally. It gladdened him that Salminen had spent time in India, the likely source of the poison, and he was delighted when Marti's record arrived from the Finnish police. At twenty-two he'd been convicted for indecent assault on a teenager, and two years later had been charged with raping an Italian student. He'd been acquitted, but the case notes the Finnish police faxed through made clear that in their view he was guilty as hell. For Hunt – no admirer of judicial process – that was as good as a conviction. He was *sure* he'd get a confession out of the boy within twenty-four hours.

When Marti first told his tale, Hunt couldn't stop himself laughing. The Finn had no kind of an alibi for the night of the murder, admitting that no one could corroborate his claim to have been at a cinema. Nor did he deny that it was Grace's death that had made him run, panicking at the thought that his letters might point the finger at him. He had the nerve to claim that the rape charge in Finland had been trumped up and he didn't want to take his chances on the British police being more honest.

For a while Marti's nerve held, bolstered by the lawyer the British taxpayers provided. Hunt probed the cinema tale, tripping him up over the timing of when the film started and finished. By two-thirty in the morning he cracked and sheepishly confessed that he'd been hanging around Redcliffe Gardens, hoping to 'bump into' Grace.

Salminen's lawyer was clearly at sixes and sevens. You could see that he no longer trusted a flipping word that the lad said. Men like Salminen made Hunt's flesh crawl, believing they were God's gift to women, so sure that when girls resisted their advances they actually wanted it. With a powerful physique like his, he would easily overpower them. Hunt would have bet a year's pay that those incidents in Finland weren't the only times he'd forced himself on defenceless girls.

Now that he'd seen for himself what sort of man Salminen was, he was pretty sure what had happened. Although Salminen hadn't molested Grace sexually that night, it was more than likely that on some other occasion he *had*. It might even have been rape. Perhaps she was too shocked, too scared or too ashamed to report it. Then something changed her mind, some burst of courage or outrage, and, fatally, she told him what she'd do. He persuaded her to see him first, having made up his sick mind that if he couldn't talk her out of it he'd kill her.

Hunt waited until exhaustion had all but overwhelmed Marti before confronting him dramatically with this theory. The angry denial was to be expected, of course. It was obvious that he was playing for time, trying to work out what to say next, wriggling this way and that like a fox with one leg in a trap. Hunt was pretty sure he would've arm-wrestled a confession out of him there and then, if the lawyer hadn't been present. And this was the system that they called justice.

Grace Chesterfield hadn't got much justice, had she? When Marti had grabbed her in the back of that cab, Grace hadn't been able to call for a lawyer to defend her. Sure, the Finn was within his rights opting for silence, as his lawyer now advised him. Hunt had some prerogatives too, though. Like to withdraw for a while, talk it over with Wear, and ignore the words of caution from that fool Long. He might not have a confession yet, there might still be a few missing items of evidence, but what he *did* have on his side was thirty years of experience screaming that this was their man. With all due solemnity he marched back in there and announced they were charging Marti Salminen with the murder of Grace Chesterfield.

They got it out on the newswires by seven on Wednesday morning, in time to capture the headlines on the breakfast news.

*

Rosco Sellars flew right off the Richter scale when he heard what she'd done. He expected loyalty, respect, obedience from anyone he hired. Before he left for Zurich on Tuesday, he sat with her for over an hour, listening patiently to her girlish worries. He assured her it was all garbage. When that had no effect, he switched to stern words about not making trouble. Though Julia didn't confirm it in so many words, by the time their meeting broke up, he was pretty sure she'd seen sense.

On the way back from Heathrow on Wednesday morning, Rosco heard the news that should have clinched it in Julia's mind: the police had arrested a Scandinavian, a guy with no banking connection. Yet before his car reached Belgravia, what did he get? A message that the police wanted his comments on something Julia Daventry had reported to Sergeant Wear.

As soon as he got into his flat, Sellars rang Wear and was mightily relieved to hear that the police were only going through the motions, taking Julia's theories with a large helping of salt. Wear was friendly to the point of being chatty. He confided that Superintendent Hunt was 'over the moon' about the apprehension of the Finn. They had been under huge pressure: London was still in uproar over the incident, with politicians, bishops, and other do-gooders weighing in. The papers were serving up stale stories of minicab assaults. Fear was in the air. This was one murder that simply couldn't be allowed to go unsolved. Under such a spotlight, to find a suspect through a deft combination of old-fashioned detective work and international cooperation was deeply satisfying. In strictest confidence, Wear told Rosco that the Commissioner himself had called Hunt to pass on a quiet word of congratulation from the Home Secretary.

Sellars added his own commendation and proceeded to bend Wear's willing ear to his view that Julia Daventry tended to get carried away. It was a bit of a woman thing, if Sergeant Wear

191

knew what he meant. They finished the call on very amicable terms. By the time Sellars began dialling Skidders's head of personnel, his friendly smile had given way to a steely-set jaw and ice-hard eyes.

*

Julia Daventry was feeling uncomfortable. She knew how cross Rosco would be if he found she'd ignored his request. She had wrestled with her conscience all night long, failed to best it and, not without misgivings, set off for her early appointment with Superintendent Hunt.

If she'd listened to the radio and heard that they'd tracked down a suspect, she would have thought better of it. She didn't know that the arrest had changed everything for the police. With Hunt now too busy to see her, she was fobbed off with a sergeant. Faced with his obvious scepticism, she wilted. Even to her own ears, her 'information' sounded hopelessly vague.

The sergeant mentioned nothing of the Finn, and she was back at the bank before she saw on Bloomberg that he'd been charged. It took a moment to realize who he was, that he was *that* Marti, the scumbag from Shipshape. Her first emotion was remorse that she hadn't pressed Grace to go to the police about those letters. Then she felt faintly surprised. Marti had been sleazy, no question of that, and it was easy to imagine him reacting badly to rejection. Did he look like a murderer, though? She had a lot of work to catch up on, and decided to put it out of her mind.

The phone call a few hours later sent a thousand volts through her. Why did the head of personnel want to see her immediately? She'd only met him once, when she and the rest of Rosco's team were finalizing their packages. And why wouldn't his secretary tell her what it was about?

Feeling suddenly chilly, the roof of her mouth strangely parched, Julia made her way to the second floor. The secretary told her to wait on the bench outside. It felt uncomfortably like being sent for punishment at school. The door to the personnel

192

guy's office was closed and had no windows. At one moment she thought she heard a New York accent penetrating the plasterboard. Her blood chilled at the thought that Rosco might be in there. Christ, what was this about? Had he found out about the police? She was badly rattled now. She had witnessed Rosco's temper before, seen him fire an associate so brutally that the poor young guy had burst into tears in front of all of them. When he got in that state, Rosco became an animal, vicious and unrestrainable. If he was in there, that room would be more like a lion's den than a head teacher's study. She was made to wait another ten minutes before the secretary told her to go in.

He *was* there. Julia's hands shook uncontrollably as she sat down to face the Inquisition. The personnel guy invited Sellars to speak. She could see that Rosco was shaking too, with a cold fury. The volcano's cap could blow at any time. She tried desperately to shore up her feelings. Whatever this was about, she had done nothing wrong. Going to the police wasn't breaking any company rules. It was a matter for her own conscience. Then Julia looked at Rosco and the icy blast of his hatred blew out the slender, flickering flame of resistance, and she felt only fear.

'Julia, I thought you said you'd drop it.'

'I didn't say that. I only agreed to think over what you said.'

'And proceed to *ignore* it?' He was near boiling point already.

'I did what I thought right. I'm not sure it's anybody else's business.'

'In case you haven't noticed, this bank's been going through some lean times. Our reputation's shot to pieces, staff morale is at an all-time low, and many of our best people are heading for the door. Then, to cap it all, we get a murder. If anyone thinks it's connected with our business, it's the final nail in our coffin. Now, we all know that there's no link whatsoever, and fortunately the police here are a lot smarter than where I come from. The case will be wrapped up in double quick time, and our clients can stop worrying that if they share a cab with someone from Skidders, they may never live to pay the fare. So everything's dandy, except

193

that one troublemaker runs along to the police and suggests they let this Finnish guy go and give everyone at Skidders the fifth degree instead.'

'I didn't say that. I didn't even *know* about the Finn.'

'Bull*shit*, no one could've missed that. It was *everywhere*.'

'Well, *I* missed it.'

'I don't believe that for one fuckin' minute.'

The head of personnel looked hugely embarrassed. Julia guessed that he'd implored Rosco not to lose his cool. She decided to address her next comments to him.

'May I ask why I've been brought down here? Are you suggesting that this is some sort of disciplinary offence? Am I about to be reprimanded or something?'

He cleared his throat.

'Not quite. As you know, Julia, investment banking is all about team play and trust. Rosco feels very let down by your behaviour and believes you wilfully disregarded the interests of the bank.'

'I'm truly sorry that Rosco feels that way. I assure you that I will do my best to rebuild his trust in me, if he'll give me the chance.'

'We feel it has gone beyond that. Rosco thinks that the relationship has broken down irretrievably, that working with you in future will be impossible.'

'So what are you saying? You want me to move out of his team and work somewhere else in the bank?'

He couldn't look her in the eye as he said it.

'We have considered whether there are any options of that sort and have concluded that at the moment there is nothing . . . suitable.'

Julia gasped. 'You don't mean you're *firing* me?' Now she was having no problem getting some spirit going. This was outrageous. 'Well, that's going to cost you. You guaranteed me two years' bonus. As long as I get every penny of bonus and salary for that period, you can do what you like.'

The personnel guy kept staring down at his desk. It was Rosco who weighed back in.

'If you think that, after what you've done, you're walking off with a huge bunch of money, you have another fuckin' think coming, lady. You're fired, *period*. At this very moment, a security guard is putting your personal things in a bin liner and bringing them down here. You'll get paid till the end of the month, and not one penny more.'

Julia's eyes flashed.

'You can't do this, Rosco. This isn't Wall Street. There are laws here to stop employers behaving that way. If you don't pay what's due to me, I'll sue the hell out of Skidders. Now, *that* would be great publicity for the bank, wouldn't it?'

Nothing could have been more calculated to make the volcano blow its top. She got the full spitting, table-thumping blast.

'You sue Skidders, and I'll make sure you never work in investment banking again. And if you *ever* threaten me again about bad publicity, you wait and see what I'll do to *your* reputation.'

The personnel man looked mystified. For Julia the meaning was immediately and painfully clear. That sexually charged, champagne-laden night in New York, they had gone back to her place. Rosco had produced from his briefcase a 'little surprise' in the shape of a Polaroid camera. For over an hour she'd refused, but another bottle and burgeoning lust had made off with whatever remained of her sense. First she posed bra-less, then pantie-less, and finally, to her later mortification, with a banana. At the time he'd promised faithfully that it was only to turn them both on, that he'd burn the shoots in the morning. And so he did – some – having stealthily concealed the most exotic snaps in his jacket pocket when she went to the bathroom.

Julia had never done anything so shaming in all her life, and the knowledge that the pictures had been destroyed only partly removed the horror of that memory. Rosco had let several months go by before letting her know, with a cruelly lascivious look, that he'd preserved one or two for his 'collection'. As she sat opposite him now, her hatred for him growing by the minute, she had no doubt what he meant, nor that if she crossed him again nothing would stop him posting those pictures in glorious colour on the

Internet and making sure that every banker in the world checked out the site. She was beaten.

She went very quiet as a document was produced describing the severance process. As soon as she'd signed her agreement, Sellars left the room without so much as a glance at her. The personnel man mumbled a half-apology and stood up himself to indicate that the meeting was over. Very slowly, Julia rose, shuffled out, and saw there on the bench a bin liner bag containing all that remained of her investment banking career.

*

As Einstein drew up outside Len's house in the early afternoon, he could see Terry's cab coming down the street. They nodded to each other and waited for Len to come to the door, both subdued and aware that this would be their grimmest and maybe last counsel of war. Even without what they'd heard on the news, the outlook was bleak. Jowell's share price had weakened again. Deprived of Daphne's vital input, getting fares with the key players at Skidders was difficult and their hunger for new information went unsatisfied. Now things were getting worse. Poppy's condition had worsened again. She didn't sleep and had lost more weight. From the first moment they learnt of the hunt for the Finn, the pall of troubled conscience hung heavily on them all, and the news that he'd been formally charged removed any hope that this was a clever police feint.

Jean was out shopping, so Len made the tea himself, sat them down in the lounge and opened proceedings.

'So . . . what the 'ell do we do now?'

Einstein tried to keep open a crack in the door.

'Look, he may be a gym attendant, but that doesn't mean he couldn't know about Jowell. Perhaps *she* told him. Perhaps he has rich friends who invested on the strength of that. If cabbies can invest, why shouldn't gym attendants?'

They didn't believe a word of it, and he got no response. Terry was feeling especially miserable.

'It's okay for the both of you. What 'appens if they find out I

196

told them a load of old bollocks? I didn't mention this before, 'cause I reckoned there were enough other things to worry about, but I think I'm bein' followed.'

Len laughed dismissively.

'Bollocks. You've got a James Bond complex, that's all. Terry Thorogood, licensed to ply.'

Terry didn't join in the joke. In fact, he was well narked.

'I *mean* it, Len. And if the coppers are followin' me around, they'll soon work out we're in this together. As long as we can 'elp Poppy, I'll take me chances, but if them options ain't worth the paper they're printed on now, I'm for tellin' the truth.'

Einstein tried again.

'I know it's looking bad, but the options don't expire for more than three weeks. We'd be *mad* to give the game away before then. What d'you say, Len?'

'I don't really know *what* to say, to tell the truth. We're in pretty deep doodoo, Terry in particular. And if this Finn they've nicked is innocent, we're aidin' and abettin' the real murderer gettin' away.'

'Can I make a suggestion, then? For a few more days we try to get information on what's happening with Jowell. If we fail, we sell the options quickly for whatever they're worth, and draw a halt to the whole racket. And if it looks like they might find the Finn guilty, we find a way to let the police know they've got the wrong man.'

Terry shrugged.

'It's your call, Len. Poppy's your gel. If you want to keep goin' a bit longer, I'll stick with you.'

Len nodded. 'Okay, let's do like Einstein says.'

Suddenly came another sound.

'*No.*'

All three tensed. The door to the hall was very slightly ajar. Terry was first out of his seat to get at the door handle. He pulled it open.

'*Bleedin' 'ell.*'

She was huddled on the floor, a crumpled little bag of bones.

The effort of dragging herself down the stairs had exhausted her, but from somewhere she'd found the strength to fight back the coughs while she listened. All three men were standing in the doorway now. Len pushed past Terry and leant down to her.

'Jesus, Poppity, what the 'ell are you doin' down 'ere?'

She glared back.

'Carry me in there. I want a word with you three.'

'No way, pet, I'm takin' you right back upstairs to your bed. You'll catch you death down 'ere.'

'*NO.*'

There was a passion in her voice and eyes that cowed him. Without another word, he picked her up and carried her through to one of the easy chairs. Terry needed no bidding and nipped up the stairs to fetch a blanket from her room. She waited impatiently while Len arranged it around her. Then she opened *her* meeting.

'You all think that 'cause I'm sick I've got no idea what's goin' on. Well, I know more than you think. You lot was involved in the cab murder, wasn't you? *Wasn't you?*'

She was in no mood to be messed around, and took her Dad's silence as agreement.

'And it was Terry what was drivin', wasn't it? That's why you and Mum were up the whole night and why Einstein and Ruth came over. I'm right, ain't I?'

Terry nodded sheepishly.

'That Finnish fella didn't do it, did 'e? You know that and you're not tellin'. That's what you was sayin' just now, I 'eard you. Well, if this is what you're doin' to get me to California, I ain't *never* goin' there. Unless you go and tell the truth, I'll call the police meself and I'll never talk to any of you again.'

Einstein had a stab at appealing to her reason.

'Look, Poppy, if we tell the truth, it doesn't only mean that you can't go to America. Terry may go to prison, and your Dad'll lose his job. Where will we all be then?'

Poppy scrunched up her fists into tight little balls and yelled as loud as her damaged lungs would permit.

'*I don't CARE.*' Tears began to roll down her face. Len knelt in front of her.

'Okay, love, we'll do what you want, if that's all right with Terry.'

Terry nodded again.

''Course, if that's what Poppy wants.'

Len picked Poppy up and took her upstairs to bed. It was twenty minutes before he came down again. He looked in a bad way.

'Terry, I'm not lettin' you do this alone. It was all on account of *my* gel. If you're goin' to tell the coppers the truth, I'm comin' with you.' He turned to Einstein. 'No need for you to get caught up in this, mate.'

Einstein slowly shook his head,

'D'you think I could live with that? Taping the punters was my idea. It was me that got us into this mess. Can it wait till tomorrow, though? Ruth's at work and I don't want to tell her over the phone.'

'Don't see why not, if it's all the same to Terry.'

Terry managed a brave smile.

'Yeah, I'll go and find some gel to give me a last shag before Pentonville. 'Ow will Jean take it, Len?'

'She'll be bleedin' *thrilled*. I think I'll go out for a while, and collect me thoughts before she gets back.'

20

Terry *was* being followed. He'd only been gone from Len's house for two or three minutes and was driving towards Gant's Hill roundabout when he saw in his mirror another cab steaming up behind him, its headlights flashing off and on like a firework show. He slowed enough to let it catch up, to see what the song and dance was about. As it drew level on the outside of him, he saw it was Einstein, signalling urgently for him to pull over. What the hell did he want now?

Terry braked to a halt. Einstein darted in behind him, jumped out of the cab and scampered like an excited puppy the few yards along to where Terry sat.

'Any idea where Len would have gone, Terry?'

'To Tommy, most likely.'

'You know where that is?'

'Yeah. Why?'

'I've had an idea. Let's get after Len. I'll follow you.'

He skipped back to his cab, flashing impatiently at Terry to get moving.

It took ten or fifteen minutes for them to get there. It was situated depressingly, without dignity, on a slight rise above a noisy road. Buses and lorries rumbled by, doing their best to wreck the contemplation of visitors. Most of the graves were still covered in the grimy remains of the weekend snow. The two of them made their way along long rows before they saw him standing in a far corner, wearing only a sweater against the biting wind.

Len didn't turn around as they approached and, stopping a few feet behind him, they stayed quiet until his reverie ended. Even when he sensed they were there, he kept on staring at the stone.

'He would've been twenty-one next month.'

Terry nodded, unseen by Len.

'Yeah, we would've 'ad a right old knees-up for 'im down the Spreadeagle . . . Len, mate, Einstein's got another idea.'

'Bit late for that, ain't it?'

'Give 'im a chance, Len . . . We don't want to drag you away from Tommy, but in case this takes a while, would it be all right if we sat in one of the cabs? It's bleedin' brass monkeys out 'ere.'

They sat in Len's cab for more than an hour. Len took a hell of a lot of persuading even to *think* of trying it on Poppy. However, twenty minutes later the little delegation was trooping solemnly into her room.

Poppy looked hostile, unyielding. Her eyes were still red from the tears, and her mood hadn't softened one jot. It was obvious they were going to try something on, try to wriggle out of their promise, and she was damned if she was going to let them get away with it. She set the tone right away.

'What the 'ell do you want now? I've *told* you what I've decided. You try to back out and I'll call the police, you see if I don't.'

Terry sat down on the bed and took one of her hands in his. She tried to snatch it away, none too convincingly. She had a big crush on him.

'No one's backin' out of anythin', Poppy. It's just that clever old Einstein's thought up a way we can do what's right without landin' your Dad – *and* me – in deep shit. All we want is for you to listen. If you don't agree with Einstein's plan, I'll go straight to the police, like we promised. See what you think, that's all.'

Poppy pulled a grumpy face.

'I'll give 'im five minutes.'

Einstein smiled gratefully.

'Thanks, Poppy. My idea . . . it's simple really. How clever d'you think the average policeman is?'

Poppy frowned. 'Pig-thick.'

Einstein grinned.

201

'*Exactly*. So even if we tell them everything we know, it doesn't amount to much. For instance, we have no idea who did it, what age he is, or what he looks like. All we can say for sure is the murderer may be involved in business with her. And if you're right that the police aren't so smart, it's pretty unlikely that such a small piece of information will help them catch the murderer.'

Poppy looked doubtful. 'At least they won't keep that Marti fella in the nick, if they know 'e 'ad nothin' to do with it.'

Einstein shook his head vigorously. 'We can't even be sure of that. After all, he *could* have had business dealings with her.'

'*You* don't think so.'

Einstein was willing to concede that one.

'True. However, what *we* think may not interest the police very much. Don't forget, they got all that credit for catching him. It'll be hard for them to admit they were wrong.'

Poppy crossed her arms.

'So what *is* this brainwave of yours, Einstein?'

'It's that we should solve the murder ourselves.'

'*What*? *You* three? When I said coppers was stupid, I didn't say they was any thicker than cabbies. You may be smart, Einstein, 'cause you're a nerd, but Dad and Terry can 'ardly sign their own names. What do you three know about detective work?'

Einstein had anticipated that one, and slickly supplied his answer.

'There are so many detective programmes on TV, we all know how to go about it. It's easy: lots of legwork and a little deduction. I've always fancied myself as a bit of a Sherlock Holmes.'

'Oh *yeah*? So Dad's that divvy doctor, is that it? And what does that leave for Terry to do, eh? Bonk all the gels on the jury?'

Terry looked miffed. Einstein rubbed salt in his wound.

'You know, that's rather a good idea, Poppy. Shall we call him Sergeant Shagger?'

This time Poppy couldn't prevent a smile escaping.

'You see, Poppy, the only clue we have is a deal the girl was working on for her bank. Either the bank doesn't know about this

202

connection, or they may be keeping quiet about it. No one will find out the truth unless they get closer to Skidder Barton. Now, there we *do* have a head start on the police, because we know which people worked with her on that deal. Apart from that, the real beauty of my plan is that, while we're hunting down the killer, we could hang on to our little investment and try to get you to San Francisco after all.'

They all waited tensely for the verdict. Still she said nothing. Len spoke up.

'Poppity, love, if you don't like Einstein's plan, or don't think we've any chance of pullin' it off, you just say, and we'll go right to the police, like I promised.'

'I'll give you two weeks. All right?'

Terry pleaded.

'These things take time, doll. Give us a couple of months.'

'*One* month, that's my best offer.' She turned and looked at the Liverpool calendar up on her wall. 'That takes you to Christmas. If Green Badge Valley's answer to Scotland Yard ain't cracked it by then, it's over to the police. Promise?'

They all said 'Promise' in unison. Len gave her a big kiss, and Terry and Einstein lined up to do the same. Then it was back downstairs to the lounge for a strategy session.

Len's euphoria evaporated as soon as he began to think about the practicalities.

'Just 'ow *are* we goin' to work out what's goin' on at Skidders, Einstein?'

'Yeah?' contributed Terry.

'Give me time. I haven't had a chance to work out a plan yet. Come to think of it, Poppy's suggestion for Terry may make sense.'

'What you mean, Einstein? I'm in enough bother already. I ain't tamperin' with no jury.'

'Don't worry, I wasn't thinking of the jury; it's *secretaries* I had in mind. We could find out the name of the secretary to that Ford, and you could do a Daphne on her.'

Len chortled. 'Gives a whole new meaning to "private dick", don't it?'

Terry wasn't sure he would take much more of this.

'You can both piss off. At least at Control Cabs I got me pick of the gels. I ain't goin' on no blind date. What if she's married?'

Len knew too much about Terry's track record to let him get away with that one. He recited some of the residents of Green Badge Valley known to have been cuckolded.

'Whatever you both say, I'm not doin' it. I've got me principles too . . . Unless you can prove she's under thirty and tasty with it, I ain't droppin' me pants again.'

*

Julia Daventry sat alone in her flat. The bottle of Peter Michael *Point Rouge* Sonoma Chardonnay that she'd kept for a special occasion stood empty. She checked what else there was to drink. Two fingers of vermouth. Plenty of gin, and no tonic. An almost-full bottle of whisky. She hated the stuff; it was only there for guests. Nothing else. She looked at her watch. Past midnight. The little shop down the street might still be open; they would have something. She made it as far as the front door, where the sight of the pouring rain put her off. She turned on her heels and went to the fridge, snapped half a dozen ice cubes from the white plastic tray and drowned them in a huge tumblerful of Scotch. The first gulp provoked a great grimace. After a few more, she began to get used to the taste. Either that, or too anaesthetized to care.

She felt very friendless. Apart from Grace, there'd been no one at the bank she was close to. If she told her parents, they would be sympathetic, of course, but they would worry themselves silly. This would affect them, too. The two years of guaranteed bonuses from Skidders would have paid off the last of their debts, as well as providing the start of some net worth for herself. Now all that was gone. Oh *fuck*, what a mess. If her parents asked what she planned to do next, she wouldn't have an answer. She'd have to keep it from them, play for time, until she had some sort of game plan. She should make sure they didn't call her at work and find out that way. Better say she was away on a project or something.

As she swallowed more whisky, the wish to strike back at Rosco grew. But as long as he had those photos, he'd have a hold over her. Where would they be? Since he boasted about having a 'collection', perhaps he kept them with proof of other conquests in an album? Would he risk leaving them in his apartment in New York where his bitch of a wife might discover them? No, they *must* be in London; possibly in his desk at work, more likely in his flat. She fantasized about breaking in there and taking them.

She'd been to Rosco's place for his flat-warming party. There was a concierge who would be hard to get past. Even if she managed that, there was still the problem of getting into the flat and finding the album.

She poured herself another whisky. For all that she'd so far knocked back, she wasn't yet properly drunk. She had no sleeping pills and, in her emotional state, nothing but alcoholic stupor would provide any prospect of rest that night.

As she put on a CD of Chopin nocturnes, her mind drifted to why Rosco had reacted so venomously. She could see why he might not want her on his team, but why had he been *so* determined that she shouldn't be offered another job in the bank? What the personnel guy had said was garbage. Skidders were leaking people like a sieve; to suggest that she couldn't add value somewhere was ridiculous. So why? The more she thought about it, the more convinced she grew that he *must* have something to hide. The nagging doubt wouldn't leave her. Marcus had been a bit odd, too. He'd seemed ill at ease, almost *too* quick to deny any knowledge of what might have troubled Grace.

She thought more about the creepy Finn. Were his fingerprints in the cab? Had the cabbie identified him in one of those line-ups, or picked up his foreign intonation? There had to be something of that sort: surely it couldn't only be those pervert letters? How she'd love to have a chat with that cabbie.

Was there any way she could find out his name? There was no point in asking Control Cabs. The police would have warned them to tell no one. Hang on, though. The cabbie would surely have told other cabbies; by now, quite a few of them must know his identity. If she could find just one of those. It would take luck, perseverance and, winter weather notwithstanding, a very short skirt.

How would she do it? Book a whole host of rides and ask every driver? Or try one of those green cabbie shelters you saw all over town? Were ordinary people allowed in there?

She'd damn well give it a crack in the morning. Feeling better for having some sort of plan of action, she crawled off to bed. By two-thirty she was still wide awake. At three she got up, put on something very figure-clinging, went out in the rain, flagged down a cab and astonished the driver by asking him to drop her off at the nearest cabbie shelter.

It turned out to be the one opposite the Victoria & Albert museum. The cabbie did better than drop her off. After taking a good look at her in his mirror, he developed a sudden thirst, decided he needed a cuppa, and gallantly escorted her in. Inside it was surprisingly bright, with a little kitchenette at one end and a few narrow formica tables at the other. When one older cabbie looked up and saw Julia come in, he spilt his tea all over himself. The others were edgy and unwelcoming at first, but her long slim legs and plunging neckline gradually worked their own magic. They weren't able to answer her question, but the encounter cured her of stage fright and gave her the confidence to go on her own to another fourteen shelters in the next twenty-four hours.

*

Normally, Dieter Manz expected hired help to come to him. However, since he was passing through London on other business on the twenty-seventh of November, he had no objection to calling into Skidders's offices for lunch. On hearing his plan, Ernst Lautenschutz immediately flew over from Zurich to join them.

In the bad old days in the City, business was never discussed until the port or brandies were poured. When brandies disappeared, the critical moment switched to the coffee, and later to the main course. Now it starts at the starter. Manz asked his first question before taking even one mouthful.

'So gentlemen, how do you think the Jowell share price will perform between now and the time we launch?'

Rosco deferred to Marcus on this one.

'The price has been weak for the last two weeks. If the market knew what we know about the big orders Jowell will win, you'd expect it to rise very sharply. Luckily, those orders shouldn't be confirmed in time to have any effect. And as we've agreed, if the price *does* start moving up, we'll leak the information our special source also provided about the poor yields in their semi-conductor division. That should dampen things down again for a while.'

Manz looked pleased. 'Good, so it's all under control. We will not have to pay too high a price.'

Neither Marcus nor Rosco were certain that Manz had understood their many patient explanations. It was Rosco's turn to try again.

'Dieter, did we run the concept of a takeover premium past you last time? Jowell's shareholders have a high degree of loyalty to Austin. To get them to forget about that, we'll have to offer a *minimum* of forty per cent above market price. Think fifty and you'll be safer.'

Manz looked sharply at him.

'Mr Sellars, I am well aware that, since investment bankers are paid by success, you try to persuade clients to pay a high price to ensure that the deal goes through. This strikes me as a strange definition of success. I will regard this transaction as successful *only* if Burlikon pays not one penny more than is absolutely necessary. And let me tell you right now, I have no intention of paying a premium of anything *like* fifty per cent. The highest I would contemplate is thirty per cent over market. So you'd better make up your mind. Can Skidder Barton earn its extortionate fees by delivering Jowell to me at that price, or shall I go to another bank?'

What a goddam jerk, thought Sellars. He *hated* doing business with Europeans; give him Americans any day. At the sort of price Manz was proposing, there was only one sure way to be successful: get lots of dirt on Jowell and their top management and leak it judiciously, so their reputation was trashed and the fight was knocked out of them.

'It'll be tight, *very* tight. However, I think we can pull it off. What d'you say, Marcus?'

By now Marcus had learned enough of Rosco's methods not to take everything too literally. Rosco must have a reason for this wild optimism, so he'd better go along with it.

'I agree.'

Manz was pleased. He'd shown these Anglo-Saxon mechanics that he was not to be fooled with.

'And our proposed timing is no problem either, Mr Sellars?'

'We would've preferred to go sooner. The longer we wait, the bigger the chance of a leak or a rise in the Jowell share price. However, we accept you have your reasons to wait until after Christmas.'

Manz turned to Ernst.

'Herr Lautenschutz, I presume from this comment that the gentlemen are aware of your own plans for Skidders.'

Lautenschutz nodded.

'Ja, Herr Doktor Manz, in the circumstances we concluded that it was important that they *should* know. However, they are the only two personnel here to know that we will buy Skidders. Mr Sellars will have a significant role to play in the new organization.'

'So the schedule is unchanged? Zuricher will bid for Skidders on the twenty-ninth of December, and we will launch the next day?'

'Correct. If the Barton family will not sell, we will postpone our own bid for some months and wait for some fresh disaster to persuade the fools. Either way, nothing will delay your launch on the thirtieth.'

'Good.' Abruptly, Manz put down his knife and fork. 'Now, if you will excuse me, I must leave. Herr Lautenschutz, would you accompany me to the elevator? I want a word in private.'

Stiffly, he shook hands with Sellars and Ford and left. A mystified Lautenschutz followed him. Ernst was concerned that something had displeased Manz, so the explanation, delivered in guttural Swiss German as they rode down in the lift, relieved him mightily.

'Forgive me for rushing out like that. I could not stand the American's barbaric table manners one moment longer.'

Lautenschutz smiled.

'We hire them for their talents, not their social skills. They are like the guard dogs at my house: provided they bark loud and bite hard, who cares if they slobber a little? If you have time, why don't we lunch at the Savoy?'

'An excellent idea.'

*

'Einstein, you workin'?'

'What d'you want, Terry?'

'I just got a call out of the blue from the Daventry girl. Says she wants to book a cab for the whole of tonight, and will I do it? So I ask, why don't she just ring Control Cabs? She says it's too expensive – which is fair enough, I s'pose – and will I do a deal?'

'What did you say?'

'Said I'd think about it. Told 'er to ring back in a few minutes. D'you think the coppers put 'er up to it?'

'Definitely. How else would she have found out your number? They probably want her to get you talking about Grace, to see if you know more than you told them.'

'Should I say no, then, Einstein?'

'Hold on.' Einstein put his phone down while he negotiated Hyde Park Corner. It gave him time to think. 'Saying no would be safest. On the other hand, she does work at Skidders, and we *do* need to get more idea what's going on there. As long as you're on your guard and say nothing more than you told the police, it's hard to see what the danger could be. And you might

209

be able to turn the tables and get something out of her. Be careful what you say, though. They might have wired her for sound, like in films.'

'Okay. I'd better get off, in case she's tryin' to get through.'

'Best of luck, then. Oh, Terry.'

'What, mate?'

'You'll find your brain works better if you keep your under-wear on.'

21

Julia found her frustration rising. It was midnight, and they'd been driving aimlessly around for three and a half hours, from landmark to useless landmark. He turned down her offer of sharing a bite to eat. He didn't seem to want to talk, and looked preoccupied and nervous. She virtually had to *order* him to join her for a drink at a bar in Brompton Cross, and then all he would take was a fruit juice. Had she put him on the defensive by admitting that she'd tracked him down deliberately? Julia couldn't see any other way she could get him talking about the night of the murder. However, he seemed to have little to say beyond what had been reported in the papers. She'd hoped he harboured doubts about whether Marti was guilty; he seemed to have no opinion either way. Every time she raised it, he wriggled off the subject of the murder and turned the conversation to banalities, like life at Skidders. Had that been another mistake, pretending she still worked there? Perhaps if she'd explained why she'd been fired, he might have opened up more.

Might he have alerted the police about her call? Was that what he was doing when he asked for time to think about it? Had they told him to go ahead, but to take care what he said? Could they be trying to find out she was up to, telling him to quiz her about Skidders? They might even have wired him for sound, like in the movies. She'd better be careful, and above all steer clear of names. If she voiced any suspicions about Rosco, and the police passed them on, her naked body would be international public property within the hour.

What should she do now? There wasn't much point in continuing this purposeless, expensive journey round London.

She told him to head for her flat, and fell silent until they arrived. Terry turned round.

'Okay, love. 'Undred quid, we agreed.'

'Of course.' She rooted around in her handbag and took out six twenty-pound notes. 'Thank you. Would you do me a favour? . . . We've had a lot of break-ins round here recently. I'm rather frightened, especially after the murder. Would you mind coming up to the flat, to check everything's all right?'

Terry wasn't sure he should. He hadn't found out anything, but so far he hadn't screwed up either. She was a definite looker, this one, and he could never trust himself when he got indoors with a tasty number. On the other hand, she was so proper, so upper-class, it was less likely he'd find his hand up her skirt. He parked, locked the cab, and trailed up two flights of stairs.

He'd never been in a place like this. It wasn't that it was big: it was the way it was done up. It was real tasteful – in a girlie sort of way, admittedly – all gentle colours and soft lighting. Smelt nice, too, like her. As soon as they got in, she announced she was making some coffee and disappeared into the kitchen. Terry filled in the time by going for a piss, then settled down in a comfortable armchair.

Should he make some excuse and leave quickly? He no longer felt quite so keen to rush away. It was nice here. As long as he stayed on his guard, like Einstein had said, what was the harm in having a coffee?

She brought in a tray, and spooned in three sugars for him. She took hers black and curled up with it on the carpet right beneath him. As she sipped it, she looked gently up at him. That made him feel kind of . . . well, something or other.

'Terry? Is it all right if I call you that? There's something I wasn't quite honest about. I don't work at Skidders any more.'

'*What*?' If Terry hadn't been sitting, he could've been knocked over with a feather.

'I was sacked earlier this week.'

'Why the 'ell . . . ?'

'For asking questions about Grace.'

Terry gulped and spilt coffee on the carpet.

'Shit . . . sorry.'

'Don't worry.' She ran off and got a cloth. 'There, it won't show. You see, the day she died, Grace told me that something at work was worrying her. I told the police, and Skidders fired me for that.'

'What a bummer.'

'I've been wondering if they did it to stop me digging around. I thought maybe you could help me understand what *really* happened that night.'

Terry frowned. What the hell was he supposed to say now? This could be a trick, to lull him into telling more. What did she take him for? She wasn't going to fool him *that* easily. Then he had a brainwave, one worthy of Einstein. If it was true what she'd said, there was no reason for her not to level with him about the Jowell bid.

'What was Grace workin' on when she died? Was it a takeover bid?'

Julia was perplexed. Why should a cabbie care about that? This must be something he'd been put up to, to see if she would divulge confidential information. On the other hand, if she refused to reply, she wasn't going to get much out of him, either. In this case it helped that she truthfully didn't know.

'I *think* it was some sort of bid. For a Continental client, if I recall. You see, we have to keep things secret in that department, even from each other.'

Bollocks. They'd been on the same team, hadn't they? Terry decided to go for broke.

'She was in the cab once before, you know, with some other fella. I thought they mentioned a bid for a company called Jowell.'

Julia's intake of breath was audible. This was definitely a put-up job and, in case he *was* wired, she'd better make absolutely clear that this project was no longer alive.

'Oh, there was a project called something like that, and Grace *did* work on it. Me too, as a matter of fact. But that project died a death before Grace did.'

213

'Oh, I see.' What a lying bitch, Terry was thinking. Julia tried again.

'That night, did Grace mention anything about work?'

'Not that I recall.'

Bullshit. She could see from his eyes he was lying. She would damn well find out if he was wired. She moved an inch or two closer, and dropped her voice an octave to super-husky.

'Terry, I don't suppose I'm the first woman to find you rather handsome.'

'*What*?'

Julia reached up and put a hand on his thigh.

'You *are. Very.*'

He couldn't stop himself gurgling contentedly. He looked down at her legs. Her short black skirt had sort of ridden up and there was a lot of thigh showing. Soft, slim, *nice* thigh.

'You're not bad-lookin' yourself. Who's your squeeze? Some rich banker, I s'pose?'

Terry was sitting with his legs spread wide apart. Julia slid gracefully forward until she was all but nestling between them.

'I don't have anyone at the moment. I only moved here from New York a few months ago, and I was so busy at the bank that there wasn't a lot of time for social life.'

'Well, that'll be easier now, eh?'

Julia laughed. 'That's true. Is there someone special in *your* life?'

He had to play this one carefully. Better not sound *too* available.

'Well, yeah . . . sort of. Depends 'ow special you mean.'

Julia's head moved to one side until it rested on one of Terry's knees.

'Are you in love?'

'Nah, nothin' like that. I *was* . . . with me ex-fiancée. At least, I *think* I was. Tell the truth, I didn't 'ave much choice in the matter. She would've given me 'ell otherwise.'

They both paused to take sips of coffee. Julia looked up at him again. A few moments later, Terry felt himself beginning to tingle. Ever so delicately, she was using the fingers of one hand to

214

kind of massage his thigh. He tried to put it out of his mind: the last thing he needed was to lose control now. On the other hand, he *did* need to touch her to feel for any wires that might be taped to her. Where would she have them? Didn't look like it was on her legs. They could be on her back, of course, somewhere around her stomach, or in the tit zone. The very thought of that started him off again, and her fingers were still weaving their sultry magic. Better get on with checking her out while he still had a cool head.

He reached down, took hold of her shoulders and pulled her bodily up to him. She looked into his eyes, put her hand round to the back of his head and drew it gently to her. The kiss wasn't like the ones he was used to. It wasn't tonguey, or gobby, and her teeth didn't bang into his. It was soft, but very sexy. When she finally pulled way, he found himself craning forward in search of another. That one was nice, too. He didn't want to stop, and scarcely noticed her slipping open the top button of his shirt. What was she up to? He couldn't work her out. So posh and ladylike, but pretty flipping forward with it. Ten seconds later, she had all his shirt buttons undone and her hands were getting to grips with his chest and sides. She was kneeling upright now, working her hands all the way round to his back, while kissing him more. It gave her the perfect chance.

His back felt slightly spotty, but definitely unwired, and his black leather trousers looked too tight for a microphone to fit. She could stop now, she supposed, before he got too much of the wrong idea. Only she wasn't sure she wanted to. She felt his hands roughly yank the back of her blouse free of the thin black belt and start to stroke the base of her spine. It was over a month since she'd been touched by anyone. Another two minutes wouldn't hurt. He didn't look the date-rape type, so the downside was getting yelled at for being a prickteaser. Oh, that felt *nice*.

His hands were voyaging northwards now, and she felt his leading finger make landfall on her bra strap. Was it her imagination, or was he fingering the strap between his thumb and first finger? If he thought he'd slip it off one-handed, James Bond-style, he was in for a big surprise. She tried to suppress a grin.

215

Terry explored for a few more seconds before accepting that it really *was* just a bra strap. He looked at her. What was *she* smiling about? Oh shit, she must've thought he'd tried to get it off and failed. What was he meant to do now? Back off completely, or get his hand back up there and show he could do it? Male pride won out, and his hand shot up. He hadn't been trying for the clip before; where the hell was it? . . . Oh *no*, not a front-loader! Now she was giggling away openly.

'Need a little technical assistance, Terry?'

Before he could think of some cool reply, she began sliding loose her blouse buttons.

The bra was black, and the wiring was for uplift, not sound. The occupants looked . . . lovely. Sizewise, they were halfway between peaches and grapefruits. She smiled at him, saying nothing. He would have liked to return her steady gaze, but his eyes couldn't spare the time. His fingers began to twitch. He closed his eyes and thought of Einstein.

When he reopened them, she was pouting a little.

'Don't they appeal to you . . . ?'

Terry's throat had gone very dry, and he only managed a meaningless croak.

'You don't feel like touching them?'

He emitted a strange little squeak.

'Or is it that you're still not sure how bras unfasten? Shall I show you? . . .'

This time no sound would come out at all.

'It's easy, really.' Her hands met in the middle of her chest. 'You push it ever so slightly together, and it just pops open . . . like *this*.'

It was the first upper class deck he'd seen, and they were absolutely bleeding *magnificent*. These were tits worth missing a home game against Tottenham for. A massive force surged through him: it was as if her breasts had become magnetically charged and his hands were being pulled towards them by the power. He strained to keep them away. It was unbearable. Suddenly, the iron filings in his fingers flew at them.

216

Julia was shocked at herself for allowing it to go this far. Though he was more of a grabber than the well-schooled caressers she was used to, he was pretty damned sexy with it. She really had to stop it right here, or be willing to go to the brink and hope that it loosened his tongue.

Terry's brain was slowly being scrambled. With a superhuman effort, he wrenched his hands away to recover the power of thought. Len and Einstein would never forgive him if he told them that, instead of finding out anything, all he'd done was bonk her . . . Then again, what if he went ahead, showed her a bit of the old magic and made her lose some of that cool control? He was preaching to the easily converted. His hands went back to work and the kissing started in earnest.

There was little holding back on either side now. Julia unbuckled his belt, yanked his zip open and slid her hand inside. Terry let himself groan for a while, then reached out a hand to reciprocate. Instead, Julia stood up, took him by the hand – and led him through to the bedroom.

The contrast with his own bedroom was acute. In the low light from the two bedside lamps, everything looked so tidy. Julia let go his hand and stood back for a second to look at him properly. He grinned shyly, at a loss what to do. Oh, to hell with it, she *was* a girl, wasn't she? As fast as he could, he pulled off his remaining kit and, without much ado, did the same for her. They kissed again, much harder now. This was nearer to familiar territory for him. He marched her backwards over to the bed and, before he remembered about foreplay, there he was, bang inside her.

She'd meant to ask if he carried condoms. All the men she knew performed routine ten-minute touch-ups, so there was plenty of time to pop that kind of question, or propose other solutions. His direct approach took her totally by surprise. This was bloody risky. Risky and goddam wonderful. She was in serious danger of forgetting completely why he was here. Wasn't she supposed to be using his passion to get more info out of him?

217

'Terry, Terry . . .'

He froze.

'What is it, doll? Am I doin' somethin' wrong?'

She shook her head. 'Not at all. It's just that . . .'

'Julia?'

'What?'

'Be a good gel and give it a rest. I'm tryin' to concentrate . . .'

And he started again, putting an emphatic end to her questions.

They lay silent for a long while, her head resting gently on his curly-haired chest. He had almost drifted off when she said gently, 'Terry, can I tell you the truth?'

' 'Course, doll.'

'I thought that maybe you'd told the police about my call, and they'd asked you to check me out. Sounds silly, I know, but I thought you maybe had a microphone under your shirt.'

Terry snorted.

'What a daft idea.' Then his pride took a tumble. 'Is that the only reason you . . . ?'

Julia smiled. 'Yes. Though I *did* get a little carried away with my checking.'

Terry felt rather hurt. 'Well, I've got news for *you*. I thought the same.'

'*What*?'

'Yeah, when you gave me a bell, I thought it was the boys in blue puttin' you up to it. That's why I was makin' a berk of meself with your bra strap. I thought that was *your* wire.'

'Why would the police would set *you* up? You're not a suspect, and you told them everything you know . . . You *did*, didn't you?' Julia raised her head and looked carefully into his eyes.

'Yeah, yeah, 'course I did.'

Disappointed, she put her head back down on the pillow.

'I met him once, you know, that Finnish boy, Marti Salminen. He was odd, all right, and definitely a sleazeball. Grace told me he wrote her some weird letters. I imagine that's how the police

218

got hold of him in the first place.'

'I dunno. They never said nothin' to me about it. When I told 'em I didn't clock the geezer proper, they didn't even get me to do one of them – what you call 'em?'

'Identity parades?'

'Yeah, that's it.'

'You know, Terry, I haven't a shred of proof, but my instinct tells me that the Finnish boy isn't the murderer. Think about it, if you'd sent weirdo letters to some girl's home address, would you bump her off without checking that the letters had been destroyed? You'd be pointing the finger right at yourself, wouldn't you?'

'Yeah, don't make sense, do it? But if Marti ain't the murderer, then who *is*? Someone at Skidder Barton?' It was dawning on Terry that, if Julia wasn't a police stooge, she was just who they needed to get closer to the bank. Bonking her might've been a brainwave.

'If I knew that, I'd be back to the police at the speed of light. What I'd hoped was that there was something you saw or heard that night that would help me work out whether I'm on the right track.'

What a dilemma. Say nothing and he was safe. That would be the end, though. He'd get nothing more from her, and never see her again. He already knew he wanted to.

So how about taking his chances and spilling the beans? It *might* work, or it might land him in the nick. Could he borrow her dog-and-bone and ask Len or Einstein what to do? No, no, it might be bugged.

The conversation tailed off, and Julia propped herself up. Terry sensed that she was about to send him home. It was now or never. He decided to spill one bean.

'There *was* one thing. It's just come back to me. That company, Jowell–'

Julia's head swung round.

'I'm not altogether sure, mind, but she might've mentioned it again that night.'

219

'*What*? Grace mentioned Jowell – in your cab – that night? Terry, this is important. Did you tell the police?'

'Nah – I must've forgot.'

'*Forgotten*? – Are you *mad*?' There was fire in her eyes. Terry was regretting his move. *Shit*, why had he opened his big mouth? She jumped on top of him and stuck her face six inches from his.

'Why didn't you tell them?'

'Can't remember.'

'Answer properly.' Her right hand shot down and grabbed hold of his balls. '*Answer* . . . or I'll . . .' She squeezed harder. Terry yelped.

'*Leggo* . . .'

Even harder.

'O-*kay*.' His voice was falsetto. She relaxed her grip a fraction.

'Come on, then.'

'Give me a second to get me breath back.'

She rolled off him and let Terry nurse the bruised prisoners. He felt all hot and squeamish. It was the last time he would tangle with a posh gel. Even Marcie never grabbed him as hard as *that*.

'So, let's hear it. How come you didn't tell the police?'

'I didn't think it was important.'

'You didn't think it was *important*? You hear that the murderer has a connection with Grace's work, yet you don't think it's important? Just what *is* your game, Terry? Clearly there's something going on here that I don't understand.'

Suddenly she shuddered and voiced the thought before realizing the risk.

'My *God*, you weren't *involved*, were you? You didn't–' Christ, she might be lying naked beside a cold-blooded murderer.

They looked at each other.

Julia flew out of bed and ran naked from the room. All in a panic, Terry tore off the duvet and chased after her, reaching the sitting room just as she was trying to dial 999. As he approached, she paused and yelled fiercely at him.

'*Stay away from me.*'

She went back to dialling. Terry had his wits about him and

220

dived for the wall socket, ripping it out before she could punch in the third digit. Now she was truly terrified. She picked up a porcelain vase and flung it at him. As he swayed to avoid it, she skipped past, got to the bathroom, and bolted the door behind her.

She was hyperventilating, trying frantically to think. What the hell was she going to do now, stuck in a flat with a murderer, in a bathroom with no windows? He could outlast her, or break the door down and kill her at his leisure.

Terry stood impotently outside the bathroom door. What the hell was he going to do now? What a tosser! In five minutes flat, his big mouth had converted him from lover to murder suspect. Unless he talked her out of it, the moment she got out of that bathroom she'd be straight on to the police. He put on his softest voice.

'Julia?'

'. . .'

'Julia? You in there?'

'You keep away from me.' She was fully ready to lie her way out of trouble. 'If you leave now and never come back, I won't go to the police.'

'Julia – it's not what you think.'

'Go away – *please*.'

Bollocks, what was he supposed to do? If he went, she'd be on that phone before he started the cab's engine.

'Julia, I wasn't involved. Not at all. You listenin'?'

He kicked himself. Of *course* she was listening. What else would she be doing in there? Filing her nails?

'I don't know who killed Grace. The Jowell bit was on this . . . tape.'

'What d'you mean, "*tape*"?'

'I won't tell you unless you come out of there and promise not to tell the police.'

Inside the bathroom, Julia was shaking her head vigorously.

'Don't you think you can trick me like that. I'm not going out

221

there, and if you try to break down the door, I'll open the bathroom window and yell for help.'

She prayed he hadn't noticed.

Terry relaxed a little. 'Must be a magic bathroom, then, 'cause
there weren't no windows when I was in there.'

Shit. What could she do? Would she have a better chance out
there, after all? Still very scared, she wound a towel around
herself and pulled back the bolt.

Terry was sitting on the carpet, trying hard not to look
threatening. That didn't stop Julia deciding that sternness was the
best policy.

'Right. We're going to sit down, as far apart as we can. And
you're going to tell what you mean about a tape.' Terry nodded
docilely and followed her through. She perched defensively at
one end of her sofa and imperiously indicated a small, hard chair.
He sat obediently, snatching up a green cushion the size of a fig
leaf.

'What's the story about this tape?'

'You promise not to tell?'

Julia nodded curtly. If he'd suppressed vital evidence, she
would have no qualms about shopping him.

'Occasionally when I'm in the cab, I make tapes of what
punters say. Some of 'em give me tips for the 'orses, for instance.
Obviously, I can't take notes while I'm drivin', so the tape's to
remind me.'

'And are you saying that there's a tape of *that* ride?'

'Part of it.'

'But if the police have that tape, don't they? Maybe I've been
unfair to them, if Marti Salminen's voice *is* on it . . . I get it, they
took the tape from your cab at the hospital, right? Before you had
a proper chance to listen to it.'

'Not *quite*. You see, tapin' punters like that ain't quite kosher.'
Julia looked puzzled. 'I mean, it ain't altogether *legal*. If the boys
in blue found it, I'd lose me badge.'

Julia's eyes went wild.

'Are you saying to me that, to stop yourself losing your taxi

222

licence, you didn't even *tell* them about it?'

Terry nodded lamely. It seemed like he was only digging himself in deeper.

Julia shook her head in bitter disbelief.

'Right, where do you keep this tape? Wherever it is, you and I are going to collect it right now and take it to the police.'

'You *promised* you wouldn't tell.'

'To hell with that. When I promised, I didn't know you'd done something *so* low, *so* despicable, to save your own miserable skin.'

'It wasn't just my own skin, honest it wasn't. There was another reason . . .'

'Terry, I don't give a *fuck* about your other reason, because whatever it was, it cannot possibly justify what you did. Tell me *now* where it is.'

'Okay, okay, it's at a mate's house, another cabbie.'

'Does he have any idea what's on it?'

'Yeah.'

'Oh brilliant, so he's in on this too? Is that it, or are half the cabbies in London involved?'

'One more, that's all. And we did 'ave a good reason.'

'Terry, go and get dressed. We're going to your friend's house.'

'It's gone two. We can't barge in there and wake the whole family.'

'Oh yes, we can. He'd better get used to it. I dare say they wake people up early in prison.'

'Can I at least ring and warn 'im we're on our way?'

'So he has lots of time to wipe that tape clean? You *must* be joking.'

22

It took an age for lights to come on, and more for the frosted glass to suggest the shape of Len lumbering sleepily down the stairs. It took still longer for him to locate the straying dressing-gown cords and tie them around his bulging pyjama-clad form. Terry waited nervously. Behind him, Julia bit her lip. The door opened.

'Sorry, mate.'

'Bleedin' 'ell, Terry, what you want this time of night?'

Terry stepped aside to reveal his companion.

'Len, this is Julia. She booked me for tonight.'

'Einstein told me.'

'Yeah, well we . . . got to talkin' about the murder and I sort of . . . mentioned the tape.'

'*Jesus*, Terry . . .' He caught himself before he said any more. His face had said it all, anyway. 'So what does she want? To listen to it?'

Terry shook his head sadly.

'Nah, she wants to take it to the police.'

'And you *agreed*?'

'I didn't 'ave much choice. She said she would tell them anyway.'

'Fuckin' ace. Well, I s'pose you better both come in.'

Switching lights on as he went, Len showed them through to the lounge and gestured Julia to a seat. Primly, she announced she'd rather stand. Julia didn't want to show it, but she was terrified. She had no idea how these people would react. They *might* let her waltz in and take their precious tape, or they might get difficult. And difficult could mean dangerous.

All Len could think about was how badly they needed Einstein. When he went over and picked up the phone, the girl had the nerve to try to stop him. His dander was slowly rising too, and he simply turned his back on her and made the call anyway. Einstein promised to be there in fifteen minutes.

Julia was horribly afraid that Len had sent some coded message, and this 'Einstein' person would turn up with a knife or a gun. She *had* to get out before he arrived.

'Give me the tape.' She held out a shaking palm.

That narked Len even more. Since Terry had let the cat out of the bag, the girl had them over a barrel: that didn't mean she could push him around in his own house.

'You get nothing till Einstein arrives.'

Julia glared at him, desperate to maintain a coolly righteous demeanour, scared she was losing control of the situation.

'Okay. While I'm waiting, play me the tape.'

She sat down and stared pointedly at the hi-fi.

Len thought about it. It was hard to see that playing her the tape could make things any worse, and it *would* buy some time. He walked to the Technics, put it on, and picked up the remote control so he could turn the volume up and down in the key places.

The first moment Grace's voice came on, Julia's knuckles tightened. She stared at the machine, transfixed. When the tape ended, she said simply,

'Again.'

Len did as she asked. During the second playing, Einstein rang the door chime. Julia seemed unaware of Terry scooting out to let him in. Len kept on with his work on the volume control, and stole a sideways glance at Julia. She looked like she was in shock: tears were streaming down her face. Len couldn't stop himself softening a little.

When Terry brought Einstein in, Julia refused his outstretched hand. He shrugged and turned to Terry to fill him in properly. At the end, Einstein nodded.

'Okay, give it to her.'

Len looked aghast. Even Terry was expecting more than *that*. Einstein was unfazed.

225

'But before she gets it, she has to go up and see Poppy.'

Julia frowned. 'Who's Poppy?'

'Len's daughter.'

'And what's this got to do with her?'

'A lot.'

'I don't understand.'

Einstein's instincts told him to say no more.

'Just go up and see. What are you afraid of? She's only thirteen. She won't bite you. Terry'll take you up.'

'I don't see any reason to . . .' Julia looked at the three cabbies' faces, and her nerve wavered. 'Won't she be asleep, anyway?'

Len shook his head. Reluctantly, Julia stood up and followed Terry out.

Terry stuck his head round her door. The little night light was on. She was wide awake, and coughing painfully.

'Hi there, Poppy, love. Sorry to bother you in the middle of the night.'

'What you want, Terry? You landed yourself in *more* bother?'

He pulled the door fully open.

'I want you to meet a friend called Julia.'

Poppy took a look at Julia, and thought she looked beautiful. She didn't mind visitors like this, even in the middle of the night.

'Okay, she can stay – and *you* can piss off.'

Terry did as he was told. Julia walked over and sat down on the small bedside chair.

'Hello, Poppy.'

''Ello. You can switch the other lamp on if you want, it's brighter.'

Julia leant over and pressed the switch. She looked around the room, festooned with posters of Michael Owen and the Liverpool football team. Poppy levered herself up an inch or two.

'So, what's this about? Why've you come to see me?'

'I don't know. Einstein said I should.'

''Ow long you been Terry's friend?'

'Only tonight.'

'Did you go out on a date?'

Julia smiled. 'Oh no, nothing like that.'

Poppy smirked. 'I bet he bonked you, all the same.'

Julia swallowed hard and put on a shocked scowl. Poppy crossed her arms.

'Well, *tell* me. Did 'e or didn't 'e?'

Julia flushed scarlet. This was *outrageous*. She didn't even know why she was meeting this strange, skinny child, yet here she was, getting the fifth degree on her sex life. Poppy laughed a knowing laugh and looked up at the ceiling. Julia wasn't going to take any more of this. She summoned up her severest tones.

'Now look here, young lady–'

This only prompted giggles. Poppy looked back at her.

'Don't worry, you already gave me the answer.'

'No, I didn't.'

'Oh yes, you *did*.'

'This is getting ridiculous. Terry and I merely–'

Poppy rolled her eyes.

'Don't be pathetic, it's *obvious* he bonked you. He bonks all the gels . . . Was he good?'

Julia was seriously flustered. She would have stormed out immediately if she'd had any idea why she was there in the first place.

'I, I don't know what you're talking about.' Poppy looked back, saw the blush, and chortled happily. Julia cratered. 'It's none of your business anyway.'

'Tell me, 'as Terry got a big one? I always wanted to know.'

Julia contrived to look even *more* horrified. Then the smile in Poppy's eyes defeated her, and her face relaxed into a shy grin.

'Oh, I'd say about normal.'

They both laughed, but Poppy's laughter tailed off into a terrible hacking, convulsing cough.

'Poor you, that sounds bad. Have you got a cold?'

'Something like that. I'll be all right in a minute.'

The coughing continued. Unsure what to do about it, Julia scanned the room for another topic of conversation.

227

'Oh, look at all your Barbie dolls. I *love* Barbies.'

Julia walked over and picked one of them up. Poppy had to wait for her splutterings to subside before she could reply.

'I liked 'em till I was four or five. Now I think they're sad. I've just never got round to throwin' them out. If you want, I'll put the lot down for you in me clog book.'

'That's nice of you. What's a clog book?'

'It's where I write who gets what when I pop me clogs.'

Julia smiled at this childlike thought, and tried not to look too patronizing.

'Now, what sort of talk is that from a girl your age?'

Poppy looked unimpressed.

'Wasn't you told? I'm goin' to die soon.'

Julia blundered cheerfully on.

''*Course* you're not, don't be silly.' When Poppy didn't laugh, her own smile started to fade. 'You're not being serious, are you? Die of what, for goodness' sake?'

'Cystic fibrosis. Like Tommy, my big brother.'

Julia bit her lip. She was getting out of her depth here, and had the first uncomfortable inkling of why she was in this bedroom. But she didn't know how to ask the question. Before she could formulate anything, Poppy put her on the spot again.

'Why did you come 'ere tonight? Is it to do with the murder?'

She looked hard at Julia, who nodded hesitantly.

'You a copper?'

'No, I'm a banker. *Was*, anyway. I worked with Grace, the girl who was killed.'

'And now you've found out what they're up to?'

'Not all of it. I know about the tape.'

'So you're goin' to grass on 'em?'

Julia felt her skin tingle with embarrassment.

'I have no choice. It's vital evidence. It's for Grace I'm doing this.'

'Good. They should've told the police *ages* ago.'

'I don't want to be rude about your Dad, but it *does* seem selfish of them, thinking their licences mattered more than catching Grace's killer.'

228

'Oh, so they didn't tell you why they made them tapes?'

'It was instead of writing things down, wasn't it? Betting tips and so on.'

Poppy shook her head.

'No, it was for *me*. They was buggin' City punters and investin' on the side. It was all to send me to San Francisco. There's a clinic there that has some new treatment for CF, only it costs an arm an' a leg. Don't matter, though. Prob'ly wouldn't've worked any-way . . .'

Julia squirmed. Of course, nothing excused standing by while an innocent man was convicted, but the cabbies had a more honourable reason than she'd thought. Poppy began spluttering again, and her sentences came through painful hacks.

'They 'ad the divvy idea of investigatin' it themselves. Einstein's clever, all right, but 'e can't do it alone. Terry's got the gift of the gab when it comes to gels, but basically 'e's thick, and my Dad ain't a whole lot smarter. They'll never solve it. No, you're doin' the right thing, gel, don't you let 'em change your mind.'

'How can you say that, Poppy, if it stops you going to that clinic?'

'I wanted to go, but I can't, that's all. It's no big deal. Shit 'appens.'

She suffered new convulsions. Julia had no idea what to say next. She stood up, squeezed Poppy's hand, and walked very slowly downstairs to the lounge.

They were sitting in glum silence, and their eyes turned towards her as she came in and sat down. She looked very ill at ease, but didn't speak. Len concluded that there was no point hanging around. They might as well get it over with.

'Okay, me and Terry are ready to go. There's one other thing – I want you to keep Einstein out of this.'

Einstein shook his head violently. 'Len, we talked about this before. We're all in this together. I'm going with you.'

'No way, mate.'

'*SHUT UP!*'

They stared open-mouthed at her.

'Thank you. Before you go *anywhere*, I want to hear all you know about Jowell. I told Terry the truth: that deal died long ago. But from what Grace said on the tape, she must've been working on another bid for the same company. If I think you're telling the truth, and if you convince me that you have some chance of finding the killer, I *might* be persuaded to take leave of my senses and lend you a hand.'

*

The next day dawned miserably. Rain had begun falling in the early hours, and was now turning into evil sleet. The north wind hurtled down Cardigan Bay and hurled itself angrily at the thin, cracked defences of the ancient control-tower windows. The single contoller watched as the great galumphing wings of the military transport were sprayed with de-icer, and thanked his lucky stars he wasn't aboard that machine.

Inside they waited patiently. If they were concerned by the weather it didn't show. A few chatted quietly. The rest checked their equipment again and kept their own counsel.

Ten more minutes and it was done. The crew got the okay, started up the engines, and the plane lumbered unconvincingly away from the apron, like an elderly, arthritic Saint Bernard. At the end of the long runway, it paused long enough to wind its propellers into a desperate, wheezing fury, and inched forward.

Gathering speed with painful slowness, it covered three, four, five hundred yards, looking like it couldn't possibly mean it. Another six, seven hundred. Just when it seemed the attempt must end ignominiously at the edge of the airfield, the great vibrating craft struggled to its haunches and shuddered clear of the ground.

Guy Barton was one of the quiet ones. Training with the Special Boat Squadron was the most special of privileges. He had learnt to parachute in the Foreign Legion, acquiring a badly smashed ankle on one of his first jumps. Rather than putting him off, the accident had spurred him on, making him all the more determined to master the technique and the treacherous winds. He had never given it up, jumping regularly in all seasons.

However, since he discovered HALO parachuting, his passion knew no bounds. Jumping at over twenty thousand feet and free-falling down to one thousand doused him in adrenalin, the only drug that he'd cared for since his youth. When he heard how much further the SBS pushed this practice, he wanted to jump with them. His fame, fortune and fitness proved persuasive advocates, and opened doors which normally would be barred. Not that they let him do it without putting him through a battery of medical tests that would have defeated most younger men.

The SBS used HALO jumps to minimize the chance of being detected by radar when landing on an enemy shore. They left the plane at very high altitude and screeched down to a mind-numbing five hundred feet, when an altitude sensor released a tiny black chute. This provided only six seconds of braking effect, and they smashed into concrete-hard seas at sixty-five miles an hour. Nothing – not even their specially designed helmets – could save them from momentary unconsciousness. Normal men would be killed instaneously by that impact or knocked out for so long they would drown. The superfit SBS men blacked out for ten seconds or less, their physical condition better able to cope with the shock, and their will-power so strong it would punch its way back to consciousness.

That was why Guy needed this practice. For his world record attempt, he planned to jump from nearly twenty miles above sea level. Falling through the thin upper air at more than the speed of sound, he would certainly black out. As he fell further, his speed would slow, and he *might* come to. The entire descent would take five minutes. If he remained unconscious all the way down, even with an automatic parachute release, his landing would be totally uncontrolled, and he could sustain serious injury. Guy Barton wasn't planning on taking that chance. He would carry no altitude sensor, no automatic release gear. If he didn't come to, he would rather crash into the desert floor like a sack of potatoes than run the risk of being paralysed.

Tough as he was, when he looked through the tiny window down at the stormy-grey Irish Sea, Guy was glad that, unlike the rest of the team, he would have a boat to scoop him up and take him to the Welsh shore. The others would have to unstrap their harness and swim over two miles, to simulate a landing.

The co-pilot warned them that they were approaching the drop area. Guy felt a growing dryness in his throat and a moistness in his palms. This jump would be the scariest he'd ever tried. Five minutes from now he might be dead. It was a knife-edge risk: crazy, pointless and fantastic. The perfect way, in fact, to take your mind off a swelling sea of troubles.

*

The murder team had been pruned back to eight. Formally, a team had to stay in existence until a conviction was secured; in reality, once a suspect was charged, they were wound down. In the rare case that the judge or jury was too dim or soft to secure the right outcome, they would rev themselves up and start over again.

The Chesterfield team still maintained some activity, but were mainly going through the motions. The lead came from Superintendent Hunt. Any information that would not help put Marti Salminen away was to be given only cursory attention. However, disappointingly little new evidence against the Finn had come to light. It made them uneasy, and even Hunt occasionally looked fidgety beneath his swagger. This was by far the most high-profile case he'd handled and, if all went well, it could re-open the issue of promotion to senior command. Nothing must be allowed to get in the way of convicting that Finn.

All he needed was a little bit of luck, he was thinking as he marched in to chair the evening meeting. DI Long was due to report on the surveillance of the cabbie. The fact that the Finn was remanded in custody might not prevent him arranging a pay-off. After all, his need for the cabbie's continuing silence was greater than ever. How sweet it would be if they caught the Finn's accomplice in the act! Hunt was regretting putting that fool girl in charge of something so key. Still, he had to give her *something* to do.

The meeting got under way. After a few routine comments from Wear, it was over to Mary Long.

'We've maintained a twenty-four hour watch on Thorogood and, after getting the formal authority, monitored his home phone and his mobile. We've also kept in touch with his bank.'

'Well, get on with it. What have you found? Are there any signs he's been paid off?'

'No, sir. No suspicious movements in his bank account, and no sign of him flashing money around.'

'What about the people he socializes with?'

'Early in our surveillance he went several times to pubs or bars, and sometimes he emerged with young women.'

'Did he fuck them?'

Hunt simply adored embarrassing her. All the men grinned.

'Hard to say, sir. According to the reports, he took some of them back to his flat. Maybe he needed help with the ironing . . .'

Hunt frowned. He hadn't knocked her off her stride as easily as he'd hoped. He'd slap her down harder next time.

'He continues to meet regularly with the two other cabbies we identified after we first released him. If there's anything going on, I wouldn't be surprised if they know all about it.'

'This is all pretty dull stuff, Inspector. Anything else?'

'Yes, there *is*, sir. One *very* interesting thing. Thorogood was phoned a couple of days ago by none other than Julia Daventry. If you remember, sir, she was the girl from Skidder Barton who came in and saw DS Wear. She had a theory that the murder might be connected with Chesterfield's work.'

Hunt grunted. 'I remember. Right load of feminine crap that was.'

This was too important for Long to react to his barbs.

'Daventry booked Thorogood's cab for that evening. They drove all over central London for over three hours, stopped off at a bar, then went to her flat. Thorogood went inside with her . . .'

Hunt leered. 'So what? Wear said that girl needed a good rogering.'

'However, one and a half hours later, they emerged again together and drove over to one of the other cabbies' house.'

'Don't tell me she bonked him, too.'

'I have no idea. A little later, the *third* cabbie arrived there. At three-thirty a.m., she and Thorogood emerged together . . .'

Hunt laughed out loud.

'Not *again*. I can't stand any more emerging. Don't tell me, they drove back to her flat and went in together . . .'

'Yes, sir.'

'And at five a.m. they emerged together again?'

By now all the men were chuckling away with Hunt.

'No, sir. Thorogood emerged on his own at eight-thirty.'

'Hooray. Free at last!' He surveyed the whole room, delighted with the pleasure he was giving. 'Tell me, DI Long, what do you deduce from this magnificent detective work? How will it help us put Salminen where he belongs?'

'What I deduce, sir, is that we should take Julia Daventry more seriously.'

'We *did* take her seriously, DI Long. We followed it up by the book. Sergeant Wear raised it with one of the people at Skidder Barton. There was nothing in it.'

'Well, Daventry doesn't think so, sir, or she wouldn't have made the effort to track down our cabbie.'

'Track down, *balls* . . .'

Hunt was pissed off by her attitude. Her whole demeanour was bordering on the insubordinate.

'Thorogood works the City a lot. Chances are she's been in the back of his cab before, and made a note of his cab or badge number. If she had either of those, finding out his name would be child's play. She probably fancied a bit of rough. From your own evidence, it's pretty bloody obvious she opened her legs for him last night.'

Mary took a couple of deep breaths, trying to keep her cool.

'If this was only a meeting between Thorogood and Daventry, I agree it might be meaningless. But for him to take her to meet his cabbie friends in the early hours . . . What could that be for, except

234

to discuss the murder? There *has* to be something going on here, sir.'

'Something involving Skidder Barton, I suppose? DI Long, we have charged Marti Salminen. Are you proposing opening an entirely new line of enquiry?'

This was the crunch point.

'All I propose, sir, is that we invite Julia Daventry back in and find out what she was up to with Thorogood. Or, if you prefer, we could interview the other two cabbies.'

Hunt cracked his knuckles ominously.

'DI Long, how many murder teams have you served on?'

The cheap bastard. 'Sir, you are perfectly well aware that this is my first.'

'Well, might I suggest that you pay more heed to the views of a senior officer who's served on *scores* of them? I'm telling you there's *nothing* to investigate at Skidder Barton. I have no interest in either the sex life *or* the far-fetched theories of Julia Daventry. All you will achieve is to take her feminine intuition, add it to yours, and build a shitheap of pre-menstrual garbage.'

Mary fell silent. She had lost. Hunt rumbled on.

'The surveillance of Thorogood has cost tens of thousands and yielded nothing. I'm terminating it with immediate effect. And you are on no account to approach Julia Daventry or any of those cabbies. Do you understand, DI Long?'

'Yes, sir.'

'And since the surveillance is over, I will need to assign you to new duties within the team. Beginning with collating the inputs from members of the public.'

He could have sacked her from the team altogether. This was more humiliating, and humiliating her seemed to be his aim.

23

Einstein's attempts to hack into Skidders's computer system got nowhere. They simply *had* to get inside the bank. And that meant getting help from Julia.

Julia was doubtful. She insisted that, come what might, she wouldn't go back there unless she first recovered some mysterious 'papers' an ex-colleague kept in his flat. And anyway, how was she going to get past the security guards in the lobby of Skidder Barton or into the corporate finance department on the eighteenth floor without every head spinning round?

Einstein saw right away that they needed to harness the wider skills of the Thorogood clan. There wasn't a flat in London that could resist the charms of Mike Thorogood's skeleton keys, and Terry's sister, Lorna, should be able to disguise Julia nicely. Terry called Lorna's salon and got her round to Len's house for a first assessment. She sat Julia down in the lounge and ran a comb through her hair. They all waited for the verdict.

'Yeah, it needs to be cut and layered, then dyed a nice blonde . . .' She sensed the squirming shoulders below her, and patted Julia. 'Don't worry, love, I'll dye it back afterwards.'

Terry could see there was something else troubling his sister and asked. Lorna hesitated.

'It's not the clothes – she can borrow some of mine – and I'm not *too* bothered about the way she talks: you say she's a good mimic, so she'll soon pick it up . . .'

Terry was still confused.

'Then what *is* it, Lor?'

'Didn't you see the way she walks? Like she's got a snooker cue up 'er arse.' She patted Julia again. 'Don't take it personal, love. It's not *your* fault, it's the way you was brought up. And the way she stands on them 'igh 'eels, so *straight*. Gels round 'ere never do that: we all point our 'eels in at an angle.'

Terry chimed in.

'Yeah, Jules, our gels are like the wheels on old cars, they've got what's called "positive camber": the top of the tyres stick out more than the bottom.'

Julia looked witheringly at him.

'Terry, you're the only man on the entire planet who could work cars into a discussion about high heels. Why not shut up and leave it to Lorna?'

Lorna nodded approvingly. 'You tell 'im, love. Now, watch me, then stand up and 'ave a go yourself.'

She marched up and down the room, her scuffed white heels leaning out like yachtsmen in a stiff breeze. Julia observed her doubtfully.

'How *do* you do that?'

Julia got up and tried a few faltering steps. Then one of her ankles, unused to the strain, turned over.

'*Christ*, this is difficult. It's like learning to walk all over again.'

Terry was smirking away.

'If you find it too 'ard, why not start on all fours? Lorna can get another pair of shoes for your front legs.'

Julia ignored him. She was concentrating on mastering this strange form of motion. Lorna tried to sound encouraging.

'*That*'s better. You'll soon pick it up. When you do, you never forget. It's like riding a bicycle . . . Now, as soon as you manage the 'eels, we'll start on your 'ips.'

Julia stopped and swung round.

'My *hips*? What's wrong with *them*?'

Lorna scratched her head, wondering how to say it.

'There's nothing *wrong* with 'em. You 'ave lovely 'ips, matter of fact. So why not *use* 'em? Swing 'em a bit.'

'Show me what you mean.'

Lorna did. To Julia it looked even harder than the heels.

'Show me again . . .'

Lorna completed another lap of the lounge, exaggerating the

swing to illustrate the point. Terry's expression had become lascivious.

'Your turn now, Jules. Don't forget, a swing like that could be useful in lots of situations.'

'Terry, get *out* of this room.'

'You can't red-card me, not when I'm 'avin' so much fun.'

'Then *shut up* . . .'

Julia walked a few paces, feeling like she was imitating Marilyn Monroe in a game of charades. The rhythm was all wrong, unnatural. Lorna decided on direct action.

'Try one more time, love. Relax as much as you can. I'll put me 'ands on your 'ips and move 'em from side to side as you walk, till you pick it up.'

Lorna took up station behind Julia and together they gently advanced. Steering her by the hips proved trickier than Lorna had guessed, and it proved easier to hold Julia's buttocks. *Now* they were making progress. Terry forgot about staying quiet.

'This is better than lap dancin'. You gels ought to charge for this.'

The two girls skidded to a halt. Julia pointed towards the door. Lorna pronounced the official sentence.

'*Red card.*'

*

The pressure on Charles Barton was relentless, and he couldn't take much more of it. His taunting demons had made him seek sympathy and break the taboo on discussing Skidder Barton. Without a word, Patricia and the girls stood up, took their plates from the dinner table and left him to stew. He was so incensed and unhappy, he drove straight back to London late on Saturday night and spent a miserable Sunday alone. Everything was falling apart. His nerves were in tatters, his hair was falling out, and his sudden weight loss made him look ten years older. And whenever he opened a paper, there was his brother, grinning at him.

Coming back to the office on Monday, he was called by Skidders' head of global markets, who confessed that his gamble on Mexican bonds had gone disastrously wrong. Instead of selling and taking a moderate loss a week ago, he'd clung on. A speech by the Chairman of the Federal Reserve had washed away the last fragile dykes of support and, ever since, the bonds had been in free fall. The bank had lost eighty million dollars. Charles knew what spin would be put on this when it came out: another catastrophic failure of top management at Skidder Barton.

If this wasn't bad enough, Richard Myers, Julian Lithgow, and three other corporate finance directors marched into his office and announced that they were decamping to Schroders.

'Why?' It was the only place to begin.

'You really need to ask?'

Before now, Myers had always been deferential to Barton. His tone was different now: harder, cocky almost.

'Okay, Charles, I'll tell you. The reputation of this bank has fallen so far, it's becoming an embarrassment to work here. No one in the City believes we'll be independent in a year's time and, frankly, the five of us don't want to work for the Swiss.'

Barton went through the motions. 'Ernst Lautenschutz has assured me that Zuricher will remain a supportive shareholder.'

Myers snorted, brushed aside this remark, and pressed on.

'We might have soldiered on if the department was still a pleasant environment to work in. However, since you brought in Sellars, the collegiate atmosphere has been destroyed. His team won't even tell the rest of us what deals they're working on.'

'They say the same about you.'

'Why should we tell them, when *they* won't?'

Barton asked a few more questions, playing for time, trying to gauge whether they were definitely leaving or using this offer to negotiate. He *had* to keep them if he could, not because they were particularly talented but to stop more hullabaloo in the press. As delicately as he could, he led up to the key question.

'So, Richard, are you determined to go to new pastures, or can we talk about it?'

Myers smiled triumphantly. He would have been crestfallen if

239

Barton had simply accepted their resignation. Like all City terrorists, this quintet had their list of demands ready. The offer they'd got from Schroders was acceptable, if not as jam-filled as they'd hoped. It was good enough, however, to put them in a strong position with Charles Barton. They had his nuts in a vice and could twist as hard as they pleased. After all he'd had to bear in recent months, Myers wanted to enjoy every minute of this.

'Basically, Charles, we're committed to go.'

'Have you signed?'

'Not yet. However, we could only *contemplate* staying if you satisfied us on various fronts.'

'Such as?'

'Well, first there's remuneration. The offer from Schroders is generous. They're guaranteeing us a million pounds each for three years.' Barton guessed, correctly, that this was a wild exaggeration, not that he could prove it. Nor did it help him now: this wasn't the moment for brinkmanship.

'If it's mainly a question of money, I'm sure we can work something out.'

'I wouldn't say *mainly*. Things here can never work while Rosco Sellars is around. If we are to stay, *he'll* have to go.'

Barton had half expected this. If it had been up to him, he might have agreed there and then. Sellars had achieved precious little so far. The problem was the Swiss: they were still in love with him.

'I'll have to think about that. Is there anything else?'

The five looked at each other. Barton sensed that whatever else was coming would be the toughest condition of all.

'Our last question concerns the top management of the bank.'

'What about it?'

'You know perfectly well what the papers and analysts are saying. For you to continue as both Chairman and Chief Executive is impossible.'

Barton's tone became chilly. The *cheek* of this third-rater.

'What are you suggesting?'

'That you remain as Chairman, but hand the day-to-day running of the bank over to . . . someone else.'

'Such as?'

'We've given a lot of thought to that. We can't think of anyone suitable at another bank who would be willing to come and sort out the mess.'

'So what *are* you proposing, Richard?' Barton had a pretty good idea what was coming.

Richard Myers asked Julian Lithgow to take over as spokesman.

'We think the only way Skidders can rebuild its reputation is by putting more emphasis on corporate finance. Appointing Richard as Chief Executive would send the right signal.'

Myers studied his hands demurely while Charles Barton struggled to control his fury. What with the Mexican losses, they had timed this ambush to perfection. He wished he could tell them to rot in hell. Unfortunately, it wasn't that simple.

'Can you give me some time to consider this?'

Myers smiled magnanimously. It sounded like the putsch had worked: they were going to get everything. My *God*, the man's nerve had cracked. It wasn't done and dusted yet, though; he had to keep the pressure up.

'We have to get back to Schroders by the end of today. We can give you until five o'clock.'

Barton had to interrupt a Zuricher board meeting to speak to Lautenschutz. He told him of the first two demands, but kept quiet on the third. He didn't want to discuss his own position unless it was unavoidable. The matter was resolved rapidly. Lautenschutz had no hesitation in insisting that Sellars must be kept at all costs, and seemed unperturbed by the loss of the Englishmen.

They both put the phones down. In London, Charles Barton called the head of press relations to work out a damage-limitation strategy. Only when that was done did he call a surprised Myers to say he would not to contest their decision to leave the bank. In Zurich, Ernst Lautenschutz waited until the end of the regular board agenda before announcing a welcome development.

241

Publicity of trading losses and staff defections should drive the Skidders' price down and rattle the nerves of the Barton family in the run-up to Christmas. The timing for their strike should be perfect.

*

Julia banished Terry to bed and spent another couple of hours practising the walk. After a few glasses of wine, it felt more natural. She still had a little time to perfect it. In the meantime there were more pressing things to worry about.

At past two she crept in beside him. He turned towards her, gave her a token boob-squeeze, then rolled back the other way and snored contentedly on. He didn't seem worried about the plans for the next day, but then *he* wasn't breaking and entering, though he was driving the getaway cab. Julia lay awake worrying. What if the police had the building surrounded when they came out? And what if Mike had lost his knack, or they got captured on some video in the lobby? Would the sunglasses and headscarf safeguard her? On and on she worried, until she fretted herself to sleep.

At least they didn't have to get up early. They needed to be sure that Rosco had left for the office and decided to wait until ten.

Mike came round at nine and over a cup of tea they ran through the plans once again. Terry wasn't so fussed about plans: there was something else on his mind.

'Jules, if me and Mike are riskin' our liberty over this, I think we ought be told why you need them papers so bad.'

Julia sipped her tea and said nothing. Terry had been on at her about this for days, and had come uncomfortably near the truth.

'Love letters, I reckon, prob'ly *dirty* love letters. Or pics, maybe. Yeah, could be nude pics. What you reckon, Mikey?'

Mike grinned a friendly, toothy grin. 'Don't make no odds to me.'

'If they're nude pics, maybe we could use 'em on our Christmas cards, eh, Jules?'

Julia looked at her watch.

'Isn't it time to go yet?'

It wasn't. She had to endure another twenty minutes of waiting first.

Terry dropped them off a hundred yards away, pointing to the little side street where he would be waiting. As they walked towards the handsome stucco block, Julia cast a sideways glance at Mike. Their best efforts at dressing him hadn't worked very well. He looked as comfortable with a tie as with a hangman's noose, and he kept tugging at the chafing collar like a boy on his first day at school. Julia hoped to God that the porter wouldn't look too closely at her 'assistant'.

It was quite a chance she had taken, calling half an hour before, pretending to be Mr Sellars's secretary and informing the porter that Lucinda Nightingale, an interior designer, and her assistant would visit the flat. When the porter insisted that if they wanted to be let in, he would have to hear it direct from Mr Sellars, Julia airily assured him that Miss Nightingale had spare keys. As she spoke, she was casting a doubtful eye over the old credit cards and the range of metal spikes that Mike had arrayed on the kitchen table.

As they strode up the steps, Julia's heart was beating furiously. Mike seemed very calm by comparison. She had to perform first, talking their way past the porter. Her glasses were so dark, she found it hard to see whether there was suspicion in his eyes. Could this be a trap? Had he double-checked by ringing Sellars back at the bank? It was too late now; he had already pointed them towards the rickety old lift and told them to go on up.

Coming out on the fourth floor, they walked along the wide corridor until they found Flat G and rang the brass bell. If Rosco's cleaner was there, they were buggered.

No one came. They looked left and right. Julia nodded to Mike, who pulled out one of his tools and started wiggling it around in the keyhole. Ten, fifteen, twenty-five seconds. It didn't work. He tried another spike. Come *on*. Still nothing. Then there was a click, and the first lock yielded. On to the second. Another half-minute, more. Julia thought her heart would burst right out of her chest. *Please*, Mikey. The lift started moving back up. What if it was a resident coming up to the fourth, or, worse still, the porter checking them out? Do it Mike, do it *now*.

He gave up on the spindly tool and switched to a plastic card, working it up and down in the jamb. The lift was nearly there. They'd have to make a run for the stairs.

The lift doors motored open at the very moment Mike teased the lock free. Whoever emerged from the lift would have seen only an elegant female back disppearing.

Drrriiiiiiiiiiiiiiiiinnnnnnnnggggg . . .

Christ, why hadn't she thought of this? It should've been *obvious* that there would be an alarm in the flat. Thirty seconds from now all hell would break loose.

. . . *dddrrriiiinnnnnnggggg* . . .

Bloody Mike, *he* should have guessed. He must have come across alarms before.

Mike had. It was such a common hazard, he hadn't bothered to mention it. Without a word to the furiously panicking Julia, he calmly followed the trail of the high-pitched whine, opened a wooden cupboard, and punched four digits into a keypad.

The noise stopped. In the strange silence that followed, Julia could hear no sound but her own thumping heart. She whispered.

'How did you know the number?'

Mike grinned widely. 'You said this place was rented, right? Round 'ere they all use the same agent. While you was sleepin' last night, I took a little gander in the agent's filing cabinet. There was no keys there, but they *did* 'ave a note of the alarm combination.'

Julia smiled, impressed, and they spread out to look round the flat. She had an unpleasant instinct that Rosco might keep the collection close to his bed, so she first hunted high and low in the master bedroom.

Nothing. Nor in the two other bedrooms. Meanwhile, Mike

had made a beeline for the antique partner's desk in the small study. The drawers stayed locked for all of ten seconds. Since he had no idea what he was looking for, he waited for Julia to finish up in the bedrooms and come through to inspect the contents. She flicked as fast as she could through the piles of papers, her gloved hands slower than naked fingers, then shook her head.

They moved on and checked the big sitting room. Rosco had furnished it minimally, so it didn't take long. They were running out of places to look. Mike went for the dining room and Julia did the rest. Kitchen? No good. Bathrooms? Ridiculous, but she tried the medicine cabinets anyway. She was almost despairing when there was a yell of triumph from the dining room. Julia dashed through. Mike had looked behind a purple abstract painting and had discovered a wall safe. It had a single knurled dial. Julia knew that Mikey was carrying a stethoscope, but it seemed that this sad device didn't warrant producing it. His unaided ear detected the tiny clicks as the gears slotted into place, and he had it open in two minutes. As he stood back to let Julia peek inside, the phone started ringing.

Could it be the porter? If so, would he come up when they didn't answer? They'd better get out of here soon. The safe's aperture was small, but it widened out inside as a precaution against someone trying to remove the whole thing. Like a dog digging a hole, Julia shoved her hands in and scooped out great armfuls of paper, letting them fall to the ground. The doorbell rang.

Oh *fuck.*

'Mikey, you answer it. Say everything's fine and we're leaving.'

Scoop, scoop, scoop. More fat wodges of papers spilled out. Right at the bottom, could that be it? It was a small, leatherbound album. She tore it open. Women, women, women: all naked, all naughty. Jesus, there were a lot of them. Where was she? She flicked further on through the pages.

From the hallway outside, she could hear Mike trying to fend off the porter. It sounded like his suspicions were aroused, and Mike wasn't convincing him. Flick, flick, more blondes, more redheads. Flick. *There*: a whole dreadful page of herself. Peeling back the transparent covering sheet, she plucked the photos clear and stuffed them in her jacket pocket. She was about to toss the album back into the safe when she realized that other girls might be in the same boat, and she could spare *their* blushes, too. The whole album went into her handbag.

She stopped and listened. Mike had lost by the sound of it, and the porter was insisting on checking the place over. Which room would he look in first? Good, it sounded like he was starting at the other end. Furiously she began picking the papers up from the floor and shoving them back in the safe. They were mostly share and bond certficates, doubtless worth a fortune.

Was that him coming? Mikey was trying one last conversational ploy to slow him down and win her vital seconds. She thrust the last pile in. As she was about to close the safe, her eye was caught by a large vellum envelope with 'Hawk International' printed on the front. What the hell could Rosco have to do with *them*? She reached back in, grabbed it, closed the little door and twiddled the dial furiously to lock it.

The porter was getting twitchier and twitchier. He didn't like the look of this 'design assistant' one little bit, and the man's nonsense about giving him tips for the horses was irritating him. What was his game, and why was trying to stop him going into the dining room? There was nothing for it but to brush him aside, and barge his way through.

Odd. What was going on here? The room looked normal enough. He couldn't see anything missing. Why, though, had the woman turned sharply away as he walked in and put her dark glasses back on? He took a good look round. Everything looked in order, apart from the horrible purple picture being slightly skew-whiff.

He went over to straighten it, then eyed the girl. Her glasses made her look rather sinister. He noticed her hands. He knew it was cold outside, but wasn't it strange that she still had gloves on twenty minutes after she had come indoors? Hang on, they couldn't be . . . ? Then common sense grabbed hold of him again.

If they were burglars, surely they'd have cleaned the place out by now. All the same, he didn't trust them one bit.

'If you don't mind, Miss, I'm going to get Mr Sellars's personal confirmation that it's all right for you to be here. I tried him a few minutes ago after you arrived, but his secretary at his bank had her voice mail on. I'll ring the operator there and ask them to track him down. Shouldn't take long.'

Julia smiled coldly.

'That won't be necessary. We're finished. Thank you for your help.'

The porter nodded and shepherded them towards the door. He was glad he'd checked. With Christmas just round the corner, it was a good time to show concern for tenants' property. Some of them were very generous, and if Mr Sellars was paid as much as he'd heard, he might be worth a couple of hundred. The funny little assistant irritated him by reminding him to switch the alarm on. The porter was having none of that, and told him to do it himself. Then they had the barefaced cheek to march out and down the corridor, leaving him to use his own master keys to lock up.

He rode down in the lift with them and made sure they left the premises. As he watched their retreating backs, he felt pleased how he'd handled it. If they were legit, they couldn't complain: he hadn't been rude to them or stopped them doing their work. And if they were crooked, he might have prevented a burglary. For a moment he toyed with phoning the police. What could he say, though, when there was nothing obviously missing from the flat?

No, he'd mention it to Mr Sellars when he came home that night, and suggest that if there *was* anything wrong, he should contact the police right away. He hadn't seen much of the girl, but he *had* got a good look at the man.

Rosco came home at about nine that night. When the porter told him the tale, his face went thunderous. Without so much as a word of thanks, he raced over to the lift and, when it didn't come right away, fairly flung himself up the stairs.

247

Ten minutes later, he rang down, wanting to know what they'd looked like. Naturally enough, the porter majored on the man's appearance. Mr Sellars sounded mightily annoyed when he was unable to say much about the woman. He'd even forgotten what colour hair she had.

The strangest part of all was that, though he seemed to be frantic, he didn't want to bother the police. Odd buggers, Americans.

*

Mary Long sat twiddling her thumbs. There was damn-all for her to do. Twice she'd asked Hunt to release her from the team, and twice he had refused. She was sure he was paying her back, not only for her mild insubordination but for all she represented. For her, too, Hunt was a cipher, representing an old 'beat 'em up and lock 'em up' approach that left justice to play the percentages, with innocent men getting caught in the net along with villains. Respected as he was by most of the rank and file, Hunt had picked up a reputation for not letting lack of evidence stand in the way of a solid conviction. His years on the drugs squad were the stuff of legend: they said that his imaginative recycling of packets of crack had helped put away many an anguished dealer.

Mary was less naive and loftily idealistic than Hunt thought. In her six years on the force, she'd seen too many credulous juries, too many smooth-tongued barristers talking clients off a charge to believe that the judicial system worked reliably. She understood why her colleagues got frustrated and were tempted to cut corners. But she wanted no personal part in wrongdoing. Reaching the highest levels of the Force would give her no satisfaction if she got there by breaking the law she'd sworn to uphold.

For the umpteenth time she thought about Marti Salminen. Nasty bit of work though he was, it didn't feel right. She knew that the Crown Prosecution Service were worried that the evidence was too weak, and she feared how Hunt might react if

248

they threatened to abandon the case. Would he just shrug his shoulders, release the Finn, and kick the enquiry back into life? It would mean eating a giant-sized portion of humble pie, and would bring down the curtain ingloriously on his career. She sensed that Hunt hankered after a grander swansong, or maybe an extended run on the boards. If he was cornered, might he conjure up a new, vital piece of evidence that magically converted a shaky case into a compelling one?

What were the possibilities? Not fingerprints in the cab, it was too late for that. Unearthing a murder weapon would be risky unless Forensic were willing to be implicated. A new witness, perhaps, who would testify to seeing Marti leaving the cab? If Hunt wanted that badly enough, it would be easy to arrange. He had hundreds of underworld contacts who would help in return for a past or future favour. And there would be nothing she could do to stop it. Unless . . .

She was off duty that evening, and had no particular plans. Should she see if Terry Thorogood was around and in the mood for some impromptu socializing?

*

Julia skimmed the *FT*'s Lex column about Myers and friends as she prepared to go under the scissors. After the criminal exertions of the morning, it was soothing to sit in the salon awaiting alchemic transformation to bright blonde via medieval-looking bowls of chalky goo.

She turned to the main story reporting the defections. Skidders' attempts to spin it had been mocked, making everything worse. Clearly Myers or his cronies had got to the journalists first and talked up the sow's ears of their reputations into silk purses of stardom. Julia couldn't help feeling pity for Charles Barton. Granted, the poor man should never have been running an investment bank in the first place. Who would want to be in his shoes now, though? Friendless, assailed on all sides, waiting limply for the axe to fall. Why on earth didn't he just walk away, and go and live happily ever after in that lovely Gloucestershire house? Was it vanity? Stubbornness? Inertia? Or a misplaced sense of *noblesse oblige*?

How dire would the atmosphere be in the corporate finance department now? Banned from contacting any of them, Julia was starved of gossip. Never mind, she'd find out soon enough. Einstein's plan would be put into motion next Monday. A friend of a friend of Jean Bishop worked in the agency which supplied temps to Skidders and had been watching out for a vacancy in that department.

Would Rosco be in the bank then? Would he have noticed that things were missing from his safe? She was damned glad she'd taken the other things. How could she have been so stupid as to *think* of implicating herself by taking only her own pictures? Now any of the girls could have done it, even if she was probably suspect number one. The Hawk papers had inadvertently provided further camouflage. The thief could have been after those, and taken the pictures for a giggle.

What *were* those Hawk papers about? Julia couldn't read a word of German and had handed them over to Einstein. He'd promised to try to work it out. She knew that Hawk's services didn't come cheap. Whatever those German papers were about, they might be interesting.

In the mirror, she saw Lorna coming back.

'Okay, Jules love, this is the big one. You ready?'

'Ready as I'll ever be, Lorna. Go on, do your worst.'

'Right, one Romford Special coming up. After that we'll 'ave a cup of tea and do some more talk practice.'

24

Again, Julia hardly slept. If anything, she was more nervous than before the burglary. Between getting up at five and leaving Terry's place at eight, she had about ten espressos from the Gaggia machine she'd bought him.

It was the weirdest feeling, being back in that personnel department. Not that she was seeing the head this time; the girl who signed on the temps and gave them their instructions and security passes was much more junior. There were six of them that morning, all headed for different parts of the bank. As they sat together on two benches, it gave her a chance to get into the linguistic swing. Lorna's final words after the days and nights of language practice rang in her ears: you've got to get into the *rhythm* of Essex talk. She made her chant it like a mantra: 'She says to 'im, and 'e says to me; she says to 'im and 'e says to me.' As she walked up Throgmorton Lane from the Tube station, Julia recited it over and over, making it more musical with each repetition. She was only fifty yards away from Skidders when she remembered about walking properly. She pushed out on her heels and tried to induce that elusive hip sway. The mantra came back into her head, and she realized it helped with the swing. As long as she recited it under her breath whenever she walked, she would automatically swing her hips.

Julia was called in to be processed. She did her best to keep up the accent. Fortunately, the personnel girl was full of talk herself and didn't seem to require much in return except nods and grunts. Julia's biggest concern was which secretary she'd be replacing. Much as she needed to get into that department, she hoped that her boss for the week wasn't someone she knew well.

The girl looked up the list. Oh, God, *no*. Jo Silkin, Marcus Ford's secretary! Julia swallowed hard, shakily accepted the security pass, said goodbye to the gaggle outside and headed for the lift.

The doors opened on the eighteenth floor. Okay, girl, go for it. She stepped forward, confident as a church mouse. Damn, she'd forgotten the walk. Rhythm, rhythm. That's better. *She says to 'im and 'e says to me . . .*

She was concentrating so hard on the walk, she nearly marched straight over to Marcus's desk. Just in time, she stopped herself and picked a junior executive she'd never seen before to ask the way. He pointed. Then it was the real gauntlet, straight past four of the Americans from Rosco's team. This would *never* work. Surely they'd recognize her, even with the hair, the glasses, the scarlet lipstick, and the pink and white hooped dress. She went by, avoiding eye contact. There was no obvious reaction. So far, so good. A bit more confident now, she went the last yards, with better swing and heel angle. As she walked over, she stole a glance towards Rosco's glass box. Good, he wasn't there.

Marcus was on the phone, his feet in their usual position up on the desk. Off-handedly he waved her to the empty desk beside another secretary, Janice. This would be a bigger test: Janice had done some work for her on the Furnival bid. Where was Janice from? South London, perhaps. As long as it wasn't Gant's Hill, or anywhere near there, she might be all right. After Terry's whistle-stop tour of local places of interest – the Spreadeagle, the Chinese restaurant, and Faces night club – she had enough ammunition to survive a superficial test, but not an in-depth examination from someone with a PhD in the subject.

'Scuse me, is this Jo Silkin's seat?'

'Oh 'ello, you the temp? Janice, Janice Johnson.'

Janice held out a hand. Julia smiled back.

''Ow d'you do. Shirley Mason.'

Janice jerked a thumb over her shoulder in Marcus's direction. At precisely that moment he brayed with laughter at some joke.

'That's who you're workin' for. Marcus Ford.'

'What's 'e like? Okay, is 'e?'

252

'About as okay as Genghis bleedin' Khan. Pompous prat . . .'

This was interesting. Julia couldn't remember Janice saying anything like this before. Maybe secretaries were only candid with other secretaries.

'Jo 'ates his guts.'

'Why don't she leave, then?'

'The mortgage, of course, just like me . . . Watch out, that's 'im off the phone now. You better get sat down and switch your machine on.'

Julia did as bidden, only to bob back up when Marcus approached.

'Hi, Marcus Ford. You're . . . ?'

'Shirley.'

'Okay, Shirley, I don't have time to tell you what's what, so Janice will have to sort you out. I'm off to a meeting in the Avon room on the twentieth floor. While I'm there, I want you to type up these handwritten notes. Then I need a taxi at around twelve o'clock to take me to the Berkeley for lunch, and another to pick me up at two-thirty. Don't interrupt my meeting unless there's a call from Switzerland. Got it? Good.'

He grabbed the jacket from the back of his chair, gathered up a file of papers and dashed out.

Another test passed. This could be fun. As she sat down again, Janice brought her up short.

'You temped at Skidders before?'

Julia shook her head emphatically.

'I can't 'elp feelin' I seen you somewhere before . . . Never mind, must be my mistake. Married, are you?'

Their preparation hadn't got that far. She had to busk it.

'Yeah, no kids, though.'

'What's 'e do, your fella?'

''E's a cabbie.'

'That's nice. Good job it is, being a cabbie. I'm always on at Pete to do the Knowledge. Pete drives a JCB, one of them big ones. It's all right when the buildin' trade's goin' well, but when it's quiet, there ain't the work to go round. 'Ow long did it take your fella to

253

do the Knowledge? . . . What's 'e called, by the way? I can't go all week callin' 'im "your fella", can I?'

' 'E's Terry. Can't think 'ow long it took 'im. Normal, I s'pose.'

'So 'ow long's "normal" nowadays?'

Julia hadn't the faintest clue how long it usually took. A year? Two? Ten? Better pick something in the middle.'

'Can't remember. Six years, was it?'

'*Six*? I've never 'eard of anyone takin' *six*. 'E can't be very bright, your Terry.'

Julia managed a grin.

'That's my Terry . . .' Better get off the gossip and on to information gathering, starting with getting up to date. 'Janice, why are those desks over there all empty?'

Janice grinned. 'Right palaver that was. Last week, five of the directors left and took six executives with them. All over the papers, it was. They called us into one of the big meeting rooms so the boss, Charles Barton, could tell us there was nothing to worry about, and that there'd be no more departures. Load of old bollocks. See them three over there in the corner – the ones who're chatting together? – rumour is they'll resign this week.'

'What about Marcus? Will 'e leave?'

'No, Marcus is the blue-eyed boy at the moment. 'E's workin' on a big takeover.'

'What's a takeover?'

'It's when one company does a smash-and-grab raid on another. They're all confidential, but this one's top secret.'

'But you and Jo know?'

' '*Course* we do. The secretaries *always* know.'

'*Really*? So which company's goin' to get took over?'

Janice smiled conspiratorially, looked carefully left and right, and whispered.

'It's called Jowell. Don't you go buyin' shares, mind, or you'll land us all in the shit.'

At the mention of Jowell, Julia's eyes widened before she could catch them. She struggled to pull back a blank look.

'Me buy shares? You must be jokin'. Who'll buy this Jowell company, then?'

Janice leant right over.

'That's supposed to be the biggest secret of all. It's a Swiss company called Burlikon . . . What's the matter? You look odd.'

'No, no. I was thinkin', that was all. I'm always on at Terry to take me to Switzerland. Must be *lovely*, all them mountains and cows.'

'Yeah. Nice chocolate, too. Shirley, you better get on with that typin'. Marcus 'as one 'ell of a temper if things ain't ready on time.'

'Okay.'

It was hard to concentrate on typing after hearing that. When they'd done the bid work for Furnival, they'd identified Burlikon as one of the obvious white-knight bidders. Once Furnival's bid plan collapsed, had Marcus and Rosco taken the same idea to Burlikon? *Or* . . . ? No, surely not even Rosco would do a thing like that? Hang on, though, Rosco got a big share of any fees he brought in, didn't he? Could the slimy scumball have *deliberately* arranged for the Furnival financing to fail, so he could offer Jowell on a plate to Burlikon and cash in personally? If Janice could help her access the files on Marcus's computer, she would see when the contact with the Swiss began. If there was a decent interval after Furnival's bid ended, he and Rosco deserved the benefit of the doubt. But if work on the second bid started immediately the first one stopped . . . Another thought came to her. Grace had been working for Marcus on some big project, and she was abroad the day before she died. Could she have been at Burlikon?

Her reverie was interrupted by Janice's friendly voice. 'Want a tea or a coffee, Shirley? I'm off to the machine.'

'Oooh, I'd *love* a cup of tea.'

As the day wore on, Julia's nervousness eased to the point that she got rather bored. The phone hardly rang. There were no calls from Switzerland. Marcus's wife snarled one ill-tempered

255

message down the wires, and a man rang to say a batch of Marcus's shirts were ready. That was about it.

The biggest excitement was when Julia finished some work at the photocopier, swung round – and bumped straight into Rosco. Fortunately, he behaved in character, swearing at her under his breath and not even *thinking* of helping her pick up the papers she'd dropped. He marched across to his glass box, made a few phone calls and disappeared again.

None of the executives, who a few weeks ago had all been so keen, even noticed her existence. If secretaries were a low form of pond life, then evidently temps were even lower. Not being spotted was one thing; making progress was another. Janice had no idea when the Jowell bid was planned. Even more of a shame, she didn't know Marcus's computer log-on code word. She said that he'd recently changed the code word and wouldn't give Jo the new one.

Julia looked at her watch. Ten past six. Janice was switching off her PC and preparing to leave. The phone on Julia's desk rang.

'That you, Jules? It's me, Terry. I'm at the back of Moorgate. Thought I'd take you for a drink . . .'

Julia didn't notice Marcus return from a long meeting and walk up behind her.

'Shirley . . .'

She didn't respond.

'*Shirley* . . .'

Christ, Shirley was *her*. She turned round, all of a fluster.

'Sorry, Marcus, I didn't hear. Turnbull & Asser called. Your shirts are ready.'

Marcus stopped and stared. Janice turned too. *Fuck*, she'd said it in her normal voice. In a panic, she clamped the receiver back on the side of her face, and said down the line to a mightily puzzled Terry,

'. . . So, she says to 'im, and 'e says to 'me . . .'

Marcus's impatience trumped his curiosity.

'Shirley, will you please get off the phone right *now*. I need to dictate something urgently.'

Julia was in even deeper shit now. He would *hate* this.

'Oooh, didn't the agency say? I don't do short'and.'

Janice kept looking at her, her expression still strange. Marcus ground his teeth in fury.

'That's just fucking *great*.'

He grabbed the receiver from Julia's hand, and dialled Personnel, planning to tell them to get him a *proper* secretary. Janice intervened and saved Julie's bacon.

'I'll do it, Marcus. You run off 'ome, Shirley, see you tomorrow.'

Julia picked up her bag and fled.

Tuesday passed uneventfully. Julia began to appreciate Janice's earthy humour and was fascinated by her input on the department's sex life. How come she'd never heard all this when she worked here? Like that Marcus Ford had bonked at least three of the female executives, and wasn't above bedding a secretary if the spirit moved him. It gave her a natural opening to ask Janice innocently if she had known that girl from Skidders who's been murdered.

'Grace Chesterfield? Course I did. Sat right over there, next to that brown-haired lad. I liked Grace. Northern lass, bags of personality. Not stuck up like most people in this bank.'

'Did *she* 'ave a fella?'

'Grace? I wouldn't know. I never 'eard talk of anyone regular. Tell the truth, Grace was a bit of a slapper.'

'*What*?'

'Like the rest of 'em, she thought she could get away with it, that no one would find out. Within two months of comin' to Skidders, she got rogered by two of the fellas from Fund Management. What I 'eard was . . .' She lowered her voice. '. . . they had 'er in one of the meeting rooms on the twentieth floor, takin' turns to bonk and keep watch.'

Janice laughed a dirty, infectious laugh, allowing Julia to bury her astonishment by joining in.

'That's *naughty*. What else did she get up to?'

257

'About a year ago, she 'ad a fling with someone from global markets, David Asquith. After that, I can't think. She seemed to 'ave quietened down a bit. There was a rumour that she and Marcus 'ad a thing goin' on, but I've no idea if it's true. Terrible shock it was, Grace gettin' bumped off.'

'Ooooh, I can *imagine*.'

Janice got up and suggested a visit to the ladies. While they were checking their make-up, she slipped in a question of her own.

'You always lived in Gant's Hill, then, Shirley?'

Julia gulped, but recovered fast.

'Yeah, born and bred.'

'Pete's from Gant's Hill. Which school was you at?'

At last it was something they'd worked out: Terry's own school.

'Fairlock Compr'ensive.'

' 'Ow old are you, then? Twenty-eight, twenty-nine?'

No reason to lie on this one. 'Oooh, do I look that young? That's nice. No, I'm thirty-one.'

'Then you'll know Pete's kid sister. She'd be an age with you, and she went there. Bridget Johnson.'

'*Bridget Johnson*? I remember the name all right. Can't put a face to it, though. She must've been in another class.'

'Barrel of laughs, Bridget is. She's always goin' on about that PE teacher, the fat woman with great 'airy armpits. I forget now, what was 'er name?'

'Oh, '*er*? Yeah, she was *funny*. Name's on the tip of me tongue. No, can't think of it. These days I got a memory like a sieve ... Oh well, back to work, I s'pose.'

Julia led the way back, swinging for all she was worth, and breathing a sigh of relief to have squeaked through that one. Janice followed, the tiniest hint of a smile on her face.

When they got back, Marcus was waiting impatiently. He announced that he had to fly to Switzerland the next morning and would be there for the rest of the week. She should book him on the first flight to Zurich. He needed to send some e-mails right away; after that, he'd be gone to a meeting for the rest of the day.

If any papers came in later from Findlaters, the lawyers, she should bring them round personally to his house after work.

This was desperate. If he was gone for the rest of the week, how could she get his log-on out of him? Then, too late, she saw the last chance. There he was, sitting down and turning his PC on. If she moved quickly behind him as he tapped in the code word, maybe she could read it.

Damn, the screen was already on. These machines were so quick, there was almost no start-up procedure. She got there as fast as she could, but he was already beginning to pick out the log-on letters with his index finger. It would be in and gone before she could see it.

She was in luck. Marcus couldn't touch-type. His index finger rose and fell slowly and deliberately. Furiously, she concentrated on which keys it hit. Middle row left end, middle row five from the left, second row down four from the left, middle row left end again. That was it. She scuttled back to her own desk and checked them: A,G,R,A. Agra. As in Taj Mahal? No, it couldn't be that. Log-ons had to be at least five letters. She must have looked over too late and missed one key, or even two. What short word ended in 'agra'? She found herself running through the alphabet. Bagra, cagra, dagra, fagra . . . If it had six letters, there were more possibilities. It shouldn't be *that* hard, though. Einstein would solve it.

The parcel from Findlaters didn't turn up until seven, and was sealed so securely that any tampering would have been obvious. Rather than bothering Terry, she took the cab that Skidders provided over to Chelsea and told it to wait while she made the delivery.

Marcus brushed aside her objections, insisting that she come inside and wait till he'd read through the papers, in case he needed to respond immediately. He sent the cabbie away, took Julia's coat, ushered her into the drawing room and poured her a glass of Chablis.

Julia sat in silence, looking around the room. The taste was

259

decidely chi-chi, which made it harder to keep a suitably awed look on her face. Marcus ran through the pages, snorting once in a while, then put them down on a side table. Julia, who'd whiled away the time playing with the gold-plate clasp on her emerald-green handbag, looked up.

'Everthin' okay, is it?'

'Yah, fine. Nothing to do tonight, anyway.'

'I better be off, then.'

'Take your time, finish your drink . . . Like wine, do you?'

'It's very nice.'

'Not your usual tipple, though?'

'No, I drink Bacardi and Coke most of the time. Does your wife like wine?'

'Only red. She's allergic to white. Allergic to lots of things, my wife. Smiling brings her out in a rash.'

'*Really*?'

'No, just kidding. I would introduce you, but she's away. When she heard I was going to Switzerland, she buggered off with the kids to her father's place.'

He got up from his armchair to replenish his glass and, as an afterthought, wandered over to the sofa and filled Julia's too. He sat down at the far end of the sofa, slurped half a glassful and, with a faintly amused air, proceeded to examine her. She smiled back shyly.

'What you lookin' at?'

'You.'

'What for?'

'You have a lovely figure.'

'Oh, *go on*.'

'I mean it. You go in and out in all the right places.'

'My 'usband Terry says I'm scrawny.'

He lunged across and tested one of her thighs for scrawniness.

'No, you're just right. Terry's talking through his arse.'

Marcus withdrew the hand, but moved to the middle of the sofa, giving her no more than token breathing space. She inched back as far as she could.

260

'I bet you've got nice breasts, too.'

Julia didn't need to fake the blush.

'The things you say . . . They're all right. A bit small, maybe.'

'What size bra do you take?'

'Thirty-four B, if you must know.'

His hand flashed out, slipped deftly through her panic defences and squeezed her left breast through her cardigan.

' 'Ere, you can't do that, I'm married.'

'So am I. Who cares? As long as neither of us mentions it, where's the harm?'

Julia was calculating as fast as she could. The way he was behaving, it was perfectly possible that he might throw himself on top of her. She doubted he would be mad enough to rape her, but it could get unpleasant, and in the mêlée her specs or her accent would slip and the game would be up. However, make a fuss now and the petulant brat might stop her working at Skidders for the rest of the week. If she knew Marcus Ford, flattery would be the best policy. Like flicking a switch, she banished her scowl and replaced it with a winning smile.

'I think you're *really* impressive, you know.'

Natural modesty stopped Marcus accepting the accolade too lightly.

'Impressive? Why so?'

'Janice says you're the biggest star in the bank.'

'Oh, I wouldn't say that.'

'*Really*? Who is then?' Julia was finding it hard not to grin.

'Well, if you put it like that . . . I don't suppose there's anyone else in Skidders who's as well regarded in the UK market. There are a few guys in other banks, like Goldman Sachs and Morgan Stanley.'

'But none of them's *better* than you, surely?'

'Not . . . better, no. Older. Some clients like grey hair.'

'Not me. I think you've got *lovely* 'air . . .' She raised her glass to her lips and looked at him seductively as she took a sip. 'So why are you off to Switzerland? Is it some big takeover, or only a teensy-weensy one?'

Marcus smiled condescendingly. 'Shirley, I *never* do teensy-weensy deals. I leave those to the juniors and the old farts.'

'So is this one medium-size? By your own standards, I mean.'

Marcus was wearying of this. He wanted to get back to discussing her body. The easiest thing was to kill it stone dead.

'Shirley, my Swiss deal will be the biggest Skidders has ever done and one of the largest the whole London market has seen.'

'Oooh, will it be in the papers, then?'

He moved his hand forward again, more slowly this time, and rested it on her thigh. She didn't protest. He looked into her eyes.

'It will be all over them. Guaranteed banner headlines.' His hand began to slide up under her dress.

'Oooh, how *excitin'*! I must watch out for it. Will it be this side of Christmas?'

The other hand moved to unbutton her cardigan. His voice went huskier, more distracted.

'No, but don't stop reading the papers between Christmas and New Year. Prepare to be impressed.'

Bingo. Now she had to get out of here. Her cardigan was wide open, and she was down to her last line of nylon resistance. Memories of Rosco Sellars flooded her mind; the thought of Marcus Ford touching her breasts – even if he didn't know they were *hers* – was too much to bear.

'Marcus?'

'What is it, Shirley?' He wasn't going to be put off now: it was *obvious* she wanted it.

'I *can't*.'

'Don't give me any more of that "married" bullshit.'

'No, it's not that . . . it's the wrong time of the month.'

'Doesn't bother me.'

'Men think it's *dirty*.'

'No, we don't.'

'Well, *I* do. Let's do it next time your wife's away . . .'

Shit. Still, what did he have to lose? She might be worth waiting for. She had a tarty charm and would fuel his fantasies about

262

Essex girls. Plus, she was only a temp, so it wouldn't get back. He was pretty sure that none of the bank girls he'd screwed had been dumb enough to blab, but you could never be sure. Now that he was becoming so senior, he would have to be even more careful.

'Okay, leave me a note of your phone number and I'll call you next time she's away.'

'All right . . .' Julia looked at her watch. 'I got to run. Terry'll be wonderin' what's 'appened to me.'

Marcus stayed seated. He was on heat, and wanted something from her on account.

'Shirley, before you go, how about a mouthful?'

'I'm not 'ungry.'

'That's not what I meant.' He unzipped his flies, and closed his eyes in anticipation.

Julia knelt in front of him and closely examined the enthusiastic protuberance.

' 'Ow big does it get when you 'ave an 'ard-on?'

Marcus's eyes flashed open in fury and hurt. He looked down defensively at his weapon.

'What d'you mean?'

Before he could recover his wits, she scrambled back to her feet, gave him a little wave and departed, leaving him cursing for hours and fretting for days.

*

It was Poppy who cracked it. Einstein had said he would rig up a program to find all the six-letter words in the dictionary ending in -agra and bring it round to their nightly counsel of war. Of late they had got in the habit of holding them in Poppy's room. It made her feel part of it all and spared Len and Jean her tantrums for not being informed.

Einstein arrived with the printout. There *were* only three such words in the whole dictionary, none of them very likely-sounding. If it was some obscure acronym or random series of letters, there wasn't a lot they could do. Einstein threw the printout down on the bed and switched excitedly to his news about the Hawk papers. He'd deciphered the elaborate references in the handwritten letter, and worked out that the recipient had played a part in handling works of art looted from Jews. And who was that recipient? None other than Gerhard Muller, Chairman of the mighty Alps insurance company. Len and Terry failed to cotton on to the relevance of this until Einstein breathlessly informed them that the papers also identified Alps as Burlikon's leading shareholder.

Julia's eyes sparkled. 'Brilliant, Einstein, absolutely bloody *brilliant* . . .'

She grabbed hold of his cheeks and gave him a huge wet kiss right on the lips. Einstein's glasses steamed up, blinding him briefly, and his whole face went deep pink in grateful embarrassment.

'That's so *typical* of Rosco. He's got Hawk to find dirt on Muller so Burlikon can't shaft him.'

Terry looked puzzled. 'Shaft like 'ow, Jules?'

'Like back out at the last minute, or refuse to pay Skidders's fee.'

They all been so rapt listening to Einstein, none of them had noticed Poppy picking up the printout. From the top of the bed, a small voice piped up.

'Bleedin' obvious, in'it? Thought you was meant to be smart, Einstein.' They looked at her, not sure whether she was joking. Len asked,

'If it's so obvious, Poppity, what the 'ell *is* it?'

'I'll give you a clue. It's somethin' *you* could do with a truckload of, Dad, but if Terry got 'old of it, all the gels from Romford to Wanstead would run for cover.'

'What you on about, love?'

Len was nowhere, and nor was Terry. Einstein and Julia were already grinning.

*

Though Marcus was away, there were too many people around for Julia to try logging on before lunchtime. Luckily, Janice went

264

out for a bite with some of the other girls; even then the floor was far from deserted, and she was acutely aware of eyes watching her as she sat down casually at Marcus's desk, switched the computer on, and typed in 'Viagra'.

Bullseye! Quickly now. She scrolled through the files. There they were, a whole bunch of them. There was no time to try out the contents, so she hit the 'print' button for the lot.

This would take a while. While she was waiting, there was another thing she could do: call up his electronic diary and download that too.

It was a fast printer, and in twelve nervous minutes it was all done. Still aware of the risk that she was being watched, Julia collected the pages, carried them over to her own desk and stuffed them in two big brown envelopes. Five minutes later, she looked furtively about her, and when no one was looking her way, slid them into her oversize handbag. Now to get out of here. She should leave a note for Janice to thank her. She grabbed a pen and a 'Post It' sticker and started to scribble something.

No. It felt underhand, after all Janice had done. Counting the seconds, perspiring more than a little, she waited until two o'clock came round and the girls bounced back in, still chirruping away. Janice sat down with a thump.

'That was fun. We do 'ave a laugh, us gels. Pity you didn't come too, Shirley'.

'Yeah. Janice, I got a bit of a problem. Me Mum's been took sick.'

'Nothin' serious, I 'ope.'

'She fainted while she was out shoppin'. I ought to go and see 'er.'

''Course you ought. Don't worry, I'll cover the phones for you.'

'Thanks, Janice. Thing is, though, if she's *really* poorly, I might 'ave to look after 'er for the rest of the week.'

'That's okay, love. Tell you what, you run off, and I'll let Personnel know.'

'Thanks ever so, Janice, you've been real good to me. I'm sorry we won't meet again.'

'Me, too. Remember on Monday I asked if you'd worked 'ere before?'

'Yeah.' Julia's pulse accelerated.

'I realize now why I thought that. You remind of a gel who used to work 'ere. Not a secretary, an executive. Posh gel, but friendly. Julia Daventry, she was called.'

Julia felt her throat constricting. It was hard to get words out, in *any* accent.

'What . . . what 'appened to 'er?'

'Got the shove. Marched 'er right out the door, they did. I never got a chance to say goodbye. Pity, that. Never mind, at least *you* didn't skip off without sayin' goodbye, did you?'

Janice held out her hand. Julia took it. They both smiled warmly.

'Bye-bye, Shirley, and good luck with whatever you do next.'

And, barely noticeably, Janice winked.

25

Early on Wednesday evening they gathered back in Poppy's room to hear Julia's pronouncement on the papers she'd downloaded.

'Okay, Burlikon's definitely the bidder, and Skidders's work for them began *immediately* after the Furnival bid collapsed.'

'What else did you find?' Einstein was fascinated.

'Well, there's something truly odd here. As you know, I worked on the Furnival team, and I remember exactly how much information we had on Jowell. It was all publicly available material, which in Jowell's case isn't a lot. It gave us quite a headache, putting together a financing plan with such skimpy data. Yet, when I look at this, Marcus has all manner of detailed numbers, including full breakdowns by sector, plant and product. Not only that, there are weekly sales and profit figures here that can only have come from Jowell's internal management accounts. It's *amazing*. Any takeover bid would be easy to plan if you had info like this.'

Len scratched his head.

'But Jules, don't banks 'ave ways to get stuff like that?'

'Not legally. No target company is just going to hand it over.'

It was Einstein's turn to challenge her.

'Couldn't they have hired an ex-employee of Jowell with a lot of that knowledge in his head? *That* can't be illegal.'

'True, but it can't be the case here. For a start, it's much too detailed. It's also too up-to-date. We're what? – the ninth of December. The last of these reports is dated the first. That's Tuesday of last week – The only explanation is that Skidders have got a mole inside Jowell. They must be *crazy*. If they get caught, the bank's reputation would be destroyed and the individuals involved might end up in jail. They'd certainly never work in the City again.'

Terry looked doubtful.

'Jules, from what you've said about Marcus Ford . . . I mean, I know 'e's a plonker, but is 'e the type to take that big a risk?'

'I wouldn't've thought so, Terry, unless Rosco Sellars has some sort of hold over him.'

'What, like nude pics?'

They all smirked. Poppy laughed out loud. Julia had never admitted what she'd wanted from that safe, even after the burglary. All the same, they *knew*. She had the grace to smile shyly.

'Something like that. Anyway, if he *is* up to no good, there could be a link with something that's in his electronic diary. Since mid-November, every Tuesday has an "F" marked. On the tenth of November, it seems he met "F" in Brussels, and on the seventeeth in Stockholm. After that, there's no venue mentioned, but the diary says Tuesday midnight every week until the middle of February.'

'Anyway we can check this out, Jules?' Len felt he hadn't contributed much recently, and was impatient for action. Poppy provided the orders.

''Course there is, you div. Next Tuesday night you can follow 'im. Terry can go with you and take pictures.'

Len bristled. 'It'll be *dark*, smarty pants. And if we use flash, they'll see us, won't they?'

Poppy couldn't think of a good answer, but rolled her eyes anyway. Einstein said they could go to a spy shop and buy an infra-red camera.

'*See*?' declared Poppy conclusively.

Einstein was anxious to get on. 'What about timing?'

'That's the bad news. Marcus was telling the truth last night. It's planned for the thirtieth of December. Your options will have expired by then. There's only one way to get us out of this hole . . .'

Len raised one hand reprovingly.

'Jules, I've told you before. We won't 'ave you borrowin' money for this. We know you're nearly as skint as we are.'

Julia shook her head.

268

'Len, that's not the problem. When you three bought the options, you were being pretty naive. The authorities are always on the alert for unusual dealing patterns before a bid and they might well have picked you up. As long as they didn't twig your little recording habit, you *might* have persuaded them that it wasn't true insider dealing, that you'd simply overheard something and put two and two together. This time it's different. Information doesn't come much more "insider" than what I've stolen today from Skidders's computer, and if the authorities ever got to the truth, you really *would* go to prison. So would I.'

Terry's voice was plaintive.

'So what *can* we do, Jules? We got to do *something*.'

'I agree, and I have a suggestion to make. I propose that tomorrow we establish a boutique.'

'A *boutique*? What would we sell?' Terry was well confused.

'Brain power.'

''Ow d'you mean, "brain power"?'

Poppy chortled. 'She don't mean *you*, Terry.'

Julia smiled. 'Yes, I do. I mean all of us. This sort of "boutique" isn't a shop; it's the name they give to a miniature investment bank.'

Einstein waited patiently for this exchange to end.

'Tell us, Julia, what would we use the boutique for?'

'To become Jowell's advisers.'

'And advise them to do what?'

'To make a takeover bid for Burlikon, *before* Burlikon moves on them.'

Einstein grinned at her cheek. 'I can see that Jowell might welcome that. How does it help Poppy, though?'

Julia had reserved her broadest smile for this moment.

'Fees. For a bid of this size, we'd want to charge . . .' She paused maliciously. 'Guess. Terry, you go first.'

'I dunno. Ten grand?'

Julia shook her head and turned to Len. From Jules's reaction, Terry must've been way too low.

'Fifty grand?'

269

Another smiling shake of the head. Einstein had no idea at all, and was trying to calculate it. Unless banks received more than Terry and Len were saying, how could they afford to pay those famous bonuses? Also, Julia was looking so pleased with herself, this *had* to be a knockout idea, enough to pay for the whole Poppy thing.'

'Half a million.'

Julia reached out and took Poppy's hand.

'That's the trouble with cabbies, isn't it, Poppy? They all think so small. I wouldn't *dream* of taking on a bid of this size for a penny less than five million pounds.'

Terry's whistle could be heard halfway down the street.

*

All three of the cabbies were badly behind in paying their bills and decided to work that night. Julia didn't feel like trogging all the way back to her own flat, so she decided to stay on with Poppy for a while and let herself into Terry's house later. She'd had a few chats with her now, and they'd struck up quite a friendship. Sooner or later, the conversation always got onto Terry. Poppy gave a fuller and funnier account of Terry's sexual adventures than he volunteered himself, and she could do a hilarious imitation of Marcie in a temper. Tonight she related the tale of Daphne and the dose Terry had given her, which very nearly brought Julia up to date.

'Jules, what would *you* do if you found out Terry was playin' away from 'ome?'

'I'd cut his balls off.'

'And do what with 'em then?'

'Cook them in a Bolognese sauce, and eat them with lots of spaghetti.'

Poppy laughed. 'Will you miss 'im, Jules?'

'What d'you mean, Poppy? Why should I miss Terry?'

'It's *obvious*, in't it? It's all very well you two bonkin' like rabbits durin' "Save Poppy Week", but after you've raised the money and caught the murderer, you'll be off, won't you?'

270

'Why d'you think that?'

'Come on, Jules, I wasn't born yesterday. You're 'avin' a bit of fun with the workin' classes, that's all. I don't blame you. That's prob'ly the attraction for Terry, too, shaggin' an upper-class gel like you.'

Julia didn't look thrilled. 'Is that what Terry says?'

'Nah. Normally, Terry tells me everythin'. Not about you, though. All 'e says is 'e likes you.'

'I like him too, Poppy.'

'Maybe you do. Won't last, though, will it? You wouldn't want your friends to meet 'im, you'd be ashamed. And what about your Mum and Dad? Terry says they're lords or somethin'.'

'They're not lords. Daddy is a "Sir", and that makes Mummy Lady Daventry. The "Sir" came from Daddy's job: he wasn't born with a title.'

'What about your Mum?'

'Mummy's called "Hon", but that's only what they call a courtesy title. She got it because her father was a Viscount. He died a long time ago.'

'Does that make your Gran a Viscountess?'

'That's right. She *was* exactly that. After my Grandad died, though, she got married again, to a very grand man with no money at all. She got a new title from him, so now she's a Duchess. He died, too. I suspect she poisons them. I'll be seeing her at the weekend: she's visiting Mummy and Daddy for her eighty-third birthday. They're having a party for her, and the old dragon insists that I go.'

'Are you takin' someone? . . . Don't worry, Jules, I won't shop you.'

'No, I am *not*. Mind you, my mother hasn't given up hope of marrying me off, so she's probably invited one or two Hooray Henrys.'

'Why don't you take Terry? 'E'd see them off.'

Julia chuckled. 'I'm sure he would.'

'So, why *don't* you?'

'Oh, Terry wouldn't enjoy it. He'd be bored rigid.'

271

'Ask 'im. Let 'im decide hisself.'

'It's too late now. There wouldn't be room round the table for another person.'

Poppy snorted.

'*See*? I was right, wasn't I? You *are* ashamed of 'im. You'll drop 'im the moment you find out who murdered your friend.'

'No, I *won't*. And I won't have you saying I'm ashamed of Terry, 'cause it's not true.'

'Prove it then.'

'How?'

'Take 'im with you.'

Julia hesitated. Poppy turned away and faced the wall.

Shit, she couldn't *believe* she was being cornered like this. Poppy was the sneakiest, most manipulative, cleverest kid she'd ever met. Couldn't she think of some decent excuse to get out of it? Inspiration didn't strike.

'Oh, *all right* then.'

Poppy turned back and giggled, so infectiously that Julia's irritation dissolved. All the same, she was horrified at her stupidity in agreeing. What on earth would her family make of Terry, especially her brother? It didn't bear thinking about.

*

Julia's Thursday was a big day, arranging for business cards to be printed, showing Einstein how to run numbers and analyse data, probing Len's memory banks until they yielded recollections of long-lost rag-trade friends, and dispatching Terry on a succession of minor errands. In all her years in banking she'd never worked so hard, kept so many balls in the air, achieved so much.

Friday was different. To Hertz at seven a.m. and on the M1 by eight. Something Janice had said about Grace and Marcus kept echoing in her mind, and, unresolved, it pushed her north to Beverley.

She knew she should ring ahead, yet somehow she couldn't. Was it the fear of censure, spoken or unspoken, for her absence from Grace's funeral? Or the risk that Beth and Tom would rail against her painful prodding of a raw-red wound, and beg her to stay away? Hard-hearted as it might be, she couldn't take that chance, and drove on through the miles.

The eyes behind the opening door were haunted, sunk, defeated.

'Mr Chesterfield? Do you remember me? Julia Daventry?'

He stared, glazed, uncomprehending.

'I worked with Grace. I stayed here. Don't you remember?'

Still he looked blank.

'We don't want no . . . interfering. We've been through enough.'

He started to close the door. Julia surprised herself by blocking it with her foot. Tom was too surprised, too bewildered to resist and he pulled it back open.

'Mr Chesterfield. I really need to speak to you. Is your wife in?'

From somewhere in the house she could hear a voice asking who it was. Limply, Tom Chesterfield turned sideways, looked down at the worn hall carpet, and mumbled.

'It's a girl. Says she knew Grace.' He spoke far too softly to be heard in the kitchen.

Again came the disembodied voice, clearer now, approaching.

'Who *is* it, Tom?'

Through the kitchen door, her hands clumsily pulling off the apron, Beth Chesterfield came into view. She went on the attack before she got a proper sight of the visitor.

'If you're from the papers, we've told you we won't be bothered.'

As she got closer, Julia saw the glint of recognition in her eyes.

'Mrs Chesterfield, it's *me*, Julia Daventry.'

There was a nod, a half-smile, still a large measure of doubt. She pushed her husband gently back towards the parlour, leaving Julia standing on the step.

'Hello, Julia. I'm sorry if Tom didn't recognize you. We've been through a lot, and we don't like being bothered nowadays. Visitors upset us, especially Tom. They mean well, I don't doubt, but they all want to talk about it.'

273

'Mrs Chesterfield, I'm so sorry to drop in on you unannounced in this way . . . To be perfectly honest, I thought if I called you'd say no.'

Beth nodded in agreement with that.

'I'm sorry if we seem unwelcoming, Julia. I know you've come a long way, but if it's to talk about Grace, we simply don't *want* to. We want to be left in peace.'

'Mrs Chesterfield, I *must* speak with you. It's about the man who murdered Grace.'

Her eyes narrowed.

'I hope he rots in hell, the pervert. All we do is thank God they caught him, so he won't cause pain to the Mums and Dads of other poor girls. After they've locked him up, they should throw the bloody key away.'

Julia looked left and right up the bleak street, wondering how best to phrase it, afraid of what was coming.

'Mrs Chesterfield, I don't know how to say this well, and, anyway, I can't come near proving it to you . . .'

'What? . . . *What?*'

'I don't believe that Marti Salminen did it. I think the police have got the wrong man.'

Rage flashed across Beth Chesterfield's face.

'The only thing that gives us peace is knowing that the devil who murdered our girl is behind bars, and you have the nerve to come back here and . . . Go *away. Now.*'

The door slammed violently. For a few seconds Julia stood there, wondering if she had the courage to try again.

No. It wasn't only a matter of courage, either. She saw the harm she was doing. She and the cabbies might be right or wrong; it didn't give them the licence to do this to these people. Feeling more than a little ashamed, she turned round, walked a few steps and began fumbling for the car keys.

It took her time to outsmart the immobilizer system and get the engine going. Before she moved off, the green door opened again and Beth Chesterfield came towards the kerb. Julia put the car back into neutral and pressed the window button. They looked at each other for a moment, Beth's expression half-accusing, half-pleading.

'You better tell me.'

'Okay.'

'Have you got a coat with you?'

'In the back.'

'All right, put it on, we'll go for a walk. I don't want to trouble Tom.'

*

'I know it must've seemed cold of me. I just *couldn't*. I'm terrible at occasions like that, I go to pieces.'

'D'you think we'd have cared? I was sad you didn't come. You were the only one of her London friends we ever met. None of them came, except for Mr Barton. I suppose he felt he had to, being head of the bank. All the same, it was a kind gesture. We appreciated it.'

'I hadn't realized he did that. You're right, though, it was decent of him. Did he say anything to you?'

'I can't remember. I don't recall a word anyone said that day.'

'Mrs Chesterfield, there's something I need to ask you. Grace told me she was having an affair with a married man. Could it have been someone at the bank?'

There was no answer. They walked on.

'You see, the day she died I had a coffee with her. Something at work was worrying her, and she hinted it was tied up with her relationship. I'm *convinced* that her death is linked to whatever this was and, if I'm right, Marti Salminen may be innocent. Don't get me wrong, I'm sure he's not a good person. But being bad doesn't make you a murderer.'

They walked on for a few hundred yards. They had left the body of the town behind and were skirting the racecourse. Mrs Chesterfield seemed unembarrassed by the long silence. Eventually, she broke it.

'Julia, will you give me your word that you'll tell no one about this? Not the papers, not the police?'

'You have my word.'

She took a deep breath before starting.

'It *was* someone at the bank. A married man with two children, that's all she told us.'

'Was it serious?'

'Grace thought so. She said he would get divorced and marry her. She was very happy about it. We weren't sure *what* to think. Breaking up a marriage is a terrible thing. Grace's case was . . . unusual, though.'

'Unusual in what way?'

'Oh, Julia, I don't know if I should be saying this. Grace was odd about boys ever since she was a slip of a thing. It wasn't that she was bad, she was just a bit – well there's no good word for it – *easy*. I don't know what we did to make her that way, God rest her soul.'

Julia tried her best to laugh it off.

'Yes, Grace told me about her great teenage love. I had one of those, too.'

'There were lots of others besides him. I dare say she didn't tell you about the trouble he got her in.'

'Trouble?'

'He got her pregnant when she was sixteen. She had an abortion. Tom and I were beside ourselves at the time. Later we thought it was a blessing in disguise. It gave her a hell of a shock. She began to work hard at her studies and got to Cambridge and all that. We thought she'd grown out of those bad ways, but we thought wrong. Going to London went to her head. She got involved with a bad set there and ended up pregnant again. She told us, bold as brass, that she didn't know who the father was.'

'What happened this time?'

'She had another abortion, only that one didn't go well. The doctors told her she wouldn't be able to have children of her own. So she made her mind up to go out and find what she needed.'

'What on earth do you mean, Mrs Chesterfield?'

'She thought that no successful single man would want her if he knew she couldn't have children, so she decided to go after a man who already had kids. Not just any man, mind. She wanted a man to be proud of, that's what she said, and for Grace that meant rich, I'm afraid. The way she saw it, time wasn't on her side. If she was to catch someone grand, she had to act while her looks were still there. She was terribly scared of turning thirty without being married. The poor lass doesn't have to worry about that now.'

Beth began to cry, and had to stop and hold on tight to Julia's arm.

26

He ran down the platform and, ignoring the command to stand back, wrenched a moving door open and jumped sweatily onto the six-forty-four. Terry was pissed off with Julia. At first he'd been pleased, as well as gobsmacked, when she'd invited him. Then came the doubts and the to-do, spending half Friday morning in Moss Bros in Covent Garden hiring a dinner jacket. It was the first time he'd worn one, and as far as he could judge from the shop's mirrors, it made him look more like a waiter than James Bond. The assistant's patient explanation of how to tie a dickie bow fell on stony ground, and Terry abandoned the unequal struggle in favour of a ready-made royal blue job.

Julia was supposed to be back in good time for them to drive there together. Then came call after whispered call on her mobile phone. It was the Chesterfields asking her to stay Friday night, to have Saturday lunch, to visit Grace's grave. She murmured that she'd found out something vital, but couldn't say what it was. After she finally left, she ran into serial roadworks and told Terry to go from Waterloo, promising to meet him at Salisbury station if she could get there in time. He was regretting agreeing to go at all.

At ten to eight the train rolled into a rain-soaked Salisbury. No Julia, and a long queue for cabs. It was freezing cold and the wind was angling the rain under the useless canopy, drenching him. He yanked his coat out of the canvas bag and put it on over his DJ. He'd *kill* Jules.

Fifteen minutes later, the battered Vauxhall set off towards the house of terrors: the Old Vicarage, Milton Parva. It took the driver three wrong turns and a question in a pub to find the place. What kind of cabbie was this? When Terry thought of his four years of hard labour on a moped, it riled him that a fella like this could get some sort of badge without knowing the first thing about the area. He paid him the fare of eight pounds fifty, climbed out and crunched his way up the long gravel drive to the ivy-clad house, nervous as a kitten. Jules had promised to tell him what to do, to watch out for him, and generally be his minder. Oh to hell with it, they were only people. He pressed the polished brass bell.

The door opened, revealing a tall, elegant man, his silver hair swept back. Framed by the glow of the warm light inside, he looked effortlessly superior in his beautifully tailored dinner jacket. Already, Terry was no longer so sure that people were only people.

'Hello. You're Terence, I presume. I'm Julia's father. I'm afraid she's not here yet.'

Terry dropped his bag and stuck out a hand.

Sir Sydney shook it quickly. 'Come on in, man, you must be getting soaked out there.'

Terry stepped inside, reached down and pulled a box out of his bag. At Waterloo, it had occurred to him that he should bring a gift. Finding something had almost made him miss the train.

'I brought some Milk Tray. That okay?'

'That's . . . very kind, Terence, but perhaps it would be better if you gave it to my wife. Better still, it's Lavinia's mother's birthday, why not give it to *her*?'

'Good idea.' Terry grabbed the box back.

'I *was* going to show you up to your room to change, but I see you've done that already. You can leave your bag and jacket here if you like. Why not come through, and meet everyone? Do you need to wash your hands?'

Terry checked: they were okay. Sir Sydney led the way to the drawing room, with Terry trailing after him, clutching his chocolates.

The first thing his eyes were drawn to was the Duchess herself, sitting holding court to a posse of guests. She was wearing a big black dress and gallons of pearls. Terry was surprised she didn't have one of those tiara jobs that Princess Di used to go in for. As he came in, the Duchess looked up, took him in, then carried on playing Queen Bee.

Nearer the door was another group, with a skinny older lady in a white dress, two girls in their twenties and a red-faced geezer who was banging on about Tony Blair. Julia's father put a hand on the skinny lady's arm and prised her away. Red-face rattled on regardless of the depleted audience.

'Darling, this is Terence.'

Lady Daventry smiled cautiously.

'We're *so* glad you could join us, Terence.'

'Nice of you to invite me, your ladyship.'

'Oh, don't bother with that "lady" nonsense. My friends call me Lavinia.'

'Thanks. Me mates call me Terry. No one's called me Terence since I got baptized.'

Sir Sydney gestured at the slender box.

'Terry kindly brought some chocolates for you, darling. I wondered if he should give them to your mother instead.'

She looked at the box, and back at her husband. He had a wicked twinkle in his eye.

'What a nice idea. Terry, why don't you come across and be introduced? But you haven't got a drink. Sydney, you're neglecting our guests.'

Terry's request for a beer was met with a glass of champagne. Lady Daventry walked him over, and they stood there for a minute or more while the Duchess finished a childhood anecdote. Only when the polite laughter subsided did she look up. So did her audience of two late-middle-aged women – one mousy and the other haughty – three young men, and a particularly pretty girl.

'Mama, may I introduce Julia's friend, Terry?' The grand old lady nodded curtly, though not coldly.

'Pleased to meet you, Duchess.'

Two of the young men giggled; the third looked daggers at him.

Lady Daventry continued.

'These are my sisters, Alice and Charlotte . . . and this is Julia's younger brother, Giles, and two friends of his, Will and Nick.'

''Ow d'you do?' Terry did his best to smile at the whole group.

'And this beautiful creature is Giles's new girlfriend, Davina.'

Davina flashed a brilliant smile at Terry.

'Mama, Terry has a birthday present for you'

To make it more of a surprise, Terry had held the box behind his back. With a flourish, he produced it.

''Appy birthday, Duchess.'

The two young men seemed so taken aback, they broke off from the group and went and stood together by the window, sharing some private joke. Giles looked stunned, making Terry wonder if this had trumped *his* present. Davina seemed absolutely delighted. The Duchess paused for a second before accepting the offering.

'Thank you, young man, that is very kind of you. It's a long time since I've been given Milk Tray.'

Terry was pleased. 'Yeah, it's not easy to find them. I 'ad to search the length and breadth of Waterloo.'

The conversation was interrupted by the sound of the doorbell. Lady Daventry clapped her hands and looked imploringly upwards.

'Dear *God*, let that be my daughter.'

It was. Julia rushed into the room, greeted everyone at double speed and dashed over to Terry, whispering in his ear.

'*So* sorry. I ran out of petrol. Are you all right?'

''Course, Jules, I can 'andle meself. Everyone's being real friendly, even the Duchess.'

'Marvellous . . . I must go and change. I'll be as quick as poss. Can you manage till then?'

''Course I can, doll, take your time.'

She didn't leave without whispering again.

'Grace was having an affair with a man at Skidders, someone married with two kids. Marcus has two, and Janice thought they might be having an affair. Rosco has a couple of kids, too.

281

It *has* to be one of them, and they could've got the poison through Hawk.'

Before Terry could ask more, she was gone.

For a moment he was left on his own. Then the two young fellows, Will and Nick, marched over to him from the window, both wearing wide grins. Will went first.

'Julia's been keeping you a big secret, Terry. How long have you two been together?'

'Oh, two or three weeks, I s'pose.'

'Do you work in the City, too?'

'Yeah, quite a lot of the time.'

Nick looked puzzled.

'Did you meet through work, or socially?'

'Neither, we met in a cab.'

'What, were you *sharing* one?'

'In a manner of speaking. I was drivin' it.'

'I don't follow you.'

'It was me own cab. That's what I do, I'm a London cabbie.'

'*Really*? How utterly delicious. Well, good for you, that's what I say, eh, Will?'

And off they went again, this time in Giles's direction, and muttered something to him. Terry saw him grimace and, with wild, fierce eyes, storm out of the room. The sound of stairs being taken furiously two at a time was audible throughout the house.

Julia forced the black dress over her head, and wriggled it all the way down into place. She'd have to get her mother to do up the top hook. She began putting on make-up. The door was flung angrily open.

'How *could* you do this to me?' His eyes were like burning coals.

She looked defiantly at him, then back at the mirror.

'Do *what*, exactly, Giles?'

'Bring that thing here for Grandmother's birthday, when you *knew* how much I wanted Davina to get the right impression.'

'Oh, is *that* it? Well, sorry if I've let the side down.'

It had been a very long time since Julia had liked her brother. He'd been a selfish brat throughout his childhood and had shown few signs of improvement since.

'I can't believe it. My sister going out with a fucking taxi driver. And why, may I ask, didn't you at least have the decency to warn Mummy and Dad what he is? You've made them a laughing stock.'

'Balls. If there's any laughing being done, it's at *my* expense, not theirs. Mummy and Daddy aren't half as big snobs as you. I admit I should have told them so they weren't surprised. I thought I'd get here before him.'

'Well, if I'd been told, I certainly wouldn't have come. I can't stop you having your bit of rough, but I'll thank you not to bring a lowlife like that again when I'm here.'

'I'd better keep away myself, if you're going to be so worried what your girlfriends think; *I* might say the wrong thing too. Now, piss off out of my bedroom and let me finish my make-up. And Giles . . .'

'What?'

'If you're rude to Terry, I'll never forgive you.'

Giles replied with an ugly smile, spun on his heels, and left.

Lady Daventry had hidden Terry as best she could, between her mousy sister Alice, and the doddery wife of an old friend of her mother. More important, he was as far away as possible from Giles, his pals and Davina. The Duchess sat in state on the right of Sir Sydney, with Lord Warburton, the Duke's best man, on her other side. The cleaning ladies, who doubled as waitresses on occasions like this, brought in the prawn bisque.

The soup was accompanied by hushed conversation and many glances. Davina kept looking diagonally at Terry, watching with amusement as he followed Julia's distant leads on how he should eat, while doing his best to engage the biddy next to him in talk of the weather. Davina found the whole situation delightful. She was far from sure that Giles Daventry was an interest she planned to pursue. For all his good looks, she saw in those pouting lips traces of petulance, and she didn't care too much for his braying ways when his friends were around. It was hilarious how he'd reacted when his sister's boyfriend had turned up. What business was it of his? She rather admired the girl for having the nerve to bring a cabbie to a party like this, especially as he was not altogether un-cute. Before he arrived, the party was dull as ditchwater. At least he might provide some amusement. The whole thing was clearly irritating Giles beyond measure. Perhaps she might add to the spice by catching the cabbie's eye and having a tiny flirt with him.

It took until the duck for the unspoken truce to be broken. Predictably, it was one of the agents provocateurs, Will, who did it. The distance down the table didn't bother him.

'So how much does a cabbie make these days, Terry? Enough to keep a girl like Julia in the style she's accustomed to?'

Julia flashed a look at him. All other conversations dried up. Lady Daventry tried to cut it off.

'Terry, you pay no attention to Will or Nick.'

Terry shrugged good naturedly.

'It don't bother me, Lavinia, I'll tell them if they want. I make around fifteen quid an hour.'

'That's a lot of money,' said Nick with mock approval. He worked for a big law firm in London and was vastly proud of his salary. 'What do people get up to in the back of London cabs? Do they have *sex*?'

'Last year a couple wanted to do it round Gant's Hill roundabout. Offered me fifty quid if I'd drive round and round till they was done.'

Nick and Will guffawed. Davina giggled prettily. Apart from that there was slight, nervous embarrassed laughter. The Duchess didn't join in. She was looking very closely at Terry. Lord Warburton tried to interest her in a question about dogs.

Giles had been furious when Nick and Will started up, knowing full well that it was aimed at him. However, Davina seemed fairly amused by the situation and mightn't hold it against him as much as he'd feared. Perhaps he could demonstrate a sense of humour by joining in. Davina looked at the cabbie, and the oaf had the nerve to grin back at her. *Right*, that did it. Giles's foghorn voice cut down the shoots of conversations that had begun to grow again here and there.

'Hard to become a cabbie, is it?'

Terry nodded. 'You got to do the Knowledge, that takes time.'

'What about education? Are GCSEs or 'A' levels needed?'

'Nah, nothin' like that.'

'Did you get many of those, Terry?'

The Duchess put down her knife and fork and listened carefully.

'No.'

'What, none at all?'

'I got one GCSE. Geography it was, I think.'

Terry was burning with shame. Now he'd understood the game, he wanted to punch the snotty prat in the mouth. He saw the colour rising in Julia's face, too. Giles looked for approval at Nick and Will and, reassured, pressed on.

'Aaahh, well, with a GCSE in geography, driving a cab's the ideal career, eh? What sort of school was it, anyway? Charlie, Nick and I were at Marlborough. Where were you, Terry?'

Terry looked down as he answered.

'You wouldn't 'ave 'eard of my school.'

'Oh, but I'm *sure* we would. What was it?'

'Fairlock Compr'ensive.'

Giles looked triumphantly at Nick and Will.

'No, you're quite right, Terry, we *haven't*.'

The three young men shook with laughter. When his eyes cleared, Giles smirked at Davina. She was taking a forkful of duck breast and didn't seem to find his joke as funny as he'd hoped.

Lady Daventry was horrified. Giles and his wretched friends were in danger of ruining the whole party. Julia's eyes were filling with angry tears and she looked like she might run from the room any moment or throw something at her brother. At the

285

far end of the table, her own mother's jaw had a set look to it and that usually meant trouble.

The last few mouthfuls of the main course were consumed in something approaching silence. As the plates were being cleared away, the Duchess's voice boomed forth.

'Lavinia, since it's my birthday, I have a special favour to ask. I don't want to spend the whole dinner talking only with Sydney and Alan Warburton. Can we change places?'

'Of course, Mama. Is there anyone you'd particularly like to have sitting next to you?'

The old lady nodded.

'Yes, there is. I'd particularly like to have that pretty child up there come and sit on my left . . .' She pointed a heavily-ringed finger towards Davina. Giles looked very pleased. 'On my other side, perhaps the young man who gave me chocolates.' Giles's smile faded. 'As long as I get those two, I don't terribly care whether the rest of you move around or not.'

Lady Daventry made one other token swap but essentially left the table as it was. Julia looked fiercely unhappy. Giles was still playing along with his friends' badinage, while keeping a weather eye on events at the far end of the table.

'So, young man, you're a London cabbie, are you?'

'That's right, Duchess.'

The haughty Charlotte on his right side leant in and corrected him with a noisiy whisper.

'Not "Duchess"; one says "Your Grace".'

The Duchess wasn't as deaf as Charlotte had reckoned. She patted Terry's arm.

'Don't listen to my daughter. You call me "Duchess" if you like. Or, if you prefer, you can call me Margaret, but only if you put your hand on my knee. I haven't had a man's hand on my knee for over twenty years.'

Terry put his hand under the table and gave her a little squeeze.

' 'Ow's that, Margaret?'

286

'It feels *very* nice. It makes me more than a little jealous of Julia. Now, I want you to promise me something.'

'Anything at all, Margaret.'

'I don't go up to town very often these days, but if I do, I want to book you for the whole day. You'll have to meet me at Waterloo and take me everywhere.'

'It's be a pleasure, Margaret, a real pleasure.'

'Good. Well, I'll let Julia know when I'm going.' And with that she ate a spoonful of pudding and turned to her left. 'Now, remind me what your name is, child.'

'Davina.'

'Of *course*. I want to congratulate you on your admirable taste in choosing my grandson.'

Davina smiled wanly. Giles relaxed a little.

'I must say it's very good to see him with such a pretty girl. It means I don't have to worry so much.'

Davina looked puzzled – and Giles looked concerned. Julia stopped paying attention to her neighbour's dronings.

'I used to be dreadfully concerned, but I never felt I could mention it, even to Lavinia or Sydney.'

Davina sensed that something good was on the way.

'How *awful* that must have been for you.'

'Yes, it was. It was something that happened when Giles came to stay with me when he was fifteen or sixteen . . .'

By now you could hear a pin drop. The other two young men looked nervous. Giles's face had turned clammy.

'He brought a couple of friends with him. Those same two boys up there, if I'm not mistaken.'

'And what happened?' Davina was enjoying her walk-on part.

'One afternoon I went up to Giles's bedroom. Cook was wondering whether there was anything the boys specially wanted for supper, so I thought I would go and ask. The three of them were there, but they didn't hear me come in. I got *such* a shock.'

'*Why?*' Davina's eyes were sparkling. Julia's mouth was relaxing into a grin.

'Well, you see, the little devils had stolen my maid's under-wear, shoes and so on. They were all dressed up in knickers, brassieres and suspenders, *and* they had make-up on . . .'

Davina flashed a glance at the trio and started to giggle uncontrollably. The young men didn't look happy at all.

'And do you *know* what they were doing to each other?'

Davina could hardly speak through her laughter.

'No . . . *what*?'

'Well, I'd like to tell you, but it should probably stay a secret between the boys and me . . .'

'Oh, *do* tell.' Davina clasped her hands together. The three looked like they wanted the ground to open up.

'I tell you what, Davina, why don't we let Terry decide?' She turned to her right. 'Terry, what do you say? Shall we let the boys off the hook, or shall I invoke an old woman's privilege of being indiscreet?'

Terry glanced round the table. All eyes were on him. He turned back to his immediate neighbours.

'Well, Davina, what you think? Them three must look pretty fetchin' in women's underwear, eh?' Davina beamed expectantly at him. She was going to have *so* much fun telling this one back in London. 'But as to my decision, Margaret. Weighin' one thing up with another . . . on balance, and after full consideration . . . I think we should let them off this time.'

Lady Daventry's sigh of relief was immense. Giles looked shaken but pathetically grateful. Will and Nick had gone very quiet. Davina was disappointed, but caught Terry's eye and gently nodded her approval. Terry winked back. When he looked down at Jules, he saw her smiling radiantly, with more love in her eyes than he'd seen there before. The Duchess saw that exchange, and whispered.

'She's a lucky girl.'

And one old hand reached below the mahogany table and gave Terry's left thigh a squeeze.

27

Terry and Julia left Hampshire bright and early on Sunday morning. They had to get back to London to see Einstein and Len and to prepare in case they got a meeting with Jowell. As she drove home, Julia got Terry to read out a story from the *Sunday Times* about Skidder Barton. It was the same dull stuff attacking Charles Barton and recommending that Guy step in, spiced up by speculation that a South African combine might buy Elixir. The *Mail on Sunday* provided an amusing counterpoint, running a particularly glamorous picture of Guy in his parachute gear beside a claim from a French actress that she was carrying his love child.

Such gentle distractions stopped as soon as they got back. They worked until midnight, then reconvened first thing on Monday for Julia to put in the call. It was quite hopeless at first: Albert Austin's battleaxe secretary was used to resisting boarders. The fact that her boss had little time for investment bankers made her decisions easier. Julia was left with no choice but to reach for the nuclear button. It worked. Four minutes later she was put through.

'This is Albert Austin. Who's that?'

'Julia Daventry. I'm an assistant director at Upton Advisory.'

'Never heard of it.'

'We're a boutique investment bank.'

'What's this you were saying to my secretary?'

'Jowell will soon be on the receiving end of a hostile takeover bid.'

'What makes you think that?'

'I can't go into that on the phone, but we're deadly serious and we have proof. We could come up to Manchester this week if you like. How would Wednesday suit you, the sixteenth?'

'I'm in London this afternoon. I can see you at four. Where are your offices?'

Shit. Where could she say? Suggesting a hotel would sound phoney. Time for a favour.

'We're at number 21 Ravenscroft Court, EC3. Fourth floor.'

'See you there.' The phone went dead.

They'd been listening in. They all swore: Len and Terry about the timing, Einstein about the venue.

'Julia, where and what is Ravenscroft Court?'

'It's Executive Express, a headhunting firm run by a cousin of mine. It's a glorified one-man band. He doesn't know it yet, but, courtesy of a little emergency signwriting, Executive Express will have changed its name by four o'clock. Make that three-thirty. We don't want Albert Austin turning up early and catching us with our trousers down.'

'Or whatever', said Terry, grinning at Julia. She looked sternly back at him.

'*You*, my lad, will take care of signs and pick up our business cards. They should be ready by now. Len, you'll have to make your mate lend you those suits today.'

Len shook his head very doubtfully.

'Jules, you better keep me and Terry out of this. We'll only balls it up. Why don't you and Einstein do it without us?'

'Bankers always hunt in packs. Besides, we need him to think we're a proper little bank, *and* we're giving him top-level attention. The Albert Austin types never believe that a mere girl is important, and even your Savile Row friend will have his work cut out to make Einstein look like a director. I know from Saturday night that Terry cleans up very nicely, and we can pass him off as an eager young executive, provided he doesn't open his mouth. However, that still leaves the problem of our senior person. We need grey hair.'

Terry grinned. 'Len's no good then, Jules: 'e ain't got none at all.'

'You know what I mean. In a nice suit and tie, Len will look the perfect chairman, and we'll do some work on his accent. The thing I'm most worried about is our presentation. I've run some basic numbers, but I haven't had time to take a serious look at Burlikon's businesses.'

'I had a quick look at the weekend.'

'No, Einstein, you don't know what I mean. Banks always prepare very carefully for these meetings, with pages and pages of detail to blind clients with science. We'll have to busk it. Let's hope he doesn't ask any tricky questions at the first meeting.'

The day flew by. The suits took ages. Len's tailor friend was lending them bespoke suits that were ready for clients' final fittings, but were still not properly stitched in places. Cursing Len under his breath as he worked, the tailor tacked them together so they would hold for a few hours, provided the wearers didn't move too violently. And they'd *better* not damage them, or it was more than his job was worth. By the time Len got back with them, there was only one hour for talk practice. Julia had written out a few lines for him to memorize, and answers to simple questions. Len had a go: it was hopeless.

'Okay, Len, forget the list. You'll have to introduce us, though. Don't forget the names on the cards. I'm using my own name. You are Christopher Smythson, Terry is Jason Hayward-Cole, and Einstein is Adrian Witherspoon. After that, we'll keep it to a couple of phrases that you throw in wherever appropriate, okay?'

Len nodded.

'Whatever you say, Jules.'

'Right, say after me: "I'd like to hand over to Julia here." '

'I'd like to 'and over to Julia 'ere.'

'No, no, no. *H*and and *h*ere, not 'and and 'ere.'

' 'And. Hhh . . .' and. I can't say it.'

'Of *course* you can. Practise. Exaggerate till you get used to it. Try saying Harry, habit, Horlicks . . .'

' 'Arry, 'abit, 'Orlicks. 'Ow the 'ell d'you manage to say it like that?'

'I've no idea. Let's try . . . If I say . . . " 'ang", my tongue lies completely flat, whereas when I say "hang", it sort of curls up. Try doing that.'

Len tried rolling his tongue right up.

'. . . Ccchhhh-ang. Sounds like I got catarrh.'

'Okay, forget it. Let's avoid anything with an aitch. Switch to "I'd like to bring Julia in on this".'

He had a go. It was still pure Romford.

'You have to *drawl*. Try it more like this. "I'd laik to briiiing Jooolia in on thiiiis.'

After the third or fourth attempt he was getting there.

'Brilliant. Now one more. "I belieeeve Bahlikon is a maahvellous opportuuunity for Jaawell".'

This time he got the hang of it faster.

'Fantastic. Stick to that. Einstein, your voice is more or less okay as it is. Now, where's Terry got to with those business cards?'

*

Julia's cousin was bribed with a case of Lafite. Executive Express had a panelled meeting room intended to impress the smartest job seekers. At four on the dot, Albert Austin strode in, took a look around the reception area, asked the girl at the desk, and was shown through.

Outside the meeting room, Julia inspected them one last time. Bothered by the stiffness of his new cream shirt, Terry had undone his collar button; one look persuaded him to reverse that decision. Einstein's trousers were too long, and Len's pinstriped jacket a touch tight. Other than that, they looked grand in their Hermes ties, double cuffs and silk cuff links. She smiled, gave them the thumbs-up, and pushed Len through the door first. Their visitor stood up and reached across the table.

'Hello. Albert Austin.'

'I'm Chriiistophaa Smaithyson, Chahrman of Upton. This is Joooliah Daaventry, Ayydrian Wiiithahspooon, and Jaayson Haaay-wahd Cole.'

Austin sat back down.

'I've only got half an hour. Let's got on with this.' He eyeballed Len. 'What do you know, and why are you telling me it?'

'I'd laik to briing Jooolia in on thiis.'

'I don't care who tells me, as long as *one* of you does.'

Julia leant forward.

'Mr Austin, before I joined Upton, I was with Skidder Barton. While I was there, I worked on a team that was helping Furnival Industries prepare a bid for your company.'

Austin snorted.

'Furnival, eh? I'm not surprised. I've thought for a while that Robert Quilley might have a run at me. He's a good manager, but don't worry, I'll be ready for him. So that's it, is it? You've jumped ship and now you want to sell your old employer's information for thirty pieces of silver.' Austin looked harshly at Len. 'Is it any surprise that businessmen have contempt for investment bankers? They'd sell their own grannies if there was a fee in it.'

Julia reddened, but pressed on.

'Mr Austin, I'm not surprised how you feel about bankers. However, that's not why we wanted to see you. Furnival's plans collapsed: they couldn't raise the finance.'

'Good.'

'Not so good, actually. Now another of Skidders's clients is planning a bid for you. This is *not* something I was privy to when I worked there, by the way.'

'So you're giving me fair warning are you? Well, that's good of you, but if you think that I'm going to pay you a fat fee for that, you're mistaken. Thanks all the same, though.'

'Mr Austin, we believe that this bidder may have access to private Jowell information that they are using illicitly.'

'*What* private information?'

'Your internal managment accounts. Take a look at this print-out. This came from a Skidder Barton computer.'

Austin glanced at it. His expression hardened.

'If I catch the *bastard* who's given them this, I'll– Hang on, that's against the law, isn't it? I can have Skidders for this, can't I?'

'In principle, yes. There's a problem, though. The way that paper reached us wasn't massively legal itself. Also, the information could have been sent to them unsolicited by one of your staff. Unless we can prove that they *used* it, they can't be prosecuted. In the meantime, Jowell will be long gone. The bid for your company is planned for the thirtieth of December. The bidder is the Swiss conglomerate, Burlikon. In our opinion, there is only one way you can stave off defeat: counter-bid for them first.'

Austin laughed a derisory laugh.

'Bid for Burlikon? You *must* be joking. Do you people know anything about Switzerland? It's not like England, you know. They don't let foreigners walk off with their crown jewels. All their top companies are protected by webs of cross-share-holdings.'

'We know that. Nonetheless, there are ways we could help you get a majority of the shares in Burlikon.'

'And how much would that cost us?'

'For fifty-one per cent, about fifteen billion pounds.'

Austin looked straight at Len.

'Mr – what was it? – Smythson. Do you truly think this could work?'

Len looked him right back in the eye.

'I thiink Bahlikon is a maahvellous opportuuunity for Jaawell.'

'Give me one good reason why?'

'I'd laik to briing Jooolia in on thiis.'

Julia turned to Terry.

'Jason, please give Mr Austin the analysis you prepared. *Yes,* Jason, the one with the blue cover.'

Terry stretched across the table. One of his jacket sleeves was coming away at the shoulder.

'Now, take a look for yourself. The acquisition would be positive for your cashflow, and would enhance Jowell's profits per share.'

Austin scarcely troubled to look.

'Miss Daventry, I'm an industrialist, not an accountant. I don't approve of financial engineering, and I don't believe that the synergy benefits you bankers talk about ever turn out to be real. Unless you can tell me why this makes proper sense – and I mean *business* sense – I'm simply not interested.'

Len and Terry looked at Julia. This was what she'd been afraid of.

'I'm sorry – we haven't had time to–'

'Julia?'

The quiet voice came from the end of the table.

'What is it, er, Adrian?'

'That work you asked me to do on how Jowell and Burlikon would fit together. Would it be all right if I mentioned it to Mr Austin?'

Julia didn't know what to say. How could Einstein *possibly* know how these things were done? It would be *so* embarrassing.

'Um, okay. Briefly, though.'

'Thank you. Mr Austin, I know the market doesn't see it this way, but of Jowell's twelve business streams, we think only four are really viable in the long term. Defence electronics, telecommunications hardware, jet-engine nacelles and turbine blades. In all the others, you will have increasing pressure on margins. Two of them – clutches and friction materials – you should get out of altogether. That leaves another six where you're heading for trouble because, as the world goes more global, you'll lack critical mass.'

As Einstein paused for breath, Austin glanced at the other three Upton people. They were looking about as impressed as he was.

'Now, essentially, Burlikon have the same problem. They share every one of those six areas with you. However, if you could get hold of their operations, you would be in the top two or three in the world in each sector. The savings on research and development would be huge, and the margins would double.'

Austin grimaced; he didn't want to give too much away, and wild horses wouldn't have made him admit that this was the sharpest analysis of Jowell he'd ever heard.

'You may not be far off the mark, lad. But, even so, I don't think our shareholders would approve such an enormous bid, especially abroad.'

'Then share the risk.'

'What d'you mean by that?'

'It's simple. You have no need for Burlikon's automotive businesses, and they must be worth four or five billion alone. It's obvious who needs them: Furnival. You could bid jointly with them.'

Austin looked outraged.

'You mean tie up with that young devil who was going to make a bid for us?'

'Why not? If you agreed to sell you own car and truck parts businesses to him at the same time, you could save yourself another two billion.'

'You have a nerve, lad, I'll give you that. Well, well, well, I hardly know what to say. You're the oddest bunch of bankers I've ever met. Before I do *anything* else, though, I'm going right back to Manchester to find out who Skidders' mole is and have his guts for garters.'

'No, please don't do that yet.'

He couldn't believe it. What was the girl's problem now?

'We first need to *prove* that Skidders are up to no good. We might be able to do that tomorrow night. More important, your action could alert Burlikon and make them bid before you have a chance to attack.'

'Young lady, I haven't so much as *hinted* that I might accept your madcap scheme. Just in case I *did*, though, when were you thinking of?'

'You should hit them when they're least expecting it. How about Christmas Eve?'

'That's next week, for God's sake. Surely you can't get all the finance in place by then?'

'I think we can.'

'In that case Upton must be one hell of a bank. It really is odd that I've never heard of you.'

'We like to be discreet.'

'So I see . . . Well, I'll have a think about it and let you know. I've never actually *met* Robert Quilley. If I needed to have a one-to-one dinner with him tomorrow or Wednesday, could you arrange that?'

'It'd be a pleasure.' Julia was hoping to God that Quilley would take her call.

'I have one last question for Mr Smythson, and this time, if you don't mind, I don't want you "bringing Julia in on it". I want a straight answer.'

Throughout the meeting, Len's pulse had been racing. Now it went into warp drive.

'As you may have gathered, Mr Smythson, I don't care overmuch for investment banks, and I don't hold with the huge fees they charge. If I go ahead – even if we succeed with the bid *and* you raise all the finance – there's a limit to what I'll pay you, and I want the amount settled right now. Is that okay?'

Len nodded; his heart capsized. If Austin was only going to offer them ten or twenty thousand, this wasn't worth the candle.

'I won't pay one penny above twenty million pounds. Take it or leave it. What do you say?'

Terry muttered an unbankerish 'Jesus'. Miraculously, Austin interpreted that as genuine horror that the fees would be so low. Einstein's eyes rolled uncontrollably. Julia tried not to grin. Len had a spontaneous coughing fit.

'Well?'

Len finally succeeded in clearing his throat. Then you could hear a pin drop.

'I think Bahlikon is a maahvellous opportuuuullty for . . . *everyone*.'

'Does that mean yes?'

'Yaaas.'

As Len leant across the table to shake on it, two buttons popped right off his jacket.

297

28

At five past eleven, Marcus Ford pulled his Barbour from the coat-rack by the front door, pocketed the keys to the BMW and went out into the chilly night. The last time he'd used the car, it had been hard to find a resident's parking spot and he'd had to leave it three hundred yards away. He cursed, turned his collar up against the piercing wind and began the short walk.

Len let him get fifty yards down the road before pressing the button on his phone.

' 'E's walkin' your way.'

'Okay, mate.'

They couldn't be sure whether he'd drive or travel some other way, so between the two of them they were covering both options. Terry was parked within twenty yards of Marcus's car. He started his engine immediately and put his lights on, so it wouldn't look as suspicious as doing it at the same time as Ford.

He needn't have worried. Marcus was more worried about being cold than being followed and impatiently squeezed the remote unlocker, cursing foully when it took three pushes to work. Inside, the black leather seats were freezing to the touch. Shit, in this temperature it would take forever for the car to warm up.

He was boxed in by the over-intimate parking of the cars to front and rear, and had to thump his way out, caring little whether the frail chromium bumpers of the old MG behind would withstand the treatment. Then he was out and heading for Hyde Park Corner and Marble Arch.

'I'm tucked in right behind 'im. You stay back a bit.'

'All right, Terry, mate.'

They tracked him up the Edgware Road, past Lords, Swiss

Cottage and Finchley. How far was the bugger going? At Hendon shopping centre he went left, then up the slip road to the M1. Bollocks. As soon as the road flattened out, Marcus accelerated smoothly away. Len knew at once he was finished. His old crate struggled to reach sixty-five. Terry's was marginally quicker. Len called through.

'Don't bother about me. Try to stay with 'im, even if your bleedin' engine explodes.'

'I'm doin' me best, mate. 'E's almost out of sight already.'

The motorway was damp but fairly clear. A few dawdlers baulked him now and again. Other than that, he settled to a steady eighty-five. There was no need to bust a gut. It wasn't yet quarter to midnight, and the last thing he needed was to be stopped by some bored police.

Terry called again. 'No use, mate. I've lost 'im altogether now.'

Len was finding it hard to hear Terry's words over the protesting roar of his engine. The message was clear all the same. He yelled back.

'If it's midnight they're meetin', it can't be far. Try the first services, it's our only 'ope.'

'What? I can't 'ear you above this racket.'

'The services . . . *try the services.*'

'Okay.'

At six minutes to midnight the BMW pulled into Scratchwood services and nosed into the car park beside the brightly-lit restaurant complex. There was no sign of him yet. Marcus parked, leaving the engine running against the cold. He drummed his fingers on the steering wheel. The waiting made him nervous.

*

'I've pulled off . . . I'm goin' into the car park now . . . . I don't see 'im yet . . . Bleedin 'ell, you was right. You better get 'ere with the gear.'

*

299

Marcus had to wait until twenty minutes past midnight before the grey Mondeo appeared, circled the car park and came to a rest alongside the BMW. Both drivers' doors opened simultaneously.

Eighty yards away, the high-powered directional microphone from the spy shop in Mayfair was being tested to the limits of its range.

'Sorry. Roadworks south of Birmingham.'

'That's okay. Have you got it?'

'Of course, but I don't think I can do this any more. What if they have a witch-hunt after you launch your bid and trace it to me?'

'Why should they do that? No one will know we've used non-public information.'

'I want to stop. Surely you've got enough by now?'

'Not if you want the hundred thousand. We need at least two more weekly reports, maybe three or four.'

'I thought you were launching on the thirtieth.'

'That's the plan. Our client still wants information after we launch, so we can rubbish Jowell's defence right up to the end.'

'No way. I won't do it after you've gone public with it. If they suspect, they'll be watching me like hawks.'

'You're being well paid for the risk you're taking, *and* you're going to get a big job. Plus revenge on Austin for not promoting you.'

'It's not enough. I want more. Otherwise, I won't go on doing it.'

'You have no choice, you're in this up to your neck.'

'So are *you*, don't forget. If I get caught, I won't go down on my own. I'll take you with me.'

Ford would have loved to smack him in the mouth for that cheap threat.

'How much – to keep your reports coming till the end of the bid?'

'Quarter of a million. Plus the down payment goes up to twenty-five thousand a week.'

'You must be *joking*.'

'You don't see me laughing, do you?'

300

'Well, you can go and fuck yourself.'

'Fine. Then I'm off back to Manchester.'

He opened his door and clambered in, still in his sheepskin coat. Marcus followed and stood by the open door.

'I'll go to a hundred and fifty thousand and a weekly of fifteen.'

'Nothing doing.'

With that, the man closed the door and put the key in the ignition. *Jesus*, thought Marcus, Skidders should use this guy to negotiate their fees. As the Mondeo's engine whirred into life, he tapped on the window.

'Frank.'

He pressed the button and let the electric window down a few inches.

'What?'

'Okay. I agree. You can't have the extra this week, though. I've only got the ten thousand with me.'

'So make it up next week. Forty in total.'

'O-fucking-kay. Now, give me the papers.'

The man smiled, reached to the back seat for the manilla envelope, passed it through the window, and held out an open palm for the smaller but still bulging envelope that Marcus produced from his Barbour pocket.

'Nice to do business with you, Marcus.'

Marcus waited for the window to roll up, and the car to move away before replying.

'Fuck you, too.'

Frank didn't hear him, and it wouldn't have bothered him unduly if he had. However, the microphone caught it beautifully. The infra-red camera did its job well, too, the little tripod attaching perfectly to the open cab window to ensure razor-sharp images of faces, envelopes, and registration numbers.

*

Rosco Sellars's breakfast meeting at Claridge's proceeded satisfactorily. Plan B looked in good shape.

It had taken him one very long night alone with a bottle of Jack

301

Daniels to figure out that burglary. His initial terror at finding that the safe had been opened receded when, to his profound relief, he discovered that the millions of dollars in bearer bonds were still there. The circumstances in which he'd acquired them were not matters he wanted to discuss with the forces of law and order. Then he saw that his personal album was missing, and guessed it must have been one of the girls. Cheryl, maybe, or Diandra. Or Julia. He had used it to threaten all three of them recently. They could easily have guessed that he kept it in his apartment and hired a professional to get it back. The loss was grievous: half a lifetime's work. He might start a new one. It would be quite a challenge to see if he could surpass the original. Apart from the album, everything else seemed to be there, until it had dawned on him that the Hawk papers were gone. Those were a much more serious loss.

As the night wore on, he concluded there could be no other explanation. That sonofabitch from Alps Insurance must somehow have found out who'd stolen them. How he wished he'd photocopied the papers. Of course, the Hawk guy had explained their significance, but knowing it and *using* it were different things. Now he had to worry what Muller was planning next. Would he let it go at this and call it quits? After all, it made a barrel-load of sense for Burlikon to buy Jowell; blocking that would be cutting his nose off to spite his face. What about after that, though, when Zurich had got hold of Skidders? Would he pull some kind of stunt to block Rosco's bonus, or stop him from getting a senior management position there?

Rosco Sellars didn't believe in leaving things to chance. One insurance policy had been stolen from his safe, so now he needed another. Discreetly he put the word out to a few well-positioned headhunters and explained how he felt about things. He wasn't enjoying life in London. His teenage boys were getting kind of rowdy in New York and needed to see more of their Dad. And maybe it was time for a switch to another area of banking, like private equity. It didn't take long for the offers to roll in. There was always some foreign sucker desperate for a big name.

This particular sucker had flown in from Amsterdam to clinch the hiring over breakfast, appointing Rosco as head of a new outfit being set up in New York by his Dutch bank. The deal was sweet: a sign-on fee of five million dollars, an annual basic of a million five, and a ten per cent share of any capital gains the fund made.

Over his second croissant, Rosco accepted in principle, subject only to talking it over with his wife during Christmas. He'd be back in touch soon afterwards and sign up by the first of the year.

They shook hands and walked out into the watery sunlight of a Mayfair winter Wednesday.

*

For reasons that Mary Long couldn't yet fathom, Hunt's twitchiness had disappeared, and he now seemed sure that Salminen's trial would start at the Old Bailey in March. Mary had abandoned the last vestige of hope that Terry Thorogood would provide any leads, so she was surprised when he called her, astonished when he suggested meeting, and utterly blown away when he said he'd been freelancing on the case himself and needed to share something with her.

As she sat opposite him in the East End café, she had to admit to herself that she'd underestimated this cabbie. She had him down as a brainless yob whose idea of bliss was an afternoon on the terraces, six pints of lager, a curry, and a burpy bonk. It wouldn't have occurred to her that he was the type to concern himself about a miscarriage of justice, let alone have the gumption to *do* something about it.

True, he didn't seem ready to confide in her fully about how much progress he'd made. That was fair enough: with a brother like his, he had reason to be wary of coppers, and winning his trust would take time. The snippets he *did* provide were interesting, though, and it was clear that they were thinking on parallel lines. The Finn might have had nothing to do with the murder, and it could be that someone at the bank was involved. Thorogood had a theory that it could be tied up with a big takeover that Skidders were working on. Mary had little understanding of business, but hesitated to admit this for fear that Terry would lose confidence in her. Rather than challenge him too much, she found it easier to agree to his request to trace someone he thought was connected with these arcane dealings: the owner of a Ford Mondeo, registration T48 KER. It was a simple task for her, and neither Hunt nor anyone else would know she'd done it. Terry promised that if he got that, he could tell her more, and that together they might be able to uncover the murderer.

Mary left the café both excited and confused. Terry's apparent ingenuity and social conscience were at odds with his thick-sounding voice. His looks were actually not bad, if you were attracted by the Jack-the-lad type. As for herself, she wasn't sure if she was or she wasn't.

*

The legal-aid solicitor parked his car outside Pentonville prison and patiently put up with the bureaucratic procedures to get to the interview room. He was feeling vexed. If he disliked anything more than clients who lied, it was clients who lied stupidly. Before this, he'd been half willing to believe that his client really *was* innocent.

He didn't bother to get up when Marti was led in. The boy looked worried, and had every right to be.

'What is it, Mr Davis? Why do you want to see me again?'

Marti looked thinner. Prison food didn't suit him and, though Pentonville boasted a gym, they couldn't take the risk of letting Marti near it to keep his muscles toned: feelings were running high about the murder of Grace Chesterfield and Marti might have another 'accident'. His first cell-mate had given him a good working-over, and they'd moved him in with a thief who was due for parole and probably wouldn't take the risk. Later an edict was issued that even that level of risk was too high, and he was put in a cell on his own. Starved of company, and without any visitors,

Marti felt desperately isolated. Even so, the message that his lawyer needed to see him was unwelcome: it didn't sound like good news.

'I came because we have a problem. The prosecution have a new witness.'

'Who?'

'You shared a cell with someone called Sid Finch, right?'

'Yeah. He was a funny guy. A robber. He showed me some of his tricks.'

'I understand you discussed Grace Chesterfield with him.'

Marti looked abashed.

'A little, maybe.'

'You told him about the letters you wrote to her?'

'He was interested. I saw no harm.'

'And you admitted to having been obsessed. Did you say that?'

'Possibly. What's wrong with that? I said the same to you and the police, no?'

'True. However, you *didn't* tell us that you raped Grace and, when you couldn't talk her out of going to the police, you stabbed her with a poisoned spike.'

Marti's mouth gaped.

'I *never* said that. It is nonsense, it is *garbage*.'

'Not according to Sid Finch. He is going to testify. If he's convincing, his evidence will tilt the balance hopelessly against you. I'm sorry to have to ask this, but if it is true, it would be better all round if you say so now. If you are convicted, you will get life either way. However, if you admit guilt and make a show of contrition, you may be released much sooner than if you deny the charges.'

Marti's face reddened with anger.

'Mr Davis, I will not say I am guilty when I am not.'

'Very well, then we must try to think how we can undermine and challenge his testimony. Could he have misunderstood what you said?'

'No, he is making this up, I *tell* you. The police must be forcing him, you must say that.'

305

'Marti, you are not very sensitive to how our system works. We cannot go round accusing the police of being corrupt. Unless we can prove it, it will only make matters worse.'

'Then *prove* it. He must have a reason for telling these lies. It is your job to find out what that is.'

'Marti, you are asking the impossible.'

'And you are saying that, based on the word of a thief, your courts will send me to prison for many years?'

'Yes, it could swing the balance.'

Marti punched his right fist hard into his left palm.

'Mr Davis, I do not wish you to represent me any more. I want a new lawyer, one who will believe me and help me.'

'I did *not* say I don't believe you.'

Marti stood up.

'Please leave me now. Find someone else, that is all I ask.'

Davis sighed and began putting his papers back into his shabby black briefcase.

'Very well. I will pass on your request to our authorities. They will propose a replacement to you.'

He stood and offered a hand. Marti declined to take it. The lawyer sighed once more. He was not unhappy to be out of this one. It looked unwinnable now.

'Good luck, Marti.'

He went to the window and gestured to the warder to let him out.

*

This time she was put through immediately.

'Hello, Julia.'

'Hello, Mr Austin, we have the name of your mole.'

'Good. It's Albert, by the way.'

'Thank you . . . Albert.'

'So, out with it, girl, what's the name? I'm on the edge of my seat here.'

'Francis Makepiece.'

'*Frank Makepiece*. Well, I'll be damned. The little *bastard*.'

'Who is he? What does he do?'

306

'Group Treasurer. Reports to Brian Sewell, my Finance Director.'

'Are you surprised?'

'*Surprised*? I'm bloody horrified. Frank knows everything there is to know about Jowell. He's worked here, man and boy, for twenty-five years.'

'Is there any obvious reason, apart from money, why he might be doing this?'

'Possibly. When the old FD retired last year, Frank put in for the job. I told him he didn't have a chance. He has no experience of dealing with investors or the City. He's a good enough book-keeper, but no more than that. I thought he understood, though he wasn't very chuffed when I chose someone so much younger. Maybe he resented it more than I realized. I'll *murder* him.'

'You may not have to. The law may do that for us in due course.'

'So what should I do about him now, Julia? Surely he shouldn't have access to our internal data?'

'If you block it, he'll let them know right away. Albert, I've got another idea. *You* know how good your figures are looking. If I were at Skidders, I'd want to get that bid launched right away, before your share price starts motoring. I was wondering, is there any way you can doctor the information that Frank is seeing?'

'How d'you mean, Julia?'

'If, for example, Burlikon believed that a black hole was developing in one of your businesses, they might decide to wait until that was public so your share price would plummet, your credibility would be damaged, and they could buy Jowell at a bargain-basement price. At a minimum, it would discourage them from bringing things forward.'

'I see what you mean. I suppose I could get one of my divisional chiefs to submit bad news to head office. Mind you, I doubt we could keep it up for more than a couple of weeks without Frank smelling a rat.'

'That may be enough. Now, I also need to have a word about *our* bid. I've had some initial talks with banks. The indications are encouraging. I need to tell them how things stand between you and Furnival. Did last night's dinner go well?'

307

'I liked the fellow, and I appreciated him offering to trek all the way up here.'

'Robert's a class act. Did you talk details?'

'We didn't only *talk* details, we settled them. I've always believed that things go better when there are no bankers or lawyers involved. We wrote down what we agreed on the back of our menus, initialled it, and took one copy home each. The waiters weren't too pleased.'

29

That Thursday night Poppy coughed so bad she didn't come near sleeping. When Len got back from work at half past two he had a cup of tea, and took over from Jean, sitting with her, holding her hand if she felt like it. It had been getting worse again. Jean had got the doctor in again early that evening, and he gave her a talking-to for not sending Poppy to hospital. Jean got him to wait in the lounge while she tried to reason with the little girl. She knew before she started that she was wasting her breath. Poppy wasn't going back to hospital, and that was that. Jean had no cards to play with a child who scoffed at scoldings, swore back if sworn at, had no use for treats, and was even willing to stare death down if it got in her way. The doctor left shaking his head, absolving himself loudly from responsibility, and having to bite his tongue not to blame the parents for killing the kid.

It began to feel as if every day might make a difference. While he'd been out driving that night, Len had been wondering whether to swallow his pride, get Jules to borrow the down payment, and send Poppy out to California on the first available flight. He waited for a break in her coughing to raise it. None came, so at three-thirty he went ahead anyway.

'Poppity, doll.'

'*What*?'

She was having to fight to get any words out. He should keep it simple, and be firm.

'You're in such a bad way, the worst you've ever been. Me and your Mum are beside ourselves with worry.'

'I can't 'elp that, can I? Worry about somethin' else. Did you know Julia's pregnant?'

Len looked aghast.

309

'She's *not*?'

'No, she's not, but it took your mind off it, right? See, you can do it.'

'You cheeky little so and so . . . Poppy, remember last Christmas?'

' 'Course, Dad.'

'Bleedin' awful, weren't it?'

'Yeah. You and Mum 'ad that barney about the amplifier you bought without 'er say-so.'

'That's right, and – remember – there was *nothin'* on the telly worth watchin'. Terrible Christmas it was . . .'

Poppy's coughing erupted again. Len tried to take her hand, but the convulsions were too great this time and she clamped them to her chest. He waited.

'When you think 'ow 'orrible Christmas can be, makes you think what's the point, don't it?'

Despite all her coughs, Poppy was listening carefully.

'What I was thinkin', Poppity, was maybe this year we shouldn't bother with a turkey, or presents, or Christmas crackers. Treat it like an ordinary day, why not? At least then we wouldn't 'ave no barneys. I could go out and do a spot of work. You can make good money Christmas Day. *Massive* tips . . .'

'Dad.' He ignored her.

'. . . See, if we agreed to treat Christmas like that, there'd be no reason for you not to go to California right away, would there? Imagine all that sunshine. You'd 'ave a *much* better Christmas in San Francisco.'

'Dad.'

'What?'

'Piss off. I'm stayin' 'ere. And so are *you*. You go out working' on Christmas Day and I'll *kill* you.'

'Poppity, it'd be for the best, don't you see?'

'Dad, I ain't goin' before Christmas, and that's *that*. Now stop bein' so bleedin' aggravatin' and tell me what's goin' on. No one's been 'ere today, not Terry, not Einstein, not even bleedin' Jules, and Mum ain't got a fuckin' clue.'

Len shrugged his shoulders. There were times when he thought Jean and he had been too soft with Poppy. They should've been stricter when she was small. It was a bit bleeding late now.

'Okay, I'll tell you. It's all gettin' a bit tense. With them infrared pictures, we've got Ford by the short-and-curlies and, from what Jules found in that safe, Sellars must be in on it as well. That gives the both of them a motive to bump Grace off, and, after what Jules picked up at the weekend from Grace's Mum, one of 'em was probably shaggin' the gel too.'

'So which one of 'em done it?'

'That we're goin' to find out. We'll do it like in them Agatha Christie films, when that Poirot gets all the suspects in one room. Old Einstein's ordered a couple of lie detectors through the Internet, and another machine what analyses voices. Einstein's plan is, first scare the livin' daylights out of 'em with the pictures, then clamp the lie detectors on them, ask them a few leadin' questions, and trick 'em into saying the words the murderer said on the tape, so the voice machine can compare. Then we march the guilty one to the Tower of London and say "Off with 'is 'ead." Not bad, eh?'

'Oh *yeah*? And 'ow will you catch 'em in the first place? March right into Skidder Barton, sayin' "I'm Len Bishop, the cabbie detective, and you're all under arrest"?'

'You don't give your old Dad much credit, do you? I may be no Einstein, but I'm smarter than you bleedin' well think.'

'Crap, you're a thick as a plank . . . Go on, then, Mr Smarty Pants, impress me.'

'We're goin' to see if we can borrow a police station.'

'Bollocks. They don't rent 'em out by the hour, you div.'

'Not normally, but you've reckoned without Terry's charms. The lad's got a new friend in the police, a detective, no less.'

'Another gel, I s'pose. And she'll lend you a station?'

'We're not sure. She don't actually *know* about it yet. Nor does Terry, matter of fact. Einstein and Jules only thought of it tonight. Terry was workin' late, too. Jules'll be tellin' 'im about now.'

'Sounds like it's all down to them other three. What are *you* doin'?'

'I'm to be the top copper. You should be proud of your old Dad. Quite a life I lead, eh? Chairman of a bank one minute, Superintendent the next.'

'And a daft pillock the rest of the time.'

'You watch your lip.'

'Or *what*?'

A coughing fit carried her away again, too brutally for any more talk. At five o'clock Jean brought Len a cup of tea and told him to go and get some sleep.

*

On Thursday, Rosco took Marcus to Zurich with him to see Ernst Lautenschutz. With each passing day, Rosco was growing more nervous of what Muller might do. According to the deal he'd cut with Charles Barton, half his share was payable as soon as a transaction was *announced*, so he would bank a cool twenty million the day Burlikon launched. However, if Zuricher got control of Skidders first, that money might never get paid. There was only one answer: force Lautenschutz to let Manz go first.

There were other reasons, too, for bringing the bid forward. Their mole was getting edgy, and you could never rule out him being caught. Marcus was concerned that Jowell's share price might soar. From their last three weeks' management accounts, you could see that most of their businesses were trending back upwards. If the stock market cottoned on to that, the price would quickly wake from its current slumber at around 450 pence. It was goddam obvious that Dieter Manz was one of life's cheapskates and if the price got too rich he would walk away, leaving Rosco and Marcus high and dry.

'Ernst, as I keep saying, it's only Zuricher's interests we have in mind . . .'

Lautenschutz believed investment bankers only ever had three things in mind: salary, bonus, and stock options. He took every word they said with great barrels of salt. On the other hand,

Sellars *did* have a reputation for being able to read markets, which was why he would give him a hearing.

'If you take a look at the private data we get, Jowell looks seriously undervalued. When the investment analysts work this out, they'll all put out "buy" recommendations to investors and that share price will start motoring. How far d'you reckon it might go, Marcus?'

'Six hundred, at least.'

'Right. As you know, Ernst, Dieter Manz is determined to keep the takeover premium down to thirty per cent. We've always said that's tight, but they might get away with it. Now, I don't have to tell you that thirty per cent on four fifty is . . . what, Marcus?'

'Five eighty-five.'

'Exactly. Whereas, the same premium on a market price of, say, six hundred is . . . *way more*'

'Seven eighty.' Lautenschutz had a better head for numbers than Sellars.

'And you may know different, Ernst, but I'd say that Dieter won't pay that much. He'll pull out, depriving Skidders – your future London subsidiary – of a massive fee, *and* he'll blame you for screwing up his deal by delaying the timing.'

Lautenschutz glared at Sellars. The nerve of the American! The fact that he had a point made him even angrier.

'I hear you, Rosco, but the answer is no. We'll all have to take our chances. It's exactly one week to Christmas. The whole world goes on holiday, including all the analysts. After that, it will only be a matter of days.'

Sellars glared back at Lautenschutz. This Swiss fuckwit was as stubborn as a mule. Okay, he'd have to rough him up.

'Ernst, I'm afraid there is one other factor. Ever since you told us about your intention to bid for Skidders, Marcus and I have been in a very difficult position. We've both taken legal advice about whether we have a duty to inform our employers . . .'

Marcus's eyes went out on stalks. What kind of bullshit was Rosco spouting now?

'We've been advised that, in principle, the answer is yes.

313

We would've been willing to ignore this, but our lawyers say that if there's evidence that we're actively synchronizing Burlikon's bid with your own, we could land in serious trouble.'

'So what exactly are you saying, Rosco?'

'If you don't agree to de-couple the two transactions and invite Manz to bid first, we'll have no option but to follow our legal advice and inform Charles Barton of your plans.'

'This is *intolerable* . . .'

Lautenschutz's fist crashed down on his desk. Marcus was horrified, Rosco looked cool. Ernst's temper held no fear for him. He remembered his early days at Salomons: any of the bosses there would have had this Swiss jerk for breakfast.

'I wish you both to wait outside while I discuss this with my colleagues.'

The secretary brought them some coffee, then some sandwiches for lunch, then more coffee.

*

'I don't *care* if it's the only way to solve it. You're crazy.'

'No one will ever know, love. You're so gorgeous, I'm sure there's plenty of coppers who fancy you and would turn a blind eye.'

'And unless you tell me everything you know, how am I supposed to interrogate your suspect?'

'Oh, I wasn't thinkin' that you'd actually *do* that. Not in *person*, like. I reckoned it'd be better if I interviewed 'im on my tod.'

'I can't believe your nerve, Terry. It almost sounds like you just want to *borrow* a police station.'

'Yeah, that *is* the idea, more or less.'

'D'you have any *idea* what I'd get for aiding and abetting you impersonating a police officer?'

'Three points on your licence?'

The phone was slammed down, hard.

*

'Janice?'

'Yeah, who's that?

314

'Julia Daventry. Remember me?'

Janice smiled. ''Ow could I forget? What can I do for you, Julia?'

'I need a little help. Are Marcus and Rosco in the bank today?'

'No, they're abroad together. And tomorrow Marcus is in Birmingham and Rosco's off to Paris.'

'*Damn.*'

'What?'

'Oh, nothing. Janice, would you do me a huge favour? What flight are they coming back on tonight?'

'If you 'old on a minute, I'll check . . . Julia, you still there? It's the BA 276 from Zurich; it gets into Heathrow at nine twenty-five.'

'Thank you *so* much, Janice. Can I take you out to lunch one of these days?'

'I'd like that. Then you can tell me if that Mum of yours is better.'

They both laughed. Julia pressed 'End' and punched in the short code for Terry's mobile.

'Hi, it's me. Bad news, I'm afraid. Tonight's our only chance. They're both flying in from Zurich. If Mary definitely won't help, we'll have to make do with second best. Between Terminals One and Two at the airport there's a business centre that rents out conference rooms by the hour. Book one of them and get all the gear set up in there.'

*

Ernst Lautenschutz could see all too clearly how disastrous it would be if Charles Barton found out about his plans now. With Guy Barton away at Christmas on his ludicrous parachuting adventure, it would give Charles every chance to rally the support of the family. No, Sellars and Ford held the upper hand for now. When Zuricher got control of Skidder Barton, he would fire them both immediately.

He took his decision and consulted his board colleagues within half an hour. Making Sellars and Ford cool their heels for a further

315

five hours was done out of pure spite. He then had his secretary summon them back in and deliberately began the call to Dieter Manz before they came into his office. He stayed talking in Swiss German for several more minutes before switching into English.

'Herr Doktor Manz, my colleagues have joined me now, so I will put you on the loudspeaker . . . Can you hear all right?'

'*Ja, kein Problem*. Good afternoon, gentlemen.'

'Hi, Dieter, how you doing?'

Marcus also muttered a greeting. Lautenschutz was determined to keep control of the call and steamed right in.

'As I was saying, Dr Manz, we are concerned that the market in Jowell shares could strengthen sharply. Mr Sellars and Mr Ford think you should launch your bid sooner.'

'I see. When do you recommend, Mr Sellars?'

'Every day counts. We think it should be very soon. Realistically, the earliest we could do it is . . . what do you think, Marcus?'

'Next Monday.'

Manz was consulting at his desktop calendar.

'The twenty-first? When are you due to get another of your special reports?'

'I'm seeing him on Tuesday, as usual.'

'And you cannot bring that forward?'

'No. That's the day the numbers are collated in Jowell's head office.'

'I would like to see one more set.'

Marcus shook his head into the telephone. 'Dr Manz, they're very unlikely to look much different from last week's figures.'

'I will *not* launch this bid without having absolutely up-to-the-minute information. Is that clear?'

Rosco gestured to Marcus to back off, and stepped in himself.

'That's fine, Dieter. Marcus will get one more set on Tuesday. That'll give us Wednesday to digest the data and we can launch first thing on Thursday morning.'

'Mr Sellars, Thursday is Christmas Eve.'

Rosco laughed.

'As far as I know, Christmas Eve isn't a public holiday any-where. Not in England, not even in Switzerland.'

'Technically, that may be true, but very few people are at work. *I* will not be, for example. I shall be in my chalet in Gstaad. And Herr Lautenschutz will be my guest.'

'In my opinion, Dieter, Christmas Eve is the *perfect* day to launch a hostile bid. Hit them when they're least expecting it. And what you do with your vacation plans is up to you, but if you *do* launch, you really ought to be here in London. It'll make it easier to get that information to you, and you'll need to be available on Thursday to speak with the press.'

'Mr Sellars, I agree with you that we should not delay. I will postpone the start of my holiday and come to London on Wednesday. If next week's figures from Jowell look good, you will have the green light to launch the bid on Thursday.'

'Great. Thanks, Dieter.'

Rosco couldn't stop himself casting a gloating glance at Ernst Lautenschutz.

30

Guy Barton stood alone at the window of his elegant office next to the Howard Hotel and watched the last faint streaks of yellow-grey afternoon light disappearing beyond the Thames.

He'd had a bruising, emotional encounter with his head of finance. The man was crumbling under the pressure from the banks, and was beginning to rebel against his boss's insistence on creative accounting. Barton had stopped him resigning only by promising to raise more capital or sell the company before the floodgates burst.

Guy knew that for much of the last two decades he'd been less clever than he'd been given credit for. The ochres, zincs, tints, unguents, stones and perfumes of Africa, India, Araby and Asia had been stalwart friends, rising erratically but consistently in value, shaming by comparison the returns from Europe's industrial giants. Now all that had changed, and the tide was running against him.

Years ago, the threat of collapse would hardly have worried him. Back then, he was branded a rogue, villain and charlatan so often that it amused more than bothered him. Now he felt different. Success and celebrity were seductive, and he enjoyed being courted by politicians and welcomed by royalty. His feelings towards the wider Barton family had changed, too. Rather than taking pleasure from cocking a snoop at them, he felt the resonance of being part of a dynasty and was glad not only to have redeemed the indiscretions of his youth but to be seen as the family's shining star.

So far, by hook or by crook, he'd kept most of it out of the press, and the banks didn't yet know the true scale of the problem. However, selling Elixir to those hard-nosed South Africans now would be crazy: the price they had tabled was a joke. It all made Lautenschutz's offer attractive. The two hundred million pounds could be channelled through the back door to repair the hole in Elixir's balance sheet. The banks would be reassured, and he'd gain vital breathing space.

It would mean having to spend a couple of days a week at Skidders. That interested him little, but at least he would make a better fist of banking than his useless brother.

There was still the question of whether he could persuade his father to sell the family shares. If the old man refused, and Elixir collapsed, he might have to slip quietly into exile. He had recently purchased a lush ocean-front estate near Dakar, and had squirrelled enough away in Cayman and Liechtenstein banks to be able to indulge his taste in fine carpets and fine women. Over the years he had done enough favours for prominent Senegalese to be confident of being protected from the attentions of creditors or authorities abroad.

All the same, he hoped it wouldn't come to that.

*

Rosco and Marcus started on the champagne in the British Airways lounge in Zurich airport, and kept it up throughout the flight back. The inevitable winter air-traffic delays had them circling southern England for an age. Although the bar service was officially closed, Rosco created a stink until they got one more drink each.

They were both as pleased as punch. Marcus kept complimenting Rosco. Never in his short career had he witnessed such breathtaking chutzpah. Rosco was forced to agree that, when push came to shove, not many bankers, even on Wall Street, possessed balls the size of his.

They played back their exchanges with the two Swiss, their mimicry of the accents growing louder and more outrageous with each passing bubble. Now that Rosco had blown that jerkhead Lautenschutz out of the water, they could get this motherfuckin' show on the road. *Yeah.*

319

When they were decanted into Terminal One, Rosco railed noisily against the length of the queue for non-Europeans, proclaiming to anyone listening – and they had little choice in the matter – his resentment at being required to wait in line with a bunch of smelly savages from flyblown republics. Marcus waited patiently beyond Immigration, faintly embarrassed by Rosco's antics, not quite drunk enough to be impervious to the reactions his colleague was provoking.

Finally Rosco was through and, delivering one last volley of curses at the inadequacies of this airport, they marched briskly past the carousels and the Customs officers and out to the waiting sea of faces. Rosco's uniformed chauffeur was among them. As they walked towards him, they found their way barred.

'Mr Sellars and Mr Ford?'

'Yeah. Who the hell are you?'

It was two youngish guys in suits and old macs. The one who looked like a comic-strip nerd spoke up.

'I'm Detective Sergeant Sharp from Scotland Yard. This is Detective Constable Reilly . . .' They flashed police ID badges that they'd bought from a tourist shop in Oxford Street. 'We'd like you to accompany us. There are some questions we'd like to ask you.'

Marcus blanched and his gut tightened. Oh fuck, the nightmare had come true. The colour fled from Rosco's face, too. This might be real *bad* shit. He had to keep his nerve and act cool.

'What's this about?'

'We'll tell you that later.'

'Bullshit. I ain't going nowhere till I've spoken to a lawyer.'

They'd thought about that one. Getting hold of a lawyer at ten forty-five p.m. isn't all that easy. The smart thing was to let them try.

'Very well. Make it quick.'

They both flipped open their mobiles. The effort collapsed quickly. The only private attorney Rosco knew was in New York, and was travelling. Marcus tried one firm that he'd heard specialized in criminal law and got only an answering machine.

Rosco swore.

'Okay, how long will this take? I have my driver waiting.'

'Unless you want a very big bill, I'd send him home.'

Rosco dismissed the chauffeur and walked off with the officers, his mind already whirring, trying to formulate a plan for handling this. He was horrified when, almost before they'd set off, they stopped.

'Hey What the fuck are we doing in the business centre?'

'We thought you might find this more convenient. Would you prefer it if we took you to the police station right away? It's easily arranged . . .' Terry'd been practising that line all evening and delivered it pretty coolly. Marcus elbowed Rosco, reminding him there were bigger things to worry about. Terry and Einstein marched them briskly on past the reception desk and up to the de Havilland room.

They all squinted as they went in. The dimmer switch on the main lights had been turned well down, and most of the illumination came from three brilliant table-top lamps that were shining towards them. From out of the shadows, a bulky silhouette rose and stepped forward.

'Superintendent Branagan . . .' He gestured them to sit. 'Thank you for coming.'

Rosco decided instinctively that attack was the best form of defence. As they'd agreed on the plane, he had steel balls, and this wasn't the time to lose them. Whatever this was about, the only hope was to bluff and act outraged, as if he really did have nothing to hide.

'Superintendent, I wanna speak with your superior immediately. I tell you: this is the worst career move you've ever made. Do you have any idea who you're dealing with? We come back from a hard day's work propping up the invisible earnings of this pathetic country, and what happens? We're harassed at the airport in full view of hundreds of people. Do you understand how traumatic and *humiliating* that is? I tell you right now, I'll be suing the police for millions.'

The superintendent cracked his knuckles and stared back

impassively. In the half-light his round features looked strangely menacing.

'Frankly, Mr Sellars, I don't give a damn.'

Shit, it hadn't worked. Better try another tack.

'So what the fuck is this about, anyway?'

'I'll get on to that, if you'll keep quiet for one minute.'

'Okay.'

'We'll be recordin' this interview . . .'

The two bankers watched while the curly-haired constable switched on a tape machine. When it was spinning satisfactorily, Len continued.

'We 'ave reason to believe that you two are engaged in illegal conduct concernin' a corporate transaction . . .'

Jesus, thought Marcus, they've caught Frank. What should he do? Admit they received the information but claim they never used it? The cash payments were untraceable. The papers that Frank gave them went straight to Manz, and the data was stored electronically only on his own computer. No one else could access it.

Fuck, thought Rosco, they found the mole. Thank God he'd made Marcus play go-between. There was nothing on his own computer, the mole didn't know his name, and as long as Manz and Lautenschutz kept their mouths shut, no one could prove he knew about it. Marcus would have to swing for it.

'What . . . transaction?' You could have heard the nervous catch in Marcus's voice half a mile away.

Len turned to his right.

'Sergeant, will you explain?'

Einstein nodded. 'Of course, sir. We've been informed that you're working on a takeover of a company called . . .' He pretended to consult his notes. '. . . Jowell.'

Marcus looked like he was going to vomit.

'In connection with this, you solicited information from an employee of that company . . .'

Marcus leapt in pleadingly.

'That's not *true*. Someone sent us some stuff anonymously. We couldn't return it to Jowell without alerting them to what we were planning, so we shredded it. Didn't we, Rosco?'

Rosco's face was all puzzlement.

'I don't remember you mentioning *anything* about this to me, Marcus.'

Einstein looked across at Terry.

'Constable Reilly, can you pass me the photographs?'

Terry slid the folder across and Einstein pulled the photos out, arranging a selection in front of the horrified bankers. The pictures were beautifully in focus: there could be no mistaking Marcus's chiselled features. While Marcus was trying to think up another tale, Einstein went for the jugular.

'Before you make matters worse, Mr Ford, I should tell you that we have a tape recording of your discussion with Francis Makepiece. Do you want to hear it?'

Marcus shook his head. Frank must have set him up, the bastard. For a moment anger overcame his terror.

'It was Frank who informed, I take it?'

'No, he is entirely unaware of all this.'

Rosco leaned back, adopted his most statesmanlike pose and picked up a photo to scrutinize.

'Marcus, I cannot believe this. Surely you don't mean to say that you've stooped to *this*. In all my years investment banking, I have never seen anything so low.'

Marcus turned on him, trembling with rage,

'Fuck you, Rosco.' He looked straight at Len. 'Superintendent, I admit what I did. But *he* . . .' – an accusing finger jabbed out sideways – '. . . knew all about it. He made me do it in the first place.'

Rosco looked hurt.

'Marcus, how can you *say* such a thing? I've only been in the UK for two months, and I've never visited Manchester or met anyone from Jowell. I understand how you feel, but dragging down innocent people with you won't help, can't you see?'

Rosco glanced at Len for agreement. Len didn't react. And Marcus wasn't going to be suckered *that* easily.

323

'As you know very well, Rosco, I didn't know Frank Makepiece – or anyone else at Jowell, either. You made me speak to the London office of Hawk International, and *they* found Frank and set the thing up. And you've been providing half the cash advances to him ever since.'

'May the good Lord forgive you, Marcus. I will be perfectly happy to make my bank account details available to these gentlemen . . .'

Rosco always kept large amounts of cash to hand. The money could never be traced to him.

'As for – what did you call them? – Hawk International, I don't believe I've ever heard of them. Check with this London office that Marcus mentioned; you'll soon find I've had no dealings with them.'

Einstein looked at Rosco.

'What about abroad? Have you ever used Hawk in America or on the Continent?'

Rosco shook his head emphatically.

'Never. Let me be quite clear, Sergeant. It's true that there *are* some banks that use private investigation agencies. Personally, I find the very idea repugnant. If you check out my resume, you'll find that I have worked only for banks with impeccable credentials, firms that would never *countenance* having anything to do with them. I'm not sure I've even *heard* of Marcus's agency.'

Marcus swore under his breath. It looked like the bastard was going to get away with it.

Einstein slowly pulled some more documents out of the folder.

'Mr Sellars, are these papers familiar?'

Fuck, how had they got those? Rosco took the envelope from him. The Hawk logo was writ large on it. He had to keep his nerve, and make like he was examining the contents. Einstein let him take his time and watched a cruel sparkle come back into Marcus's eyes. Rosco shook his head decisively.

'Never seen them before. What are they? I don't read a word of German.'

'They're stolen property.'

'Stolen in Germany, I presume, sergeant?'

'No, in Switzerland. At least, that's where they were stolen the first time. Then they were taken again, right here in London.'

'Really?' Now Rosco's voice and his act were beginning to crack.

'Yes, *really*, Mr Sellars. We recovered them from a thief who says he stole the envelope from a safe in your flat.'

'Well, he must be mistaken.'

'I don't believe so. At the same time he stole a photograph album of a rather *personal* nature. You appear in a number of the photographs yourself, together with some female acquaintances . . .' Earlier that day, Julia had handed the album over, knowing how important it might be.

Rosco was fresh out of road.

'I'm not answering another question until I see a lawyer.'

'That's your prerogative, of course. And ours is to arrest you and issue a press statement.'

Marcus tried desperately to intervene. Rosco waved his objections away and looked Einstein right in the eye.

'Go ahead. You won't get another word out of me.'

'Very well. Perhaps you'd like to hear what we'll be saying.'

It was the decisive moment. If Sellars called their bluff, they were finished. Len and Terry watched, hearts in mouths, as Einstein began to read the statement he'd drafted earlier.

As the sergeant proceeded, Marcus hung his head. Visions flew before him of the lurid headlines, the ritual humiliation, the ignominious divorce – and the unspeakable horrors of prison. Rosco was listening intently, making his own calculations. He was all too aware how damaging this statement would be: whatever the final verdict, enough mud would stick to wreck his career. However, right now he was more concerned with keeping himself out of jail. If the only charge was spying on Jowell, a smart lawyer might help him pin all the blame on Marcus. He winced when the statement mentioned extradition for the theft in Switzerland. He didn't fancy Continental justice one little bit.

325

As he put down the document, Einstein sensed a change in the Sellars body language.

'As it happens, it's not mainly these crimes that we're interested in. Indeed, we might be willing to overlook them, provided you answer certain questions under a lie detector.'

Marcus's eyes widened with bemusement, and he looked imploringly at Rosco. Rosco was having none of it; this could lead *anywhere*.

'I'm not doing *that* without legal advice.'

Len sighed and turned towards Terry.

''Ave it your own way, Mr Sellars. Constable Reilly, call Scotland Yard and tell them to put out the statement right away.'

Marcus lunged forward.

'Superintendent, if *I* cooperate, will you take my name out of the statement?'

Len pondered, then nodded.

'I don't see why not. Reilly, get them to change so it only mentions Mr Sellars.'

Rosco grimaced. If he had no one else to blame, he'd be in even worse shit. He wavered and cratered.

'Okay, okay, I'll do it.'

Quietly, Len breathed a sigh of relief. Quickly, Terry and Einstein set about wiring Rosco and Marcus up. They had practised on Ruth and Jean to get the hang of smearing the jelly evenly and connecting the electrodes in the right places. Saved from one fate, but now facing an unknown ordeal, both bankers were sweating buckets.

When it was done, Einstein shone the lights directly in their faces and began the questioning.

'Okay, I'm going to ask you some questions concerning the murder of Grace Chesterfield . . .'

Both men started. Marcus stared wildly ahead, Rosco's chest constricted painfully. Stealing information was one thing, murder was another.

'First question to you, Mr Ford. Did you have an affair with Grace?'

Marcus paused. Trying to fool the system was pointless; he'd only antagonize the police. He looked down at the table, all hangdog.

'Yes.' Rosco looked sideways at him, in a distinctly unfriendly way.

'How about you, Mr Sellars?'

'What d'you mean, how about me?' Rosco tensed his toes as he spoke. He'd read in some airport thriller that you could trick lie detectors by twitching your toes when you said true or meaningless things. Then everything registered like a lie, and they couldn't tell what was true and what was false.

'Did you have an affair with her?'

He untensed his toes.

'No way.'

Einstein looked over to the darkest part of the room at Terry, who was monitoring the read-out.

'Lie, sir.'

Rosco swallowed hard. Jesus, this thing seemed to work. Did that mean he had no choice but to tell the actual, motherfucking truth?

'I didn't have what I would call an *affair* with her. I fucked her on business trips to Zurich and New York.' It was Marcus's turn to look daggers.

'Were those the only times?'

'Absolutely.'

Lying was such second nature to Rosco, he'd gone and forgotten about the machine. Terry chimed in again.

'Lie, sir.'

'Okay, *okay*. A few more times back in London. Look, we're not talking emotion here, we're not talking significant interpersonal involvement, we're talking sex, that's all.'

'So you never mentioned anything about divorcing your wife and marrying Grace?'

'I don't recall. Hey, I might have said *something* about it, but I wasn't serious. Sometimes you have to share those fantasies with girls to get them in the mood. It was no big deal.'

'So she never raised it again?'

'Maybe once, yeah. She could be persistent, that gal. I told her straight, though, when she pushed the point. She was in no doubt where I stood.'

'How about you, Mr Ford?'

Marcus was looking down grumpily, biting his nails. The bitch, the slapper!

'We talked a bit, too. Grace knew my marriage wasn't easy. Once I went too far, and regretted it immediately. I told her it was impossible . . . eventually.'

Einstein pretended to be writing notes.

'Right, next question. Mr Ford, did Grace know about the mole?'

'She wasn't meant to. She found out by a freak chance, when she was at our Swiss client's office. My flight was delayed, she got there first and the client showed her the papers.'

'When was that?'

'I don't remember exactly.'

Terry was watching.

'Lie.'

'O-bloody-kay, it was the day before she died.'

'And what did she do? Confront you?'

'Yes, all the way back on the plane she gave me attitude. I thought that by the time we landed I'd talked her round. Then she asked me to spend the night with her, but I couldn't because my wife was in town. She stomped off in a rage, wouldn't even share a taxi into town. By the next afternoon she was threatening to go the police unless I left my wife and married her.'

'What did you reply?'

'I said I needed to think it through. I promised to call her the next morning.'

'So she was killed before you could give her your answer. What would it have been?'

'I honestly don't know.'

Rosco was muttering darkly to himself, and it took Einstein a few seconds to get his attention.

'Were you confronted too, Mr Sellars?'

'Yes, I goddam-well *was*. The day she found out, I was in New York. I flew back overnight and went directly into the bank. The moment I arrived, she marched into my office, closed the door and started on me.'

'She wanted you to marry her too?'

'Yes. She made out like I was the only one for her, and all that shit. Un-fuckin'-believable. At least she threatened me before she threatened Marcus. Whatever, I turned her down, point blank. I don't take shit like that.'

'So you thought she *would* tell the police?'

'No way. She'd never have worked in finance again if she had. As a pure sop, I offered her some extra cash – fifty thousand pounds – to back off.'

'Did she accept?'

'If I remember correctly, she told me to go fuck myself. Okay, I admit I low-balled it. I was tired and I wasn't thinking straight. Fifty was a bit of an insult. I figured we were negotiating, and you lose any negotiation if you start too high. She surprised me by storming out of my office without making a counter-proposal. I was planning on calling her the next morning, and upping the offer.'

Good, thought Einstein. There was no doubt that both of them were in this up to their wealthy necks. It was Poirot time. He'd promised to hand over to Len for that.

'Well, it seems both of you 'ad a clear motive for wantin' Grace Chesterfield out of the way. And we know for certain that the murderer knew about your Jowell bid. Mr Sellars, who at Skidder Barton was aware of it, except you two and Grace?'

Rosco looked aghast. He nearly began lying again, but remembered in time.

'No one, I admit it. But hold on here, what about the gym instructor?'

Len slowly shook his head.

'We don't think Marti done it. Grace Chesterfield was

329

murdered by one of you two, and we're about to find out which one . . .'

Simultaneously, Rosco and Marcus cast imploring glances at the lie detectors, *willing* them to be on their side. It all got too much for Marcus and he began to sob. Len was unmoved.

'Right, we'll do this alphabetical. Mr Ford . . .'

Marcus wiped his nose with his suit sleeve.

'. . . Did you murder Grace Chesterfield?'

There was a pause before he spoke.

'No, I didn't.'

They hardly listened to him, so sure were they that he'd deny it. All eyes and ears were directed at Terry. The couple of seconds the machine took to register felt like an eternity for all of them. Terry checked to be sure.

'No lie, sir.'

Rosco went grey at that verdict, then white at Len's next question.

'In that case, Mr Ford, who do you *think* murdered Grace?'

Marcus shrugged. 'I've always assumed it was Rosco.'

Sellars waved his arms frantically in denial and gulped for air. Len closed in for the kill.

'Okay, let's find out. Your turn, Sellars . . .' Now that he was all but convicted, it seemed wrong to keep calling him "Mister". 'Did you murder Grace Chesterfield?'

Rosco struggled to compose himself.

'*No*. I thought *Marcus* did.'

Eight eyes swivelled round towards Terry again. Rosco's expression was defeated, hunted, piteous.

Terry tapped the machine.

'It 'ain't worked properly. You'll 'ave to ask 'im again, sir.'

Rosco yelped like a wounded animal

'No fuckin' way. What happened to the benefit of the doubt?'

Len had no truck with such niceties.

'Sellars, you'll answer anythin' I ask, as many times as I bleedin' well want you to. Now – once again – did you murder Grace Chesterfield?'

330

'No.'

Terry frowned and shook his head.

'Machine says 'e's tellin' the truth, sir.'

Rosco slumped in his chair, his eyes closed, like he'd fainted with the strain. Marcus was clearly astonished; Len looked horrified. To cover his confusion, Einstein jumped up and busied himself removing the electrodes. Could one of the lie detectors have malfunctioned? Should he double-check with the voice analysis? He decided to try it.

'Okay, that's it for tonight. We may need to speak to you again. There's one last thing I'd like to ask tonight. Mr Ford, in round numbers, what's eight hundred thousand dollars in sterling?'

'*What*?' Oh fuck it, he didn't care any more. 'Half a million pounds, about.'

'Mr Sellars?'

'He's right, goddam it.'

'Say it, please.'

'For Chrissakes . . . okay, half a million. Happy?'

'Thank you. I think that's about it. Sir, is there anything you want to add?'

Rosco interrupted before Len could speak. His brain might be addled now, but it hadn't stopped functioning altogether.

'Hey, what about our work? Do we have to stop the Jowell bid?'

Einstein hadn't thought of that one. They'd only used the mole stuff to frighten the bankers and find out which was the murderer. He hadn't realized that this might stop the bid altogether. If the threat to his own company was over, Albert Austin would *never* attack Burlikon, so there would be no fee – and no California for Poppy.

'No, Mr Sellars, we definitely want you to continue. If you two are not responsible for the murder, then someone else connected with the bid *is*. It's important that it goes on as planned. However, you must make no mention of your interview here to anyone. Not to wives, colleagues, friends, or lawyers. If we find that you have, we will immediately arrest you and put out that statement.'

331

'Superintendent, how about indemnifying us against prosecution in return for cooperating with you?'

Len was confused. What in buggery did that mean? He turned to Einstein, who, like Marcus, was blown away by the man's cheek. He ought to be strung up just for asking. Einstein had to remind himself that he wasn't really a policeman, so it didn't matter what he promised.

'We can't give you any formal document. However, as we said, our team's concern is investigating Grace Chesterfield's death. Your illegal activities are the domain of the Serious Fraud Office. We haven't yet shared our information on Jowell with them. Provided you carry on as normal, do nothing to interfere with our investigation, and keep the contact between us confidential, we may be able to help you.'

Rosco nodded. It was better than nothing. He joined the others in being impressed by his own chutzpah. It boosted Marcus's composure enough for him to venture a question of his own.

'Sergeant, what should I do about Frank Makepiece?'

'Meet him on Tuesday, as usual, and say nothing of this.'

Len wrapped it up.

'Okay, that's it. Thank you for cooperatin' with our enquiries, Mr Ford and *Mr* Sellars. You can go 'ome now.'

Two severely shaken bankers stumbled along the corridor and back into the terminal. Rosco pulled out his mobile to summon a limousine. Marcus grabbed his arm and marched him towards the taxi queue. He wanted to get far away from that place before the police changed their minds.

31

As soon as Einstein had loaded all the machines into his cab, he ordered Terry to page Mary Long. For the moment they seemed to be stymied, but whatever happened next, preserving the contact with her had to be a priority. Terry wasn't sure he agreed, but he obliged anyway and during a ten-minute call talked Mary into a drink at a club after she got off her late shift. She was still in high dudgeon when she arrived.

'I can't believe you asked me to do that.'

'Got a bit carried away in the search for justice, didn't I?'

He reached over and put a friendly arm around her.

'Get your filthy hands off me.'

He pulled his arm back. 'You're edgy, ain't you? 'Ow about another vodka and tonic to settle your nerves?'

She rolled her eyes in amazement at his cheek, then thought what the hell, and accepted. Terry queued at the bar and brought the drinks over.

'There you are, pet.'

'I'm Detective Inspector to you, not "pet".'

'Okay, love. Cheers.'

She couldn't bring herself to say 'Cheers' back. She took a sulky sip before asking,

'So, *are* you making any progress?'

'Oh yeah, I'm gettin' much warmer.'

'Is that bullshit?'

'*Nooo*. Cross me 'eart and 'ope to die.' He crossed his heart, then with a quicksilver hand crossed hers too. She was so surprised, she spilt her drink.

'Jesus Christ, Terry. If you do that again, I'll *castrate* you.'

For a while they sat in silence, Terry taking manly slurps of

333

lager and Mary hugging her glass defensively to her impugned chest. It took ten minutes for her to clamber down from her high horse and speak again. She had come with one nugget of her own that she wanted to share.

'I've been doing a bit of digging myself . . .'

'Oh yeah?'

'I found out that there's a new witness who'll testify against Marti Salminen. Name of Sid Finch. East End villain doing time in Pentonville. He was a cell-mate of Marti's for a week or so and claims that Marti confessed to the whole thing.'

'So Marti done it after all?'

'Maybe . . . *if* Finch's telling the truth.'

'Why should 'e be lyin'? Would they cut 'is sentence?'

'No, it can't be that. He's due out on parole in a few months anyway . . . I was wondering, though, if there could be any other reason. That's why I started asking a few questions.'

'What you find out?'

'Sid's got a younger brother who was picked up recently for GBH. Knifed a fellow in a pub fight. He's got some previous, too, so he could go down for six or seven years . . . But guess what?'

'What?'

'Around the time that Finch grassed on Marti, the charges were dropped. Funny coincidence, that. I'm trying to get hold of the case files, to see if there's any obvious reason why.'

'So you think that your boss might've . . . ?'

'I don't think *anything*, Terry, not yet anyway. Later on, I might very well think something. Now be a good lad, and get me another vodka. You're right, it does calm the nerves.'

*

Julia was dismayed by the cabbies' news about Rosco and Marcus, but she had no time to dwell on it. Her entire Friday had to be spent getting the financing numbers together. It wasn't until early evening that they were in good enough shape to show them to anyone.

She'd decided that the speed and the scale of the deal meant there was no point in going to banks who were unfamiliar with Jowell. It would take them too long to get up to speed. Unfortunately, the banks that Jowell normally used didn't have the firepower to lead such a vast financing.

There was only one answer: BankManhattan. They were big, and had done all their homework on Jowell for Furnival's bid. It was handy that Julia had accessed Marcus's computer and confirmed that Zuricher were planning to fully finance Burlikon's bid. That meant that BankManhattan wouldn't have been approached to join in any syndicate, and should be free to look at another proposal.

She put in the call to Lex Gunn, the head of acquistion finance at BankManhattan. Lex was absolutely the right man for a deal like this: quick, decisive, and always able to carry his internal credit committee. The only downside – and it was a big one – was that Lex was a big buddy of Rosco's.

'Hi, Julia, good to hear from you. How ya doin'? You and Rosco kickin' some Brit butt?'

Good, that meant he hadn't heard.

'Rosco is, I'm sure. We're not working together any more, though.'

'No kiddin'? What happened?'

'I didn't enjoy Skidder Barton as much as I'd thought, and I got an offer from Upton. D'you know them? It's a boutique over here that's really going places.'

'I heard of them, of course.' Lex hated not being au fait, and lying was better than sounding dumb. 'but I've never done anything with them.'

'Well, I hope I'm about to change that. Can I try something on you?'

'Shoot.'

'As we say over here, I'm a poacher turned gamekeeper. One of Upton's clients is Jowell. Remember? Furnival's target.'

'How could I forget?'

'Well, Jowell's planning a mega-bid of its own, and I was wondering whether BankManhattan would be interested in leading the financing?'

'In principle, sure we would. Jowell seemed like a neat company. Is Rosco in on this, too?'

'No. Of course, I would've liked to bring him in. Problem is, the target's Swiss. In view of Skidders's relationship with Zuricher, the risk of a conflict of interest is too big. Jowell has insisted on keeping them out of this.'

'Pity. I would *love* to help Rosco with his first big European deal.'

'I'm sure he's cooking up some deals of his own.'

'Okay, Julia, what's the plan?'

'I'm going to send you some information on the target, and on Jowell. There's another wrinkle. Jowell may co-bid with Furnival.'

'*Furnival*? I thought they had some problem with their profits.'

'That was the rumour. It turned out to be totally groundless.'

'You sure of that?'

'Their accountants have crawled all over it. They'll be happy to speak with you direct, if you want comfort.'

'So Furnival's bid could've gone ahead after all?'

'Correct. However, all's well that ends well: they and Jowell are now the best of friends.'

'What's the timing on this?'

'That's the snag. I'm afraid that you're going to have to forget about Christmas shopping this weekend. We're planning to launch this next Thursday, Christmas Eve. I need your response no later than Tuesday. Monday would be better.'

'That's tight.'

'I know, but do you want to be in or not?'

'Why did you have to pick this weekend, Julia? Candy's sister is getting married in LA. If I don't go with her, she may run off with some musclebound beach bum.'

'That's the problem with trophy wives, Lex. You should've picked someone nearer your own age.'

'You may be right, Julia, but you can't legislate for falling in love. I guess I'd better run along to Tiffany's and buy a big rock to make her feel better. In the meantime, can you get those numbers over to me?'

'You'll have them in the next five minutes. Thanks, Lex.'

Julia put the phone down. She looked at her watch. Seven p.m. She'd better e-mail this to Lex quickly, so she wasn't too late for the session at Len's.

*

She was the last to arrive. Ruth and Jean had decided that since Poppy was too sick to be carried downstairs, they should move the Christmas tree up to her room. They were still arranging the decorations and the fairy lights when the meeting convened.

Einstein was wide-eyed.

'That's *great*, Julia. When will BankManhattan confirm officially?'

'Tuesday, I think. Naturally, it'll be conditional on us being able to buy the Alps stake in Burlikon. We always knew that.'

'So you'll fly to Zurich when?'

'Wednesday. *If* the Alps boss, Muller, isn't somewhere else. Wherever he is, I'll go. I have a feeling that'll he make time to see me when he hears that I have those papers . . . Can we get back to what you've been doing? You're absolutely *sure* that the voices didn't match?'

'Not even close. What I've been thinking is this: Sellars and Ford were adamant that no one else at Skidders knew about the Burlikon bid. Yet we know that the killer *did*. There's only one logical way the murderer could've found out.'

'How?'

'Grace must've told him. Now, we know that Grace only found out herself about it the day before she was killed. That gave her only one more day to tell the killer, threaten him with going to the police, and get killed.'

'Don't forget the night, Einstein, mate: Grace's last night before she got killed.

337

Julia looked dismissively at Terry. 'It wasn't much of a night. She was up since around five in the morning, and wouldn't have got into central London before ten-thirty. I bet she went straight to bed as soon as she got home.'

'What if she didn't go 'ome?'

Len tipped in. 'Terry, mate, what *are* you bangin' on about? We *know* she didn't spend the night with Ford or Sellars. 'Course she went 'ome.'

'Not accordin' to Mary Long. She says there was still post unopened from the day before, and messages on Grace's answer machine. Mary reckons she never went back there . . .'

All around him tongues were preparing to let fly. Terry suddenly looked defensive.

'What? Didn't I tell you before? It's not *important*, is it?'

Poppy fired the opening volley.

'What a div!'

Julia followed. 'Terry, you are a king-size moron. Of *course* it's important. If she stayed the night with some man . . . in the state she was in, she would certainly have told him what she'd found out. And if it was someone from Skidders, that means there's a *third* possible murderer at the bank.'

'Oh, *yeah*, I 'adn't thought of that.'

Einstein was looking quizzical.

'I don't get it. Julia, you'll have to help me on this. I can see why Grace could threaten Sellars or Barton with going to the police: they were the guilty ones. Even if there *was* a third man that Grace told, why should it bother him, as long as *he* hadn't broken the law?'

Julia shook her head. 'I have to admit, I don't see it either.'

'And, anyway, is there anyone else at all in the corporate finance department who's likely to have been having an affair with Grace?'

'Not someone with two kids. There are only two other guys with the magic number. One was away in Croatia on a privatization assignment, and the other practically slobbers over his wife.'

'If this *had* come out, were there other people in the bank who

338

stood to suffer, by losing their bonuses or whatever?'

'It's possible, but I doubt it. The bank's reputation would have been hammered, of course, and the whole firm could've gone to the wall. Provided they survived, though, they would *never* have cut staff bonuses. If Skidders lost any more good people, top management's position would be untenable, because–'

Julia froze in mid-sentence. Her hands flew up to her mouth, and her eyes opened wide in alarm.

'Oh, my *God*.'

Len thought she was having a seizure. 'What's the matter, Jules?'

Still she couldn't get the words out. Terry reached over and put a protective arm around her shoulders.

'You all right, pet? You look like you seen a bleedin' ghost.'

She took her hands down from her face.

'The Sunday before I joined Skidder Barton, I went to lunch with Charles Barton, the Chief Executive. He had his whole family there, his wife . . . and his *two* daughters.'

*

Albert Austin and Robert Quilley spent the weekend all but stapled together. Austin was so scared of leaks that he refused to let anyone – even his own Finance Director – into the secret. Not only would he handle it by himself, he insisted that Robert Quilley did the same. That didn't bother Quilley one jot. There was no manager in England who had a better grasp of his own business, and as they ran through the long catalogue of Burlikon's operations, carving them up this way and that, he positively enjoyed the feeling of flying solo. By Sunday night they'd reduced it all to four sides of foolscap, including the bare bones of the contract governing how everything would work. It was written in plain man's English; after they initialled it, they handed it over to their respective legal eagles to work round the clock, expanding and embellishing the agreement until *no* plain man could understand it.

*

339

Julia had quite a weekend, too. She was on the phone practically non-stop to the people at BankManhattan, and was busy hiring lawyers for Jowell by the truckload in London, Switzerland, and New York. Together they laboured like an international ant colony, running hither and thither in some unfathomable, genetically programmed way, making draft after draft, checking fact after fact, until by slow stages the most important documentation began to emerge, like a shapeless mass of marble morphing to human form under the sculptor's relentless chisel.

Julia's biggest sigh of relief was occasioned by their Swiss lawyer, Bruno. With a twinkle in his eye, he opined that it was indeed unconventional and very un-Swiss, but yes, it *would* work. Switzerland might have adopted elegantly Anglo-Saxon takeover rules, but the regulators had reckoned without a situation where the leading investor in a company might deliver effective control to a foreigner *before* the takeover bid was officially launched. If Alps decided to sell – for whatever reason – there was nothing Burlikon could do to stop them.

*

Marcus was delighted that Monday's papers were filled with more speculation that Guy Barton might sell Elixir. Skidder Barton's share price moved up four per cent on the news: surely he must be clearing the decks to succeed his brother at the bank.

For Marcus, this was almost the last brick in the wall. Guy Barton wouldn't come to Skidders without a game plan, and the bank was too obviously too weak to have a credible independent future. He must have ensured that the family was willing to sell so Zuricher could take over. Marcus wondered whether Rosco had really thought this through. A personality as strong as Guy Barton would never take a back seat as Chairman and let the Chief Executive have a free hand running the place. Sooner or later, there would be a titanic clash; he would need to work out which gladiator would be the winner and align his own loyalties accordingly.

Fortunately, he didn't have to worry about that yet. He was

now only three days from launching his mega-bid. The documentation and financing were ready. As long as Frank's report tomorrow contained no surprises, they were home and dry.

How he would enjoy his in-laws' reaction. Sophie's father had paid them the regal honour of visiting them for Sunday lunch. As usual, he had laid down the law about this, that, and the next thing, and it had got right up Marcus's nose. In the past, he'd always played along, humouring the man. He didn't feel like doing that any longer. Some pre-lunch champagne and a couple of bottles of Chambertin teased away the last glimmers of obsequiousness. Once he'd warmed to his theme, Marcus spoke fairly but firmly, told the man what was what, and put him in his place. From the way he reacted, it was laughably obvious that no one else had spoken to him that way for decades. As her father got angrier, Sophie kicked Marcus furiously under the table. He ignored her and kept right on, rather as Rosco might have done. And when the absurd little man suddenly shot up and demanded his coat, Marcus left it to Sophie to see him out.

Things were changing, and it was high time that Sophie's father – and Sophie herself – started recognizing it.

32

The cabbies spent much of the weekend thinking about Charles Barton. This would be trickier than with the other two bankers. They wouldn't catch *him* half-cut off a plane, and this time there would be no evidence of wrongdoing to throw in his face.

Whatever they did, it had to be soon. They were running out of time. Marti had become Poppy's crusade. Pervert or not, Marti was good-looking and she'd made Jean stick his sultry newspaper mugshot up on her wall beside Michael Owen. Poppy was fretting that the real killer would leave Marti to carry the can, and was blaming herself for letting her Dad and his friends play detectives. She even wondered if it was all a trick so they could keep raising the money, that they never meant to solve the murder. The thought that Marti might be sacrificed to pay for her treatment haunted her long, lonely hours. Nothing, and she meant *nothing*, would stop her contacting the police if they failed. When Terry came to plead for more time, Poppy sent him away with a flea in his ear. They had until Christmas Day and that was that.

They wondered if they could call Barton on some pretext and ask a few questions. Julia was sure they'd never be put through. It would have to be the police, and that meant Mary Long. She wouldn't have to *meet* him: all they needed was a recording of his voice. Would she agree to do it? From what Terry had gathered, if she did that without Hunt's permission and he found out, her career would be in tatters.

The conversation started well enough. Excitedly, Mary told Terry that she'd finally got hold of the file on Sid Finch's brother. It was an open-and-shut case. The evil little thug had been in a fight outside a pub in Stepney and had used a flick knife to settle it, sending his victim to hospital with a badly slashed face. Three witnesses had given statements.

Yet the police had dropped the case, apparently for lack of evidence. Mary couldn't *prove* that Hunt had intervened to force that decision. But it was one big coincidence that the decision was taken around the same time that Sid Finch decided to grass on Marti Salminen, and another that the Chief Inspector responsible in Stepney, Sam MacNally, had once worked for Hunt on the drugs squad. It wasn't enough proof to move against Hunt, but it convinced her that she was on the right track.

Terry praised her to the skies, hoping it would soften her up. No chance. When she heard what he wanted *this* time, she slammed down the phone with such a bang it broke.

There was nothing for it but to impersonate her. Julia would have to do it.

*

Julia placed the call at eleven on Monday and, after holding for a few minutes, was put through.

'Mr Barton, thank you for taking my call.'

'That's quite all right. What can I do to help, Inspector? I have already discussed this matter with your colleague, Superintendent Hunt.'

'Yes, I know. He was very appreciative.'

'I'm glad to hear that. So, what *is* it you want?'

'We're trying to tie up a few loose ends before Marti Salminen goes to trial. One of the matters the defence may focus on is Grace's movements in the last hours before she was murdered. I supervised the inspection of her flat myself, and it didn't appear that she spent her last night there. We have statements from Salminen's flatmates that he slept in Earls Court, so she wasn't with him.'

'Is that important?'

'Perhaps not. However, it suggests that Grace had a lover. Whoever she picked up in the cab was known to her. The defence will want to persuade the jury that, unless that lover can be identified and eliminated, he could have been the murderer.'

'But haven't you got plenty of other evidence to convict Salminen?'

'Yes and no. The fact that he fled is persuasive, of course. Other than that, what we have is uncomfortably circumstantial. There's no weapon, fingerprints, or anything solid. That's why we have to be especially diligent checking other avenues. The strange thing is Grace seems to have kept pretty quiet about her lover. Girls usually confide in others about these things. It suggests she had something to hide. Was she having an affair with a married man, for instance? Or could it have been an office romance that her colleagues might have considered unprofessional? We've talked to some of her friends: they know nothing.'

'How unfortunate.'

His voice sounded very controlled. She'd have to go further, and break the promise she'd given.

'Her parents, on the other hand, are aware that Grace had a relationship . . .' She stopped and listened for any sound. '. . . With a colleague at the bank, someone married with two children.'

There was a long silence. Was he being cool, or was he struggling to keep his composure? Finally he spoke up.

'Inspector Long, Monday is a particularly busy day for me. Can we get to the point? What can I do to help?'

'I'd be grateful if you could let me have a list of all male members of staff at Skidder Barton who have two children.'

'Inspector, it may be Christmas, but do we *really* have to behave like King Herod?' Getting no response, he sighed. 'Very well, I'll have it drawn up. I presume you are only interested in the department where Grace worked?'

'No, I see no reason to limit it.'

'Very well. The list will cover all the departments in the bank.'

'Actually, we want it to cover *everyone* in the bank. Including top management.'

He hesitated for a second, but there was no giveaway gulp. 'Very well, I'll fax it through to your office.'

Damn, she'd planned to ask him to leave it at reception for

collection. This would cause real trouble with Mary. How could she refuse, though?

'Thank you, that'll be fine. Mr Barton, I have one last question. How much did Grace earn?'

'I'm not sure. Probably about eighty or ninety thousand, including bonus.'

'And over the next four or five years – if she'd survived – how high would that figure have gone?'

'She was in line for promotion. It would depend how she fared as an Assistant Director, *and* on the bank's overall profits, of course.'

'How much will your top Assistant Directors make *this* year?'

'Three or four hundred thousand. Half a million at most . . .'

Bingo.

'Well, thank you very much for your cooperation, Mr Barton.'

'Goodbye, Inspector.'

They looked at each other, all nervous excitement. Einstein was already rewinding the tape of the call to the right place to try it against the murderer's voice. Julia grabbed Terry's arm.

'Better get hold of Mary Long as fast as you can. Tell her to expect a fax and to make sure that none of the rest of the team intercepts it. And arrange to meet her as soon as possible afterwards. If we get a match, she's *got* to go into action for us.'

Terry nodded and went over to dial. By the time Einstein had the voice-trace machine set up, Terry had done his stuff. Mary was grumpy as hell, but offered to call him as soon as the fax was in and go straight to his favourite caff in Romford to hear what it was all about.

As Einstein fiddled with the dials and switches, Len wrung his hands with nervous impatience.

'Come on, mate, my old ticker won't stand much more strain.'

The machine had two small screens. On one, the murderer's voice was frozen like a jagged mountain range. Einstein had to fine-tune it more to get the two taped snatches synchronized. At last it was done. Before their eyes, a second crazy mountain range flickered into view.

Julia jumped clean out of her seat. Terry punched the air. Len roared his approval. The three of them did a little jig.

Only Einstein stayed seated, staring intensely at the screens. Len didn't want him to miss the moment.

'What's the matter, mate? We got the bastard, ain't we?'

Einstein was still busy scrutinizing.

'I *think* we have . . . it's *almost* a perfect match. There are just two points . . . here and here . . . where it's *fractionally* different.'

The rest of them had another look at the peaks and troughs. Terry thought Einstein was nit-picking.

'Near as makes no difference, if you ask me.'

Julia chipped in. 'Couldn't nervousness alter a voice, Einstein?'

Einstein nodded thoughtfully.

'Yes, I hadn't factored that in. I suppose it *could* change the trace slightly.'

Len's smile returned. 'So it's a "yes", then?'

'Yes, I probably *am* being too cautious. I think he's our man.'

'Great. What should Terry tell Mary Long?'

Julia covered that one.

'We'll have to be more open with her or she'll never do it. Tell her we're certain that Charles Barton did it. Say you listened in to a phone call with him, and you're convinced it was the same voice as the murderer. Add that we know Grace was having an affair with a married man with two kids, which tallies with Barton. Plead with her to make an excuse to go and see him, and get her to ask what he was doing on the night of the murder. If Einstein's voice machine is right, he *can't* have an alibi. By the way, you'll have to admit to Mary that we used her name. D'you want me to come and own up?'

Terry shook his head and grinned.

'Nah. Mary fancies me rotten, so 'avin' another gel around won't 'elp. I'll tell 'er it was my sister puttin' on a posh accent. Anyway, you got to phone that bank in New York.'

Julia glanced at the time.

346

'You're right. Lex Gunn gets to work early. I said I would call at seven o'clock eastern time. Keep your fingers crossed for me. And you, Terry, keep your fingers to yourself, as well as crossed.'

Terry smirked. 'I'll play it by ear, doll.'

*

'Hi, Julia. How was your weekend?'

'Busy – like yours, I imagine.'

'Sure was.'

'How's Candy?'

'She's not back from LA till tonight.'

'Did the rock do the trick?'

'It quietened her down. Didn't stop a major-league pout, though. Julia, I'm goin' to put you out of your misery right away. We're not goin' for your deal.'

'*What*? Why *not*, Lex? All the numbers stack up, don't they?'

'Sure they do, Julia. The numbers look just fine. It's not that.'

'Then what the hell *is* it?'

'Rosco Sellars and I go back a long way. I called him a few minutes ago. I felt I had to check out with him whether he minded me doin' business with you, now that you've left Skidder Barton.'

'Lex, you didn't tell him about our project? That's a *total* breach of any kind of–'

'Hold your horses, Julia. Rosco wanted to know, of course, but I didn't breathe a word, other than to say we were considering a proposal you put to us. All I asked was whether it was okay with him in general terms.'

'And he said no, presumably.'

'Between ourselves, he said more than that. He said that if I did *anything* with you, that would be the end of his relationship with me, personal or business. He said he fired you for unprofessional conduct and wants to warn everyone off you.'

Julia groaned. There was no point arguing the whys and wherefores of her firing.

'Is your decision final?

'I'm afraid so. I stick with my buddies. It's not such a big deal, is it? From the numbers I've seen, you should have no problem getting some other bank to put up the money.'

'Lex, we don't have the time. You *know* we're launching the bid on Thursday.'

'Won't it keep until after Christmas? A few days won't change the world.'

'In this case they will. Lex, will you do me one favour?'

'Sure. What is it?'

'Have dinner with me.'

'Any time.'

'How about tonight?'

'*Tonight*? I thought you were in–'

'I *am*. If I catch the seven o'clock Concorde, I can be in Manhattan by early evening.'

'Julia, any other night I'd be happy to, but tonight I've promised to take Candy to a new Thai place.'

'Then take me instead.'

'Sorry, Julia. I can't stand up my gorgeous little wife again.'

'Then don't. A drink will be fine. I'll see you in the bar of the Four Seasons at six-thirty.'

'Okay, if you insist, but you're wasting your time.'

'I'll take my chances.'

'See you later, then.'

*

As Julia was stepping onto the Concorde, Mary Long was being shown into a meeting room on the twentieth floor of Skidder Barton. It seemed that, at long last, Terry had really levelled with her. She was amazed that he could recognize a voice so clearly, but he did seem *very* confident about it. It was a calculated risk. She would soon find out the truth: either Barton would have an alibi or he wouldn't.

Charles Barton marched in, looking decidedly hostile, shook Mary's hand cursorily, and coldly gestured her to sit down.

348

'So, Inspector, what is it now? I presume you got my fax?'

'Thank you.'

'I'm beginning to find this all *very* odd. I intend to raise it with Superintendent Hunt.'

If Hunt heard about this, there'd be hell to pay. For the moment, though, she must hold her nerve and not look worried. If she nailed him, though, everything would be okay.

'That's quite all right, Mr Barton. Actually, I'm only here as a matter of courtesy. We intend to ask all of your male staff who are married with two children to account for their movements around the time of the murder. I thought it might overcome any resistance if I could say that you volunteered to go first . . .'

Barton scowled, but his Adam's apple bobbled slightly.

'Very well, Inspector. Can you remind me what time the murder took place?'

'About nine-thirty.'

'I was dining in a Japanese restaurant called Kiku, from around eight until after eleven.'

'And where is that restaurant?'

'St John's Street.'

'Rather near Holborn, isn't it?'

'Are you implying that *I* . . . ?'

'No, Mr Barton, I'm not implying anything. Though don't you think it's ironic that, at the very moment Grace was killed, her boss was only a stone's throw away?'

'You'll have to forgive me if I don't see the relevance.'

'Did you leave the restaurant at any time during the meal?'

'Certainly not.'

'Can anyone vouch for that?'

Mary hoped desperately that he wouldn't have a good answer.

'The restaurant staff should remember, and my guests *certainly* will.'

She tried to keep her disppointment from showing.

'How many guests *were* there?'

'Three. My brother, Guy, and two of his parachuting friends.

349

We met to discuss a question of sponsorship. I suppose I can get their details from Guy, *if* you absolutely insist.'

'That would be kind, if you don't mind.'

'My secretary will fax them through. Now, if that's all . . . ?'

'Thank you, Mr Barton.'

He escorted her to the lift and stood in silence beside her until it came. The tone of his farewell was wintry.

As Mary rode down in the lift, then stepped out into Throgmorton Lane, her mind was in turmoil. What if Hunt heard from Barton and called her to account? He would now have the ammunition to have her demoted or even drummed out of the force. Should she resign on the spot, or fight back and confront him with her suspicions about Sid Finch? No, she didn't have enough proof of his wrongdoing, and now she needed to find it bloody fast.

Why had she been so stupid as to trust Terry? She'd *kill* him. The weird thing was, up to the moment that Barton produced his manicured alibi, all her instincts had told her he was guilty as hell.

Charles Barton went back to his office and stood by the window for a while, looking out over the dark City. Normally, his loyal secretary would still have been there but that day he had let her off early to do some Christmas shopping. He checked the number and picked up the handset.

*

Lex Gunn walked, flustered, into the crowded bar, carrying several expensive-looking carrier bags, and made his way over to the corner table where Julia was nursing her third gin and tonic.

She was feeling sick, both with worry about the deal and with a grisly conscience over what she was about to do. Lex put the bags down, gave her two big cheek-kisses, and sat down. A waiter materialized and he ordered a Becks.

'Sorry, Julia. The traffic was terrible, and I had to stop off and get some more Christmas presents for Candy.'

350

Julia smiled tightly back. They waited for his beer to arrive and clinked glasses.

'Chin-chin. Happy Christmas. Candy and I are going up to our house in Maine. The snow's five feet deep there. What about you?'

'I'm not sure yet. Maybe I'll stay in London.'

'Workin' on your deal, eh? I'm real sorry I couldn't help out on this one. Maybe in a few months, when Rosco cools down a little, we can do some business together . . .'

Julia nodded politely.

'Now, tell me what brought you all the way to New York.'

'Lex, I have to explain: we're *desperate* to do this·deal. It's not so we make money ourselves. There's a sick kid back in London who needs expensive treatment right away. We're donating part of our fee to pay for it.'

Lex looked sceptical. That wasn't the kind of thing bankers did. However, when he saw the intense look on Julia's face, he didn't feel inclined to challenge her.

'Hey, if that's it, can I help personally, with a cheque for five or ten thousand? Maybe I could round up a few buddies as well.'

'That's a kind thought, Lex, but the treatment costs far more than that and there isn't time. I have something to show you, but I'd much rather not. It's something you'll find very hurtful.'

'Something to do with Rosco, I guess?'

'Yes.'

Lex laughed and relaxed.

'Well, if you're goin' to show me that he double-crossed me on some deal, I can handle that. Rosco's a rattlesnake: he double-crosses everyone. *I've* put a few things over on him in my time. Sorry if you've had a wasted journey, Julia, but that sort of stuff won't make an ounce of difference to my decision.'

Julia shook her head. 'It's not about business, Lex. It's *personal*. And I tell you, it's something you'd be happier not seeing. I want you to take my word that Rosco isn't a true friend to you.'

'And you expect me to drop Rosco and finance your deal on your say-so alone? You *got* to be kiddin'.'

'Okay . . .' Julia reached down to her handbag and pulled out an envelope. 'Lex, I hate myself for stooping to this, and I swear, if I had *any* other choice, I wouldn't do it.'

The smile had gone from Lex's face. His mind was racing with what the envelope might contain. He was sure his old buddy Rosco wouldn't do anything *that* bad to him, but Julia looked pretty grim.

'What's in there?'

'Before I show you, I have to tell you about something that's a very hateful memory for me. Back in the spring, I had a brief fling with Rosco.'

'I know.'

'The scumbucket *told* you?'

'He tells me about all of them. If it's any consolation, he rated you pretty highly.'

Julia all but retched. She grabbed her glass and gulped a great mouthful. Lex waited patiently while she recovered from the news.

'Not only did we have a fling: Rosco took some pictures of us together – with no clothes on, I mean.'

Lex smiled. 'Come on, Julia, loosen up. What's the matter with taking some sexy pictures? Candy and I do it sometimes. It's fun, for Chrissakes.'

'The "matter" is that Rosco used them to blackmail me. When he fired me, he threatened to post naked pictures of me on the Internet if I kicked up a fuss.'

Lex nodded sympathetically.

'That's not too nice.'

'I knew I couldn't go on with that hanging over my head, so I decided to get the photos back. I broke into his apartment in London and took them.'

Lex whistled, impressed.

'You sure got balls . . . I'm sorry, Julia, I still don't see what this has to do with me.'

'You will. I found the pictures in an album, among photos of all his other conquests. Some were of girls on their own – always

352

naked, of course – and some had Rosco in them as well. I stole the whole album. This envelope contains three of the pictures from it.'

Unable to look Lex in the eye, she handed it over. He drew the snapshots out, looked at them for a moment, then shoved them roughly back in and threw the envelope on the table. He glared angrily at Julia, then slowly closed his eyes and covered them with his hands.

Julia waited in wretched silence for two or three minutes. Finally Lex's hands came down. He looked homicidal.

'That's our own fuckin' bedroom. I'll *kill* him . . .' He clenched his large, powerful fists till the fingernails drew specks of blood from the palms. 'I'm goin' to call him *now*.'

He stood up and knocked his beer flying. Julia grabbed his hand.

'No, Lex, not *yet*. Not if you want *real* revenge. There's a better way to do that.'

33

Julia stayed half an hour too long with Lex, and narrowly missed the last London flight out of Kennedy. With time so precious, holing up overnight and waiting for the Tuesday morning Concorde was an appalling waste of it. She tried to make it up by rising at four and running up a calamitous phone bill to Einstein and the lawyers in London and Zurich. Now that BankManhattan were in, the funding itself should fall into place. But there was still a mountain of things to be done in two days if the bid was to be launched on Thursday.

By the time she got back into London, it would be seven p.m. and Tuesday would be all but gone. Any thought of helping on the murder would have to be set aside: the bid would need her full concentration. Especially the approach to Gerhard Muller of Alps Insurance.

She tried ringing his office in Zurich, and soon was cursing herself for letting this slip down her long list of priorities. Somehow she'd assumed she'd be able to charm, bludgeon or trick his whereabouts out of his office. Both he and his secretaries were already on holiday, and the switchboard clearly had a standing instruction to obstruct any caller. If she couldn't track him down by tomorrow, their whole fragile edifice would collapse. How on earth could she get hold of his home address?

Ah. Hawk wouldn't have closed for the holidays yet. She called their Swiss office. A mere three hours later, Jowell's expenses had risen by a million francs, in return for a fax with a smart address on the banks of Lake Luzern, coupled with an assurance that Mr and Mrs Muller would be there entertaining their daughter and grandchildren throughout the Christmas holidays.

354

The Concorde was full, and Julia had to endure the company of a ghastly banker from Goldman. To get a rest from his piercing voice, she passed up the beluga and foie gras and feigned sleep.

That didn't stop her mind cranking. Even if Muller was around, there must be a risk he would go out for the day and scupper her best-laid plans. Rather than spending the night in London, it would be better to catch the last flight to Zurich and be in Luzern by the crack of dawn.

Terry would be pissed off, having trundled out to Heathrow to meet her. Maybe they would have time for one drink together. What more news would he bring? From her last phone conversation before leaving JFK, it sounded like Mary Long had given him a royal roasting. She'd refused point blank to check with Guy Barton or his friends, since Charles would hardly have given their names if they wouldn't corroborate his story, and told Terry to his own dirty work at the restaurant.

As she sat in seat 22A, eyes tight closed, it occurred to Julia that there *was* a sort of silver lining in the failure with Charles Barton. In their headlong zeal, she and the cabbies had chased blindly after the truth. But who were they doing this for? Wasn't the Chesterfields' greatest concern to protect what remained of their daughter's good name? How would they feel about catching the real murderer, if the price was having Grace's affair smeared all over the papers? And if her lover and killer was the head of a famous bank, the press would have a field day. Might Beth and Tom prefer to let Marti Salminen take the rap, or even let the crime go unsolved? Julia was flagellating herself for the havoc she'd wreaked on the Gunns' marriage, and wasn't sure she could bear much more guilt.

*

Guy Barton's household staff were in a state of shock. For weeks now, the newspapers and magazines had been full of articles about what he'd do next. Some said he'd be given a special position by the government; others said he would take over the reins at the family bank. Rumours had strengthened that he might sell Elixir. However, *no one* had suggested he might not be in London at all.

And yet here was was, three nights before Christmas, summoning them all to his study, and announcing that he was selling not only Elixir but also the house. True, they were getting a dazzling Christmas bonus, and the offer to follow him if they wanted. But had they left their villages in Asia to end up in Dakar?

It wasn't just their jobs, it was that Mr Barton was their headman, their protector, their family. He'd always done more than look after them. If any of their relatives got in trouble back home, he would make a phone call or two and sort it all out. How naked they would feel, shorn of that cover. Nor did they have time to get used to the idea. After his parachute record attempt, he was flying straight from Morocco to Senegal.

Before issuing instructions for the remaining thirty-six hours, he solemnly abjured them not to reveal to the media or *anyone* his intention to leave England for good.

*

That same Tuesday evening, Ernst Lautenschutz felt he was doing Rosco and Marcus a great honour, taking them to dinner at the Savoy Grill. He had decided to overlook their insolence in pressing Manz to bid before Christmas. Although Burlikon's bid would push up the Skidder share price, it would also demonstrate usefully to Guy Barton and his family how the bank would be boosted by Swiss ownership.

'So, gentlemen, Dieter Manz will be arriving tomorrow afternoon?'

Rosco kept chomping on an oversize morsel of steak, happy for such minutiae to be left to Marcus.

'He should be with us by three-thirty. We'll take him through the last batch of numbers, which I'll get at midnight tonight. Everything else is in good shape. You've signed off on the

356

financing, of course, the PR people are primed, and the press release with the bid terms is finalized.'

'So there should be no problems with the launch. What about the outcome?

Rosco thought this sufficiently worthy of his attention to interrupt Marcus's answer. He slowed his own chewing and chipped in.

'At first Jowell's share price will shoot way above our bid level, because the market will expect us to increase our offer. That will change when Jowell's defence is undermined by a few judicious leaks.'

'Leaks of what?'

'We're still working on that. But don't worry, we'll get there.'

'Excellent.' Lautenschutz held up his glass of Margaux. 'Gentlemen, to success.'

*

Hunt had blown his stack. Charles Barton had phoned him, making a polite, but pointed comment about Detective Inspector Mary Long, and knocked him completely off balance. He was caught between embarrassment at pissing off Barton and embarrassment at admitting that he didn't know what his subordinates were up to. In fact, he had never been so bloody embarrassed in his entire career.

Long was for the high jump, or maybe the pole vault, and he would personally stick the pole right up her arse. He screamed at Wear to find her. They paged her repeatedly. When she didn't respond, he sent the whole team out on the streets looking for her. Now it was gone nine p.m. and she was still nowhere to be found. My God, he would have her for this.

*

Len had to wait for Terry to get back from Heathrow before they could drop in on Kiku. The manager was less than happy to see them, and wasted no time examining their warrant cards.

'Yes, Mr Barton come very often to Kiku. Very good customer.'
Len wasn't interested.

357

'Look, matey, we're policemen, not waiters, and we don't give a monkey's whether he's a good customer or not. All we want to know is this: do you remember 'im bein' 'ere on the night of November the eighteenth?'

'The night girl was killed in taxi?'

'Correct.'

'Let me check reservation book . . . Yes, Mr Barton was here with three guests.'

'What time did 'e get 'ere?'

'Eight o'clock.'

'Until when?'

'Eleven, maybe half past eleven. Mr Barton always order *kaiseki-ryori*. That takes long time to serve.'

'And did 'e leave the restaurant durin' the meal?'

'No'

''Ow can you be so sure?'

'I always stand here by entrance.'

'And if you go to the toilet or somethin', who takes over?'

'Hanako. One of our waitresses.'

'Is she 'ere now?'

'Yes, but she speaks not so much English.'

'That's okay. Can you get 'er, please?'

Len and Terry hung around while the manager fetched Hanako. Terry suggested that if she was pretty, he should take over. She was, but the manager stuck to her like a limpet throughout the conversation.

'I have explained to Hanako what you want to know.'

'Oh.' Terry wasn't sure what that left to ask. '*And*?'

'She also say Mr Barton not leave that night.'

Terry frowned and shrugged. Len wasn't going to be broomed off that easily.

'We want to 'ear it direct. You recall that night, love?'

The girl looked at Len, uncertain, then turned to the manager for help. Before the cabbies could stop him, he was translating into Japanese. The confusion disappeared from her face.

358

'*Hai*. Yes. Sorry, not used to Cockney accent. Please speak in Queen's English.'

Len swore under his breath.

'So, did 'e go out or didn't 'e?'

The manager helped out again. However, this time his translation didn't seem to do the trick. She answered back to him.

'Barton-san denakatta kedo, *ototo-san* ichido . . .'

The manager snapped back at her.

'Sore wa kankei nai.' He turned back to the cabbies and smiled. 'She is certain Mr Barton not leave until late.'

Len looked doubtfully at her.

'You sure?'

The girl nodded.

There was nothing for it but to leave, closing the Barton chapter. There were only two more days left before Poppy's deadline, and now they had no hope at all.

They drove in silence back to Newbury Park to pass the word to an exhausted Einstein. Originally, he had planned to go with them. But, in Julia's absence, he stood in for her at a long series of meetings with Albert Austin, Robert Quilley and Macfarlanes, the lawyers. Julia had done her best, briefing him what to say, and discreetly asked the lawyers to take the lead whenever possible. Several times Austin and Quilley had looked at Einstein strangely, making him break out in cold sweats so often he must have lost pounds.

Ruth went to the door, let them in and put the kettle on while Len reported.

'No good, mate. They both say 'e never left the place.'

'Who d'you mean when you say "both"?'

'The manager and a waitress called 'Anako. The manager did all the talkin': the gel 'ardly speaks a word of English. They rabbited on to each other in Japanese, and of course we'd no bleedin' idea what they was on about. It was a pity, that: we both thought she 'ad more to say than the fella."

Einstein took his glasses off, rubbed his face, and put them back on.

'Well, on the brighter side, I think I've just about won my spurs as an investment banker.'

Terry looked amazed.

'*What*? In one day? Jesus, when you think of all the years I took to do the Knowledge. If I'd known bankin' was so easy . . .'

Len stood up. 'We'd better leave you to it then, Einstein. I s'pose we should tell Poppy the truth about not solvin' the murder.'

Einstein scratched his chin.

'What's the big rush? We've still got tomorrow and Christmas Eve.'

He sat back down at his computer, leaving Terry and Len to see themselves out. When they were gone, he rummaged through his heaving bookshelves until he found a thin paperback. It was a Japanese primer, which he'd taken along on their honeymoon as light entertainment and had never got round to opening.

*

Marcus left the Savoy early. He didn't want to risk arriving late at the rendezvous. Frank Makepiece was on time, too. It was absolutely freezing, and they drew their cars up head to tail, so they could talk without getting out. Marcus was surprised by the look on Frank's face. It was more than his normal nervousness: there was some new strain of queasiness, too. Frank pushed the envelope out of his window.

'You won't like this.'

Marcus felt his gut tighten.

'Why not? What's wrong?'

'Give me my money first.'

Marcus passed over the cash.

'What *is* it?'

'It's the car-brakes division. There's been a fault in production, and the defect may have caused fatal crashes in America. The companies we sell to will have to recall all their cars. They'll sue the shit out of us. We may have to provide for a liability of one or two billion.'

'One or two billion *pounds*?'

Makepiece nodded.

'Yes, it goes well beyond our insurance limit.'

'Fucking hell.' Marcus thumped the steering wheel, then tore the envelope open. There it was, in ghastly black and white. A provision like that would wipe out Jowell's profits.

'It won't stop the Swiss bidding, will it?' Frank looked sick with worry. He had been *so* looking forward to his new position as head of finance for Burlikon's UK operations, promised blithely by Marcus without reference to Manz.

Marcus shook his head and said quietly, 'I don't fucking well know.' He was already wondering if he could doctor this information. 'I'd better get back.'

He slammed the BMW into reverse, spun around in a great shriek of tyres, and raced off towards London.

34

It took Mary until lunchtime on Wednesday to find Bernie Finch. All Tuesday she'd played cat and mouse, knowing from her pager how infuriated Hunt was, and that they'd be searching frantically for her. Since Monday, she hadn't gone home or used her own car. Instead she rented from Hertz and stayed in a crummy hotel on the fringes of Essex.

She didn't dare try Bernie's house either, for fear they'd be watching for her there, and instead hung around clubs and pubs in Hackney and Stepney, hoping to run into him. At least she had a recent file photo.

It was after one-thirty when he ambled out of the Coral betting shop in Marchelsea Street and, without a glance at the red Ford parked across the road, shouldered open the grimy door of the Dun Cow. He had settled down among friends, with his pint of lager and a fag, when Mary Long marched purposefully over to his corner table.

'Bernard Finch?'

Bernie looked up and smirked. He could smell coppers a mile off. Thanks to good old Sid, he had a 'get out of jail free' card for a while, so he had no reason to take any lip.

'What you want? Can't you see I'm busy with me mates?'

'I want a word.'

'I'll give you two. *Fuck off.*'

His friends laughed. Most of them had been in trouble over the years and had no love for the police. Mary was trapped between nerves and anger at the young brat's attitude. Obviously playing it by the book wouldn't work.

'Okay, lad, play it that way if you want . . . Bernard Philip

Finch, I'm arresting you on suspicion of committing grievous bodily harm on the twelfth of November.'

'*What?* You stoopid or somethin'? I've already *been* arrested for that, and let off for lack of evidence.'

'We've changed our mind.'

'You can't do that.'

'Says who?'

'Says *me*. MacNally told me I was in the clear.'

'There wasn't a *lack* of evidence: it just got mislaid. Now it's turned up again. I'm no lawyer, Bernie, but with your previous, I'd say you'll go down for six years minimum.'

Finch's friends looked less cocksure now, and his own mouth was hanging half open.

'This is a load of fuckin' bollocks. My brother Sid was told . . .'

One of Bernie's friends kicked his ankle, silencing him.

'Told *what*, Bernie?'

Bernie glared sullenly at her. 'Can't remember.'

'Okay, let's get you down to the nick and see if you have better memory recall there.'

Bernie slowly stood up, defiantly finished his pint, then followed her out to the car. Mary knew that if she took him into any police station, Hunt would be alerted in minutes. It all turned on whether she could get him to talk in the car. She started the engine.

'Do up your seat belt, like a good lad. You wouldn't want to break the law, would you now?' She pulled out into the traffic and accelerated off. 'Where did you do your last stretch, Bernie? Pentonville, was it?'

Bernie nodded sullenly.

'You'll get to know it even better if you're in there for eleven or twelve.'

His eyes flashed aggressively.

'What you mean, eleven or twelve?'

'Like I said, you'll get six or more years for the GBH, but you've got to be looking at another five for conspiracy, haven't you?'

'What the fuck you talkin' about?'

363

'Still, Sid'll be there to keep you company.'

'Bollocks. Sid's comin' out in three weeks.'

Mary filtered left at a junction. '*Was* coming out. Not any more. Conspiracy to pervert the course of justice. That's five more for Sid, too.'

She flicked a look sideways. Bernie looked gutted. She couldn't risk him realizing that she was driving aimlessly, so she decided to head towards Hackney nick, falling silent to give Bernie time to think. Soon he spoke up.

'You ain't one of MacNally's, are you?'

'No, I'm from internal investigation. We've had our doubts about MacNally for a while. With your case, we can nail him . . .'

They turned into Cartwright Road. The police station was two hundred yards away. Mary stole another glance at Bernie. His skin looked encouragingly clammy.

'Yes . . . MacNally will go down, too, I expect. Likely to have a tough old time inside. Maybe you could watch out for him. After all, he *did* try to do you a favour . . .'

She stopped the car in front of the station and switched the engine off.

'There's only one thing we haven't worked out yet. *Why* did MacNally do it? Were you bribing him? Were there any other senior officers involved? If there *is* another big fish caught up in this, his name would be worth a lot to us . . .'

She turned to Bernie with a conspiratorial look.

'In fact, if we knew why Chief Inspector MacNally dropped the charges against you, and who asked him to do it, we might be willing . . .'

'Willin' to *what*?'

'To let those charges stay dropped. Still, I don't suppose you'd be interested in a deal like that, would you?'

'What would I 'ave to do?'

'Write down what happened and who was involved, then sign it and date it. That's all.'

'I'll think about it. Are we goin' in, then?' He nodded towards the police station.

364

'As you like. Here in the car will do just as well. There's a pen and some paper there in the glove box.'

*

For the fourth time on Wednesday afternoon, Julia called Einstein from her hotel in Luzern. He was at Macfarlanes. He could hear the rising tension in her voice.

'He *still* hasn't called me. It's been six hours now since I left him. I understand why he needed time to think, but this is ridiculous.'

'D'you think you went too far insisting he get those other insurance companies to accept our offer as well?'

'That's what I've been thinking. I wanted to make absolutely *sure* we got over fifty per cent. Maybe it was a mistake.'

'Well, it's too late now. Just sit tight.'

'How are things going your end?'

'The lawyers are doing a great job. Austin and Quilley went out to lunch together and haven't come back yet.'

'Einstein, you don't suppose Muller would do something *bad* to me, do you? Like have me killed or whatever? He's a nasty-looking bit of work.'

'I doubt it, but you better take care. When does your flight leave Zurich?'

'Nine-thirty, though if Muller doesn't make up his mind pretty soon, I'll be stuck here for the night. If so, I'll barricade my door.'

*

Marcus and Rosco sat in the meeting room, waiting for Manz and Lautenschutz to arrive. Lautenschutz had disappeared for Christmas shopping all morning, so they hadn't had a chance to brief him separately.

All day the two bankers had been squabbling. Marcus couldn't believe that the chalice of riches might be dashed from his lips at the last moment. After getting back to London, he'd gone straight to the bank and worked through the night on the numbers. The analysis convinced him that coming clean with Manz was suicidal. He had another idea: why not tell only *part* of the truth, by admitting that replacing all those defective parts would dent Jowell's operating profits but keeping quiet about the legal liability? When the full truth came out after the bid was complete, they could always claim that Manz had misunderstood them.

Marcus had expected Rosco to go breezily along with this, but had reckoned without Americans' bottomless fear of personal lawsuits. Rosco guessed Manz was the vindictive type who, if he felt shafted, wouldn't rest until he'd made the culprits pay. He said they would have to find some other way to make Manz go ahead, and assured Marcus that he had one more card up his sleeve.

As soon as the Swiss came into the room, it was obvious that Dieter Manz had changed. He seemed almost *friendly*. Though he would never have admitted it, he was looking forward to his hour on a wider stage. Running a Swiss company had much to be said for it, including many perks, not too much pressure and invulnerability to nasty things like takeovers. However, Swiss captains of industry got little public glory, and he was secretly looking forward to having his photograph splashed across the world.

'So, Mr Sellars, is all in order? How was the last set of figures?'

Rosco put on a cheery smile.

'Fine, Dieter, fine.'

'May I see them?'

'Sure you can. Before you look through them, there is one little glitch in there I want to draw to your attention.'

A shadow passed across Manz's face.

'What sort of glitch?'

'It seems like Jowell have screwed up in their brakes-parts business. Looks like they'll take a bit of a hit.'

'How big a hit?'

'Replacing the affected parts will mean that their operating profits will fall by ten per cent next year.'

Manz nodded. 'That is . . . disappointing, but I think we can live with it.'

'There is one other angle we need to run by you. It appears that

366

there is *some* risk that they may be sued by their customers or by victims of car crashes.'

'Surely their insurance covers that.'

'Partly. It may not be enough.'

'How high could the liability go?'

'Hard to say. Probably a few hundred million. A billion or two, tops.' Rosco was doing his best to make it sound a mere trifle.

Manz rocked back in his seat.

'A *billion pounds*? And if we bid for Jowell, who pays for that? Is it their current shareholders?'

Rosco was getting bored of delivering bad tidings. He flipped this one to Marcus.

'Unfortunately not, Dr Manz. A successful bidder would inherit the liability.'

'Are you *crazy*? This is *absurd* . . .' All friendliness was gone now, as was his normal steely detachment. He was red-faced with fury. 'Then we must abandon the bid.'

Marcus looked at Rosco. He had no idea what that last card looked like but if he turned Manz round now, he would deserve the all-time investment bankers' bullshit award. Rosco affected a puzzled frown.

'I'm surprised you think that, Dieter. You should think of those figures as worst-case. In all probability, the hit will be lower.'

He smiled confidently at Manz and got an icy glare in reply.

'And this means we could save you two or three hundred million by lowering tomorrow's offer.'

Manz leant forward and locked his radar on Rosco's eyes.

'Mr Sellars, are you *mad*? Even if we have *any* interest in Jowell after hearing this, we will *certainly* wait until the news is made public and their share price collapses.'

Rosco shook his head.

'Dieter, let me give you three more reasons why you're wrong, why you *should* go ahead on schedule. First, Jowell might settle any legal dispute quickly and cheaply. Second, we know that all their other divisions are doing real well and that's not reflected in the current share price.'

Manz was only getting angrier, egged on by a stony-faced Lautenschutz.

'Neither of these reasons is sufficient for us to take such a risk. What is the third?'

'The third is more private. Since the end of last week, I have hired an agency to keep a discreet watch on Albert Austin, to make sure we get no surprises.'

'*And*?'

'He has spent a ton of of time at his lawyers, Macfarlanes, and he's been seen on a number of occasions with Robert Quilley, the man who plotted the first bid for Jowell. The obvious conclusion is that Jowell are working on a deal of their own. It could be a merger with Quilley's company, Furnival, or they might be planning a joint bid for some large target. Either way, Jowell will grow in size and be a bigger bite for you to swallow in future.'

'I am not concerned about that. With the support of our friends at Zuricher, we will manage, *if* we still wish to.'

So far Rosco hadn't dislodged Manz; he had kept his biggest stick of dynamite till the end.

'Dieter, there is one more thing that the agency picked up. They can't be sure, but when Austin and Quilley were dining last night, someone at the next table heard them mention Switzerland more than once. For both Jowell and Furnival there's only one Swiss company that can possibly be of interest: Burlikon. I know you'll hate to hear it, but you could be putting your own independence at risk if you don't bid tomorrow.'

Manz roared something in Swiss German to Lautenschutz, and swung angrily back at Sellars.

'Sellars, you are an idiot, a *clot*. Burlikon is impregnable. *One hundred per cent . . .*'

He slammed the table with his fist.

'I will not be bullied by investment bankers. It is not my job to keep you in Porsches. Herr Lautenschutz, it is time you and I left for Gstaad.'

Rosco made one final try.

'Whatever you think, Dieter, you're making a mistake. Please

368

sleep on it. If you change your mind, we could still launch tomorrow morning, even if you're not here in person. Everything's ready. Just call us before eight-thirty UK time, and we can press the button.'

Manz stood up.

'Mr Sellars, as you Americans say, don't hold your breath.'

'Just *think* about it, that's all I'm asking.'

'Very well. If I have any more to say, I will call you by eight-thirty tomorrow.'

*

Len spent the evening fending off Poppy's increasingly searching questions, and resorted to a new-found interest in the news. On one channel or another, there was always *some* bulletin being broadcast, and it broke up their conversation nicely. Sadly, there was bugger-all happening in the world. Inflation was up, and the euro was down. There were Christmas carols at the White House, a flu epidemic in Scotland, and much coverage of Guy Barton's Christmas escapade. Today's announcement that he was selling his company to some South Africans had piqued media interest even more.

Every damn bulletin was the same. When Poppy got too suspicious, he claimed it was the Barton story he was interested in. It was handy that he happened to be the brother of their suspect, though why Len should need to watch the same footage so many times was harder to explain. At least it was better than claiming to be interested in the euro.

*

Mary Long spent the afternoon and early evening checking up on her rights in the event she was disciplined. She didn't doubt that Hunt had mugged up as well, and she didn't want to be caught out. At eight she called in to the team phone and told Wear to arrange for her to see Hunt at nine.

Hunt's face was a mix of rage and vicious coldness. His way of keeping control was to tell himself how much he'd enjoy this.

369

'All right, Inspector, I'm going to do this by the book. I have several complaints to make about your conduct, and I intend to recommend that you be suspended without pay from midnight. Before I indicate the full nature of the complaints I will make, you have the right to–'

'Superintendent.' Her voice sounded so sweet and reasonable, Hunt wondered if she was daft enough to think she could talk him out of it. Some bloody chance.

'I haven't *finished* yet.'

'Superintendent . . .'

This was getting aggravating.

'I said *shut up*, Inspector.'

'Superintendent. Before you say another word . . . perhaps you should look at this document.'

'What the hell *is* it?'

He grabbed it from her. As he read it, his face began to turn pink, red, then vermilion.

Mary Long's voice became colder and harder.

'That's a photocopy, in case you should think of destroying it. The original is in a very safe place.'

He stared back at the paper, unbelieving.

'You bitch. You devious, back-stabbing *bitch*.'

35

They gathered at Macfarlanes at six. No one had slept much, the lawyers and Einstein because they'd worked most of the night, and Austin and Quilley because they were overwhelmed with nervous tension.

Austin had taken Robert Quilley into his confidence about Makepiece's treachery and the false information they'd fed him about a problem on brakes. Would it do the trick, convincing Burlikon to back off, or encourage them to pounce when they thought Jowell were at their weakest?

And what on earth would happen if *both* bids were announced simultaneously? Jowell could still carry the day, as long as Julia got hold of a majority of Burlikon shares. However, there would be chaos in the market, with the Jowell share price racing up to the offer level, then crashing again. Jowell's shareholders would be livid. And, of course, if Julia failed to persuade Muller to sell, Jowell was history. However bravely Austin might man the defences, ultimately Burlikon had too much firepower. Everything hinged on Julia.

Over in Luzern, Julia was in a zombie-like state of advanced exhaustion, but hadn't so much as *thought* of sleeping. Muller had called her again before midnight and told her he would give his answer in the morning. Over the next seven hours, she chewed her nails half away.

Time was now ticking by worryingly in London. Six-thirty, seven, seven-thirty. Three times they checked with Julia: three times she still hadn't heard. Quilley paced the room like a caged panther. Austin managed to stay seated, but snapped half a dozen pencils, drank fifteen coffees and chain-smoked so fast he was lighting two at a time.

At last, at six minutes to eight, came the call. Muller had telephoned Julia and asked her to come round to his house. She was on her way. It would take about ten minutes by taxi.

More awful waiting.

Now Austin was pacing too, lapping the room in the opposite direction from Robert Quilley, hardly noticing when they passed each other. It was quarter past eight, for God's sake. She *must* be there by now. Didn't she realize the urgency? Had there been a problem getting a taxi, or a jam on the road? Come on, girl, come *on*.

*

Nearby at Skidder Barton, Rosco and Marcus were gathered around a telephone too, with their own bunch of lawyers and PR people. Marcus's mood was gloomy. Rosco was less despondent, though he knew it was a long shot. Overnight he'd done what he could, phoning Lautenschutz more than once, urging him vociferously to talk Dieter Manz round. Ernst was making no promises, but had agreed to raise it.

Rosco got up again and marched round the room. What was keeping the man, goddamit? They *knew* eight-thirty was the deadline. It was eight twenty-one, and they'd heard diddly squat. If Manz didn't come through in the next few minutes, it was over.

*

At eight twenty-four the phone rang. Einstein was first to reach for the loudspeaker button; Quilley and Austin raced over to hear. It was *her*.

'Okay, I'm here with Gerhard Muller. Mr Muller has been explaining his personal situation to me. We don't have time to go through it in detail now. The nub of it is this: if he sold us the shares in Burlikon, he'd be a pariah here. He'd have to quit and move abroad.'

Quilley looked at his watch.

'Get to the point, Julia, does that mean he won't sell?'

372

'Not quite. He *will*, but only if he gets a large sum of money paid into an account in the Caymans.'

'How much?'

'Fifty million Swiss francs for him and twenty more each for the heads of the other two institutions, if you want him to guarantee that they sell too.'

Albert Austin's face swelled with disgust. He cracked another pencil clean in half, and muttered under his breath,

'I'll see him in hell first. Anyway, we bloody well can't. An inducement like that's illegal.'

He looked at the Macfarlanes lawyer, who nodded agreement. Robert Quilley wasn't giving up so easily.

'That's certainly true in the UK. What about Switzerland, Bruno?'

At the far end of the table, their Swiss lawyer pondered.

'I think we might be able to structure something legal.'

'Good. Albert, what do you say?'

'I want nothing to do with it.'

'Julia, can you hold on for a minute? I need a quick word outside with Albert.'

*

What little excitement was still in the room was fast draining away. If Burlikon wanted to bid, they would've let them know by now.

At eight-twenty-eight, their adrenalin surged back as the phone rang. They clustered around the little loudspeaker.

'Good morning, Mr Sellars, it is a beautiful morning here in Gstaad. Ernst Lautenschutz and I are already on the slopes. I am calling you from my mobile.'

Rosco made a fast winding motion with his right hand. Who cared about the goddam weather? Get to the point, you Swiss fuckwit.

'So, Dieter, what's your decision?'

'I have considered carefully. Herr Lautenschutz and I discussed this late into the night . . .'

373

'And?'

'It is too risky to bid today . . .'

Around the table at Skidders they groaned and rolled their eyes. Marcus's heart sank through the floor.

'However, I am not ruling out the acquisition. I want you to arrange a leak of the brakes news today. We will see how their share price falls. If it goes low enough, we *might* bid later, at a far cheaper price, naturally.'

'When would that be?'

'Perhaps early January. Well, it's time to return to the piste. Goodbye, gentlemen. We wish you a merry Christmas.'

*

On the stroke of eight-thirty, Quilley and Austin walked back into the room. It was hard to read their faces. Quilley strode over to the speakerphone.

'Julia, you still there?'

'Yes.'

'Tell him we agree. We want you to buy right this moment. Does he confirm the sale?'

'Wait . . . yes, he does.'

'Okay, tell him we're putting out the announcement.'

*

'Ernst?'

'Ja, it is Lautenschutz. Who is that?'

'Charles Barton.'

'Charles, this is highly inconvenient. I am skiing.'

'Forgive me for bothering you. Something has just gone up on Bloomberg concerning Burlikon. I believe that's a company you're close to.'

'Yes, yes. What does it say?'

'They are being bid for by Jowell and Furnival.'

'Are you *serious*? Is this some kind of Christmas prank?'

'If it is, I suspect the joke is on you. I'll let you get back to your skiing.'

374

'Wait, wait . . . *Herr Doktor Manz, Herr Doktor Manz . . .*'

*

Hunt had a brief but decisive word with the head of the Crown Prosecution Service, and then had to visit the Deputy Commissioner. It was not a friendly conversation. He had hoped that a simple announcement would suffice. The Deputy Commissioner disagreed. They would all be in trouble over this, but he wanted the blame pinned firmly on Hunt. He would call another press conference for later that afternoon. Hunt would be made to admit that there was too little evidence to commit Salminen for trial, and accordingly the Finn would be released. Then the Deputy Commissioner would announce that the murder investigation would be reopened with a new officer in charge.

*

Julia raced back to Zurich and managed to get a flight. Terry should have her back into central London by half past one. After the first encounter with Albert Austin, he and Len had kept well away from the banking. With no part to play in the bid, and no murder leads left to follow, Terry felt like a fifth wheel. At least Len could busy himself nursing Poppy full-time. Now that their bid was launched and the cash was secure, he wondered if they could talk Poppy into going to California, or even sedate her so much that she couldn't say no. Probably not. If he knew his Poppy, the moment the drugs wore off, she would pay them back with interest. The fearsome mite would refuse to accept the American treatment, would *kill* herself rather than let them back out of their promise.

He reached out and stroked her hair again. Tired of getting no answers, she had closed her eyes and drifted off. Len picked up the remote control and turned down the volume on the TV.

*

The bid battle had switched to the media, with every newspaper, TV station and wire agency desperate for quotes from Austin and

375

Quilley. Dieter Manz and Ernst Lautenschutz were inundated with calls too, as they drove back in one hell of a hurry to Zurich. Their biggest priority was to speak with Gerhard Muller and the heads of Burlikon's other two largest shareholders. Maddeningly, none of them seemed to be contactable.

Einstein was no longer needed at Macfarlanes. He strolled for a while through the streets, enjoying the cold morning air, then blagged his way into the library at the City University. Last night he'd worked his way right through the Japanese primer. Now he had three hours to get to intermediate level before lunch at Kiku.

*

'I'll have the tempura and a Suntory beer. What's your name?'
'Yumi.'
'Is Hanako here today?'
'Yes, over there in the purple kimono.'
'Can I have a word with her?'
'Of course, but Hanako speaks very small English.'
'That's okay. Could you ask her to come over? Thank you . . . Hello. Hanako san desuka?'
'Hai.'
'I'm from the police. *Keisatsu.* Were you here on the eighteenth of November? Juichigatsu no juhachinichi?'
'Hai.' She looked nervous, and was casting anxious glances towards the manager who was distracted by the boisterous arrival of an office party. Einstein pressed on.
'And Charles Barton was also here that night?'
'Hai.'
'Did he go outside the restaurant during the meal?'
'Ii-e.'
'Are you *certain* he didn't?'
'Hai.' More nervous glances. If it was true, why the hell was she so jumpy? Einstein turned the heat up.
'If you don't tell me the truth, you'll go to prison.' He put his wrists tight together, as if they were handcuffed. 'Keimusho ni iku-zo! Tell me all you know. *Zenbu oshiero!*'

376

'Manager not want trouble. Mr Barton very good customer.'

There were tears forming in her eyes. Now the manager had seen it and was hurrying their way.

'Quick,' hissed Einstein. '*Hayaku*.'

She sobbed more than spoke the words.

'Mr Barton not go out. Demo kare no ototo-san wa soto e dekaketekitano.'

'*Jesus Christ*.'

At that moment the manager arrived, looked accusingly at Einstein and dragged the unhappy girl off towards the kitchen.

Forgetting to pay, Einstein rushed out of the restaurant, pulling his phone out as he ran.

'Len, where *are* you?'

'I'm with Poppy, watching the news.'

'The girl says Charles Barton didn't leave the place, but his brother Guy *did*. Has he been on TV again?'

' 'E should be on any minute. They're interviewing 'im before 'e leaves for Morocco . . . that's it coming on now. I'll turn up the volume.'

'Len, no. Just *video* it.'

'I'll try to . . . 'ow does this bleedin' thing work? Poppity, what do I 'ave to do? . . . Okay, Einstein, I got it.'

In the background, Einstein could faintly hear Guy Barton answering questions.

'. . . near a place called El Farsia, in south-west Morocco. There are ideal conditions there for wind, temperature and landing surface, very similar to Tularosa, New Mexico, where Kittinger set the old record . . . Yeah, I'll be jumping at about one hundred and ten thousand feet from a specially made helium balloon.'

'How much did it cost?'

'It certainly wasn't cheap. Several million dollars.'

Wow. Einstein had to shout into the phone to get his attention.

'Len, *Len* . . . Are you there?'

'Sure, mate.'

'I haven't got time to explain. Go over to my house and get Ruth to give you the voice machine. Bring it and the videotape to

Macfarlanes. I'll ask them to lend us a room, a TV and a video player. Come *fast*. I'll tell Terry and Julia to meet us there too.'

Einstein went straight to the lawyers, organized everything, and used the rest of the time to bluff his way through the switchboard at Sky News. They told him that Guy Barton had been interviewed at his Holland Park house. Lying some more, he milked the girl for the address.

Julia and Terry arrived next, followed by Len, who panted into the meeting room, sweating with the weight of the voice machine. Terry bunged the tape in the mouth of the player, while Einstein set about getting the machine up and running.

There wasn't time to be clever with the wiring: they simply played the videotape of the interview, while Julia held a microphone in front of the set. Einstein twiddled the dials until they had it. He picked out only the one word 'million' and superimposed the trace on the murder original.

They were *identical*.

Julia gasped. Len and Terry uttered synchronized oaths. Einstein's expression showed only disgust.

'Why didn't we think of that before? They're the same height and they look very similar, except for the hair. Put hats, scarves and dark glasses on those brothers, and at night their own mother couldn't tell them apart. Not only that: I never worked out how Charles Barton could've got hold of that poison but, if you owned Elixir, it'd be *easy*.'

Julia didn't see it. 'But why, Einstein, *why*? Guy Barton isn't married with two kids: he isn't the secret lover. Why should *he*, of all people, murder Grace?'

'I haven't the slightest idea. All I know is that, if this machine's right, he *did*. Plus, he's sold off his business and is flying abroad today. His brother may have warned him off, and I doubt he's got an explanation for why he left Kiku that night. I'd lay a pound to a penny he's not coming back.'

Terry frowned. 'But they'll catch 'im, won't they, Einstein, like what they done with Marti?'

'Guy Barton's a blooming sight cleverer, and he's had longer to plan this. He knows the Third World well. He'll disappear, or run somewhere the arm of the law can't reach. And, don't forget, we haven't got evidence we can *use*. If we can't confront him and make him confess, we're snookered . . . Come on, he's leaving his house any moment. Let's get *moving*.'

*

They raced out of Macfarlanes' offices and into Norwich Street. Julia got back into Terry's cab, and Einstein hopped into Len's. On the way up the Strand, the two passengers made frantic calls from their mobiles, trying desperately to find out when Morocco-bound flights were leaving. There was nothing more that day. That meant Guy must be using a private plane, and that could be flying from *anywhere*.

Slicing aggressively through traffic, they hurried through Trafalgar Square, up to Hyde Park Corner and onto Park Lane. There were roadworks and the traffic was heavier.

Suddenly Einstein saw Len's head swivel so hard it almost flew off his neck. Over the intercom he nearly burst Einstein's ear-drums, yelling,

'*That's 'im, that's 'im.*'

Einstein looked left and right.

'*Who, where*? What are you on about?'

'Barton's Bentley. I saw it on the telly about twenty times yesterday. Didn't you see it goin' the other way? The silver one with the reg LIX1R.'

'I'll call the others and tell them to follow us.'

Einstein got through, but the traffic was virtually at a standstill and the central reservation stopped them doing U-turns. Einstein called out to Len.

'If he's going that way from Holland Park, he can't be going to Heathrow or Farnborough. Which other airport could he be using?'

'City Airport, most likely. They'll go along the Embankment and then through the Limehouse Link.'

Einstein was thinking hard.

'He's got a head start of at least five minutes. If we go the same way, we'll never catch him. Can you think of another way to make up time?'

Len rubbed his chin.

'Only chance would be Gloucester Place up to Marylebone Road, then Euston Road, Pentonville Road, City Road, Great Eastern, Commercial Street down to the Minories, and try to cut 'im off at the big junction at the north side of Tower Bridge. If 'e gets there before us, mind, we're fucked.'

'Okay, let's go for it. At the next lights, I'm going to swap over with Julia. I need to chat with Terry.'

At the next next red light they switched. As they passed, Einstein grabbed Julia's arm.

'Get Len to give you the mobile number of every cabbie he knows. Tell them all to head for the north side of Tower Bridge, and watch out for that Bentley.'

Einstein wasted no time putting Terry to work.

'Daph? Hi, it's me, Terry . . . You're right, it '*as* been a while. Yeah, I'm still pinin'. . . . Listen, doll, I need another favour. I want you and the other gels to whistle up as many cabs as you can, and send 'em right away to the north side of Tower Bridge. If you got any mates at Computer Cabs or Dial-a-Cab, get them in on it too. The more the merrier. Only it's got to be *fast*. It's a stunt for a TV programme. It's a lark about catchin' a silver Bentley, reg number LIX1R. If them cabbies catch it, it's worth a grand a man. There's one for you too, if we get it . . . All right? Go to it, gel.'

*

Guy Barton put the car phone down, feeling troubled. On Monday, a panicky Charles had let him know that questions were being asked. Since then, he'd raced to get everything done. Matters seemed to be under control, but now, fifteen minutes after he'd left Holland Park for the City Airport, Charles was calling again, having been warned by the manager at Kiku that some fool waitress had spilt the beans.

The murder had been so perfect, so well planned and executed. Now it seemed to be unravelling, and he didn't even know why. He should still be all right, though. The whole world knew he was going to Morocco. If the police wanted to stop him, surely they would have arrested him before now. Perhaps they didn't have all the evidence yet or, more likely, were planning to question him on his return. All the same, it made him uneasy. Was it a mistake to stay in the Bentley? Should he let Shah drive on as a decoy, and switch to a taxi himself? Or was he worrying needlessly? All the same, better tell Shah to go faster.

That wasn't easy. From where they were now, in Northumberland Avenue, there was no choice but to flog along the Embankment, where the traffic was always unpredictable. The traffic lights in the shadow of Hungerford Bridge turned green and the Bentley swung left along the Thames. *Damn*, it was barely moving.

*

Einstein was keeping Terry busy. As soon as he was through with Daphne, he had him page Mary Long. She rang five minutes later.

'Thanks for callin' back, love. Listen, I think I've finally nailed our man, and I might get a confession. If I do, I thought you should 'andle it personal, so you get the credit, and you can iron out any problems about me doin' this private, like. Where will you be about four? . . . *No*? Straight up? *Blimey*! Okay, I'll try to call before then. Bye'

He switched the phone off and turned right round in excitement. Hey, *Einstein* . . .'

'Keep your eyes on the road or you'll kill us. What is it?'

'Mary's got proof that Hunt rigged Sid Finch's story. There's a press conference to announce that they're lettin' Marti go.'

'That's great. Good for Mary. Now, call Daphne back and see how she's doing.'

*

381

Len was fairly flying across London, using side streets and alleys whenever the traffic got too bad. When it was totally snarled, he gunned the cab onto the pavement, Land Rover style, wrecking his exhaust, outraging startled pedestrians, and causing two policemen to chase vainly after him for over two hundred yards. There was no rule in the Highway Code that he didn't break or bend. All that mattered was they were making good time.

One of his mates called to say he'd spotted the Bentley and was doing his best to stay on its tail as it weaved in and out of slow-moving traffic near Southwark bridge. *Shit*, Barton was already close to Tower Bridge. It looked like he'd slip through the net.

*

It was really getting to Guy Barton now. A squad car went past in the other direction. A coincidence, probably, but it made his nerves jangle. He phoned his pilot and told him to look round the terminal for any sign of a police presence, and to have the plane all ready to go. If there *was* any welcoming party, they would smash through the barrier, drive straight to the plane and take off immediately, with or without permission from the tower.

He checked his watch for the umpteenth time. They were near to the Tower of London now. From here, it should only take another fifteen or twenty minutes. As the road swung left and uphill, away from the river, the traffic started to clog again.

They crawled along the length of the Tower. Ahead, by Tower Bridge, the junction looked gridlocked. Odd that there were so many taxis: cabs parked on both sides of the road, and a stream of cabs heading back into town. He looked around. There was a long column of taxis coming over the bridge and, from the roads on the left, great phalanxes of them. He spun round to check the rear; there was *another*, tight on his tail. What the hell *was* this? A demonstration of some kind?

Three times the lights went green, but the traffic hardly moved and they only reached the mouth of the junction. Beyond the immediate seething mass of black metal, the road to Limehouse looked clear. They simply *had* to get through. Barton commanded

Shah to thump the taxi in front hard, forcing it into the thick of the scrum. It cleared a few yards. He told Shah to do it again.

Shah didn't get the chance. A cab swerved across their bows, blocking the way completely, and two others drew up tight alongside. Cabs swarmed behind them as well, hemming in the Bentley comprehensively. This looked like it was organized, as if they were deliberately *trapping* him.

He started to get scared. He'd no idea who was involved or why. All he knew was he didn't like it. He'd have to get out and make a run for it. He tried to open the door of the Bentley. It thumped hard against the side of a cab; the gap was *far* too tight for him to squeeze out. He banged it several more times, hoping that it would make the man budge it. The driver looked furious but didn't move his cab an inch. *Fuck.*

Len's mate, who was glued to the Bentley's tail, called him and guided him in. Approaching from the Minories, Len and Julia were bogged down in their home-made jam and had to abandon the cab and take to their heels. Julia had a good turn of pace. Len was soon lagging, and yelled out breathlessly to her not to wait for him.

Two hundred yards later she was in the thick of it. There was a great cacophony going on, with vans, buses and cars honking irately. Where was the Bentley? *There.* Guy Barton was trapped like a fox. Should she wait for Einstein and the others to catch up, or plunge in alone? The police might turn up any moment and start ordering the taxis to move on. She didn't have time.

Scrambling over bumper after bumper, she clambered through the black mêlée. Up close, Barton looked manic, screaming at the cabbies around him. They didn't care for his attitude and, in spite of his fame, were in no mood to do his bidding.

Julia vaulted the last hurdle, slid up beside the Bentley and said sharply to Barton.

' I want a word with you.'

'Are you police?' Julia shook her head. 'Well, are you responsible for *this*?'

'Yes. I'll tell you why, if you let me in.'

'*What*? Very well, get in, *if* you can.'

The cabbie moved his cab forward a foot or two, to allow Julia's slender frame to slip in. The instant she sat down on the deep leather seat, Barton was at her throat.

'So, what's the meaning of this? I have a plane to catch.'

'You killed Grace Chesterfield, didn't you?'

Barton snorted, then laughed loud, overlong.

'You're crazy.'

'What you didn't know was that your voice was taped that night. We compared it with your television interview today. The match is exact.'

'Pure coincidence.'

Even as he spoke, Barton's mind was whirring. If this was true, why weren't the police here? Could it be that . . . ?

'Ah *ha*, I get it. It was taped illegally, so it can't be produced in court. *Right*?'

His eyes flashed triumphantly. He was safe after all. Better be sure he wasn't being tricked now, though. He grabbed at her shirt and yanked it up violently, checking she wasn't wired.

Julia went scarlet. As she tucked the shirt back into her waistband, her voice took on a sharper edge.

'Whether or not the tape is admissible, there's *other* evidence.'

'Like what?'

'Like the fact that you slipped away from the restaurant Kiku. You might find that hard to explain.'

'Where I'm going, I won't need to explain *anything* . . . Ah, that's the police arriving. Get out of my car, before I make a complaint.'

'Very well.' Now for her last throw of the dice. 'I'd better go and keep my appointment with a journalist.'

Barton laughed in her face. 'And tell the papers I murdered her? They'll never print it, you silly fool.'

'I'll arrange that part later. I'll begin with your brother's love life.'

'So *what*? It doesn't bother me.'

'Then I'll mention Skidder Barton's illegal conduct over Jowell. After Skidders' other problems, that will be the last straw for their clients. I'm pretty sure it'll bring the bank down and the shares will be valueless. Should wipe out the whole Barton family wealth nicely.'

Julia expected a sneer at that too. Guy Barton turned away; when he looked back, his expression was drained of its cockiness.

'You have *proof*?'

'Documents and tape recordings.'

Julia looked outside. The cabs were being shooed away by an angry-faced constable and the junction was clearing. She could see her three friends standing on the pavement, uncertain what to do. There was nothing to stop the Bentley driving on. To Julia's surprise, Barton told the driver to pull in to the side. She could see he was calculating.

'I presume this is blackmail? How much do you want?'

'I don't want your money. I want your confession.'

Barton laughed, genuinely amused at her cheek.

'You cannot be serious.'

'Oh, but I *am*. If you don't turn yourself in, I give you my word that I will do everything in my power to destroy your family.'

Guy Barton sat in silence for a few more seconds, then spoke very quietly and deliberately.

'My brother, Charles, is a cretin, an incompetent fool, as pathetic at philandering as at running a bank. He called me in a great lather when Grace found out about the mole. I undertook to take care of the situation. I told him to set up the restaurant and the rendezvous. In the dark, we're hard to tell apart.'

'Did Charles know you would kill her?'

'He had no *idea* what I would do. He is too squeamish for violence, and had certain feelings for her. Ever since, the poor soul has been in torment. Would it interest you to see how I did it?'

Before she could stop him, Barton reached to the front passenger seat for a briefcase and pressed a catch. A super-sharp spike flashed out of one side. Julia flinched.

385

He laughed. 'Don't fret, silly girl. It isn't primed, and there are rather too many witnesses. A neat device, though, don't you think? It stood me in good stead in Afghanistan once.'

He clicked the spike carefully away.

'So you did it to save Charles?'

'Not at all. I care very little for my brother. It was simple. I needed the bank for myself, and I didn't want it destroyed. There were also some reasons to do with Elixir why a family scandal would have been particularly unwelcome.'

'So it was all purely selfish?'

'More or less. I suppose I did have one other motive. In my youth, I embarrassed my family.'

'They forgave you.'

'Yes, and I appreciated that, more than they know. This was a way I could repay that old debt. As you have guessed, most of the family wealth is in Skidder shares. I knew how disastrous it would be for them if the bank collapsed. For that same reason, I *might* be willing to do a deal with you. The problem, dear girl, is that you are such a poor dealmaker. If I confessed, sooner or later the whole story would come out, and the family would be ruined anyway . . . If there was another way to satisfy you, would you promise to keep both the Jowell matter and the fact that I killed Grace secret indefinitely?'

'Possibly, but I don't see what you can–'

'There is only one solution. As you know, I am going to Morocco to attempt a world record. If I gave you my word of honour that my record-breaking jump will end tragically, would you accept it?'

'Why should you do that?'

'That is my own concern.'

Julia looked out of the side window and reflected. This man was a murderer, and probably a rogue. If she agreed and got out of the car, he might laugh all the way to the airport. On the other hand, she *did* have a hold over him, if he cared at all about his family. And would life in some flyblown place pall after a while? Was his vanity such that he would rather go out in a puff of glory, reputation intact, than be branded a killer? His proposal *would* solve a whole lot of problems for her side, too. She turned back to him.

'I honestly don't know whether to trust you . . . but I believe I will. In the circumstances, I don't suppose it's appropriate to wish you luck. Goodbye, Mr Barton.'

'Goodbye. One thing. Who *are* you?'

'A friend of Grace.'

She got out of the car and shut the door. As it purred off, he was watching her.

Len, Terry and Einstein walked towards Julia. They had quietly gathered the names of the cabbies to pay them later. Their hopes had soared when the Bentley had pulled in; when they watched her letting him go, they were devastated. She walked up and said simply, 'I have a call to make to Tom and Beth Chesterfield. Then let's go and have a coffee so I can tell you what happened. For some unaccountable reason, I feel very sad.'

They had one more appointment to keep before they could go back to Poppy. Albert Austin and Robert Quilley wanted them to pass on a few messages to Skidders, and Austin's secretary had arranged for Charles Barton, Rosco Sellars and Marcus Ford to receive a delegation from Upton at five o'clock. Einstein was happy enough to accompany Julia, but Terry and Len were less sure. Julia insisted on them coming, so an unlikely-looking quartet presented themselves at the bank's reception and were escorted over to the lift.

The Skidders trio were already in the meeting room. Both Barton and Ford looked very tired and pale. Rosco was feverishly recommending how they should handle the visitors. Who the hell were Upton anyway? Probably some third-rate boutique, and they shouldn't take any shit from them. Okay, so Jowell and Furnival now controlled Burlikon, and therefore Zuricher and its holding in Skidders. That didn't give them the right to throw their weight around. Maybe Skidders could turn this to their advantage, insisting on high compensation packages to keep key staff loyal, for example. Charles Barton sighed deeply.

'Rosco, why don't we wait and see what they have to say?'

'Okay, okay, I'm trying to strategize, that's all.'

At that moment the door of the meeting room swung open to reveal one heavily-spectacled diminutive character in a very untailored suit, followed by a large, bald gent in a worn-out suede jacket and red crew neck, and a slim, youngish fellow with curly hair, black leather trousers and a denim jacket. Distractedly, Charles Barton looked up.

'If you've come to repair something, I think you may have the wrong room.'

A woman's voice came from behind. 'No, Charles, I don't think we have.'

The three men stepped aside to reveal Julia.

Barton and Ford looked astonished. Rosco laughed.

'Well, I'll be damned.'

Julia smiled thinly at him. 'Yes, Rosco, I think that's a given. In fact, as we're rather short of time, why don't we start with you and Marcus?'

Something dawned on Rosco, and he began waving a finger angrily at the cabbies.

'Hold on, I've met you before. Right, Marcus?'

Marcus was too unhappy to answer. Rosco persevered.

'Impersonating police officers is a very serious offence. I could have you put away for *years*.'

Julia smiled. 'Fine, Rosco. Why don't you do it, then? I'm sure the police will enjoy hearing why you met my friends.'

Rosco paused.

'Okay, okay. Well, have any of you guys passed the investment banking exams? That's another serious offence –'

Marcus was stirred from his tortured silence.

'Rosco, *shut the fuck up.*'

Julia smiled, more genuinely this time.

'Thank you, Marcus. As I was saying, we'll start with you two. You will resign from Skidder Barton today, and receive no compensation. If you *ever* seek another job in investment banking, your prospective employers will be made aware of your track record. Understand?'

Marcus nodded. Anything was better than going to jail. Rosco was fit to be tied.

'You goddam, scheming, cheating –'

'*Yeah, yeah, yeah*. Do you agree or not?'

'I guess I have no choice.'

'Very well, you may go. We'll let you pack your own bin liners.'

With one last defiant snort, Rosco stormed out. Marcus followed, head bowed meekly, already wetting himself over what Sophie would say. The door closed behind them. Barton waited quietly to hear his own fate.

'Charles, I've just had a conversation with your brother, Guy. Its contents will never be made public, but you can assume we know everything. Tell me, what did Grace mean to you?'

'I loved her.'

'Did you ever say you would marry her?'

'Yes, once. I got carried away. It was impossible, of course. Think of the scandal. But, believe me, Julia, I didn't know she'd be killed. I only wanted to save my good name, and the bank.'

'So what did you think Guy would do?'

'I was in such a state, I had no idea. Guy's always been able to handle women. I thought he'd do *something* to make the nightmare go away.'

Barton's head fell into his hands. Julia wasn't through with him yet.

'Why on earth did you let those two go on with the Jowell bid, when you knew they were breaking the law?'

'I needed the profits from the deal, and the success. It was my only hope of avoiding being taken over, or having Guy foisted on me by my father.'

'On that subject, I have a message for you from Albert Austin and Robert Quilley. They plan to sell Burlikon's controlling stake in Zuricher, but they will keep the shareholding in Skidders. Sentimentally, perhaps, they think it is no bad thing for *one* bank to stay British-owned. However, they want you to step down and appoint headhunters to find a successor.'

'I see.'

Julia couldn't resist a parting shot. This one was for Grace.

'I'm sure you'll enjoy spending more time with Patricia.'

As they walked back to their cabs, they ran across a group of young carollers who were going in and and out of City bars raising money for the homeless. Julia offered them five hundred pounds to come to Gant's Hill and sing for a sick little girl.

*

There wasn't enough space in Poppy's room for the singers, so they did their stuff from the landing. The rest of them all squeezed in, sitting on chairs, or the bed, or the floor. There was much ribbing of Einstein for the strategic planning job Albert Austin had offered him, and excited discussion of what they'd all do with the twenty million. They went quiet when the carollers sang 'Away in A Manger'. Ruth and Jean burst into tears and hugged each other. Poppy clung to her father's hand. She was *so* proud of the lot of them, but most of all she was proud of her own Dad.

Len looked over to where Julia was falling softly asleep in Terry's arms. Half an hour later, Einstein passed out too. The fourth glass of champagne had done for him and he lay slumped on the floor, interrupting 'Silent Night' with a stream of Japanese unconsciousness.